The Faceless Minion
Volume 1

A. E. Icalos

A. E. Icalos

Copyright © 2022 A.E. Icalos

All rights reserved

The characters and events portrayed in this book are fictitious. Any similarity to real persons, living or dead, is coincidental and not intended by the author.

Cover design by: KAZEX423

CONTENTS

Title Page
Copyright
Prologue

Chapter 1 - The Faceless Minion Begins	1
Chapter 2 - I Was Hired as the Villainess's Butler but She won't Finish Her Paperwork!	21
Chapter 3 - To Defy The Heavens!	34
Chapter 4 - What Happens Next Will Shock You!	61
Chapter 5 - The Master of Evil	74
Chapter 6 - The Spark	93
Chapter 7 - Heroes Rise Again	115
Chapter 8 - Aurora Legion on the Hunt	133
Chapter 9 - The Beginning of the End	157
Chapter 10 - The New Dawn	167
Side Story - What is a Hero?	182
Chapter 11 - The End of the Beginning	186
Chapter 12 - To Protect the World from Devastation	194
Chapter 13 - The Fall of Harmony	209
Chapter 14 - The Heist	222
Chapter 15 - An Epoch's Grave	235

Chapter 16 - The Battle of the Jurassic Cemetery	252
Chapter 17 - Showdown! Aurora Legion vs. the Boss!	267
Chapter 18 - The Fight for the World	274
Chapter 19 - To Change the World	289
Chapter 20 - And Which Desires Will You Give Me?	296
Chapter 21 - A Hero's Debut	316
Chapter 22 - Escalation	335
Chapter 23 - Blood	352
Chapter 24 - War Never Changes	367
Chapter 25 - The Captain and the Falcon	382
Chapter 26 - The End of Winter, the Start of Spring	398
Interlude - The Star and the Rose	408
Chapter 27 - New Minion Orientation	421
Chapter 28 - A Minion's Toils	437
Chapter 29 - A Beautiful Dawn	454
Chapter 30 - To Bring Down the Sun	470
Chapter 31 - Peace In Our Time	483
Side Story - And Now for a Word from Our Sponsors	499
Variant Story Chapter 1 - I was a Faceless Minion, then I was Summoned to Another World!	503
Next Time on The Faceless Minion…!	524
Characters And Organizations	526
Acknowledgements	537

PROLOGUE

On a small island in the middle of the Atlantic stood a mighty fortress of concrete and steel, flanked by air defense towers. Smoke could be seen rising above its walls, the sounds of explosions and shouts could be heard even at a distance.

And within the site itself...

Men in black military uniforms, helmets, and gas masks took up positions and opened fire with assault rifles and flamethrowers. With them were drone tanks with silver hulls, golf-cart sized robotic war machines that launched fireballs from their cannons. The men ducked as the broken turret of a tank flew through the air, smashing the drone tank beside them.

And then their foes set upon them.

A mighty triceratops made of pink light roared as it bounded through the facility, knocking over men and trampling on drone tanks. Three figures sat upon its back. In the front, there was a teenage girl in a pink combat suit, her eyes moving in sync with the dinosaur as her hands glowed with pink light. In the middle sat a teenage girl in a blue and yellow latex suit, holding out her hands. She froze the approaching bullets and fireballs midair, the projectiles vibrating in place until the trio moved out of their path. In the back, there was a teenage boy in black and purple robes, firing beams of black light from his hands. The beam swept across automated turrets and drone tanks, leaving them disabled and motionless. And to the side of the triceratops, a teenage boy in a red suit and a blue cape kicked men into walls and ripped the turrets off of tanks with his bare hands. Bullets struck him head on…and bounced right off his chest.

For this place was the lair of a supervillain.

And the heroes had just arrived.

The trio leapt off the dinosaur as it faded, joining up with the caped boy on the ground. All around them were burning metal husks and groaning minions. They walked past the battlefield and entered the large, cylindrical building in the center of the facility. They heard a loud roaring noise as they approached that sounded like a rocket launching into the sky.

The inside of the building was mostly hollow, with a large device held on three metal beams in the center of the room. The device was the source of the roaring noise, for it was shaped like a giant jet engine and firing a massive torrent of light into the Earth. Standing in front of the device was a man wearing a red cape over his shoulders and a black mask over his face. He turned to face them, showing off the volcano painted on his black armor.

He grinned at the heroes and started cackling.

"The Aurora Legion themselves! Here for humble old me, I am truly flattered! But you are too late! Even you cannot stop the Herald of Ashes!"

The boy in a cape stepped forward, pointing at the villain ahead.

"It's over, Herald of Ashes! Surrender now!"

The Herald of Ashes grinned and spread out his arms. The device behind him quieted as the torrent of light died down. The drill moved out of the way and a glowing, metal sphere lowered from a crane on the roof, positioned right above the giant hole in the ground.

"Over? Yes, it is truly over! My drill has already penetrated deep into the core! Once I drop my Geo-Oscillator into the Earth's interior it will excite the magma across the globe! On every landmass, every continent lava surges will breach the mantle, wherever and whenever I command! And the Herald of Ashes shall rule the world, reshaped in my image! Minions, release the Oscillator!"

And nothing happened.

Silence hung in the air. The Herald of Ashes cleared his throat.

"Ahem, I said, minions! Release the Oscillator!"

Still nothing happened. Aurora Legion exchanged glances with each other. The Herald of Ashes turned his head to glance at the control panel.

"Minions?"

There was nobody there.

"Um, is something supposed to happen?"

"There's no one else here."

"You ok, bro? You might be seeing things."

The Herald of Ashes turned forward, his eyes shrinking into their sockets.

"Oh."

And then the Herald of Ashes and the heroes each broke out running towards the control panel, a race with the fate of the world at stake.

This…is the supervillain, and the heroes that rose against him.

And this…is not their tale.

So whose tale is it then, you ask?

Well…

△△△

On a boat sailing away from the island sat one of the Herald of Ashes' minions. A nondescript man of average size and weight, perhaps a bit more muscular than the norm, wearing a set of black armor, a helmet, and a gas mask hiding his face.

This is one of the faceless minions in the supervillain's employ, indistinguishable from any other.

His name is Bob.

Bob shook his head as another explosion rang out.

"Cutting it real close, aren't you? You just had to show up at the last minute, didn't you? Heroes are so annoying."

Bob took out his cell phone and made a call.

"Bob!"

"Markus."

"Did you get it?"

"The Herald's blueprints are secure, I'm sending them to Kanna now. How are we looking on funding?"

"The money's not a problem. You know there's going to be interference though? A lot of people stand to lose a lot of money if this does what you think it will."

"Can't you do something about that?"

"Well I could but I'd have to actually talk with my dad, so no."

"You probably should some day."

"But Boooobbbbb, if I deal with my issues and become emotionally healthy, who will run the Bank of Evil?"

"Ivan."

"Ivan? Really Bob? You think he's the type to handle paperwork?"

"Doesn't he already?"

"What, you think I dump my work on him or something?"

"Yes."

"Hahaha you're right. But seriously, my dad's just one player. Takes more than one player to overturn the game."

"Let me think."

"I can't wait to see what you come up with."

Bob took out a notepad and flipped through it, rubbing his chin as he scanned the pages.

"I have an idea."

"That's what I love to hear."

"Approve funding for applicants 151805, 165091, and 173892."

"165091? Seriously? YES! FINALLY! Do you know how

long I've been waiting for that one? I was afraid he was going to give up."

"I'm glad you're pleased."

"Come on, Bob, live a little. You can't tell me you're not even a little excited to see *that* go down."

"...I have to make another call."

"Hahaha I knew…"

And then Bob hung up on him and got to work

This is Bob.

To most people, he's just another faceless minion.

To some, he's a hero. The man who saved their lives and gave them meaning.

To others, he's the greatest supervillain to have ever lived. The man who manipulated heroes and villains alike, who held the world in the palm of his hand.

This is his story.

CHAPTER 1 - THE FACELESS MINION BEGINS

Let's turn back the clock to when it all began. Back to the 1980s, when Bob was a strapping young lad on his first real job...

Bob heaved a sigh, the only sound other than the rhythmic clank of his boots on the metal floor. All around him were gray metallic floors with gray metallic walls and, of course, a gray metallic ceiling, lit by the occasional incandescent bulb. Bob swore those might be gray too, but he didn't know if that was the lights themselves or the tinted goggles of his helmet. Why he had to wear a helmet with a gas mask at all times was beyond his comprehension. What he did comprehend was that his nose itched something fierce.

Bob didn't know what he expected from this job, but this definitely wasn't it.

Bob winced as pain stabbed through his right foot. There was definitely a blister there. He started bending down to rub it before remembering how thick his boots were. Heaving another sigh, he leaned against the wall, taking pressure off the foot as best he could. He grimaced as that action caused a dull ache in his other foot.

Would it have killed his employer to give a five minute break on an eight hour patrol?

Giving the break might've killed his employer, but taking that break anyways saved Bob's life.

Bob wasn't sure what happened next.

He heard a loud bang.

A flash of light filled his vision.

He felt pain all over, and a floating feeling.

And then more pain as he slammed against the floor, dust and debris falling all around him.

Bob's heart raced, his stomach dropped.

Sweat began to cover his brow.

He couldn't hear anything but a high-pitched ringing noise.

He couldn't see.

He couldn't breathe.

He lifted his trembling arms with what strength he could muster, feeling as if the air had turned to mud.

He pushed his helmet up and off his head with all his might.

He gasped for breath, desperately filling his lungs.

He still saw nothing but black.

And then a red flash of light lit up the world. Bob could see the floor, suspiciously close to his face. He could see twisted and jagged pieces of metal, torn wires, and broken chunks of concrete. He grimaced as he tried to stand. One of those pieces of metal or chunks of concrete might be on top of him. He tried twisting his neck to look up and get a better view, ignoring the stabbing pain in every muscle he attempted to move.

And then he froze.

He saw a figure in a cape, stepping over the rubble.

And a moment later he saw Jenkins flying through the air.

Bob was not a small man. He could confidently say he was at least average, maybe larger than average given the amount of manual labor he had done growing up.

But Jenkins, now that was a man.

Jenkins stood head and shoulders above his coworkers with the heft to match. There was always some cocky newbie who would call him fat. And Jenkins had fat, the kind of fat that protects the truly strong. Jenkins wasn't some showy body builder with rippling muscles that were naught but skin and bones. Jenkins was a wall of mass and muscle. The ideal form of applied strength. He could and often did lift fully grown men with a single hand, as every cocky newbie experienced personally.

The guys joked that Jenkins was the most gullible man in the world, because he trusted everyone as far as he could throw them.

That very Jenkins now flew through the air like a basketball lobbed from half-court at the buzzer.

Bob winced as Jenkins slammed into the wall, grateful his hearing hadn't returned yet. Jenkins then fell to the floor, a dented wall plate falling on top of him. Jenkins lay still.

Bob pulled his gaze away from his fallen coworker. He grit his teeth as he pivoted his body and pulled on his leg. He pulled himself free, his heart dropping as the rubble shifted. He closed his eyes, holding his breath. But as the rubble settled, he felt no new pressure or pain upon his back, and so he opened his eyes.

His entire body trembled, his limbs felt like jelly and the air like molasses. But he grit his teeth and stretched his arm out. He grabbed onto a metal pole, and pulled himself forward with all his might.

Then he groaned and stretched his other arm out, grabbing yet another pole.

Then another.

And another.

Dust fell on top of him as he crawled, the very earth itself trembling. The ringing in his ears grew softer. He could now hear shouts and gunshots and something like the air itself being ripped apart.

He tried to ignore the sounds as he crept forward. He reached a larger piece of concrete, grabbing it with both hands and desperately pulling himself up.

His legs screamed in agony.

He trembled, feeling as if the slightest breeze would knock him over.

He pulled one leg up, kneeling upon it, then he ever so slowly unbent his knee until the second leg was under him as well.

He inhaled and exhaled over and over, his lungs on fire, his heart pounding in his chest, until the trembling in his limbs slowed ever so slightly.

And then Bob ran.

△△△

The next day, Bob woke up in his apartment. Fortunately, he had not been seriously hurt, nothing but a few minor scrapes and bruises, so he had simply gone to sleep.

Now he got up, made himself breakfast, and turned on the television as he sat down.

He immediately shut it off.

The news was on, showing the burning remains of a very familiar building. Bob exhaled his breath and shook his head as he tried to calm his beating heart.

Ok, he had figured his first boss was a little off, what with the random body armor and gas masks.

And the inability to return home.

And the random monologues and disturbing laugh.

The military-grade armory and the sheer number of locked doors was probably a red flag as well.

But still, he hadn't expected a *super* of all things to blow the place up.

He took a deep breath. His heart pounded as the memories of the previous day replayed in his mind.

Bob shook his head and walked over to the house phone. He needed to get out of the house…as well as figure out how to pay the bills this month. So he dialed the number of one of his closest friends.

"Chris."

"Bob, nice to hear from you! How's the new job going?"

"It exploded."

"Wait, what? What do you mean, exploded?"

"Exactly what I said."

"You mean, like, went bankrupt or something, right?"

"No."

The phone went silent for a moment.

"Well crap. Are you alright?"

"A bit banged up but ok."

"Sorry to hear that. Is there anything I can do for you?"

"I need a new job."

"...are you sure? You don't want to take some time off after that?"

Bob shook his head as he spoke into the phone.

"I'd rather keep busy."

"...if you say so. You have good timing, actually. Someone just dropped out of the job I'm on, so we're looking for someone. If you want in, I can put in a good word for you."

"Thanks, I'll do it."

"...you sure? We'll be traveling out of the country, you know?"

Bob raised an eyebrow.

"Something wrong with the job?"

"...no but, uh, the boss does prefer it if we keep things... quiet."

"I can do quiet."

"...got it. Well, it will be nice to work together again. I'll come pick you up?"

"I'll see you then. Thanks Chris."

"Anytime, Bob."

△△△

Bob walked towards a garage alongside Chris, a man slightly taller than himself. They both wore casual clothes, jeans with simply collared shirts and sunglasses.

"When you said out of the country, this isn't exactly what

I expected."

Chris shrugged.

"What did you expect?"

"Canada or Mexico. Maybe the Caribbean."

Chris grinned at him.

"What, I thought you wanted to see Tokyo someday?"

Bob yawned.

"Someday when I had time to prepare for a day-long flight."

Chris just chuckled and opened the door to the garage.

A dark-skinned woman stood in front of a table at the center of the garage, her hands crossed behind her back. Behind her stood a light skinned woman flipping through a notebook. In front of them to the left was a group of assorted men and women in casual wear. To the right was a group of men in fatigues, holding assault rifles. Bob raised an eyebrow at that.

"There you are, Chris. I was beginning to think you weren't coming."

"Sorry, sorry, cross-ocean red eyes are no fun, you know?"

"You're not here for fun."

The woman turned to Bob and extended a hand.

"You must be the one Chris talked about. I'm Cikizwa and I'm running this operation."

Bob shook her hand.

"Bob, thank you for having me."

Cikizwa nodded.

"This behind me is Linda, she helps organize things."

Cikizwa then pointed to the casual group.

"This is Sergei, Minh, Tina, George, and Kanna. Everyone, this is Bob, he'll be joining you today."

Bob greeted the group and then turned to the others. The lead man in the armed group stepped forward. Cikizwa nodded.

"This is Laurent. He and his group will be providing security."

Bob raised an eyebrow.

"Are we expecting trouble?"

Cikizwa shook her head.

"I always expect trouble, but for this operation they're just insurance."

"And what exactly is this operation?"

"Now that we're all here, we'll explain."

Cikizwa turned and nodded at Linda, who pulled out a map and stretched it across the table. Cikizwa motioned and everyone moved to join her around the table. The map showed a mountain near Tokyo.

"There's an old shrine here, whose last caretaker has recently passed. Our client is interested in something stored there, and wants us to retrieve it."

Kanna, a shorter Japanese woman, tilted her head.

"Eh, you called us all out here for that? The client wants the whole shrine, or something?"

Cikizwa shook her head.

"No, just one scroll."

"Seriously? Isn't this overkill?! I have things to do, Cikizwa!"

Cikizwa shrugged.

"You can work on your latest wonder device later, Kanna. If a client is going through me, I assume it's not that simple."

Minh, a darker-skinned Asian man, frowned.

"Is that what the guns are for?"

"You know how I operate, Minh."

"That's why I'm asking."

Linda shook her head.

"We've interviewed the client and checked out everything we could. There shouldn't be any trouble, as far as we know. This is all just a precaution given the value of the package for our client."

Tina, a dark-haired Caucasian woman, tilted her head.

"Why, how much is the client paying for it?"

Cikizwa smiled.

"Wouldn't you like to know? Anyways, the client wasn't sure as to the scroll's actual location, so you're all here to help search while Laurent and his men secure the perimeter."

Bob crossed his arms, raising an eyebrow.

"And is this legal? Sounds a lot like we're ransacking the place."

Linda nodded at that.

"Our client has secured all the necessary authorizations, and cleared things with both the Japanese government and the shrine association. There won't be any legal trouble."

Bob raised an eyebrow, but if they said that much, he'd let it go. Not that he had much choice at this point, given he was already involved with people holding guns.

Cikizwa passed around several photos to the group, along with some two-way radios.

"This is the target. Once we reach the site, we'll spread out and search. If you find it, radio it in immediately, and we'll get out of there. Understood?"

Everyone nodded.

"Good, Linda will explain which areas you'll be responsible for, and then we'll head out."

△△△

A short while later, Bob found himself walking up the stairs to the mountain shrine. He winced as pain shot through his right foot. It seemed the blister from his previous job hadn't quite healed yet, and the mountain hike wasn't doing him any favors. He heaved a sigh.

Well, at least the pain would help keep him alert. He had a really bad feeling about this job. If Chris wasn't one of his closest friends he would have ducked out a while ago.

But, well, he couldn't just quit a midnight job run by someone with a group of mercenaries on payroll.

And the pay was quite nice for one night's work, as well.

Eventually, they arrived at the top, passing through

several Torii gates before arriving at the shrine proper, several wooden buildings set up around a large courtyard. Cikizwa turned to face them and opened her mouth to speak.

"You all have your assignments, split up and start looking. Call it in the moment you find something."

And so the team split up. Bob and Chris found themselves in a small office off to the side while the others headed deeper into the shrine. Aka, the least likely place to actually find their target. But such is the fate of the new guy on the job.

It didn't take them long to comb the place. Afterwards they took a quick break, sitting on some chairs in the office.

Bob looked up at a wall and rubbed his chin. Chris tilted his head.

"What are you thinking?"

"This scroll is apparently worth a ton of money, right?"

Chris nodded.

"Right."

"So why hasn't anyone taken it yet?"

Chris shrugged.

"Maybe it's sacred, or something."

Bob raised an eyebrow.

"That's not stopping us."

"Touché."

Bob pointed out the window to where one of the guards could be seen patrolling.

"In fact, it's worth so much your boss can hire armed security just to come pick it up."

Chris nodded and crossed his arms.

"That's true, but what are you getting at?"

Bob rubbed his chin again.

"What I'm saying is, this shouldn't have been the first time someone wanted this thing. Which means it shouldn't have been the first time someone tried to take it, both by force or by subtle means. Which means...this place should have been prepared for someone to come searching."

Chris raised an eyebrow.

"So you think we're not going to find it?"
Bob nodded.
"Where's the first place you'd look?"
Chris shrugged.
"Some sort of vault, or back area."
Bob nodded.
"Exactly where they're looking now. And where wouldn't anyone think to look for some ancient scroll in a historic shrine?"
Chris shrugged again.
"If you know where it is, then stop showing off and find it already, Bob."
Bob walked over to a small rest area in the building. There was a television, and one of those new game consoles Japan had recently developed. Bob opened up the television...
He then smiled smugly at Chris as he pulled out a small wooden box. Chris groaned and slapped his forehead.
"I get it, I get it. Don't be a jerk about it."
Chris shook his head as Bob kept smiling at him, and pulled out his radio to call Cikizwa.
And then the sound of gunfire and shouting pierced through the night.
Bob and Chris's eyes widened...

∆∆∆

The wind blew along the entrance path to the shrine. Laurent and his men gripped their rifles as they scanned the path ahead.
They saw someone on approach. They raised their guns. Laurent yelled out.
"This area is restricted! Turn back now!"
The figure ignored them, and continued walking forward. They stepped out into the moonlight, coming into full view.
The men gasped.
Before them stood the most beautiful woman they had

ever seen, almost too beautiful to be real. She wore thin silk robes that fluttered in the night breeze. She seemed to glide across the ground with her smooth, graceful steps.

And then they felt as if something hit them.

Their spines went rigid.

Their eyes widened.

Sweat dripped from their brows.

They gasped for breath.

Laurent grit his teeth and bit down on his lip, forcing his body to move. He lifted his gun.

"OPEN FIRE!"

Laurent's shout shook the rest of the men out of their haze, and they too lifted their guns. The night lit up with the muzzle flashes of fully automatic assault rifles.

Spent bullet casings clattered to the ground.

As did flattened bullets.

The woman sighed as bullets bounced harmlessly off her.

She reached into her robes and pulled out something.

It was a pair of brass knuckles.

She slipped them on each hand and then slammed her fists together. A gust of wind surged forward, knocking the mercenaries to the ground.

Laurent just rose to his feet when the girl appeared before him, her fist pulled back.

She swung her fist forward...

And pierced straight through Laurent's chest, body armor and all.

The other mercenaries cried out and raised their guns.

At that moment, several figures leapt through the trees, soaring through the skies. They wore black martial arts robes with masks covering their faces, gliding through the air as they leapt from tree to tree. They landed in front of the mercenaries before the soldiers could fire their guns.

The martial artists swung swords and spears, cutting the soldiers down. One soldier got a volley off but his opponent spun his sword around, the blade appearing to vanish. Arcs of light formed around the martial artist as he moved at impossible speeds…and then several flattened bullets landed on the ground around him. Another martial artist then slammed the soldier with a mace, sending him flying into the wall around the shrine courtyard.

The woman heaved a sigh and shook her head as she wiped the blood off her fist.

"Mortals."

She turned to the martial artists, all standing at attention behind her.

"Go, tear this place apart and bring me the scroll."

The martial artists placed their fists into their palms and bowed.

"Yes, Young Mistress!"

With that, they leapt over the wall and rushed into the shrine.

But as they did, a volley of kunai knives shot out from among the trees, with paper talismans tied to them. The paper talismans had been lit on fire and burned as they soared through the air. As the kunai reached the martial artists in the air, the talismans exploded, throwing their targets to the ground.

Shadows leapt from the forest and landed in the shrine courtyard. They wore black hakamas and metal forehead protectors, with knives and katanas in hand.

It was an army of ninjas.

A vein bulged on the Young Mistress's forehead as her people groaned and picked themselves off the ground.

"So you idiots left your hiding place, huh? Just my luck. Out of the way, you cowards. This place and everything in it belongs to the Eternal Night Sect."

A woman with a katana in hand stepped forward, brandishing her blade.

"Not this time, Murderous Bloody Fist. The Village Hidden Among the Trees will stop you, here and now."

The Murderous Bloody Fist slammed her fists together, a

gust of wind surging from her as her brass knuckles collided with a clang.

"Big words from cowards who have been hiding from us for *centuries*."

The kunoichi smirked under her mask.

"Your father may be a formidable foe, but you are not him. I, the Amano Clan's Phantom Blade, am more than capable of dealing with *you*."

The Muderous Bloody Fist's face twisted in a horrendous scowl.

"Kill them!"

△△△

Bob and Chris's eyes widened as they peaked out the window.

They saw something out of a comic book. Or a horror movie in this case.

There were ninjas.

And martial artists.

And they were fighting, with fists and knives and swords.

Oh, and the martial artists were flying through the sky, and leaving craters when they struck the ground.

And the ninjas were vanishing, appearing elsewhere in an instant. Ninjas seemed to be struck by blades, only to vanish in puffs of smoke.

And one was breathing fire.

In the center, two women were fighting. One, the most beautiful woman the two men had ever seen…if it weren't for the scowl on her face and the blood covering the brass knuckles over her fists. Her opponent was a ninja woman with a katana. The kunoichi swung her blade and the martial artist woman caught it with a brass knuckle, slamming her other fist into the kunoichi's stomach. The kunoichi flickered as the fist passed straight through her…before a dozen transparent clones appeared all around the martial artist.

Metal clashed against metal. Arcs of light appeared as the clones each slashed at the woman, only to be dispelled by the woman's mighty fists. Every swing of her hands sent gusts of wind surging across the courtyard.

Chris started to tremble.

"What on Earth is going on…"

Meanwhile, Bob's eyes narrowed.

"Supers. Duck!"

He grabbed Chris and pulled him down, out of view of the window. He pulled Chris by the hand and to the side, just as a ninja crashed through the window behind them, groaning as he landed on a table. Chris snapped out of his shock just as Bob ran past him and opened the back door. The two crept along the wall of the courtyard, heading to the back of the shrine. They ducked as a sword flew overhead and *smashed* the courtyard wall to their side. Behind the next building, they found Kana and Sergei, crouched along the ground. A dead soldier lay beside them.

"Come on!"

Bob and Chris grabbed their trembling coworkers and rushed inside a door to the side of the structure. Bob then stepped out and reached into the fallen soldier's pocket, quickly grabbing something and stuffing it into his own. It turned out it wasn't a gun but he had no time to complain.

He wasn't sure what he'd do with this yet but any weapon was better than nothing.

Then he jumped up and ran into the building, slamming the door shut.

And not a moment too soon, Bob had barely closed the door when he heard stray knives thud into the wood.

In the main shrine, the survivors gathered, huddled in a circle. Minh was curled up by the wall, Tina was glancing all over the room, Linda was trembling on the ground, and Cikizwa was gripping her head and muttering.

And two martial artists stood over them, hefting their blades. Bob and Chris ducked into the shadows to observe.

Just then the doors to the structure flew off their hinges, and the martial artist woman from the courtyard marched inside.

Bob started whispering to Chris and handed him something. Chris nodded and went back towards the side door.

Meanwhile, the woman walked up to the group on the ground. A vein bulged on her forehead, and her robes had small cuts all over them.

"I hate those cowards. They're weak as crap but stupidly hard to hit. Now tell me you have the scroll."

One of the martial artists gulped and waved his sword towards the group on the ground.

"They say they don't know where it is, they hadn't found it yet."

The woman scowled.

"Then they're of no use to us. Kill them and get searching."

The men and women on the ground gasped as the martial artists turned to them with their blades.

It was at this moment that Bob stepped out towards the group, hands held high.

"Wait! I know where the scroll is."

Everyone turned towards Bob. Cikizwa and her group's eyes widened. The martial artist woman just narrowed her eyes at him.

"Do you now?"

Suddenly it felt as if the weight of the world crashed upon Bob's shoulders, as if the very air was trying to squeeze the life out of him. He could almost see an aura of light and fire shimmer around the woman. Every breath took all his effort, as if the air refused to enter his lungs, as if his chest was pushing against solid walls as it tried to expand.

The woman strode forward towards him, staring him in the eye. Every instinct in his body told him to flee, to submit. He was staring death in the face, a wholly superior being who could crush him with her very presence. Every ounce of his being screamed at him to give her what she wanted, and then drop to the ground and beg for his life. To do anything else was immediate death, his body warned.

But...

It wasn't the first such being Bob had encountered.

Bob remembered flashes of light, crumbling concrete, and the strongest man he knew flying through the air.

He remembered his trembling legs, his pounding heart.

He remembered lying on the ground, watching the being responsible walk past without even sparing him a glance.

He felt heat grow in his stomach and spread through his body.

This was the second time this week someone like this tried to take everything from him.

And that was one time too many.

Bob refused to give in. He clenched his teeth. He fought with all his might to resist his instincts, to take back control of his body.

And...

He succeeded.

It was hardly a victory. Bob could barely even move. His body trembled, he felt as if the slightest breeze would knock him over. If this woman decided to kill him, he could do nothing but stand there and watch it happen.

But that didn't mean he had to yield to her. She could take what she wanted, but it would be over his dead body.

He stood firm. He retained control over himself, if barely. He did not give into his instincts.

And so he was able to hold to his plan.

"Where is it?"

Bob moved a trembling hand to his pocket, and pulled out a small wooden box. The woman raised an eyebrow, but held out her hand. His arm trembled and shook, it felt as if the air had turned to molasses, but Bob grit his teeth and moved his arm forward, just like he had done before. He held the box above the woman's hand, just about to drop it there.

Just then, Chris stepped to the side of the building, and held the object Bob had given him. A flashbang grenade Bob had taken from the fallen soldier. Chris pulled his arm back and lobbed it at the broken entrance of the building.

The small bomb exploded with a bright flash of light and an incredibly loud noise. Everyone in the courtyard and the shrine winced and shielded their eyes. Bob dropped the box into the woman's hand and jumped to the side, the pressure fading as the woman stopped focusing her intent on him.

As the light faded, every shinobi's eyes widened as they turned towards the source of the flash. They saw the martial artist woman standing there with a decorated box in her hand. The kunoichi she had fought reappeared, a bandage wrapped around her stomach. She grit her teeth and lifted her katana once more.

"The Murderous Bloody Fist has the Scroll of Demonic Binding! Stop her!"

Shinobi leapt towards the woman, lobbing kunai and shuriken at her. The martial artist knocked them away with her fists, scowling and leaping forward to pummel an incoming shinobi into the ground.

"I'm leaving. Keep up or be left behind."

The martial artists shouted their acknowledgement and rushed to fall in behind the woman, as the ninjas moved to block their path.

And so the battle between the two sides intensified and approached its climax.

Meanwhile, when the flashbang detonated at the entrance, Bob landed amongst Cikizwa's group and pushed them to their feet.

"Move!"

The group ran to the side door, where Chris, Kana, and Sergei were waiting. Bob led them to the courtyard wall where a stray sword strike had broken a hole. They jumped through and ran off into the forest as they heard clanging metal and shouts behind them. They didn't stop running until they had made their way down the mountain and back to their cars.

△△△

The group stood in silence back in the initial garage, just catching their breath for a moment. Linda stumbled over to Bob, her legs still shaking under her.

"T-Thank you. You saved my life. You saved all of us."

Cikizwa shook her head and stood up. She walked over and extended her hand to Bob.

"She's right. We'd be dead if it wasn't for you and Chris."

The rest of the group nodded their heads as well. After that, Minh stalked towards Cikizwa, his body still trembling.

"What the heck was that?! I thought you said you weren't expecting trouble!"

Cikizwa shook her head and took a deep breath.

"I wasn't. I have no idea who those people are. Or *what* those monsters are."

Bob shook his head.

"Supers. That's what they are."

Chris swore.

"Sorry Bob, I didn't think this would happen to both our jobs. They really just do whatever they please, huh? Someone's got to reign those jerks in."

Bob rubbed his chin, and narrowed his eyes.

"Hmmm, maybe someone should."

Sergei heaved a sigh.

"But who? We all know the government won't do anything. Or can't. Not like they can arrest someone who can punch through machine gun fire like that."

Bob narrowed his eyes.

"If you want something done, do it yourself."

Sergie laughed at that.

"Hey, new guy, I'm super grateful for what you did, but

don't joke like that. You saw what they did, what they can do. They tore through professional killers like a hot knife through butter. Us normal folk? Well, we just have to let it go, and stay out of the way. There's nothing we can do about people like that."

Chris raised an eyebrow.

"I know that look. You have a plan, Bob?"

"No. But maybe an idea. Or the beginnings of one."

Sergei shook his head.

"It takes more than a plan to deal with something like that."

Bob shrugged.

"It didn't to get you all out of there."

Cikizwa heaved a sigh.

"Maybe. But there's a difference between surviving a fight and winning it. I've seen all kinds of stuff. Civil wars, insurrections, covert ops, heists gone wrong. But I've never seen anything like that, Bob."

Bob just smiled, and reached into his pocket.

Everyone in the room gasped.

In his hand was a scroll.

"You...what...I thought you handed that over!"

Bob smirked.

"The caretaker of that place had more than one scroll to hide. What I handed over was a vintage collection of... specialty literature that was stored alongside this scroll."

Everyone's eyes widened. Bob continued.

"They might be supers, they might be people who can do things we never could, but at the end of the day, they're still *people*. People can be tricked. Deceived. Manipulated. No matter how strong they might be. So I think...I think I might try to do something. Someone has to."

ΔΔΔ

Meanwhile, a shriek of unspeakable rage cut through

the night around the mountain. The Murderous Bloody Fist pummeled one of her followers as she roared.

This shouldn't have happened. Sure, the mortal had simply handed her a box. Perhaps it was foolish of her to simply accept that it held the scroll she wanted. But she had blasted the mortal with her intent, as much intent as she knew a mortal could handle while remaining conscious. It should have been impossible for him to lie to her. His body shouldn't have allowed it.

And yet he had. Had betrayed no sign of his deceit, either. And then there was that flash bomb...that was likely arranged by the mortals as well. The shinobi wouldn't have used it like that, they would have taken the opportunity to ambush her directly.

So the deception was likely planned from the start.

She grit her teeth and clenched her fists, and started to beat another one of her followers as she shouted.

"I will never forgive you! How dare you deceive me, Young Mistress Xiong Huang of the Eternal Night Sect! I will never forgive you for this insult, a thousand deaths is too good for you! That mortal, whoever he is, I will find him, and I will kill him! I swear it!"

AUTHOR'S COMMENTARY: And so our story begins! With...two jobs ending in explosive termination...and a vow of vengeance. Yep. Things are going great. But it's fine! I'm sure Bob the normal dude can definitely handle being hunted by someone called the Murderous Bloody Fist, right? Well...anyways! Can Bob do something about the problem of supers running rampant? Will Xiong Huang the Murderous Bloody Fist catch up to him someday? What can one man with a scroll and a plan do about these gods and heroes? Tune in next time, to find out!

CHAPTER 2 - I WAS HIRED AS THE VILLAINESS'S BUTLER BUT SHE WON'T FINISH HER PAPERWORK!

The first thing Bob did was flee the country. He didn't know who those people were or what their capabilities might be, but he didn't want to stick around and find out.

He figured at the very least, the ninjas might have a harder time finding him in America than in Japan.

Of course, he talked a big game, but he was just one man with some super valuable scroll. He had ended up keeping it. The group talked it over and decided that after the events of that night, they didn't want to pass the scroll off until they fully understood what it was. Who knew what Cikizwa's mysterious client might want with something supers went to war over.

Still, Bob lacked any sort of resources that he might utilize. Certainly not enough to handle the issue of supers.

There had always been legends and myths, stories of people and creatures who could do things beyond the norm. But they were just that. Stories.

Until 1945, when atomic bombs were detonated across the globe in war and in tests.

Ever since then, more and more stories began to gather. Covert black ops teams with perfect records. Soviet super suits that could fry tanks with lightning. Mad scientists building wonder devices like something out of a science fiction novel. Shadows that stalked through Japan at night. Wandering martial artists who could catch bullets with their bare hands.

Until eventually, some of these were caught on camera.

And more.

And more.

Until one day, one of them stepped out into the light. Someone who proved they could do things that everyone else couldn't, and committed to using those powers for good.

A caped crusader.

A defender of truth and justice.

The first superhero.

Like most people, Bob hadn't believed these were real. He thought it was cheap tricks and clever filming.

Until now, where he was caught in it not once, but twice.

It was clear that these supers were real.

And that they were dangerous.

And if the stories hinted at any trend, it was that they were growing ever more common.

So something needed to be done.

And to do something, Bob would need resources and connections.

So he did his homework. He looked for ways he could acquire such things.

And then, he found a way.

There was a small, anachronistic microstate in Europe known as Coflar. It was a small nation bordering France and Belgium that was small in size but rich in history and tradition. With fertile lands and a pleasant climate, its people lacked for nothing, and so were quiet and content. They did not desire grand crusades or chaotic revolutions, and so Coflar had changed very little over the course of its history. Most importantly of all to Bob, that meant the aristocracy was still in force, controlling most of the nation's politics and wealth.

And that meant opportunity.

Coflar may have been tiny, but the business of government was a big one even in a small country. And in aristocratic Coflar, government was also a family business.

Which meant if Bob could find a way to control even just one of those families, he would have access to resources and connections no normal person could even dream of.

Bob walked over to his phone and called Chris.

"Hi Bob, you doing alright?"

"Fine, yourself?"

"Same. You come up with something?"

Bob smiled.

"I did."

"Heh, I thought you might. What do you need?"

"You said Linda handled recruiting, right? You have a way to contact her?"

"Yeah, what are you thinking?"

"I just need a bit of help with my resume."

△△△

Near the capital of Colflar stood a grand estate. A golden metal gate opened a path between tall hedges, where a red brick road lead to a wide fountain. In the center of the fountain stood angels made of pristine marble, carrying horns that unleashed torrents of water. Beyond that stood a grand château with white and golden walls supporting an angled orange roof.

And within these storied halls...

Bob pushed open a large wooden door, painted white and pink with a golden handle. He blinked for a moment as the sun shone in his eyes through full length windows. As his vision cleared he could look through the window at the immaculate garden behind the château, where bushes were filled with orange and pink roses. A clear contrast to the room in front of him. The walls were covered in pink wallpaper embossed with gold designs. Around the room were pink chairs covered with a great deal of lace, all of which was also pink. To the side was a pink desk with golden highlights. The room was lit by a golden chandelier with pink lights. And around the room were the adornments, such as golden lamps, golden plates, and a golden pen with a pink center.

Bob silently swallowed to calm his stomach.

"MINION! There you are! What took you so long?"

Bob almost flinched as a piercing shriek drove into his skull, greatly exacerbating his headache. For once he was thankful for the featureless pink mask resting over his face.

"My most sincere apologies, Mistress."

Bob gave a humble bow to his current boss's daughter, Lady Anita Laflèche de Albifort. Her dark hair was tied up with pink ribbons and a golden comb, arranged in curled locks draping down the sides of her face. She had sharp, green eyes that pierced like an eagle eyeing its prey. Her high cheekbones and a sharp chin added to the effect. Altogether her features gave the air of a person in charge, on the hunt for any sign of weakness.

Or at least it would have, if she would cut down on the fluffiness of her pink dress.

Bob questioned if that much lace was truly necessary. But he held his tongue. He was a man who knew his limits and the fashion of high society was most certainly beyond them. That none of her classmates dressed like her either was simply proof of his lady's sublime tastes. Or so he had been told.

Lady Anita slammed shut the fan in her hand and pointed her finger.

"Nevermind that! Why on earth is there a dirty peasant inside my mansion?!"

Bob glanced at the man standing to the side of the room. The man was fully dressed in a suit and tie, and carried a briefcase. He had neat, trimmed hair and simple round glasses. Bob looked around but he couldn't find any other individuals in the room, much less the dirty peasant his lady mentioned. Which meant, unfortunately, she was referring to Bob's guest.

"My most sincere apologies, Mistress. I will make sure it doesn't happen again. But now that the notary has arrived, may I suggest we proceed to business?"

Lady Anita tilted her head.

"Notary? What's a notary..."

Lady Anita coughed, extending her fan to hide her mouth.

"I mean, what would the great Albifort estate need a notary for, minion?"

Bob suppressed a sigh.

"He must verify your signature to grant me power of attorney, Mistress."

Lady Anita stared into space for a moment.

"Huh, what kind of power is that? Didn't you say you don't have any powers, minion? I do not appreciate being lied to."

Bob took a deep breath through his nose.

"It is to fulfill your will, my Mistress. Power of attorney will allow me to act on your behalf, so that I may deal with the paperwork you ordered me to handle."

Lady Anita tilted her head.

"Paperwork? What paperwork? We are beyond such peasant trifles, my minion."

Bob's arm trembled as he held in the reflex to move it to his face. He spoke to himself within his mind. He reminded himself that he had stared supers in the face, withstood the gaze of beings who could end him in an instant. So he could handle anything.

Surely.

"Mistress, you wished to purchase the Mode par Éclipse did you not?"

Lady Anita just blinked at him.

"Huh? Why would I want that?"

Bob repeated his reminders to himself.

"You wished to prohibit a certain customer from having a dress tailored there, did you not?"

Lady Anita blinked a few more times. Bob took another breath through his nose and then leaned in to whisper in Lady Anita's ear.

"Miss Corriveau, Mistress."

Lady Anita jumped up and smacked Bob over the head with her fan.

"MINION! I told you never to speak that vile name in my presence!"

"My most sincere apologies, Mistress. You instructed me to purchase the Mode par Éclipse after meeting...a certain thieving vixen there."

Lady Anita ground her teeth, clenching her hands into fists.

"Hang that thieving cat! First she tried to steal my beloved Prince Lionel, then she dared to show up wearing the same dress as myself?! I'll ban her from every store in the country!!!"

Bob nodded.

"That is what we're trying to do today, Mistress."

Lady Anita glared at him.

"Then stop trying to do it and do it, minion!"

Bob grit his teeth.

"I just need you to grant me power of attorney first, Mistress, and then it will be done right away."

Lady Anita whacked him with her fan.

"I don't care about Attorney or whatever powers she has! I want that vixen to pay!"

Bob glanced at the third person in the room. Bob's stomach boiled and his face grew warm. The sympathetic expression on the man's face hurt more than a thousand whacks by a fan. But the man slowly nodded and opened his briefcase, withdrawing the documents therein. Bob walked over and took the papers, bringing them back and laying them on Lady Anita's desk.

"Lady Anita, if you sign these papers you will purchase the Mode par Éclipse."

Lady Anita sat back down and looked at the papers for a minute, then glanced up at Bob.

"And then I will make the vixen pay?"

Bob nodded.

"And then you will make the vixen pay."

Lady Anita smiled and sloppily signed her name at the bottom of the sheet. Not even close to the line. And in pink ink. Bob took the paper and brought it to the notary. The notary sighed but stamped the sheet. He then placed it in his briefcase and, with a brief nod to Bob, hurried out of the room.

"Really minion, why did you have to make that so difficult? With all that time you wasted you could've bought a hundred stores!"

Bob's left eye twitched. But Lady Anita ignored him, standing from her seat to look outside at her garden.

"Ohohohoho, I will show that vixen what it means to oppose Anita Laflèche de Albifort! I'll ban her from every store in the city, and then I will humiliate her in front of everyone at the graduation party! Then I will marry Prince Lionel..."

Lady Anita stopped for a moment, squirming about and holding her sides with a bright red face.

"And then I should get rid of that eyesore. Oh, I've got it! Daddy's doing that thing with the rocket, I'll ask him to tie her to it! I'll send her to the moon! Ohohohoho!"

Bob nodded.

"Then I should begin my work, if that's all Mistress?"

Lady Anita nodded.

"That's right, what are you standing around for, minion?! Get to work enacting my genius plan!"

Bob bowed and strode out of the room. Once outside the door he rubbed his temples with a single hand and heaved a huge sigh. After his single indulgence, Bob strode back to his own office. A simple office, clear of any adornment.

Or so he desperately wished were true. The mansion had but a single supplier of furniture and decor after all.

He sat at his desk, uncapped his pen, and began to write. He had much to do.

△△△

Ten miles past the border between Coflar and Belgium stood two figures. They were standing at the edge of a clearing deep within a forest. The night was dark, the crescent moon provided little light.

But that mattered not to Mister Dapper Tiger, for his feline eyes were six times better than a normal human's. He brushed the fur on his chin with the claws of his right hand, then took a quick sip from the cup of tea in his left. Many wished to know how the man gained the features responsible for his moniker but all he ever said was a good tailor and a tour in the jungle. What they did know is that he came back from that tour as some sort of humanoid tiger, and established quite a reputation for himself since. Which was how he entered the employ of the Coflar royal family, in fact.

"Naught but an abandoned warehouse, Your Highness."

Prince Lionel grimaced.

"She's here. She has to be."

Mister Dapper Tiger adjusted his monocle. It was true that a warehouse in the middle of a forest with no roads was more than a little suspicious. But no less suspicious than an anonymous letter delivered to the Prince's personal room claiming to know the whereabouts of his kidnapped sweetheart. Mister Dapper Tiger certainly believed Miss Adèle Corriveau might indeed be close by. After all, what better reason to kidnap the girl than to bring His Highness to such a secluded location?

Mister Dapper Tiger then heard the sound of rustling leaves. He focused his sight in the direction of the sound and caught something. A silhouette broke out of the tree line and made their way towards the warehouse.

"There is someone there, Your Highness. Please allow me to scout ahead."

Prince Lionel shook his head.

"I will not keep Adèle waiting."

Mister Dapper Tiger sighed and shook his head. Ah, to be young again. But who was he to question a young man's resolve?

"Very well, stay close. Please do not act before my signal."

Lionel nodded and the two were off, crouching low as they jogged towards the warehouse. They looped around to a wall with a window and stood against it. Mister Dapper Tiger held his hand up to stop Lionel and pressed his ear against the wall. After a few moments of silence he peeked into the window, then nodded to Lionel and slowly pushed on the frame.

In a spot of luck, it turned out the window was unlocked and could be opened quietly. Mister Dapper Tiger pulled himself up onto the windowsill, pulling up Lionel with both arms. He leapt to the floor of the warehouse without a single sound, then helped Lionel get down as well.

Both looked around the room. It was full of boxes covered with tarps. A thick layer of dust coated everything in the room and there were cobwebs growing from every corner. There was no sign anyone had been there in years, at least to the untrained eye.

But Mister Dapper Tiger was not so easily fooled.

He motioned Lionel to follow and crept towards a certain part of the room, where the dust was slightly piled up. As if someone had intentionally swept dust onto this particular spot. The tigerman pressed his claws on the floor, gently sliding until they found purchase, and pulled open a hidden door.

The two made their way into the underground tunnel and crept through dark hallways with dim incandescent lights, sticking to the shadows whenever possible. But they found naught a soul until they had reached a large, cylindrical room made of concrete. Inside armored men scrambled around and worked on various tasks. They were each covered in black armor that was adorned with an orange coat of arms. The room itself was massive, for a very obvious reason.

With a metal gate for a roof and a huge missile standing in the center, the purpose of this room could not be mistaken.

And neither could the man standing in front of the missile. He had groomed black hair with orange highlights, a thin black mustache, and a bright orange suit with a pink rose adorning his breast. Lionel could not forget Duke Gaëtan Laflèche de Albifort if he wanted to. Nor could he ever forget the person the Duke was talking with. Lionel took a step forward before Mr. Dapper Tiger pulled him back, whispering for him to wait. Lionel grit his teeth.

How could he possibly wait?

There, tied to the missile, was a young girl in a simple dress. She had a simple green hairband adorning her straight, golden hair and a cute, round face with big blue eyes. It was none other than Adèle Corriveau, the love of his life, her eyes moistening as she struggled against the rope.

"W-Why are you doing this?"

Duke Gaëtan laughed in her face.

"Bwahaha, do you not understand? Fear not, for this noble Gaëtan shall elucidate for you, young peasant! You see, this missile is aimed at none other than the Coflar Royal Palace!"

The girl glared at the Duke.

"Why would you do that?! Are you not a noble of Coflar?! How could you harm His Highness' family?!"

The Duke slapped the girl. He then jabbed his finger at her.

"Do not dare speak to me in that tone, you insolent cur! They all look down on me! The world looks down on me and denies me the respect I deserve! But when those fools in the palace are gone, I shall take my rightful place as king!"

He sneered at the girl.

"And as this missile shall fire from Belgium, all our country will cry out for war, and then I will lead them in glorious conquest! It will become a golden age for our country and then all shall sing my praises! For my name is Gaëtan Laflèche de Albifort and all who stand before me shall pay! And you, young peasant, have committed the greatest crime of all! You have angered my little darling, and for that you shall pay as well."

Lionel looked behind him to demand permission to act, only to find the beastman missing. He looked around the room until he noticed two large silhouettes in a dark corner of the room. There he saw Mr. Dapper Tiger, calmly sipping his tea next to a pile of unconscious men and giving him a thumbs up. Lionel waited not a moment longer and stepped into the light.

"Duke Gaëtan Laflèche de Albifort, you are under arrest!"

Adèle's face lit up in a bright smile.

"Lionel! You came for me!"

Lionel flashed her a smile of his own.

"I will always come for you, my love, wherever you go!"

Duke Gaëtan twirled his mustache with his left hand.

"Quite touching, young prince, but you were foolish to come alone! Minions, deal with this cur!"

And nothing happened.

Silence hung in the air. Duke Gaëtan cleared his throat.

"Ahem, I said, minions, deal with this cur!"

Still nothing happened. Duke Gaëtan began looking around the room.

"Minions?"

A light came on in the corner of the room, revealing the Duke's unconscious minions. And Mr. Dapper Tiger giving an elegant bow.

"Your Grace. You have my sincere apologies for the delayed greeting."

Duke Gaëtan turned back to Lionel, his eyes sinking into their sockets.

"Oh."

△△△

As all this occurred, no one noticed one minion exiting the warehouse, a briefcase in hand. A certain briefcase containing the coordinates for conveniently abandoned missile silos like this one Cikizwa had told him about.

Bob shook his head as he walked off into the forest. Filling the Duke's head with delusions of grandeur had been simple. Getting the Coflar royal family to act on the threat had not.

"So you ignored all my warnings about the Duke but immediately came running for the girl. Do you know how hard it was to delay that launch? How long I had to wait in that bush to tip you off? Heroes are so annoying."

△△△

And so Duke Gaëtan Laflèche de Albifort was found guilty of treason against the Colfar royal family, and sentenced to life imprisonment. His family was stripped of their titles and banished from the royal capital, including his daughter. However, the King and Queen hesitated to cut her off completely, and so the former Lady Anita was allowed to keep the substantial allowances that had been set up in her name. While some of these would be hard to access from the countryside, it turned out she had already granted her butler power of attorney, who was thus charged with managing her holdings...

AUTHOR'S COMMENTARY: So why exactly did the United States' military conveniently abandon fully-operational missile silos, you ask? Well...um...I'm sure there's an excellent reason for that that has absolutely nothing to do with the CIA! Anyways! What will Bob do with Lady Anita's holdings? Will Prince Lionel marry his sweetheart? Will Lady Anita ever learn what powers this 'Attorney' has? Tune in next time, to find out!

CHAPTER 3 - TO DEFY THE HEAVENS!

After Duke Gaetan's fall, Bob quickly took Lady Anita and stuffed her into an isolated estate in the Coflar countryside. It was a beautiful, peaceful place where she would lack for nothing, save contact with the outside world. And contact with Bob, as he immediately hired her a new butler.

And then he called up his old college roommate. The roommate who just so happened to be the only heir of a multinational conglomerate.

"Markus."

"Bob! Nice to hear from you! Here to distract me from the horrors of mundane, rich boy life?"

"I'd rather you help me join it."

"Boo, that's boring. I trust you at least have some starting capital?"

"Just acquired some, in fact."

"And I trust you'll make it worth my while?"

Bob told him what he was planning. The phone erupted in laughter.

"Oh that's great. That's rich. I'm so onboard with this. You'll let me in on it, right? No, actually, I demand to be a part of it. CEO, if you will."

"That's fine, as long as you use your own money."

"Worried my jerk of a father will get his grubby paws on it? That's...an excellent point actually. I'll be careful then, make sure it's all my stuff on the line."

"Good. Let's meet up and discuss the details then."

"I can't wait!"

With Markus's help, Bob successfully invested Lady Anita's assets, turning her and by proxy himself into one of the richest people in the world. Unbeknownst to the lady herself, but she was busy writing a book intended to sully Miss Corriveau's reputation and so couldn't be bothered with such mundane concerns.

But that was not all Bob did.

For Bob was not only aiming to acquire funds. No, his plan would require more than that. He would need help. A great deal of help.

An army, even.

And likewise, there was a huge sword hanging over his head.

He didn't know how far those martial artists and ninjas could reach, but he didn't want to wait to find out. So as he made connections with the big movers and shakers of the global economy, he asked around and researched as much as he could.

The ninjas were quite secretive and insular, based out of hidden villages in the most isolated regions of Japan, so there wasn't much he could glean about them. But the flip side of that was they were barely connected to the outside world at all. They were rarely spotted even within Japan, and never outside of the East Asia region.

The martial artists, on the other hand, were an entirely different story.

They called themselves the Eternal Night Sect. They sought immortality through meditation, body mastery, and the cultivation of qi. Even their initiates would be classified as supers compared to a normal person, their leaders were unbelievably powerful superhumans who were rumored to be centuries old.

In other words, they were cultivators, just like out of a xianxia story.

Bob would have thought it nonsense, had he not

witnessed men and women dodging bullets and soaring through the sky.

And the Eternal Night Sect had made a name for themselves within the community that acknowledged their existence, to the point that they were now known by the leaders of the mundane world as well. A sect that cultivated hatred of all things. That brutalized any rival cultivators and stole their qi, and that crushed anyone who got in their way. A group led by a killer known as the Ten Slaughters.

An evil sect, or so their rivals claimed.

A title that they embraced, and now worked to uphold.

He hadn't heard of them before, but not because they were hiding.

He hadn't heard of them because even mentioning them was a risk. They had *killed* over perceived insults, after all. So everyone who knew of them kept their mouths shut.

And no world leader wanted to admit to the public that there was a group of murderous superhumans they could do *nothing* about. Who could walk into any capital on the planet and demolish it entirely regardless of any resistance. Who wouldn't be stopped by anything short of nuclear weapons... and maybe not even that.

So everyone kept quiet and avoided all contact, praying the Eternal Night Sect wouldn't bother with them. And the Eternal Night Sect itself was uninterested in the 'mortal realm', for the most part. As were most modern cultivator sects. Apparently there had been cultivators with more 'mortal' ambitions in the past, but these had eventually been weeded out by the ones who focused their efforts.

So the Eternal Night Sect was largely content to let the mortals be...unless they were insulted or opposed.

And Bob had opposed them directly. Tricked the Young Mistress of the sect, even.

They had murdered entire *countries* for less.

Bob and the rest of Cikizwa's crew were only alive because the Eternal Night Sect rarely bothered with the mundane world, and so weren't set up to track down a handful of specific mortals. But they would find Bob eventually, not least of all because everyone they contacted would be forced to help. So they needed to be dealt with, one way or another, before they could connect Bob to that night.

So he had studied the Eternal Night Sect as far as he could, even visiting some of the rival groups incognito.

He had studied their cultivation, their organization, and the biographies of their leaders.

And he translated the scroll he had claimed, the Scroll of Demonic Binding as it was titled, which spoke of ancient techniques, foul demons, magic flowers, and mystical powers. Many secrets that the Eternal Night Sect would desire deeply, or even ones that could threaten them in the wrong hands. Bob did not have the knowledge to utilize such things himself...but the knowledge itself was enlightening.

And so he had started to form a plan.

A way to both neutralize the danger of the cultivators... and to acquire the manpower he needed for the future.

And now, he was ready to begin.

Fortunately, Cikizwa had some...less than legitimate contacts.

For to defy those who challenged the heavens above, first he needed some friends down in the dirt.

△△△

A white sedan drove along a dusty road, surrounded by nothing but cacti. The land was flat with no landmarks except the mountains rising in the distance. Which, of course, meant there was nothing to block the burning heat of the sun overhead. The car bumped along the desert road, if a hardened trail could be called a road.

The car pulled in front of a red stone building connected to a fenced ranch. The door opened and out stepped a man, his features hidden behind a black helmet and black armor.

He closed the door to the sedan and took a step forward.

Bob swore as he felt his neck suddenly stop while his legs continued forward, causing him to fall on his butt. He scooted backwards and turned his head, swearing once more as he saw the reason for his plight.

For the third time today, his mandatory red cape was caught in the door of the sedan.

He stood back up and brushed the dust off his bottom, then opened the door. This time, he gripped the end of the cape firmly in his hand and kept it far, far away from the door. Bob swore in his heart that if he ever designed a uniform, there would be no capes.

But well, that was kind of El Capa's thing.

Bob cursed as the sweat dripped into his eyes. The sun overhead beat down upon him as he stepped through the desert landscape. And for the third time today, he questioned if it was truly necessary to wear a full helmet at all times in this particular climate.

Bob walked towards the red stone building. He nodded to the caped guards as he entered into the ranch, heaving a sigh as he stepped into the shade. He greeted the serving lady as she carried the boss's refreshments, desperately averting his eyes from the drops of water forming on the sides of the drink.

Bob hesitated just a second before stepping back out into the sun. One does not wait for El Capa in the shade.

The man himself was standing in the center of a fenced area. He wore a black hat with a circular rim outlined in red, with a black opera mask covering his eyes. On his body he wore a black shirt and black pants with white socks that came high up his legs. And of course, he wore the iconic red cape he was most fond of.

"Ah, minion! It is good to see you."

Bob nodded.

"*Patrón*"

El Capa gave a bow with a dramatic flourish. The bull

behind him took its chance, the earth thundering as the beast sped towards the distracted man. But at the last second, El Capa danced around the raging mass of muscle and horns with a twirl of his cape, poking the bull with the tip of his sword. The bull cried and continued running. Once it had gained some distance it dug its hoofs in and whirled around, eyes locked upon the blade shimmering in the noon sun.

"Did you get it?"

Bob nodded and pulled a small cloth package from his pocket. He unwrapped it, revealing the plant within. El Capa turned his gaze upon the green bulb.

"One Adranis bulb, all seedless. Fifty percent more product per kilo. "

El Capa smiled as he stepped to the side. Bob bit down a curse and he jerked his hand away. The bull had been charging El Capa and stopped mere inches from the fence, very nearly squashing Bob's hand.

"Ah, with this my organization shall reign supreme. I shall have the best Soot on the planet! I can already taste the gringo cash."

"You'll taste nothing but the cold talons of justice."

All eyes turned to the top of the ranch, upon which stood a man. A handsome, muscular man. Or at least muscular, for his face was hidden. He wore a white lucha libre mask, his eyes outlined with blue wings and a golden beak painted over his nose. His torso was bare but for the long cape of white feathers covering his shoulders. His white chest hair was visible to all, broken up by the blue bird tattooed in the center. On his legs were blue spandex pants blending into his white boots.

El Capa took a bow towards the hero.

"Ah, it is a great day to be graced by the presence of Icy Falcon himself! Not only will today mark the start of my new empire, it will mark the end of my archnemesis. Minions, attack!"

Bob sighed as he and a dozen other caped minions

shuffled out into the open, pulling out their revolvers, handguns, and shotguns. Bob kept his finger off the trigger, and so was able to quickly let go of his weapon as Icy Falcon spread his 'wings'. Bob grit his teeth as a snowy wind blew past him, the cold piercing through his armor and straight to his bones. A block of ice lay at his feet, his revolver trapped in the center. The other minions who kept hold of their guns found those blocks now wrapped around their hands, stumbling to the ground from the sudden weight. Bob threw himself to the ground alongside them, and then crawled his way into the shade. Meanwhile Icy Falcon flew overhead, snowflakes falling in his wake.

"What are you doing, you incompetent fools?! Must I do everything myself?!"

"Face me, El Capa. You won't escape today."

Bob unhooked the blasted cape, wrapping it around the shivering serving lady huddled in the corner. Then he walked out of the ranch, and did not look back.

And cursed. The door and wheels of his sedan were frozen too. It seemed Icy Falcon didn't have any consideration for his admittedly anonymous informant.

"Heroes are so annoying."

△△△

El Capa leapt to the left as Icy Falcon shot past him. He grit his teeth as the chill pierced his bones, but it would take more than a cool breeze to stop him. He hid his rapier under his cape, and with a twirl launched a jab to the blind spot in his rear. A thin block of ice barely stopped the blade a centimeter from Icy Falcon's eye. El Capa sneered at his opponent.

"Come now, *Señor* Falcon. At least make it a challenge for me."

Icy Falcon flapped his cape backwards and then held it open, catching the gust of wind and gliding away from his foe. He pulled the cape back and then hurled it forward, launching daggers of ice towards his prey.

El Capa laughed as he twirled to and fro, flashes of light encircling him as his spinning blade reflected the sun. Shards of ice fell harmlessly around him, melting immediately in the desert heat. But as El Capa defended, a shadow passed him overhead. El Capa glanced up to track his foe and cursed as he looked straight into the sun. He shielded his eyes with his free arm and jumped to the side.

And then raised his eyebrow as Icy Falcon flew by...and struck the ground to El Capa's side. Somehow the hero had missed entirely.

"That's just disappointing, *Señor* Falcon. You missed your one opportunity! What were you even aiming for?"

"Your cape."

El Capa glanced over his shoulder. Sure enough, his cape was extended out, ending in Icy Falcon's grip. He felt a tug on his neck and a white gloved fist filled his view.

△△△

El Capa shivered as he came to. He couldn't feel his legs or his arms. He turned to look up and down and found his limbs encased in giant icicles growing down from the ceiling of his ranch and pillars of ice from the ground. Icy Falcon landed before him, kicking open the fence gate as he approached.

"A dirty trick, going for a man's cape, *Señor* Falcon."

"All's fair in war."

"Yes yes you win the day, congratulations."

El Capa's mouth curled upwards.

"But what have you really accomplished, *Señor* Falcon? Oh you'll take me in, I'm sure, maybe I'll even go to prison. But we both know nothing will change. I'll kick back, relax, and then be out in a week. Maybe I'll even make some new friends while I'm there. My minions will return and continue my work, and then we will continue this little dance. Round and round and round we go until maybe, one day, someone makes a little slip? It's hard to keep your balance on ice. Deep in your heart, you know, don't you? You will never stop me. Not in any way that matters."

The Icy Falcon looked up to the sky and stood still for a moment. Then he looked down and stared El Capa in the eye.

"Maybe not. But he can."

With that Icy Falcon crouched down, and then leapt into the sky with a flap of his cape. Revealing a bleeding, snorting bull that was staring El Capa straight in the eyes as it adjusted the position of its front leg.

"Motherf..."

△△△

Bob took another drink from his water bottle as he drove down the road. He could see a tower of smoke in the distance. Several army trucks passed by him, carrying green uniformed soldiers. Bob ignored them and continued on his way, driving towards the smoke. Eventually he arrived in a small town near burning fields, stepping into the local church as he pulled on his helmet. Beside the dimly lit pews stood a cop lighting a cigarette.

"Hi Miguel, looks like there was some trouble?"

Miguel shrugged.

"They need to show you *gringos* some effort, so they burn some small farms out here in Sinaloa. But what can we do? Nobody important cares about this place."

Bob pulled out a small package containing the seedless bulb, as well as a wad of cash.

"That might change, *if* you have what I asked for."

Miguel smiled.

"But of course. Anything for my new friend."

And so El Capa, the infamous drug lord, vanished, leaving a vacuum down in the Mexican underworld. At least, until a new cartel began rising to prominence in Sinaloa.

And in exchange, Bob secured the last connection he

needed. He was ready to take on the Eternal Night Sect...

△△△

Bob heaved a sigh as he climbed up the mountain. Because of course, the Eternal Night Sect was built at the very top of a mountain. And not a gentle, sloping mountain, with a nice road he could drive on. No, of course it was built into one of those stone pillar type mountains, the kind that rise nearly vertically. He had to climb sheer cliffs in some places to get this far.

But that made sense. The Eternal Night Sect was not built for mortals. No true member of the sect would have any trouble with the journey. And the Outer Disciples would find it good training...whether they liked it or not.

Once he had arrived at the top and caught his breath, Bob walked right through the gates. It turned out all one needed to do to infiltrate the Eternal Night Sect was put on the uniform of their Outer Disciples. A uniform that conveniently involved a full face mask which hid every part of the face but the eyes.

The reason for this was that no idiot would even attempt to infiltrate the Eternal Night Sect.

A cultivator capable of doing any real damage would be identified immediately by their qi. A cultivator weaker than that would be risking their life just being present within the sect. The Ten Slaughters did not care much about the lives of Outer Disciples, nor took the time to mediate the conflicts between the lower ranks. Anyone in the Eternal Night Sect can take anything they have the strength to seize, so subsequently anyone can lose anything they lack the strength to keep, including their own lives. A weak cultivator (much less a mortal) was rolling the dice that a rival wouldn't take them down just to clear the playing field. Or that an Inner Disciple wouldn't kill them just for kicks. The Young Mistress killed someone practically every day, some disciples claimed.

So to walk into the sect as a mortal? Someone who would die if the wrong disciple sneezed on them? Or if one of the Core Disciples happened to shout at someone in the same room as them?

There are much easier ways to commit suicide that don't involve climbing a stone pillar mountain.

And, of course, it goes without saying that if an intruder was actually revealed, they would be brutally murdered in an unspeakable fashion. Along with any of their relatives the Eternal Night Sect happened to come across.

So the Eternal Night Sect didn't guard the door because no one would be stupid enough to walk through it. Meaning anyone who *was* stupid enough was welcome to do just that.

And so Bob walked through the halls of the sect. He took deep and steady breaths as he stood up straight, doing his best to portray confidence.

He was, unfortunately, smart enough to understand the risks of his current actions. But not smart enough to avoid being here, apparently. So he hurried as much as he could to conclude his business before he was caught by some bored young master looking to vent.

Fortunately, the area he entered was practically devoid of people. The Ten Slaughters was known to be…somewhat temperamental at the best of times. So there was no one who dared to disturb his meditations. No one would even dare to approach his chamber while the door was closed, in fact.

Which meant, again, that Bob could walk right in and do just that.

Bob took a deep breath as he stood in front of two massive red doors.

This was it. The moment that would decide if his plans would succeed…or if he would die right here. He was committed now, there was no going back. All he could do… was hope he timed this correctly. That his new friends had come through for him. And that the Ten Slaughters was in a gracious mood and wouldn't kill him on sight.

Bob reached up to knock on the door...

△△△

In the center of a room devoid of light sat a man, his knees crossed, his hands held together in his lap. He sat completely still with his eyes closed, barely even breathing.

He took the fire in his belly and passed it through his body. Down through his right leg, over to the left. Up through his arms, swirling towards his head. His head grew light, his body trembled. He opened his eyes. He grit his teeth.

It was still not enough. A thousand years and still he lacked hatred.

Xiong Zhen closed his eyes again. He took a deep breath, pulling upon his memories. His greatest failures. The worst humiliations. The most unpleasant memories that still dwelled within him. To cultivate hatred itself was not a path for the weak-minded. But Xiong Zhen was anything but weak.

And then there was a knock at the door.

Xiong Zhen's eyes shot open. He almost admired the sheer idiotic bravery of the one who would interrupt his closed door cultivation. He glanced down. A dim pulse of red light shone in the dark, vaguely outlining the form of a blade. The side of his mouth curled upward.

It had been quite some time since the Black Blade was allowed to feast.

Xiong Zhen focused the fire in his chest. Two torches burst into flame, illuminating the jet-black blade lying in front of him. He spoke softly, but his words were full of intent. A command issued by the superior being, one that could not be disobeyed.

"Enter."

In walked a person, the black robes of a martial artist wrapped around their body and a black cloth mask covering their head and face, showing nothing but their eyes. The standard uniform of the Eternal Night Sect's Outer Disciples. And not even a hint of qi, practically still a mortal. Xiong Zhen felt a bit of the fire leave his chest as he raised his eyebrow. For an initiate of all people to dare interrupt him was truly impressive.

The disciple crouched down, touching their forehead to the ground.

"This one greets the Master."

Xiong Zhen nodded. This one at least knew his manners. Xiong Zhen decided to make his death swift.

"Speak."

"This one has something to present."

Xiong Zhen nodded as he plotted the man's demise. He reminisced fondly on the last disciple who thought he could bribe the Ten Slaughters. A shame he lasted merely a week, his screams had been most pleasant.

"Proceed."

The outer disciple reached into his robes, keeping his face upon the ground. Slowly he pulled out a small cloth package, unwrapped it, and held it out in front of him.

Xiong Zhen bit back a gasp.

The man held a small red bulb. An innocuous plant. A mere weed to the average eye..

And what Xiong Zhen's heart desired most.

A Blazing Dragon Flower. The elixir that would guarantee his ascension to the Ninth Realm. That would push him past his bottleneck and allow him to defeat the Final Tribulation. To overthrow the heavens themselves and gain immortality. And then, once he had conquered the heavens, what could the Earth do but bow before him?

His arms trembled as he took the package from the disciple's hands. For a moment, he gazed upon his prize, gently caressing the bulb.

"You have done well, disciple. Go now; await my return. You shall be rewarded for this."

The disciple rose, then kowtowed once more. One, twice, three times he bowed. He rose to his feet but kept his waist and head low as he backed out of the room and shut the door.

Xiong Zhen grinned as the torches went out.

△△△

Xiong Huang the Murderous Bloody Fist was not having a good day. The peerless beauty placed her perfectly sized hand on the jade-like skin of her heart shaped face and took a deep breath, air filling her ample chest.

Or at least that was how the bloody pulp on the floor had described her.

He was the fifth one *today* to offer her the 'honor' of warming his bed. She thought that at least *some* of these idiots might recognize the Young Mistress and Assistant Leader of their very own sect. Or at the very least check her qi before her chest but no, they couldn't see Mount Tai if it hit them in the face.

Which Xiong Huang did.

Repeatedly.

Well, the only thing they would court here was death.

She smashed the pulp with her fist once more, shattering his cultivation, quite possibly for good. She grabbed his leaking qi and pulled it into her own cultivation and frowned. Of course, he was barely even worth the effort. She heaved a sigh.

She stepped over what was left of the man and continued down the hallway.

And then she cursed in her heart.

As well as out loud.

For she saw an *Outer Disciple* approach her father's meditation room.

Just what she needed.

After murdering the disciple, her father would step outside his dungeon and blame her for the interruption, since she was in charge of recruiting and managing the Outer Disciples. He was already deeply upset about her failure to secure the Scroll of Demonic Binding, so something like this would not be forgiven. He would almost certainly conduct some 'father-daughter bonding' by training her in his hatred-fueled techniques.

The beatings were fine, she had gotten used to those. But for the duration of the 'lessons', she would be prohibited from any activities that would 'reduce her hatred', including cathartic beatings of lingering eyes. Which meant another month of dealing with idiots like the one she left on the ground.

She gathered her qi and prepared for a preemptive self-help murder when she heard the sound of a gong, the one meant to signal an emergency. She spun around on instinct before she remembered the disciple. She turned back towards her father's chamber and swore again. The Outer Disciple was gone. Since she couldn't stop him anymore, she turned around, letting her qi flare as she stalked towards the courtyard.

There had better be something for her to murder out there.

But the scene before her made her qi disperse and her eyes grow wide. The gray stone ground of the central courtyard was now checkered in red and black. Black, the bodies of countless disciples lying on the ground. Red, the blood spilling from their corpses. Her hair wrapped around her face as something blew past her, she heard a sickening crunch as whatever it was smashed through the nearby pillar. She slowly turned to look.

It was Zheng Bai, Demon of the Iron Club.

Zheng Bai was an absolute pig. He spent all day drinking. He never cleaned up after himself. Every choice he made, every word from his mouth was a stain on the honor of the sect and an affront to women everywhere.

He also beat the living daylights out of anyone who

disrespected her.

And now he was dead, blood draining from the hole in his chest.

She turned back to the courtyard. What sect had done this? What great clan had fallen upon them? What unholy alliance would dare to test them?

Her jaw dropped.

It was a single man.

A ruddy youth, no older than she appeared. His green hair was tied into a ponytail behind him. His white robes were now stained red with blood, none of it his own. He held an emerald glaive in his hands as he danced about the courtyard. He had sharp green eyes that focused solely on the man standing in front of him.

Across from him stood Fang Jing, the Unholy Blade, her father's greatest disciple. The jerk who tormented her day in and day out. How she wished to beat that smirk off his stupid face.

He was the one who never pulled his punches against her.

Who never disregarded her.

Who never underestimated her.

Who taught her the most.

Who she swore to defeat, no matter what it took.

She would never get the chance.

Fang Jing's blade moved up and to the right. His opponent stepped back and thrust forward at the same time. A green blade pierced out of Fang Jing's back. He spat blood on the enemy's face. The opponent didn't flinch, didn't even blink as he swung his glaive. Fang Jing flew through the air onto the pile of bodies, and moved no more.

Xiong Huang gripped her fists and took a step forward. And then she stopped. Her foot had hit something, something round. She slowly looked down. She saw a head, missing its body. The head of the most twisted and vile of the Eternal Night's elders. The Black Alchemist himself.

It was Old Wei.

Her vision spun. Her stomach dropped. Her heart raced.

Images passed through her mind.

Candies passed to her in secret. Nights spent reading under the covers. A constant presence as she lay in bed with a fever. Foul tasting medicines she was forced to drink. Stern lectures when she skipped her lessons. Horrible, horrible, absolutely lame jokes.

Arms wrapped around her when her father left her in tears.

The warmth and weight of his hand resting upon her head.

She fell to her knees.

She held her breath.

She swallowed.

She grit her teeth.

She shut her eyes.

A true cultivator faced the heavens alone. A true cultivator faced the world with a stoic gaze and an iron will. Much less the Young Mistress of the Eternal Night Sect, daughter of the Ten Slaughters himself.

She slowly, gently grabbed the head. She brought it up to her chest.

The dam broke as she wrapped it in her arms.

And then the world trembled.

The air drained of all warmth, as if the dead of winter had fallen upon the summer night. A chill ran down her spine. Her heart pounded in her chest. Sweat dripped from her brow. Something deep inside her told her to flee, but her legs were locked in place, refusing her commands.

Her father had come.

Xiong Zhen hovered in the air above the courtyard, silhouetted against the full moon and rocky spires, holding a jet black blade in his hand. He had no expression on his face as he surveyed the courtyard, full of the mangled corpses of his subordinates.

"Who dares?"

The youth took a step forward and readied his stance.

"I am Cao Xinya, son of Cao Zhong. The Emerald Tiger, the Lone Avenger. You slew my father, you burned down my home. Tonight, I will avenge them all."

Xiong Zhen's face curled into a twisted smile.

"You will try."

Cao Xinya leapt into the air, his glaive extended out. Xiong Zhen fell from the sky, the Black Blade pulled beside his head. As the two approached Xiong Zhen snapped his blade forward, a black streak across the moonlight. There was a high pitched ring and the two stopped mid flight as their blades collided.

And then a shattering roar blew through the mountains. Xiong Huang grunted and turned her back, shielding that which she held in her arms from the typhoon-force winds. Cao Xinya and Xiong Zhen gently landed on opposite sides of the courtyard.

"Impressive. How long has it been since I have used the Ten Slaughters?"

Cao Xinya fixed his stance.

"I have trained my entire life to defeat you. I will not fail."

Xiong Zhen grinned again.

"Then come, little avenger, and try to reach the heavens!"

Cao Xinya flew forward, like an arrow launched from a bow. Xiong Zhen slowly spun his sword around.

"I wade within a sea of blood. My fury shall open the way. The First Slaughter."

Faster and faster Cao Xinya approached. Xiong Zhen raised his sword overhead. His qi flared as he spoke the next words, and a low rumble echoed his voice.

"MY ANGER SHALL PART THE WAVES."

Down the sword swung. A black crescent tinged in red split the earth and sky.

Cao Xinya clicked his tongue and leapt to the side. A few stands of his hair floated in the air behind.

Xiong Zhen's smile grew wider. He pulled his sword to his

side until it was stretched behind his back.

"The people stretch from the mountain to the ocean. Before me is a field of heads. The Third Slaughter."

"MY BLADE SHALL CUT THE GRASS."

A black wave extended out from his sword and the pillars of the courtyard fell, cut in two. Xiong Huang threw herself to the ground. Cao Xinya flipped over the wave and continued his advance.

Xiong Zhen's mouth curled down into a straight line. His eyes narrowed.

"I step upon a mountain of bones. I shall sit upon the throne of skulls. The Fifth Slaughter."

Xiong Zhen raised his empty hand, fingers curled and palm towards the sky.

"THE FALLEN SHALL OBEY MY RULE."

Black hands reached from the ground, extending and grasping every which way. Cao Xinya leaped upwards and soared through the heavens. The corner of Xiong Zhen's mouth curled up once more. He pulled his elbow back, his blade passing by his head, his other hand extended out to the tip of the blade. He took aim.

"I cast aside the lie of love. My eyes look to the heavens above. The Ninth Slaughter."

He thrust the blade forward.

"MY GAZE SHALL PIERCE THE HEART."

The wind howled. The skies dimmed. A black lance that pulled in all the light around it shot towards Cao Xinya's heart.

Cao Xinya pulled back his glaive.

"The emerald tiger soars through the air. His prey knows only despair."

He swung his glaive as his qi filled his voice.

"HIS CLAWS CUT THE NIGHT."

A green crescent met the black lance. They spun, and intertwined. Smaller and smaller they shrunk.

The world went silent for a single moment.

And then there was a thundering roar as the mountains around them crumbled.

Cao Xinya landed in the courtyard, breathing heavily. Xiong Zhen was no longer smiling as sweat glistened on his brow.

"To think the tenth slaughter would see the light of day. Rejoice, little avenger, for this Xiong Zhen will remember you. The Emerald Tiger is worth conquering indeed."

Xiong Zhen held his sword in front of him, pointed to the sky.

"None understands the depths of my heart. None can withstand the heat of my rage. None can see in the black of night. None will stand my shattered light. None will know mercy. None will know grace. But all, all shall feel my pain. The Tenth Slaughter."

The world dimmed.

"MY HATE WILL SWALLOW THE WORLD."

The world went black.

A voice rang out in the darkness.

"The tiger stalks through the night. The predator's eyes need no light."

Green eyes glowed in the midst of the darkness.

"THE AVENGER'S BLADE SHALL FINALLY STRIKE."

A green blade shattered the night.

Xiong Zhen and Cao Xinya stood at opposite ends of the courtyard, both breathing heavily. A moment of respite for the broken mountain. Xiong Zhen's shoulders began trembling. Then he broke out into raucous laughter. Cao Xinya's eyes narrowed.

"You think this is funny?"

Xiong Zhen's face formed into a wide grin.

"Funny? It's hilarious! A mere boy matched me! I've lived more lives than you can count and I cannot end a mewling infant! Truly Cao Xinya is blessed by the heavens."

Xiong Zhen reached into his robe.

"But you are too late! Even a single day earlier and you

would have had your revenge!"

Xiong Zhen opened the package, revealing a red bulb.

"But just today, mere moments ago, I received the means to defeat you! To defeat the heavens themselves! To defeat death itself! Truly, fate has bent before me. And now, now I will never die! I will never lose! I will never be stopped!"

Cao Xinya grit his teeth, but his qi had not yet recovered. He could do nothing but watch as Xiong Zhen swallowed the bulb. Xiong Zhen's qi boiled, a dark mass becoming visible around him. He held his hands out and cackled madly.

And then there was the sound of glass shattering.

And Xiong Zhen fell to the ground.

"W-What is this? What is happening?"

Cao Xinya took a step forward. Xiong Zhen stared at his hands, his eyes growing wide.

"This cannot be. This is not possible!"

Another step. Xiong Zhen looked up.

"No...No! Get back!"

Cao Xinya's steps grew quicker. It turned into a walk, then a jog, until he was running at full speed. Xiong Zhen turned, crawling along the ground.

"It cannot end like this! I cannot die like this!"

Cao Xinya leapt into the air.

"For my father."

His blade struck true.

△△△

Cao Xinya stared up into the sky, gazing at the moon.

"It is over. Father, everyone, you can finally rest."

And then he heard quiet sobs cutting through the night. He looked into a corner of the courtyard. A girl knelt on the ground, her back turned to him. He strode over.

"Shhh, don't cry anymore, young miss. You are saved now."

The girl's shoulders trembled. She gently lay a round

object wrapped in cloth on the ground, then slowly took to her feet.

"Do you know who I am?"

She turned to face him. He nodded.

"You are Xiong Huang."

She reached into her robe, pulling out two small pieces of metal.

"Then you know I don't need to be saved."

Cao Xinya shook his head.

"I know you, Xiong Huang. You suffered at your father's hand as much as I did. Each and every day he beat you. You were surrounded by vile and evil men, forced to do terrible deeds. But I know your heart is still pure, that you can still be saved. Come with me, and I will take you from this evil place."

He extended his hand. Xiong Huang trembled.

"Are you serious?"

He nodded.

"I am always serious."

Xiong Huang slipped on her brass knuckles and slammed them together, blowing the wind past Cao Xinya's face. Cao Xinya blinked. Suddenly she was before him, her fist pulled back.

"ARE! YOU! SERIOUS?! YOU KNOW ME?! YOU DON'T KNOW CRAP!!!"

Cao Xinya jumped back, quickly pulling his glaive before him. Her fist slammed into his blade, sending him flying backwards.

"EVERYTHING I KNOW IS GONE! EVERYONE I KNOW IS DEAD! BECAUSE! YOU! KILLED! THEM!"

There were no verses. There was no qi honed into elegant techniques. There was no form. Just the wild swings and raw violence that gave Xiong Huang her name. Cao Xinya had no time to act, desperately weaving and blocking to avoid the assault.

"YOU ARE COVERED IN THE BLOOD OF MY SECT! AND

NOW YOU'LL SAVE ME?!"

Cao Xinya jumped back. Xiong Huang stood, breathing heavily.

"Well guess what, Mr. hero. I don't need saving. News flash: I liked it here. Those evil men you killed? I recruited and trained half of them myself. The one who broke the Elegant Flame Sect? Me. The one who massacred the River Dog Gang? Me. The Murderous Bloody Fist? That's me."

Xiong Huang slammed her fists together.

"You don't know me. You just don't want to kill a pretty face. Well guess what, hero, I'm every bit as bad as the lot of them. And you killed them all. Now come and kill me."

Cao Xinya's face fell, a sad frown on his face.

"So you won't turn from the path of evil? Please, I know there is good in…"

Cao Xinya gasped. A black blade protruded from his chest and a voice spoke behind him.

"Heroes are so annoying."

Xiong Huang didn't miss her chance.

Her fist dug into Cao Xinya's cheek. His eyes bulged. Teeth flew through the air.

Cao Xinya slammed into the ground. Xiong Huang jumped upon him. She brought her left fist high, and then slammed it into his face. Then her right fist. Then her left. Then right. Then left. Then right. Over and over, each blow containing all of her might.

"YOU! WANT! TO! SAVE! ME?! THEN! GIVE! BACK! OLD! WEI!"

Xiong Huang stood up. She picked up the emerald glaive lying on the ground beside them. She raised it high and spun it so the blade was facing down.

She looked down upon the bloody mess of a face.

Old Wei's smiling face flashed before her.

She brought down the blade.

Xiong Huang stood still for several moments, breathing heavily. Then she let go of the glaive, its handle cracked where her fingers had dug into it. She slowly straightened her back and turned to the only other person in the courtyard. They put their fist in their palm and bowed.

"This one greets the Young Mistress."

She frowned and crossed her arms.

"Cut the crap, I know you're not part of the sect, much less a glorified minion. You have to be in the Seventh Realm at minimum to hold my father's blade."

The man raised a hand, which was covered in gray metal.

"Not if you use a lead glove."

Xiong Huang paused.

"Wait, what?"

The man ignored her and reached into his robe. He pulled out a small package and slowly unwrapped it. Xiong Huang let out a gasp.

There laid the Blazing Dragon Flower.

The man stretched out his hand. Xiong Huang froze.

He was...offering it to her? The Blazing Dragon Flower? The elixir that would guarantee a cultivator's ascension to the heavens?

Xiong Huang trembled. She stopped her hand that was involuntary reaching for it. She took a deep breath.

She gulped as her stomach sank. What would this man demand of her? What would he want in exchange for such a boon? What could be worth such a treasure? She had a feeling she knew.

But she took another breath. She stopped her trembling and stilled her beating heart. She held her expression.

It didn't matter. Before her stood a master, with the Black Blade in one hand and the heavens in the other. She could not feel even an ounce of his cultivation, so great was his control. She could not even see the peak he must be standing upon.

This was not someone to be trifled with or denied.

So whatever he wanted, she would give to him. She had no choice. And...if he could be convinced...if he truly would give her the Blazing Dragon Flower...well she would do *anything* necessary to secure it.

She looked the man in the eyes.

"What do you want?"

She winced. She could not help her voice cracking. She prayed in vain that he didn't notice.

"You handled recruitment and training for the sect, correct?"

She stopped. She blinked. She tilted her head.

"Um, yes?"

The man nodded and tossed two items at her. She reflexively caught them both inches from her face and brought her hand down to get a better look. First was a scroll, a binding pact laying out the terms of an arrangement. The second was one of those mechanical devices the mortals were so fond of. She believed this one was called a pager?

"I will need manpower in the future."

"Um, ok?"

She read through the scroll. As the man stated, he simply wanted the Eternal Night Sect to provide Outer Disciples when asked. They would even be paid for their work, if mortal cash was of any value to them that is. In addition, there were fairly standard terms for this sort of agreement involving her and the Eternal Night Sect not harming the man.

Nothing she couldn't handle. Not even a pittance compared to a Blazing Dragon Flower. She suspected foul play or some catch she hadn't noticed but what could she do? Call him out? Raise a fuss? Everything he wanted in exchange was laid out in the scroll, which he had already signed. If she couldn't determine any hidden meanings from the words there, then that was simply her own failure.

She could not let this opportunity pass. She either had to accept the deal at face value...or admit she was afraid of something she could not see.

So she bit her finger and signed the bottom of the scroll

with her blood. She then timidly reached out her hand. The man grasped it, gave it a firm shake, and let it go. He then placed the Blazing Dragon Flower in her hand as he took the scroll. She blinked at the flower a couple of times before she looked up. The man was already walking out of the courtyard by the time she did.

"Is that really it? Is that truly all you wanted for this?"

The man stopped walking.

"Do you have second thoughts?"

Xiong Huang shook her head with all her might.

"It's just, this is a Blazing Dragon Flower. You aren't going to use it yourself?"

"I have no need for it."

Xiong Huang's body shook. No…need? The Blazing Dragon Flower was desired by every cultivator in the world. Even a mortal could gain a thousand years of life from it. Everyone in this world who had even *heard* of cultivation would kill for this bulb, would give up their firstborn child for it.

And this man declared he didn't need it, without hesitation. She shuddered at what that implied.

The peaks of the heavens were tall indeed.

Xiong Huang came to her senses just before the man left the courtyard.

"Wait, if this is the Blazing Dragon Flower, what did my father take?"

The man stopped once more.

"A custom grown Adranis bulb. It took my associates many tries to get the shape right."

Xiong Huang tilted her head.

"I've not heard of that herb, what manner of poison could affect my father so deeply?"

The man shook his head.

"It has no such effect. It is the key ingredient of the recreational drug called Soot."

"A…recreational drug?"

The man turned his head back to look at Xiong Huang. She could see the edges of his mask turn upward.

"Your father cultivated hatred for a thousand years, right? I simply helped him to relax."

Xiong Huang stared for a moment. And then rolled on the ground as she burst out laughing.

> AUTHOR'S COMMENTARY: See! Being hunted by the Murderous Bloody Fist: not a problem! Barely an inconvenience! All you need is a Xianxia protagonist who can randomly powerup and kill guys who have been training for several centuries more than him! Well, that and drugs. Anyways! Can Icy Falcon clean up the Mexican cartels? Will Xiong Huang ever learn who she has signed a contract with? What will Bob now that he is allied with the cartels and the cultivators? Tune in next time, to find out!

CHAPTER 4 - WHAT HAPPENS NEXT WILL SHOCK YOU!

With that, the Eternal Night Sect was dealt with. The Scroll of Demonic Binding had described the Blazing Dragon Flower in great detail, and so helped Bob not only find the real article, but grow a counterfeit as well.

Who would have guessed a magical cultivation elixir would look a great deal like a plant famous for relaxing narcotic properties?

Cao Xinya, on the other hand, was someone Bob came across as he visited the enemies of the Eternal Night Sect. The boy had been one of the most talented cultivators ever born, or so Bob had been told.

And most importantly, Cao Xinya had no other desire than to destroy the Eternal Night Sect.

So every other cultivator group in existence had poured all of their resources and knowledge into the young avenger, forging him into a weapon to strike at the Ten Slaughters. Bob had even contributed to this personally. The cultivator sects had long disdained the mortal world, so they were unaware that some elixirs were floating around for the taking, offered up for mundane cash by sellers who didn't know their true value.

And in the midst of his donations, Bob had spoken about the Eternal Night Sect to Cao Xinya himself, dropping some… exaggerations about Xiong Huang's personality.

And so all he had to do was show up on the right day and guarantee Xiong Zhen would fall…and then ensure Xiong Huang would get her own vengeance shortly afterwards.

And now the full might and authority of the Eternal Night Sect lay with Xiong Huang alone, so if Bob could manage her, he could manage the most powerful cultivator sect in the world. Maybe the most powerful force in the world, especially now.

Bob admitted it was a serious risk handing over the Blazing Dragon Flower to Xiong Huang, the Murderous Bloody Fist. She was powerful before, stronger than most *supers* and bulletproof to boot.

And now, with the Blazing Dragon Flower?

Well, if the legends Bob heard were true, he had just created an unstoppable and immortal demigod.

But wiping out the Eternal Night Sect entirely would have left a dangerous power vacuum. The Eternal Night had dominated an entire branch of human society for a millenium, so their sudden removal would have been immensely destabilizing.

Bob had decided to concentrate all of their power into a single person, who could maintain the Eternal Night's dominance even after most of the sect was wiped out. And who would owe him a great debt as a result.

A single person could be dealt with and managed as long as he understood them. And the Murderous Bloody Fist was surprisingly reasonable. Bob had studied her record and identified her as the best candidate among Eternal Night's elites. She was violent and temperamental…but far less indiscriminate than her title might imply. She was the public face of the sect after all, the one handling most of the mundane affairs on behalf of the elders. So she knew how to put on a smile, and reign in her rage when she needed to. Her reputation as bloody grew because she had no mercy for her enemies.

And a habit for venting her frustrations onto the disciples

she trained. They *mostly* survived without permanent harm, though.

And zero tolerance for being hit on, which given her beauty and the average cultivator's approach to women meant a trail of bodies.

So while she *did* indiscriminately beat the crap out of anyone she felt like, anyone who wasn't an active hostile and treated her with all due respect would *probably* survive the experience. Bob could even understand how Cao Xinya had misread her character so badly. Compared to the rest of the Eternal Night Sect, basic diplomacy and self-restraint seemed almost saint-like. So it only took a few minor exaggerations to convince the boy that Xiong Huang was a sheep among wolves, just waiting for a hero to come and redeem her.

It also hadn't hurt that she was *immensely* beautiful, and that Cao Xinya was a healthy young lad, whenever he wasn't consumed with his revenge that is. Xiong Huang would not have admitted it but her pretty face was a weapon unto itself.

The point being, that Xiong Huang, if treated with appropriate respect and caution, could be reasoned with and was unlikely to go out of her way to cause trouble. And with the Blazing Dragon Flower, she would reach the heavens, and immortality. She had won the prize, finished the race. She would not need to scramble and scrounge for the next magic flower any longer. So what need would she have to tangle with the masses?

And Xiong Huang, in particular, would honor agreements she had made. The Eternal Night Sect took what they wanted when they wanted it, so on the few occasions they deigned to negotiate they generally followed through. That was how a so-called 'evil' sect hated by everyone had maintained a dominant position for millenium, after all. And Xiong Huang was the most trustworthy of the bunch, as she was the one who negotiated the agreements in the first place. Bob did not need to worry about the Eternal Night Sect coming after him any longer.

And what he had gained was equally important.

The Eternal Night Sect had no lack of applicants, a practically endless source of Outer Disciples hoping to ascend. Once Xiong Huang resumed recruitment, those numbers would be restored practically overnight.

Numbers that, per the agreement, were now available to Bob for whatever task he might ask of them.

And he had also gained the aid of an unbelievably powerful ally. The ultimate insurance, should his plans one day backfire on him.

So now, Bob had money. He had connections, in both high and low places. He had a skilled group of trusted friends. And he had an army of disposable, slightly superhuman soldiers and an alliance with an immortal demigod.

At this point there was only one last thing he wanted before he started on his ultimate design.

Weapons.

And he already knew where to find them.

△△△

It was a cold winter night as the snow fell over a small town in Soviet Russia. Empty chimneys were covered in ice. White mounds hid the rusting husks of old vehicles. In the center of the town was a silent factory with broken windows. The town was almost completely empty, save for one building. Light still shone through the windows of an old school.

Bob shuffled in his seat, silently cursing at the tingling feeling that shot through his left leg. A desk designed for elementary school students was not an ideal seat for a grown man. But well, he had it better than most. He wasn't sure whether to feel more sorry for his friend Ivan or the bulging metal frame desperately trying to hold in Ivan's massive thighs.

"Ok, I will now explain the secret plan."

At the front of the room, stood the Red Colonel. He wore a red beret, a smooth red mask with no features except the holes for his eyes, and a green uniform with hundreds of metal pins and ribbons attached to the front. Surely, this was the most distinguished officer the KGB had ever produced.

Yes, Bob had joined the reds.

Infiltrating the KGB had been...surprisingly easy. Barely an inconvenience, in fact. It turned out Sergei knew a guy and Cikizwa made regular trips to Moscow, so Bob had walked right in, made some new friends, and then applied for the job with a glowing recommendation.

The Red Colonel didn't trust the suspicious new guy, of course. But the Red Colonel didn't trust anyone so that wasn't an issue for Bob.

Ivan raised his hand. The Red Colonel sighed.

"Yes, Ivan?"

"I am confused. Why are we assassinating the premier? Shouldn't KGB protect the premier? Also, why must we speak English?"

The Red Colonel sighed again.

"You see, Ivan, the current premier is actually a counter-revolutionary. He makes friends with capitalist pig dogs, ends the Cold War, and worst of all cuts the KGB budget. We must remove traitors to protect the glorious Soviet Union, whoever they are."

Ivan thought for a moment but slowly nodded.

"And English?"

The Red Colonel turned back to the blackboard and grabbed a piece of chalk.

"That is part of the secret plan, which I will now explain if Ivan stops interrupting."

The Red Colonel drew a stick figure on the board.

"Ok here is the premier, meeting capitalist pig dogs for 'peace' dinner. We will sneak into basement with the secret weapon: death ray we found in a conveniently abandoned

US military warehouse. We then use this stage lift to bring the death ray in front of the premier and shoot him while speaking English. Everyone thinks we are CIA and goes 'oh no, not the premier!' Cold War restarts and I…"

The Red Colonel coughed.

"WE get a raise. Anyone have questions besides Ivan? Yes, Boris?"

Boris put his hand down.

"What if American Death Ray doesn't work?"

The Red Colonel nodded his head.

"Da, that is a very likely problem. Which is why I have also prepared American weapons. If the death ray fails, we will rush in and shoot Premier. Be careful not to shoot any capitalist pig-dogs and remember, absolutely no Russian. Any other questions?"

The helmeted minions, err, elite KGB operatives shook their heads.

"Good. Go get ready, the plan starts tonight."

Bob walked over and patted Ivan on the shoulder.

"You all right?"

Ivan glanced up at Bob. Bob swore he could see the smile under the man's masked helmet.

"Ah, friend Bob. Da, I just have many questions about the plan. Even if we speak English, will people not notice our accents? What if actual CIA is at dinner? And if the KGB kills the premier, aren't the KGB bad guys?"

Bob shrugged.

"The Red Colonel must have his reasons, he's not the KGB's best officer for nothing. And even if we are the bad guys, it doesn't mean you are a bad guy, Ivan."

Ivan laughed and stood up, slapping Bob on the back and nearly knocking him to the ground.

"You are right, friend Bob. I think too much. I'm going to get ready for tonight, after mission we go visit my Babushka, da?"

Bob nodded.

"Da."

△△△

Voices rang out through a well-lit dining hall. Waiters in suits carried elegant glasses and dishes that looked more like works of art. Well-groomed men in pristine tuxedos and beautiful women in gorgeous gowns sat at tables covered in white cloth, candles, and flowers. An orchestra played a mellow and graceful tune upon the room's stage. At the opposite end of the banquet hall was a large table, which had American and Soviet flags draped over its front. At the table sat two older men, chatting and laughing with one another. They were flanked by men in suits and sunglasses, standing at ease and scanning the room.

The orchestra's last tune finished and a polite applause sounded throughout the room. The musicians took a bow and carried their instruments off-stage. Another suited man took the mic.

"Ladies and gentlemen, I have a special announcement. We have a surprise performance for you all! Please, direct your attention to the stage."

The lights in the hall dimmed except for the stage lights and the lights over the two leaders.

"This performance is straight from the United States of America and dedicated to the glorious Premier of the Soviet Union. A celebration of this night of unity!"

The floor of the stage swung open. Cables moved as the stage lift began to rise.

Gasps rang out amongst the hall. On the stage was a large metal cylinder mounted on a stand. At its front ran a pole, flanked by metal circles, that ended with a perfectly round sphere. The device was flanked by armored, helmeted soldiers holding M-16 assault rifles. One soldier held a small metal box with a big red button.

"Straight from the Agency of Central Intelligence, it is

Death Ray! Now die, foolish Premier!"

The button was pressed. The weapon charged. Lightning cracked around the circles and the pole. The sphere began to glow red, then orange, then purple, and finally blue.

A crackling roar sounded through the hall as the air was torn apart. A beam of blue light pierced forward and the hall was covered in a blast of smoke.

And then a metallic voice sang out.

"Capacitor's surging, checking connection."

The smoke began to dissipate. A large silhouette formed through the fog, a glowing blue circle fading on its chest where it had tanked the death ray.

"Electrodes ready, rubber shoes in motion."

Clank, clank, clank. With heavy steps from metal boots, the figure slowly stepped forward and came into view.

A large suit of bulky metal armor stood in front of the main table. It had massive gray boots, a round helmet that blended into the chest piece with a single rectangular eye slit and a glowing blue device on the back, connected with wires to the wrist mounted tesla coils. A red star was painted on the center of the armored chestplate.

"Soviet power supreme, Tesla Titan is ready!"

It was the Soviet Union's secret weapon, the living power plant. The man who channeled the power of lightning through his body, and through his specially made armored suit. The Tesla Titan.

The armored men on the stage lifted their rifles and moved to attack. The sounds of gunshots rang out and the windows of the hall shattered.

And then...

The armored figures fell to the ground.

"Chew on this!"

A figure leapt through the window, rolling on the floor. She stood up and unleashed hell from the pistols in each of her hands. She had red hair and wore a green tank top with green camo pants.

The United States' most successful operative, Special Agent Tina had arrived.

Tesla Titan nodded as he held up his hand, lightning surging from his arms into a squad of attackers.

"Ah, American woman! Good to see you arrive. Only slightly late this time."

"Shut it, commie!"

Agent Tina threw her arm back and fired behind her without even looking. An attacker that had been sneaking up on the Premier fell to the ground.

"Ah, that was nice shot."

Agent Tina smirked.

"Duh! I'm the best there is."

"Except when we fight at Budapest."

"S-Shut it, we didn't actually fight. You just called an airstrike, that doesn't count."

"Is not good to be sore loser."

Agent Tina ducked as the Tesla Titan fired a blast of lightning overhead. She spun around and gunned down a group trying to sneak behind the armored man.

"We are so having a rematch after this."

△△△

The Premier was led by two of his agents to the garage. One held his hand up and the trio stopped, the two agents lifting their guns. There was a click and the lights turned on. The Premier smiled.

"Ah, Red Colonel, it is good you are here!"

The Red Colonel stood in front of the Premier's car.

The two agents lowered their guns.

And then the Red Colonel raised his and squeezed the trigger twice.

The Premier took a step back as his agents fell to the ground.

"Colonel, what are you doing?"

"What am I doing, what are you doing, comrade Premier?"

The Red Colonel raised his gun.

"Because I know who you meet in the shadows. I know who you *truly* work for, Premier, whether you know it or not. I know what you want and I know it is not a glorious future for our country. And since you will not protect the Soviet Union, I will."

The Red Colonel took aim.

The Premier shut his eyes and shielded his face with his arms.

The sound of thunder rang through the garage.

A body hit the ground, blood streaming from the hole in its head.

It was the Red Colonel.

A squad of men in suits and sunglasses ran into the room, guns at the ready. They took up positions around the Premier. One of them stepped forward and took out a badge.

"Agent Wilson, CIA. Are you ok, Premier Gorbachev?"

The premier nodded.

"Da, thanks to you American agent. But now, I must think carefully about the KGB and the future of the Soviet Union."

△△△

In the janitor's office, an armored figure held up a radio and listened in.

"Eagle Five, this is Eagle Home. Papa Bear's with the babysitters, thanks for the tip. Over."

The figure nodded and replied.

"Eagle Home, this is Eagle Five. All in a day's work, I'll send you the bill. Over."

"Copy that, Eagle Five. Eagle Home out."

And with that, Bob put down the radio and shook his head.

"Neither of you could stick with the target, could you?

Too busy flirting, were you? Heroes are so annoying."

Bob gathered the rest of his gear and exited the closet, heading out the back door. He tread through the snow until he found another armored figure, leaning back against a building and looking up at the moon.

"You all right, Ivan?"

Ivan turned to look at him, slowly nodding after a moment.

"Da, da friend Bob. Just, a lot to think about tonight. I'm glad we fail, it did not feel right to kill the Premier. But now, Ivan is a traitor too, yea? KGB was only thing I'm good at, so now I do not know what to do."

Bob thought for a moment.

"Ever thought about the private sector? I might know somebody who can help. And who could get a nice, quiet place for your Babushka to stay."

△△△

The wind howled across an empty tundra in Siberia, both the air and ground obscured by snow. Amidst the storm, two figures walked towards a small mound, a man and a woman. The man was covered in a puffy white jacket and snow pants, trudging through the snow. The woman had no protection but a thin silk shirt and thin silk pants. Yet, not a single snowflake landed upon her head, and not a single footprint was left in the snow behind her.

The two reached the mound. Bob heaved a sigh, pulled out a shovel, and began digging.

And kept digging until the shovel suddenly stopped with a clang.

Bob put aside the shovel and wiped away the snow. He found a gray metal door, hidden beneath the snowfalls.

"It's here."

He began to reach into his jacket when the woman stepped forward, pushing him to the side. She lay one finger upon the door, then curled that hand forward into a fist. There was a sickening crunch as the doors bent open.

"That was excessive."

Xiong Huang grinned.

"You shouldn't ask for my help if you don't want excessive violence. It's my favorite hobby. Besides, you should be capable of that much, right?"

Bob shook his head.

"I told you before, you think too much of me."

The two strode into the hidden bunker, a large empty room with a single number panel on the far wall. Bob walked to the panel and input a code. The floor began dropping slowly.

As the walls of the elevator shaft dropped the two were lowered into an open underground cavern. Inside were wooden crates, stacked as far as the eye could see. There were all sorts of vehicles from cars and trucks to tanks and helicopters. The Red Colonel had even acquired some nuclear warheads for himself, heavens knows how or why. And of course, there were some more…exotic pieces the Red Colonel had gathered over the years. Xiong Huang grinned and leapt off the elevator, which was still several stories up. She had already reached one of the crates by the time the elevator reached the floor and Bob disembarked. With a single finger she flipped open the lid of a box, revealing a pile of assault rifles.

"Wow, you weren't kidding. And the mortals just leave all these weapons lying around?"

Bob shook his head.

"Not normally. The Colonel liked to handle things on his own, and was not prepared for a…sudden demotion."

Xiong Huang reached into the box and picked up one of the assault rifles. She disengaged the safety, cocked the rifle, and aimed down the sight. Bob raised an eyebrow.

"I didn't think you'd be familiar."

She grinned at him.

"Oh, daddy hated anything new. But me? I'm not so picky. In fact…"

She reached into the crate and picked up another assault rifle, holding one in each hand.

"Oh yea, I think I could get used to this."

> *AUTHOR'S COMMENTARY: Now it's time for the Soviet Union to conveniently abandon a bunch of military-grade hardware! Ivan asks how did the Red Colonel set this all up if only he knew the location? Well, you see Ivan…um…quick roll credits! Anyways! Who will win the re-match between Tesla Titan and Agent Tina? What is the future of the Soviet Union? What will Bob and Xiong Huang do with a warehouse of Red Army Surplus? Tune in next time, to find out!*

CHAPTER 5 - THE MASTER OF EVIL

And so Bob acquired a large stockpile of weapons, conventional and otherwise. Well, the Eternal Night's disciples didn't exactly need them, but appearances were important for what Bob had planned. And not everyone he worked with was an aspiring superhuman, so it was good to maintain a more mundane armory.

He also stopped the Cold War from heating up again, which was a nice side benefit.

But in any case, now it was time to put his plan into action.

△△△

And so Bob and Markus got to work, gathering up their joint capital as the decade turned and the world entered the Nineties. Between Markus's private funds and Lady Anita's holdings, they had quite the substantial amount. Enough to start their own bank.

Which is exactly what Bob did, in fact.

EL Bank. Bob had questions about the name but Markus insisted.

Bob just groaned and held his forehead. He got why Markus wanted to call it 'Evil Laughs' but he had spent too much time in Mexico to feel comfortable calling it that. And of course, they couldn't exactly explain what the letters stood for, either.

But, well, their target demographic would not

particularly mind what they were called.

A woman opened a glass door and stepped into a wide entrance hall. She wore a hat, sunglasses, and a large trench coat. She glanced every which way and pulled her collars higher.

As she did, she walked down the large, well lit hall. There were walls and pillars made of black marble, and a red carpet laid out down the center. At the end of the hall was a wooden desk. A receptionist sat there, with two large letters, 'E' and 'L', hung on the wall behind her. The woman approached the desk.

"Welcome to EL Bank, how may we help you today?"

"Y-Yes, I'm here for a loan application."

"I see, have you contacted us before?"

"Y-Yes, I called earlier..."

"Ah, Madam Toxic Kiss was it?"

The woman quickly leaned forward, trying to cover the receptionist's mouth.

"Shhh! Quiet! What are you going to do if they hear you?!"

The receptionist leaned back and put on a smile.

"I assure you, Madam, EL Bank takes the confidentiality of its clients with the utmost seriousness."

"S-Still..."

"Why don't I take you to one of our private rooms? Perhaps you'd be more comfortable if one of our clerks assisted you there."

The woman nodded repeatedly.

"Y-Yes please."

The receptionist led the woman to a hallway behind the front desk, filled with doors. She opened one of the doors and led the woman inside. The room was simply adorned, with some paintings and potted plants. On the far wall was a teller window with a bulletproof lockbox, as well as a chair. A clerk sat at the other side of the window, along with a notary.

The woman exhaled a breath, then walked over to the window.

"Hello, how may I help you today?"

She took a deep breath, and then flung her arm into the air, pulling off the trench coat, sunglasses, and hat all in one motion.

Underneath, the woman wore a black leather suit, adorned with neon green highlights. She had a mask over her eyes, and her hair was dyed bright green.

She took a pose, standing wide and tall with one hand on her hips, and the other pointed at the clerk.

"Muahahahahahaha! It is none other than I, Madam Toxic Kiss! Today you will have the honor of assisting me in my grand endeavor! I will overthrow the pathetic establishment and take my rightful place as ruler of the world! Muahahahahahaha!"

The clerk simply smiled and nodded.

"I see. We would be happy to assist you with all of your needs, Madam Toxic Kiss. Why don't you have a seat."

Madam Toxic Kiss froze for a moment, and then nodded.

"Um, ok."

The supervillainess sat down in the chair.

"So, ruler of the world, was it? I believe then our enduring investment package would be ideal for you?"

Madam Toxic Kiss nodded after a moment.

"Ah, yes please."

The clerk nodded and pulled out a bundle of paper and a pen. He placed it inside the lockbox, then sealed his side and unlocked the other.

"Please fill out the application. Real name is optional but we will need legitimate contact information for you to inform you of your application status. Please inform us of your plans with as much detail as you feel comfortable sharing."

"Ah, ok."

Madam Toxic Kiss took the bundle and began filling out the forms.

"U-Um..."

"Yes, do you have a question?"

"Is this...insurance clause truly necessary?"

The clerk nodded.

"There can be only one ruler of the world, after all. We require all our clients to invest in an insurance program in the eventuality one of them casts the other down. I imagine there might be some...individuals you have plans for?"

Madam Toxic Kiss grit her teeth.

"Oh, do I have plans for them!"

The clerk nodded.

"The insurance clause is to support that. We imagine that during your rise to power, you may inevitably cast down some of our other clients. With this clause, we can wholeheartedly support you, without concerning ourselves with anyone you may need to...handle."

Madam Toxic Kiss nodded.

"Ah, I see. Yes, that is for the best. I try to be kind, you know, but these people just keep getting in my way. My hand might be forced, you see."

"We understand completely."

Madam Toxic Kiss signed the insurance application, and then placed the papers back in the box. The clerk took them back and flipped through them, before nodding and signing the paper. The notary nodded and certified the document as well.

"Thank you, did you wish to discuss our staffing options as well?"

Madam Toxic Kiss nodded.

"Ah, yes please."

"Of course."

The clerk placed another bundle of papers in the window.

"As you may know, all EL Bank loan packages also come with a staffing option through our partner, Midnight Staffing, who offers a discounted rate if you submit a request along with your loan application. Midnight Staffing will handle all the bureaucratic aspects of your employees, including hiring, payroll, benefits, medical claims, and compliance with all relevant labor laws in your jurisdiction, all so that you can focus on what you do best. Do you wish to apply for the standard staff package or would you like to customize for your operation's requirements?"

"Ah, the standard package will be sufficient, I think?"

"Excellent, please fill out that form then. If you do have any preferences or special requests, please note them in the appropriate fields."

The clerk waited as the supervillainess filled out the form and handed it back through the box.

"Thank you, should your loan be approved we will submit this immediately. May we help you with anything else today?"

"Ah, no, that will be all."

"Thank you for choosing EL Bank, we look forward to helping you change the world."

"Y-Yes, thank you."

With that, Madam Toxic Kiss put her disguise back on, and left the room.

△△△

Up in a small office within EL Bank, Bob sorted through the new applications. He rubbed his chin as he looked over Madam Toxic Kiss's paperwork, and then nodded.

"Should have some potential."

He grabbed a phone in the room and dialed it.

"You have reached Sinn Kwaigno, Director of Placements with Midnight Staffing, how may I help you?"

"Hi Sinn."

"Hi there Bob! What can I do for you today?"

"Got another one, needs the full complement."

"Understood, another bunch just arrived from our friends out East so that shouldn't be a problem. Will you be joining in?"

"Not this time, I think the standard procedure should be fine."

"I'll let Stacey know then. Should be ready in about a week."

"Thanks Sinn."

"Anytime, Bob!"

△△△

And so a group of workers, managers, and security guards headed out from Midnight Staffing. Which was a front company for the Eternal Night Sect, managed by Cikizwa's former crew. They met up with Madam Toxic Kiss at her new research facility, purchased for her by one of EL Bank's associated real estate agencies, and got to work fabricating her proprietary neurotoxin.

That is, until one day when all the managers and technicians and other non-combat personnel suddenly took the day off. Which, of course, the managers ended up approving, leaving the facility empty save for the security detail.

Madam Toxic Kiss was just arriving for the day when the alarms went off.

"W-What's going on?! What's happening?!"

One of the security guards shouted into a phone and then turned to her.

"We're under attack, Ma'am! It's…it's…"

"Attack?! By who?!"

"It's Captain Hot Devil!"

Elsewhere in the facility, a man marched through the halls. He wore a red cape and mask over a yellow suit, symbols of flames on his chest and the cape on his back.

And his fists were coated with fire.

Three security guards rushed towards him with batons in hand. Captain Hot Devil swung his leg in a roundhouse kick, a jet of flame shooting from his heel and accelerating his attack. It slammed one of the guards into the wall. He then leapt off the ground to spin around and plant both his feet on the next guard's chest. Another jet of flame from his feet accelerated him back and up into the air, allowing him to flip backwards and land upright. The last guard rushed forward, only to meet a flame accelerated fist to the face.

As Captain Hot Devil handled the last attack, another squad of guards rounded the corner, assault rifles in hands. Captain Hot Devil pointed a palm out at the group.

A cone of flame engulfed them, setting their uniforms ablaze. *Probably* not enough to be lethal, but certainly enough to cause some serious pain.

The guards screamed, dropped their guns, and rolled about on the ground as Captain Hot Devil ran past them.

Once Captain Hot Devil had moved further inside, the guards suddenly stopped rolling about. Surges of qi passed over their bodies, extinguishing the flames. The guards from the start rose back up too, no worse for wear from the blows the Captain had given them. One of the first guards reached into his armor and pulled out a bundle of papers and blueprints.

The group nodded and then ran out of the facility.

A scene that repeated several times, until Captain Hot Devil confronted Madam Toxic Kiss at the heart of her facility.

A facility that burned to the ground later that day, as another supervillain fell to the heroic captain.

△△△

Bob walked into a sterile laboratory, wearing a full hazmat suit. Another figure in a hazmat suit was working at a lab desk, mixing a beaker together.

"How are we looking, Kanna?"

Kanna looked up from her beakers and nodded at Bob.

"Well, biology isn't my strongest field, but I think I can

come up with some medical applications for this. I mean, assuming you don't just want to sell it to some government as is."

It turns out Kanna was a bit of a supergenius herself, a fact Bob discovered when she helped him go through the Red Colonel's arsenal. EL Bank had therefore provided her with funding, as well as any patents they acquired the rights to through their insurance clauses. As such, Tanifuji Incorporated was making a name for itself with revolutionary inventions.

And making a great deal of profit, as well.

Bob shook his head.

"Civilian applications raise less questions."

Kanna shrugged.

"Well that's a bit boring, if you ask me, but I should be able to come up with something, eventually."

Bob crossed his arms.

"Can't you ask your husband to take a look? I thought he was an expert on this sort of thing."

Kanna froze.

"Ugh, don't remind me of that jerk."

Bob raised an eyebrow.

"I thought you loved him?"

"And I thought he loved me, but turns out he doesn't know me at all. Still thinks I'm at home prepping dinner. That idiot hasn't even connected my last name with the company, for goodness's sake."

"Are you sure you should be here, then? Sounds like you two have some things to work out."

Kanna shook her head.

"Tried that already, he's not interested. Besides Bob, I'm here to distract myself, so stop reminding me!"

Bob shrugged.

"If you say so."

A bit later Tanifuji Inc. entered the pharmaceutical field with a miraculous new drug, earning a great deal of profit for themselves. And for their investors, including a certain bank...

△△△

And so EL Bank became the name in funding and staffing for a...particular clientele. Which meant whoever approved EL Bank loan applications could decide when and where supervillains would arise. And could keep tabs on their progress as Eternal Night Outer Disciples filled the ranks of their evil organizations. The villains with promising designs or sympathetic goals could be allowed to progress, such that their work could be continued after their defeat. Those just out to burn the world could be directed towards parts of the globe that needed a shakeup or else taken down early. And those who were too dangerous, too powerful, too radical? Well, they could be tipped off to the authorities...or to the nearest caped vigilante.

Of course, things didn't always go as planned. Some villains were wiser than others and took precautions that forced EL Bank to play straight with them. And others never bothered going to the bank in the first place, confident in their own abilities and resources.

And contrary to popular belief, the heroes didn't always win.

But well, Bob had an answer to those cases as well...

△△△

Xiong Huang yawned as she sat back on her new couch, flipping through the channels of her newly installed television. Not that she had many channels, it turned out it was hard to get a decent signal on the top of a stone pillar mountain in the middle of China. But it was something to do, other than eat the bag of snacks she had lying next to her.

She'd trade pointers with the disciples, but they were still recovering from the last time. They were weaklings, each and every one of them. However, she *did* want an Inner Disciple or two eventually, so breaking the disciples' cultivation out of boredom would be counterproductive.

It was then that her phone rang. She raised an eyebrow.

There was only one person who would dare to call her.

...well there was only one person who knew this number in the first place. The one who had paid a great deal to have it installed.

She picked it up.

"Hello Xiong Huang."

"Hello Bob, what do you want?"

"There's a bit of a situation going on over here."

Xiong Huang flipped the channel.

"So? What does that have to do with me?"

"I figured you might like the chance to test out your power. There's someone here no one else has been able to handle so maybe they might survive a round or two with you."

Xiong Huang raised an eyebrow.

"Seriously, Bob? You're calling the Immortal Mistress of the Eternal Night Sect to come clean up a mess for you?"

"I figured as the Immortal Mistress of the Eternal Night Sect you can do whatever you feel like. And you might be interested in a novel spar."

Xiong Huang's eye twitched. If it was anyone else, she would have killed them for taking that tone with her. But like it or not, she had a contract with Bob.

And she also hadn't quite figured him out yet.

She couldn't detect even a lick of qi on him, even after her ascension to the Ninth Realm. Anytime she saw him in person, he acted like a normal mortal.

She had not seen him perform a single feat that would imply he had any sort of power, cultivated or otherwise.

By all appearances, by everything she could see or feel with all of her senses, he was weak.

And yet…

He had walked into the Eternal Night Sect without fear or hesitation. A task no one outside the sect, cultivator, shinobi, or otherwise, had ever dared to attempt.

He had confronted her father face to face, come before the master of the Eternal Night Sect on his own initiative. Something that not even the elders of the sect were willing to risk unless summoned first.

He had dared to deceive the Ten Slaughters, and destroyed his cultivation. Something thousands had tried over a millenium, and failed to achieve.

He had picked up the Black Blade, the blade with a demon of hunger sealed within that would consume anyone below the Seventh Realm, anyone not in perfect control of their cultivation. That no one save her father had managed to tame.

He had given away the Blazing Dragon Flower, all to acquire a mere *recruiter.*

She could not believe he was simply a mortal.

She could not believe that was all there was to him.

And until she figured it out, she had to treat him with the utmost care. She needed to entertain him as if he was as powerful as his deeds would suggest.

And…

She owed him a debt.

The Eternal Night Sect was beholden to no one. They took what they wanted, when they wanted it. If another person gave to them, that was their mistake.

But…

He had handed her the Blazing Dragon Flower freely, for a contract not even a fraction of its worth. He had destroyed both her father and the avenger who murdered her sect. He gave her a path to restore the sect, to go beyond their borders and inflict their will upon the wider world.

This was not an implied deal he forgot to confirm. This was not a naive do-gooder thinking the Eternal Night Sect would reply in kind.

This was charity.

Her heart burned at the humiliation. She had been helpless, weak. She was on the floor shedding her tears while he was manipulating cultivators she could never oppose. She was lashing out in rage and pain, expecting death, when he suddenly granted her the revenge she never imagined. And then he had handed her immortality and the heavens on a silver platter.

And now he dared to treat her as if she was free? As if she had a choice?

No, Xiong Huang of the Eternal Night Sect, the Murderous Bloody Fist, was not content to just walk away after all that.

She would pay him back for his arrogance and pity. And she would do so AFTER she had cleared any inkling of debt between them. She would let no one accuse her of weakness. Let no one lay claim to her ascension but herself.

She would not let it be *charity*.

And once she had taken the measure of his power, once she had confirmed his intentions and his capabilities, once she had cleared any and all debts between them...

Then she would remind him of who she was. And teach all in the heavens above and the Earth below that the Murderous Bloody Fist is not to be manipulated or pitied.

But well, that didn't mean she'd just jump at his beck and call before that time.

"What do you think I am, Bob? Do you think I'm just lounging around at home, bored?"

"You're not?"

A vein bulged in Xiong Huang's forehead as she quietly turned off the television in the background.

"Do not act as if we are friends that you are calling up for a social outing. If you need my help, ask for it."

"I need your help."

"...fine. This Great Mistress will deign to assist you. Who do I need to kill?"

"...I didn't say anything about a murder."

"You are calling me, and I have a very particular set of skills. You would not call me if you did not require violence."

"...right."

With that, Bob gave her the details. Xiong Huang rose from her couch and stretched. Then she looked down at her arm and clenched her fist.

She grinned.

Bob was right about one thing.

She WAS excited to see just how strong she had become.

ΔΔΔ

In the deserts of Mexico, at night when the stars and the moon shone in the sky, a man in a red lucha libra outfit grit his teeth and panted for breath. He was in rough shape, his clothes torn and his body covered in dust and bruises. A man in a suit stood in front of him, who had not a single speck of dirt on his clothes.

The man in red grinned even as pain shot through his body.

"Well, this might be a bit rough."

The man in the suit spread his arms out.

"Oh, done already? Whatever happened to your bravado, Mr. Red Hawk? Do you truly believe you can change things here with that pitiful amount of strength?"

Red Hawk lifted his fists.

"Heh, me? No, not at all. I'm just a coward, an idiot who can't do crap without someone else to show me the way. But that's ok. Because there's someone here who can. And he WILL change things around here. So me? I'm not going to change anything."

The man in the suit grinned.

"Oh? Then why are you here, *hero*?"

Red Hawk grinned back at him.

"To keep jerks like you away from him! Reinforce!"

With that, Red Hawk rushed forward, his fist pulled back. He strengthened his body, his skin turning hard like steel while his muscles grew elastic, the power that made him bulletproof.

The man in the suit raised a palm.

The Red Hawk cried as a huge blast of air shot from the man's palm, flinging him through the air.

"Indeed. In fact, I had hoped to meet Icy Falcon today. His powers are great indeed. You, on the other hand?"

Red Hawk groaned as he tried to lift his head, his body refusing to move. The man pointed his palm at the fallen hero once again.

"You are not even worth stealing from."

△△△

The man in the suit was strolling through the desert when suddenly he stopped and turned.

Standing behind him was a young girl in thin silk robes, barely even an adult.

"A bit late to be out and about, little miss. Why don't you run along home?"

She crossed her arms and scoffed.

"*This* is what you wanted me to kill? Some suit wandering around in the desert and picking on the weak?"

The man in the suit raised an eyebrow as he examined her more closely. His eyes widened slightly.

"Well now, this is a surprise. There's a bit more to you than meets the eye, huh? Perhaps I will gain something from this trip after all."

He raised his hand and spread his fingers towards her. Suddenly his fingers turned to wood, growing out into twisting branches and vines. They wrapped around the girl...

Suddenly the branches froze. The man felt as if the world was collapsing on top of him. As if gravity had grown several times stronger, as if the air was trying to squeeze the life out of him. For the first time in decades, he began to sweat as his heart rate quickened.

The girl hadn't moved. She hadn't done anything but release a small bit of her carefully held power.

The man activated his own powers, shielding his mind and body from foreign effects. He gasped for breath as his body fell back into his control, the branches quickly receding back into his fingers. He breathed heavily for a moment before he started to laugh.

The girl just raised an eyebrow at him.

"You dare to laugh? Your death is growing more painful by the second."

The man spread his arms as he laughed.

"You are powerful, truly powerful! Why, I haven't felt like this since…ever!"

And then he narrowed his eyes at her as he grinned.

"It seems as if I will have to get serious."

He pointed his palm at the girl. His arm swelled up to a massive size…and then a huge blast of wind cut across the desert, obscuring the girl from view.

"You have power, but only one! I, I on the other hand, have been gathering strength ever since my youth, taking the abilities of others for my own! Even here, I combined several defensive powers with the ability to create shockwaves, allowing me to generate power at a scale the original user never could! I can destroy an entire block of skyscrapers with this attack!"

The dust and sand cleared, revealing a huge trench across the desert.

And a girl, standing still, completely unharmed. Without even a single hair out of place. The sand behind her was untouched as well, the trench stretching around her position.

And she *yawned*.

"Is that all? How…disappointing."

The man grinned at her.

"Amazing. You are truly powerful."

He crouched down as he thrust another blast at her. His legs bulged and lightning began arcing around them. He left a crater in the ground as he took off, and a blast of sound thundered out as he immediately broke the sound barrier. He shot forward in an instant, traveling right behind the blast of air, and stretched out his hand. He shot through the cloud of dust and grabbed the woman's neck...

"But it's over! Now that I have a hold of you, I will take your power for my own. You will allow me to leap forward several steps, accelerate on my quest to become the ultimate symbol of evil!"

He activated his original power, pulling the energy from her body. He grinned as power unlike he had ever experienced rushed through his veins, filling them with fire. He looked forward as the dust began to fade, eagerly anticipating her face of despair...

He froze, and blinked several times.

He was not holding her neck, but her arm, raised in a block.

And she did not have a face of despair.

In fact, she was still *yawning*.

Her power surged, the flow of power becoming a mighty wave that burned his insides. The man gasped and let go of her arm in shock, stumbling back.

She cracked her neck side to side and took a step forward.

"How disappointing. I was told I might find a good opponent here, but all I found was a cheap imposter."

And then she vanished, without a sound, without even disrupting a single grain of the sand beneath her feet.

And then the man felt an impact on his back.

The next thing he knew he was flying through the air, and bounced along the ground several times.

Then the girl appeared in front of him, holding her arm out to the side. The man flew straight into her, bending forward as his stomach slammed into her immovable arm.

He spit blood as the air was driven straight out from him.

And then she flicked his forehead, sending him flying once more. She followed after him, continuing to launch and beat him. She spoke as she did, without raising her voice. Yet, he could hear her as if she was standing next to him.

"Listen up, you think you have power? No, what you have is a fluke. A quirk of genetics that lets you bully those weaker than you. But you will never develop true strength with it. You will never challenge the heavens."

She let her power loose, a visible flame-like aura appearing around her.

"I *earned* my power. I took it by my own hands, wrestled it away from those who would keep it from me, be they man, beast, or the heavens themselves. Everything I have belongs to me. Everything I take from others becomes my own. You? You're just borrowing."

The man didn't respond as he lay on the ground and panted for breath, bleeding all over. She casually strolled over to him and picked him up by the neck.

"Let me show you how it's done."

The man cried out as the girl intentionally sent her power into him. His veins burst into flames due to the raw amount of power coursing through them, but the power didn't stop pouring into him.

Nor did it stop upon arriving.

The power continued to flow…and flowed back into the girl.

As did the power he had taken from her earlier, the energy responding to the girl's command as if it had never left her.

And it carried the man's powers with it.

"See, I am not dependent on a genetic fluke I was just born with. Since I earned my power, it does not leave me unless I allow it. I do not merely steal what does not belong to me. I conquer and *take* what is now mine, through my own strength and skill. If you cannot keep me from doing so, it is simply because you are *weak*, and unworthy of that which you hold."

The man activated everything he had. Super strength, healing factors, super durability, energy manipulation, psionic powers. But nothing worked. Everything he had was like a tiny bucket against a tsunami of energy, everything he had was stripped away, broken down, and pulled into the girl. The powers floated around in his body, but as she stated they did not belong to it. There was nothing holding them within him, and so he could not keep her from taking them.

Until he was left with only a single power, the one he had been born with.

Until that, too, was stripped away, ripping apart his body as she took the one thing that *did* belong to it.

"Ultimate evil? Hah. Only the weak cry about good and evil. Only the weak surrender to the heavens' declarations of 'how things should be.' True power needs no justification or label. The truly strong simply are, no matter what the masses call them."

But the man did not respond any longer.

Xiong Huang heaved a sigh and tossed away the withered husk. She turned to the side and took a single step forward. She crossed miles with that step, appearing in front of a man with a set of binoculars. She crossed her arms and frowned.

"A test of my strength? Hah, that weakling barely survived a fraction of my intent."

Bob simply shrugged.

"A test for us both, its hard to tell exactly how strong you are."

She narrowed her eyes at him.

"Really? I'd imagine someone like you could do it."

He shrugged again.

"I've said it before, you think too much of me."

She glared at him for a moment more before heaving a sigh. Well, if he would give it up that easily, he wouldn't have taken down her father.

"If I'm going to come out personally, I at least expect a

challenge, Bob."

"Well, I'll do my best."

Her vein bulged at that but she shrugged off his insolence. Now was not the time, not yet. So she simply turned to leave.

"Thanks Xiong Huang, I appreciate the help."

She lifted an eyebrow at that. She wasn't sure if he was being sarcastic or serious. Not sure which would be worse, either. So she simply scoffed and leapt into the air.

And so more than once, heroes and villains mysteriously vanished without a trace. And the world spun on, unaware of the organization growing in the shadows.

Unaware that all would-be evildoers now answered to a master, whether they knew it or not.

> AUTHOR'S COMMENTARY: Why don't the villains realize the insurance clause creates profit for the bank on their defeat, you ask? Well, they do...but no supervillain ever assumes THEY'RE the ones who will get defeated. Remember: they're the great genius who's going to conquer the world! Anyways! Will the world ever learn of the true Master of Evil? Will Xiong Huang ever determine Bob's true powers? Will Kanna work things out with her husband? Tune in next time, to find out!

CHAPTER 6 - THE SPARK

Bob nodded as he reviewed his notes. Everything was proceeding according to plan. Which meant it was now time for the next step.

But the next step would not be so easy. He could not achieve it with what he had now. Or rather, *who* he had now.

It was not something that could be done in the shadows, but something that needed to spread openly across the world.

So he would need help. He would need a special individual to make it happen.

He started to flip through the latest EL Bank applications, checking for anyone that might be useful for his next design...

△△△

One afternoon two figures stepped into EL Bank. One was walking in front without sparing a glance for his surroundings, the other was following behind and to his side. The one in front was a man past his prime, with frazzled white hair on both his head and his face. He wore a white lab coat over a black shirt and green pants. The one behind him was a woman, wearing an armored mask at odds with her otherwise neat suit. She had dark skin, braided black hair, and carried a briefcase.

The pair walked down the EL Bank entrance hall and approached the receptionist.

"Welcome to EL Bank, how may we help you today?"

The man straightened his back and crossed his arms.

"It is I! Dr. Kayserling himself! Today you shall have the honor of rewriting the course of history!"

The woman behind him heaved a sigh. She stepped forward and passed a business card to the confused receptionist.

"Hi, as stated this is Dr. Kayserling and I'm his assistant, Londyn Green. We're here for a loan application interview. Dr. Kayserling has an appointment scheduled."

The receptionist nodded and looked down, shuffling some papers.

"Dr. Kayserling, was it? Yes, I see you have the three 'o clock. Please take the elevator on the left to the top floor, Mr. Herring is waiting for you."

Dr. Kayserling immediately turned to the left and continued walking without another word. Londyn said a quick thank you to the receptionist and hurried after him.

The pair made their way up the elevator. With a chime, the doors opened up into a bright office, the sun shining through a wall of floor to roof windows on the far side from them. The adornments were simple at first glance, but each was of the finest quality and craftsmanship. More impressive was the cabinet filled with bottles, each of them holding one of the finest drinks money could buy. On the side wall was a large picture frame, holding a...movie poster? An interesting choice, somewhat out of place with the rest of the furnishings. At the end of the office were two men, one a well-groomed young man in a suit, sitting at a large desk, the other a hulk of a man wearing a suit and sunglasses, standing to the right of the seated man. The young man smiled and stood up.

"Ah, Dr. Kayserling I presume, welcome welcome."

"Greetings, young plebeian. I, Dr. Kayserling, have decided to grace you with my time today."

Londyn resisted the urge to hold her head, and stepped forward to shake hands with the young man instead.

"Londyn Green, thank you for having us, Mr. Herring. We

are most grateful for the opportunity."

The young man beamed as he shook her hand.

"Please, call me Markus. Mr. Herring is my father. And this is Ivan, my bodyguard slash analyst extraordinaire."

"Hello, is good to meet you."

Markus nodded and began walking back towards his desk.

"Please, have a seat!"

Markus waved the pair to their seats before taking his own.

"Now let's get into it shall we? We've taken a look at your proposal and I must say it is most exciting. Would you mind if we ask a few questions?"

Dr. Kayserling let out a sigh and shook his head.

"I suppose it is hard to fully comprehend the workings of my genius."

Londyn put the briefcase on the table and opened it, removing some of the documents within. She nodded at Markus.

"Yes, we are prepared to address any concerns you may have."

Markus clapped his hands.

"Wonderful, Ivan, would you please?"

Ivan moved to a shelf and grabbed a folder. He walked over and handed it to Markus. Markus opened up the folder and took a look.

"Right, so you plan to build this, 'Mass Suppressor', you call it?"

Dr. Kayserling nodded.

"My life's work, my crowning achievement."

"And it will allow you to…"

"I shall steal gravity itself! The laws of physics shall bend to my will!"

"How exciting. And then…?"

"Then? Then what? All shall bow before me, obviously."

Londyn sighed.

"Doctor, I believe he is asking about the monetization

scheme."

"Oh, how droll. Minion, take care of it."

"Yes, sir."

Londyn separated out some of the documents. Ivan stepped forward and Londyn handed the stack to him, who passed it to Markus.

"As you can see, we've scoured the legal system and found no laws that could be implied to refer to the ownership or right to gravity. This is currently irrelevant as there is no way to manipulate gravity, which will change once the Doctor's work is completed. We will demonstrate that gravity is a resource and that we possess the means to redistribute it. We will then offer said redistribution as a service and allow market forces to allocate gravity as is most efficient."

The edge of Markus's mouth curled upward.

"And you'll capture the profits?"

Londyn nodded.

"That is the goal."

Markus nodded several times.

"Interesting, but I imagine you will be regulated fairly quickly?"

Londyn nodded.

"We've made some contacts in the government who will lobby on our behalf, so we should have ample time to profit off of the initial invention. We also have a number of follow up products that will utilize the technology once it matures. We plan to invest the initial profits to fund a second wave of research and development in order to capture the new market. And..."

"And?"

Londyn smiled under her mask.

"We have...contingencies if the public officials are not reasonably cooperative."

Markus's grin grew.

"Most interesting. I would be most curious to see what these contingencies entail, should they ever take place."

Ivan took a step forward.

"I have question."

Londyn turned to the man and nodded.

"Yes?"

"This technology, it sounds very fancy. It will take long time to make, yes?"

Dr. Kayserling glared at the man.

"You dare to question my genius?"

Markus shook his head and held his hands up.

"Of course not, my dear Doctor. Your genius is self-evident from the sheer brilliance of your invention."

Markus moved his hands back and clasped them on his desk.

"But my associate does raise a valid point. Even the best of projects can run into delays, due to unforeseen circumstances, of course. What is the timeframe on the Mass Suppressor and what will you do if you require additional funding midway?"

Londyn nodded and took out another document, handing it to Ivan as he approached her again.

"We do have a plan for that scenario. While the Mass Suppressor is the Doctor's primary focus, it is not the only invention he has produced. We imagine there would be a smaller market for some of his devices. Our projections say they will cover operational costs as well as fulfill the R&D budget fairly quickly. We simply need the initial capital to get started and for some of the larger purchases the Mass Suppressor will require."

Markus rubbed his chin as he reviewed the document.

"A well thought out plan. Any thoughts, Ivan?"

"Da, is very exciting technology. Maybe too exciting? It may attract many thieves, I think."

Londyn nodded.

"Yes, that is a concern. We heard you also provide some discounted staffing with a partner agency, correct? We would like to apply for that as well. We are aiming for a full security detail on top of engineering and administration departments."

Markus nodded.

"A wise choice. Well I think we have a good picture of your needs and plans now."

Markus stood from his seat, extending his hand forward.

"Thank you two for coming in today. We'll get back to you with our decision. A pleasure speaking with you."

Dr. Kayserling stood up, arms crossed.

"Don't keep me waiting."

And promptly turned around.

Londyn packed up her briefcase, then reached out and shook Markus's hand.

"Thank you for taking the time to speak with us today, we look forward to hearing from you soon."

As the doors of the elevator closed and the numbers atop it began to drop, Markus sat back at his desk. He grabbed the receiver off his phone, dialing in a number.

"Hi Bob!"

"Markus."

Markus began giggling, then broke out into full on laughter.

"So, what do you think? Stealing gravity itself, heh."

"It's good. They're far better prepared than the average applicant."

"And so?"

"Too good. The world isn't ready for that kind of technology."

"Too bad, I was looking forward to seeing it in action. Shall I give them the bad news?"

Bob leaned against a chair in a small break room, drinking a cup of coffee. He focused on a television in the room.

"*Next up, defenders of justice, or violent criminals? We talk with the experts to understand this new 'supers' phenomenon sweeping the globe and what it might mean for you!*"

"No, they might be able to pull it off without us, so we best keep it in-house. And...I have an idea. You still keep up with Lewis from undergrad?"

"Yea, we're on for golf this weekend, why?"

The edge of Bob's mouth curled up.

"Approve the funding for Dr. Kayserling. I think I know exactly where to put him."

△△△

Bob shuffled into a large conference room in the newly acquired Kayserling Tower, a skyscraper right in the heart of New York City. He was dressed in body armor and a helmet covering his entire face, much like almost everyone else in the room. He took his spot around the middle of the room, off to the side.

Three people stood on a stage at the front of the room. Two of them were Dr. Kayserling and Londyn Green, the third was a woman in a suit, also wearing a mask on her face.

Dr. Kayserling scoffed and walked up to a mic on stage.

"Greetings, peons and inferiors. Today you have the honor of basking in the presence of my genius, and contributing to my grand endeavors. Know that I will upturn the entire world, overthrow the very fabric of reality with my work here! As such, I expect you to display the kind of effort and drive such an achievement requires. You will not stop. You will not rest. I expect you to work at your very best for as long as is required. And I will accept nothing less than your best, anything else shall be considered failure. A genius like mine deserves no less, and I expect you all to do your utmost to meet my expectations. Now, get to it. Assistant."

With that, Dr. Kayserling marched out of the room. Londyn heaved a sigh and took the mic.

"Hello everyone, my name is Londyn Green, Dr. Kayserling's personal assistant and the Director of Operations of Kayserling Incorporated. That, as you might have guessed, was Dr. Kayserling, and he is most excited to have you all working here. We will introduce our company and overall goals to you today, afterwards I will work closely with your supervisor to assign responsibilities and shifts. Please rest assured, Kayserling Incorporated will fully comply with Midnight Staffing's employee contract, including the stipulations regarding overtime frequency, compensation including overtime pay, and performance evaluations. Now, if you'd please direct your attention to the screen here..."

After the presentation, as the minions of Midnight Staffing shuffled off to grab lunch, Bob watched as Londyn turned to the other woman on stage and extended her hand.

"I'm sorry to have delayed our greeting, but I'm Londyn Green. I'm glad to have you here."

The masked woman shook Londyn's hand.

"The pleasure is all mine. My name is Linda, and I look forward to working with you."

Bob nodded and then headed off to grab his own lunch.

Yes, for this operation he had brought in the big guns. Getting Dr. Kayserling a skyscraper in New York City was a massive investment of both money and political capital, so Bob was taking a personal hand in the operation to ensure it went perfectly. He needed this time to go exactly as planned. Too early and it may not have the payoff to justify the investment. Too late and the casualties could be catastrophic.

And beyond that risk was another concern. This assistant, Londyn Green, was highly competent, the secret behind Dr. Kayserling's success thus far. She even had her own political contacts, and was well on her way to securing funding for the Doctor before they had applied at EL Bank.

Which meant she would notice if anything was off.

So the standard tactics wouldn't work here. Londyn would be keeping a closer eye on things than the average megalomaniacal supervillain. They needed someone who could match her talent for administration if they were to achieve their goals.

So Bob had brought in Linda.

As Cikizwa's main assistant, the one who once ran the entire administrative show for a mercenary black-ops group, Linda was the very best when it came to management and legal affairs. Even Bob couldn't match her when it came to paperwork, bureaucracy, and raw organization. So if anyone could pull the wool over someone like Londyn Green, it would be Linda.

And...

Bob glanced back one more time, watching as Londyn and Linda's conversation picked up.

If Londyn and Linda built a good working relationship, there might be additional opportunities here...

△△△

And so the new Kayserling Inc. got to work, Londyn and Linda working hard to get everything in order, with Bob covering things on the ground. It had been tough, moving things into place while keeping Londyn in the dark, but Linda had proved her worth and the work continued on.

And speaking of the work...

Bob stood with his hands crossed behind him. He looked out upon the city as he rose, cars and pedestrians shrinking to the size of ants. He blinked as the elevator cleared the neighboring skyscraper, revealing the sun in all its glory. The tinted goggles of the minion uniform helped for once. His nose still itched though.

The elevator came to a stop with the noise of a soft bell, its doors opening behind him. Bob strode through the red carpeted hallway past the occasional potted plant and water station. He did question the point of buying nice carpets if Dr. Kayserling wanted to mandate heavy boots, but a supergenius's purposes were beyond mortal men such as himself. To his side were offices with glass walls, helmeted clerks hard at work. Bob shook his head. Once again, he questioned the requirement for everyone in the building to wear armor at all times.

But, well, Dr. Kayserling didn't like to gaze upon the faces of the inferior masses, and a man of his genius could not be denied.

Bob strode into an open area with tiled floors. On the far wall was a round wooden desk, a large double door to its right. Behind the desk was another armored figure, complete with a helmet. Though this one only covered the face, revealing braided black hair and the occasional hint of dark skin. The figure perked up when they saw Bob, only to drop their shoulders. Bob nodded his head.

"Londyn."

"Bob..."

The woman looked down.

"Need me to cover another shift?"

Londyn kept looking down for a moment, before looking back up and slowly nodding.

"I'm really sorry about this."

Bob shook his head.

"I know it's not your fault."

Londyn gripped her fists and let out a sigh.

"I've just about had it with this foolishness. Dr. Kayserling says he wants me to draw up a patrol schedule. I spend hours working out routes and assignments. Then he goes and pulls half the guards, leaving his *already assigned* assistants on break for half the day. Now the guards are complaining to me about the overtime and there's a massive hole in the security. Does he want a secure facility or not?"

"You all right?"

Londyn let go of her fists and dropped her shoulders before looking back up at Bob.

"I'm fine, just tired. I'm more worried about you, you going to be ok running a double shift?"

Bob nodded.

"It's not my first rodeo. The hours here are much better

than my last few jobs, thanks to you no doubt. I'm going to grab a coffee first, you want something?"

Londyn shook her head.

"I'll be fine, thanks Bob."

Fortunately, Dr. Kayserling himself had proven Bob and Linda's best ally. The lofty genius couldn't be bothered with mundane affairs such as schedules and policy. He simply did as he pleased, and expected Londyn to clean up after him. If he considered the mess he was making at all, that is. So anytime she noticed any discrepancies, the tired woman just assumed Dr. Kayserling did something without telling her. Again.

Bob couldn't help but feel sorry for her. So even as he worked his own plans, he did what he could to lift her spirits. The only good news was that she had Linda to help shoulder the burden...when she wasn't secretly adding to it, at least.

Unfortunately, Linda wasn't here today, having gone out on an urgent task.

In fact...

A lot of the staff had called out today. What Londyn hadn't realized just yet was Dr. Kayserling pulled the security guards today because he couldn't *find* the assigned assistants.

Fifteen minutes later Bob walked out of the coffee shop across the street from Kayserling Tower. He could've gone to the company cafeteria or one of the break rooms but the coffee there was truly Dr. Kayserling's most evil invention. He got a latte for Londyn too, he knew she'd appreciate a real drink after another meeting with the doctor.

And then the sky lit on fire.

A fireball blasted through the fifth floor window of Kayserling Tower, showering glass onto the streets. A few moments later, the pedestrians began screaming and running. Bob swore as he dropped the coffee and sprinted into the street.

He knew it was happening today, but this was earlier than

he expected. And now he would have to move quickly.

He jumped and slid over the hood of a honking taxi, rushing back to the tower. He slammed open the door to the tower and continued running, ignoring the scrambling guards. They had their orders and were already moving to evacuate any remaining non-super staff, except for one. Bob turned right, away from the stairs and elevators crowded with other minions, searching for the maintenance closet.

Once inside he pushed aside a cabinet of cleaning tools, revealing the hidden emergency gear. Bob grabbed a pair of metal cylinders with straps, secured it on his back and around his waist and legs, grabbed a crowbar, and then bolted to an elevator that had been closed for service. He pried the doors open and stepped inside, jabbing open one of the ceiling panels. With a leap he grabbed onto the edge and grunted as he pulled himself up and onto the roof of the elevator.

Once there he situated himself, double checked all the straps and harness, and then pulled the strap of the emergency anti-gravity booster.

Bob grit his teeth. He felt as if he slammed into a wall as the air rushed past him. For once he was thankful for the full body armor he was forced to wear. Once he saw the ceiling he began counting down.

Three.

Two.

One.

Bob pulled the shutoff lever and prayed he timed it right. The ceiling grew larger at an alarming rate. Bob ignored the urge to close his eyes, waiting for his speed to drop.

And fortunately, it did.

He came to a stop in the air in front of an elevator door. He stabbed the crowbar into the gap and pulled open the doors. Sirens blared and red lights flashed in his face. As soon as the opening was wide enough he angled forward and boosted himself into the hallway. He was immediately drenched by the sprinkler system, yet heat assaulted his entire body. Smoke filled the hallway, obscuring his view of the now vacant offices, but Bob began sprinting regardless. Soon he reached the open area, where flames now covered the round desk. Bob kept to the walls as he stepped towards a smoking hole in the double doors.

"It's over, Dr. Kayserling! Surrender or face the consequences!"

"On the contrary, Captain Hot Devil, I have merely begun! Once my Mass Suppressor activates, gravity itself shall be at my command. The universe shall be at my fingertips! The laws of physics themselves shall be a privilege, not a right, and I shall be their sole distributor!"

Captain Hot Devil stood in the room beyond, his back facing Bob and his fists clenched. In front of them both stood Dr. Kayserling himself, the mad scientist holding a remote in his hand. Behind him stood a silver polyhedron with glowing blue circles on its sides, floating between two metallic cylinders on the floor and roof. The Mass Suppressor in all its glory, just about operational. The rest of Dr. Kayersing's office resembled Bob's former roommate's room but he did not like to remember those days and so ignored it.

Captain Hot Devil's fists ignited into flames.

"You may own the laws of physics, but the fires of hell are free for all."

Bob ignored that too.

Dr. Kayserling's eyes widened and he smiled.

"Most excellent timing, minion! Now deal with the hellish captain while I finish activating the Mass Suppressor!"

Bob looked away, glancing around the room. He could feel two people's gazes but he had more important things to do. Finally he found what he was looking for.

"Heh, the great Doctor Kayserling. Says he commands gravity, but doesn't even command his own minions."

"Shut up. Minion, you are so fired!"

There was another minion in the room with braided hair,

lying underneath a smoldering table. Bob gently removed the table and checked her pulse. She weakly turned her head to face him and whispered.

"Bob...?"

There was a gash on her forehead but she was alive, and mostly intact. Bob hoisted Londyn over his shoulders and ran from the room.

Shortly after he left, the Mass Suppressor exploded, destroying the top floors of Kayserling Tower and its villainous owner.

And showering the surrounding area with smoking debris...

△△△

Bob was in a small clinic, with three beds, an old box tv, and a small window with a potted plant. Not the most advanced care in the world but clean and, most importantly, anonymous. Bob handed the physician a wad of cash, who nodded and left the room. Bob then turned his attention to the patient propped up on the bed.

"How do you feel?"

Londyn turned towards Bob. For the first time he could see her brown eyes, though mostly hidden by her narrow gaze.

"How do I feel? How do I feel?!"

Londyn took a deep breath.

"I feel like crap Bob. I hated that place. I hated my life. But now? It's all gone. All that effort, all that pain, all the late hours, all the denied raises, all the schedules ignored, all the jerks I put up with, all the gossip and whispers. And for what? So some pyromaniacal 'hero of justice' can burn it to the ground. I'm scared, Bob. I can still smell the smoke, feel the heat as that man punched through a solid wall. I looked in his eyes as he saw me, Bob. There was no pity, no sympathy, not even hate. Just nothing. Like I was just another piece of furniture, like I wasn't even there. And now I have nothing, and I don't know what to do."

Londyn held her face, quietly sobbing. Bob put a hand on her shoulder, saying nothing for several minutes.

That was all he could do.

Londyn put her hands down and wiped her eyes with her arm. She grabbed a nearby tissue and blew her nose. Bob took his hand off her shoulder and handed her a cup of water. She nodded and drank.

"I have a job for you if you're interested."

Londyn narrowed her eyes at Bob.

"Thanks but no thanks. I'm not working for another villain, Bob."

Bob removed his helmet, looking Londyn straight in the eyes.

"I'm not asking you to work for anyone, this isn't for Midnight Staffing. You'll be your own boss. I don't know if it will work, that will be up to you. And it will be harder than anything you've ever done. But I promise you this. You'll be the one calling the shots. And if it works, no one will ignore you ever again. Not even those annoying heroes."

△△△

A tower of smoke rose into the sky. The ground was covered in dust and shattered glass. Firetrucks and ambulances blockaded the street. Helicopters patrolled the skies. Medics examined people wrapped in blankets. Firefighters carried people covered in soot. On the other side of the street, countless news vans had arrived, cameras were set up, and reporters spoke.

"We're here live at Kayserling Tower, home to Kayserling Inc. There have been multiple explosions and fires breaking out in Kayserling Tower, resulting in casualties among pedestrians and in the neighboring structures. First responders are on the scene and working to bring the situation under control. At this time we have not confirmed the cause, but several eye witnesses claim the vigilante super known as Captain Hot Devil was seen shortly before the first explosion. Dr. Kayserling, founder and owner of Kayserling Inc, has produced numerous fantastical inventions and is widely suspected of having villainous intentions, so we suspect this may be the result of a fight between supers. We will continue our coverage of the event and our investigation of exactly what happened here. Now, let's hear from some eyewitnesses."

"I-I don't know, I was just walking back to work, a-and then suddenly the sky was falling!"

"I thought we were under attack. It was like, oh god, is this really happening?"

"I...I...I'm sorry, I just, I didn't want to die. So when...I'm sorry, I need a moment."

"I thought it was a bomb. So a hero you say? That's no hero. Those firefighters there, the medics, those are heroes. That? That's a menace."

△△△

Later that week...

"Good evening, all you denizens of the planet Earth. This is Global News Network and I'm your host, Brendan Baird, bringing you all the updates you need. Tonight we're here to discuss the latest on everyone's mind: the Battle of Kayserling Tower. Let's go to GNN's super-analysts, Lacey Cook and Liam Reynolds. Lacey, Liam, how are you doing tonight?"

"I'm doing great, Brendan."

"Same here."

"Glad to hear it. Well folks, let's dive right into it. It's official, Kayserling Tower was the site of battle between two supers, right in the heart of downtown New York. What are your thoughts?"

"Absolutely awful, Brendan."

"I agree with Lacey, it never should have come to this."

"I think we all can agree that what happened was shocking. Now, Lacey, what is your take on this?"

"I think we need to really ask ourselves: should strangers in masks act as judge, jury, and executioner? We've let these supers do as they please, operate outside the law, and now this is the result? Who is this Captain Hot Devil and why was he allowed to blow up a downtown skyscraper? If it was a normal person, we'd be calling this a terrorist attack and arresting the man, why is it any different in this case?"

"Liam, I believe you had something to say in response?"

"That's right, Brendan, I don't agree with my colleague on this. From what I hear this 'Dr. Kayserling' was preparing some kind of weapon, unlike anything we've ever seen. I heard he was about to activate it, so who knows what might have happened if he did? How much more damage might have been done, entirely intentionally? I think we should be thanking Captain Hot Devil for stopping him when he did. The real question we need to ask is why was a suspected supervillain allowed to set up in the heart of New York?"

"That's the thing Liam, 'suspected' supervillain. What crime, exactly, had Dr. Kayserling committed up to that point? He had no criminal record, no history of wrongdoing. What reason was there to deny a legal purchase of land? And why is it not a crime for someone to just blow him up and all his life's work in the middle of the streets? We have laws for a reason. Just cause, due process. None of that occurred here."

"It's Captain Hot Devil! This isn't his first rodeo. I think we all can say, if the Captain thought this guy needed to go then he wasn't doing anything good."

"But where's the evidence? What was the process? I can agree that Captain Hot Devil's adventures have had good results before. But this is a man acting solely on his own, outside of the law, without any authority or oversight. Who's to say he didn't make a mistake? How do we know his actions were justified? Should we really just let him do as he pleases just because of past history?"

"I think he's a hero, and I'll stand by that."

"And what exactly is a hero? And why are they allowed to conduct violent assaults without any prior justification? Why are they allowed to ignore the law, sometimes with deadly consequences?"

"Well that's an excellent question, Lacey, but let me pose you both another one: what do you think we should do?"

"We need laws and regulations. An organization. A standard we can hold these people accountable to, and someone to hold them to it. Or else we need to get them off our streets until we're sure they're needed. But we cannot permit the unrestricted use of violence by vigilantes who answer to no one, or tragedies like this are bound to repeat."

"Do you agree, Liam?"

"No, I don't think introducing bureaucracy into this process is a good idea at all. What if Dr. Kayserling activates some sort of weapon while Captain Hot Devil's waiting for permission? Are we content to let people suffer and die while some politicians discuss the issue in a committee? In these kinds of scenarios, when lives are on the line, time is of the essence and regulation is anything but timely."

"That's my point though, right now there isn't a process at all, Liam. Whether it's before the fact or after the fact, there needs to be something separating the good from the bad. And in every case involving violence, that's the law."

"What would you propose, Liam?"

"These men and women are heroes. They are laying down their lives to protect ours. We shouldn't be holding them back, we should be helping them thrive. I think we should set up something to support the heroes, to get them where they're needed. If we can get them to the scene before the villains are activating their weapons, then we can keep the damage to a minimum."

"And what will you do when a super blows up another skyscraper?"

"We should put that burden on the ones causing problems, not the ones solving them. We should proactively go after villains, those who enable them, and those who look up to them. If Dr. Kayserling hadn't been allowed to set up downtown, we'd all be singing Captain Hot Devil's praises right now. And if he had known about this ahead of time, he wouldn't have had to rush in like he did."

"That sounds a lot like a police state, Liam. I don't think it's right to punish someone before the crime."

"It's a dangerous world now, Lacey. We can't always afford to wait that long. And if it's a choice between punishing some punk who glorifies evil, or a hero who fights for my life, the answer is clear to me."

"Well whatever the case, I think all the world is starting to agree, something needs to be done. Thank you both for your insights."

"Thank you, Brendan."

"Any time, Brendan."

"This is GNN and we'll be back after a short message from our sponsors."

△△△

A few months later…

On a television screen, a well-groomed man dressed in a suit smiled and waved to the crowds as he walked down the steps of the Marble Palace. He didn't flinch as cameras flashed in his face. A reporter held out a microphone to him.

"Mayor Lewis McCarthy, could we have a moment of your time?"

"Shoot."

"Mr. Mayor, what are your thoughts on *The City of New York vs. Captain Hot Devil*?"

The mayor nodded.

"It's a great day, a historic win for the American people."

Another reporter thrust out their mic.

"Mr. Mayor, why did you fight so hard against superheroes? Haven't they saved your city countless times? Didn't Captain Hot Devil save your own life?"

The mayor's smile dropped.

"Let me be clear, I didn't fight against superheroes. I've never fought against superheroes. No one loves superheroes more than I do. I, the city of New York, and the world owe these men and women a debt we can never repay. And that's why I want them to be a part of our society, not pushed outside of it. And society is built on responsibility. We all have responsibilities, it's how we maintain our privileges and our freedoms. I want superheroes to be free to act and use their God-given abilities. And to do that we have to define what responsibilities they will have when they do so."

△△△

Jim Roberson shut off the television.

"Jerk. Shouldn't have stopped that bomber."

Jim glanced down at the papers on the kitchen table. So Mayor Mcarthy wanted him to take responsibility, eh? In Jim's opinion, that sleezebag should take responsibility for selling a prime location tower to a freaking supervillain before trying to slap him with a bill for collateral damage.

"Shouldn't have? What you shouldn't have done was skip your daughter's game to go blow up a freaking skyscraper!"

Jim glanced up at his wife. She had her brown hair up with a handkerchief, wearing a simple dress with a cooking apron. Her face would have been as beautiful as he remembered, if not for the bags under her eyes or the wrinkles starting to form.

"Dang it, Eleanor, don't harp on me now of all times!"

Eleanor gripped the baking pin in her hand.

"I should've harped on you more! Your family needed you,

Jim! I needed you, Jim!"

Jim stood up and glared at his wife.

"Those people needed me!"

"Those people don't give a crap about you and you don't give a crap about them! Don't pretend you're some noble saint! You loved the glory, you loved the thrill, you loved the people cheering your name! You don't care about them, you don't care about us, you only care about yourself! Well guess what, Jim?! Now we're going to lose our home, the home I worked for and cared for. The home you barely slept in! You know what, Jim?! Maybe they did need you. But I'm starting to think that we don't."

Jim turned and walked out of the kitchen. He kept his eyes forward, trying not to glance at the two children huddled in the hallway.

"Just where do you think you're going?"

Jim opened the door.

"For a drink."

"Don't you dare..."

Jim slammed the door.

△△△

"Another please."

Jim reached his hand out and waved it about, too tired to lift his head up from under his other arm. The bartender frowned as he wiped another glass.

"Jim, pal, I think you've had enough."

Jim groaned and reached around for his mug, hoping there might be something at the bottom. A crash and the sound of glass shattering on the floor told him otherwise. The barkeeper opened his mouth, but then closed it and shook his head as he walked to help another patron.

"Hello, Jim"

Jim peaked his head up. Some lady had sat down next to him. He put his head back down.

"Get lost, lady. I'm married."

The woman didn't budge.

"Hello, Captain Hot Devil. You've made a real mess this time, haven't you?"

Jim bolted up, then cursed as the world spun. He vaguely felt a glass fill his hand and brought it to his lips. The water tasted especially cool on his throat. When he finished he wiped his lips with his arm, and the world stopped spinning enough for him to focus. Seated next to him was a woman with dark skin and braided black hair. She wore a neat suit and a pair of sunglasses. Not someone who should be in this bar.

Jim glanced around and realized there wasn't *anyone* in this bar.

He narrowed his eyes, moved one of his hands under the bar and clenched it into a fist.

"Who are you?"

The woman placed something on the bar. A small, pale-gray, rectangular piece of paper. It was bland. Generic. It just had a bank's name, and his own.

And a heck of a lot of zeroes.

"Londyn Green. I'm here to offer you a job, Captain Hot Devil."

> *AUTHOR'S COMMENTARY: Ah yes, my surely super unique plot of superheroes getting sued! You could even say it's...incredible. Anyways! Can the heroes find a way to pay their bills and get back in the fight? Will the villains take advantage of this situation before they do? And what is Londyn hiring her attacker Captain Hot Devil to do? Tune in next time, to find out!*

CHAPTER 7 - HEROES RISE AGAIN

After the landmark case of The City of New York vs. Captain Hot Devil, it was decided that heroes could be sued for damages if they could not prove such measures were necessary. Captain Hot Devil himself was slapped for a bill for millions of dollars for the devastation at Kayserling Tower. He vanished from the public view after that day, performing no further hero activity in the aftermath.

Predictably, hero activity dropped around the country, with the heroes only acting if they could guarantee a clean and obviously necessary takedown. It turned out most heroes were not legal experts and had no lawyers of their own, and so struggled to argue their cases. And as they were generally not paid for their work, they lacked the money to handle those kinds of bills.

Even beyond the United States, heroes grew hesitant around the globe. No one knew whether they would become their country's Captain Hot Devil. No one wanted to risk it.

And, of course, villain activity grew in response.

Nothing as dramatic as Dr. Kayserling and his Mass Suppressor occurred, but a lot of minor issues began popping up. Bank robberies, heists, public damage by rampaging supers.

The people began to ask that something be done.

But the courts could not go back on their decision. To do so after the case would require specifically granting heroes immunity for damage caused, which no judge was willing to do. As for changing the law itself, Congress was caught in a standstill and unable (or unwilling) to make a clear decision on the issue. And no one was both willing and able to foot the bill on behalf of the heroes.

There was some talk of forming some sort of government organization, or bringing heroes into law enforcement officially, but this was slow to materialize. Not least of all because of leaked information about CIA super death squads from the sixties and seventies, calling into question the wisdom of heroes fighting for a flag. And of course, after being slapped with bills for collateral damage by that very government, very few heroes expressed any willingness to cooperate with such measures.

And so the nation held its breath, knowing that it was only a matter of time before a villain went unopposed. Praying that someone would come up with a solution before something truly terrible occurred.

But there was a reason these people were called heroes. No matter the odds, no matter the challenges, no matter who stood against them, no matter if they were appreciated or not, the heroes still carried on. They didn't give up. They kept fighting the good fight. They searched for a way.

They could be knocked down, but they couldn't be counted out.

And so one day, the heroes rose again.

△△△

"That's it for the weather, back to you, Brendan."

"Thanks, Terry! Oh what's that? Breaking news folks, it seems there's a super rampaging in downtown New York, right now! GNN's chopper is on the scene, let's go to the live feed. Parents, please be advised that the following footage could be disturbing."

△△△

People screamed as a bestial roar sounded through the streets. Police sirens, honking horns, and the beating of a helicopter's blades contributed to the cacophony. Every which way, pedestrians ran, desperately trying to escape the area.

And at the epicenter of the chaos…

There was a massive beast of a man, stomping around the city streets. He was nine feet tall and his arms and legs were the size of tree trunks. His bulging muscles stretched his skin to its utmost limit. He wore a black wrestling mask and wrestling suit, the material stretched taunt over his massive body. He roared as he lifted a hotdog cart over his head, pouring out its contents into his mouth.

A blockade of police cars surrounded him, dozens of officers took aim with handguns and shotguns. One had a loudspeaker held to his mouth.

"NYPD! Put down the cart and put your hands up!"

The beast ignored them and continued his feasting.

"This is your last warning! Cease and desist or we will open fire!"

Still the super ignored them. All the officers turned to the captain. The captain nodded.

"Bring him down!"

Thunder roared as the officers opened fire. Shell casings clattered as they hit the ground by the officers feet. The square lit up like the night sky on the Fourth of July.

And flattened bullet-heads clinked onto the ground, unable to penetrate the super's skin.

The assault was harmless.

But it was not unnoticed.

The man lowered his gaze from the cart overhead to the officers around him. His face twisted into a snarl. He pulled his hands back, and then with a roar, lobbed the cart into the sky.

"Move!"

The police officers dove to the ground as the cart smashed into one of the police cars. A shadow grew overhead, then with a mighty crash the man landed on the car, flattening what remained of it.

"If Hungry Smasher can't eat, then he'll smash!"

Hungry Smasher ripped the bumper off the flattened car, lobbing it into the windshield of another. The nearest police officers broke and ran. The ones on the other side of the encirclement kept up their fire. Hungry Smasher turned, and with another snarl leapt to the other side. The concrete cracked as he landed in front of the blockade, police officers gaping as he grabbed a car and lifted it high overhead. The police kept firing at point blank range, but the bullets still bounced off the man's skin. The Hungry Smasher swung the car down, and two police officers cried out and closed their eyes.

They waited for their deaths.

And waited.

And kept waiting?

They timidly opened their eyes. The car was frozen, silently vibrating midair. The Hungry Smasher blinked as he pushed on the vehicle, but it refused to move.

And standing in front of the officers...

Was a teenage girl?

She had black hair and brown eyes. She wore a blue and yellow latex suit over her thin body. A blue domino mask covered her face. She had yellow gloves over her hands, and was stretching her arms out just in front of the frozen car.

The girl grunted.

"Get out of here! I can't hold this forever!"

The police officers jumped at her cry, then nodded and ran. Sweat trickled down the girl's forehead as she groaned. Hungry Smasher grit his teeth and growled as he pushed on the car.

Just as the girl clenched her teeth a black shadow shot by the car and collided into the man. The Hungry Smasher flew backwards and crashed into a tree.

"Finally!"

The girl dropped her hands and leapt to the side. The car stopped vibrating and immediately smashed into the ground where the girl once stood. The girl dusted herself off as she stood, and walked up to another teen standing in front of her. He had short blonde hair and a red mask covering his blue eyes. He wore a red suit with a blue cape, with a 'W' written in yellow on his chest.

"Took your time, Wonder Knight! I almost died!"

Wonder Knight rubbed the back of his head.

"Ah, sorry about that, Chronolock."

Hungry Smasher stood back up from where he lay, brushing branches and leaves off his shoulder. He threw his arms to the side as he let out a roar, his muscles bulging.

"Wow, that bro's kind of ugly."

"He seems in pain, I wonder what's wrong with him?"

Two more teens arrived on the scene. One, a dark-skinned boy who wore black and purple robes that covered everything but his face, with a mask over his eyes. The second, a light-skinned girl wearing a pink and white suit and helmet. There was a clear, pink visor over her pink domino mask, and she had large white gauntlets around her wrists.

Wonder Knight took up a position in front of the group.

"All right team, let's do this. Pink Star, distract him. I'll wrap around and go for the arms. Chronolock, trip up his legs. Voidspeaker, drain him once he's down."

Voidspeaker nodded.

"All right, bro."

Pink Star pumped her fists.

"Yea, we got this!"

Chronolock narrowed her eyes at their foe.

"Got it."

"Aurora Legion, let's go!"

The four scattered as Hungry Smasher galloped forth. Pink Star held out her hands, her gauntlets glowing pink.

"I choose you, Gorilla!"

Pink light burst from her gauntlets and formed into the shape of a gorilla. The glowing gorilla beat its chest and let out a roar, before bounding into the approaching villain. Man and gorilla grabbed each other's hands and stared the other down, their muscles bulging and concrete cracking under them. Both grunted and gripped the other's hands, but the winner was clear. The gorilla took a step back, its body beginning to flash and flicker.

Just then Wonder Knight jumped on Hungry Smasher's back, wrapping his arms underneath the man's armpits and then locking his hands behind the villain's head. Wonder Knight let out a shout and pulled back with all his might. Hungry Smasher's eyes widened and he stumbled back. As he did Chronolock slid in underneath him and thrust out her hand towards his boot. The boot began vibrating and immediately stopped moving. Hungry Smasher let out a cry as he lost his balance and fell backwards, smashing into the ground.

"Gah!"

With Wonder Knight underneath him.

And then the gorilla leapt on top of them both, pinning them to the ground.

Voidspeaker floated towards the mass of bodies, closed his eyes, and held out his hands. He waved them in circles, the left moving clockwise, the right moving counter clockwise. A black substance which blocked all light appeared over his hands.

His eyes shot open when the substance had grown into large balls around his hands.

He clasped them together.

The substance formed into a large, black sphere.

"Experience nothingness!"

A black beam shot from his hands into the fallen villain. Hungry Smasher's eyes widened, he cried out and thrashed about. But his thrashing grew slower, his cries grew quieter, his eyelids grew narrower.

Until he finally stopped, and fell unconscious.

As the large man began to snore, Pink Star and Voidspeaker let down their hands. The black beam and the pink gorilla both scattered into black and pink particles of light. Wonder Knight threw the Hungry Smasher to the side with a grunt.

"Ugh. Ok, that was a stupid idea."

Voidspeaker shrugged.

"It was your plan, bro."

"Ugh."

Pink Star fidgeted a bit.

"Um, I thought it was a great idea, Wonder Knight!"

Wonder Knight just shook his head.

"Thanks Pink Star, but you don't have to humor me. I can feel exactly how good of an idea it was, ouch."

As Wonder Knight stood to his feet, police officers and news reporters slowly crept towards the group.

"Who, who are you?"

Wonder Knight looked at his team. Pink Star nodded with a wink, Voidspeaker gave a thumbs up, and Chronolock rolled her eyes. The team gathered up and faced the growing crowd. Wonder Knight stood with his legs spread, pointing a thumb to himself and winking. Voidspeaker floated in the air as he crossed his legs and assumed a meditation stance. Pink Star skipped on one leg and held her hand in a 'V' shape across her face. Chronolock just crossed her arms and leaned back.

"We're Aurora Legion, a team of heroes from the International League of Superheroes, and we're here to help!"

△△△

"Breaking news, folks. Earlier today a supervillain known as Hungry Smasher went on a rampage in downtown New York. He was stopped by a group of supers calling themselves Aurora Legion and claiming to be from something called the International League of Superheroes. They were able to defeat Hungry Smasher with no loss of life and minimal property damage. The International League of Superheroes also sent a cleanup crew to help repair the damage, and the city is as good as new. Who are these new supers, what is this International League of Superheroes, and what will they do next? Join us tonight as GNN talks with the experts to find out!"

△△△

And so Aurora Legion made their entrance into the public view, backed by an organization calling themselves the International League of Superheroes. This organization made sure to come in and clean up after all of Aurora Legion's activities, minimizing the damage left behind. Of course, mistakes happen in chaotic battlefields and so lawsuits would eventually be filed against these heroes too. But each time they were, the International League of Superheroes brought in expert lawyers that presented their cases thoroughly and professionally.

One day, for the first time since *The City of New York vs. Captain Hot Devil*, the heroes managed to win a case.

And even when they didn't, the International League of Superheroes' lawyers managed to restrain the bills to reasonable levels, which the organization then paid off on Aurora Legion's behalf. And they stretched the cases out, as well. In fact, many of Aurora Legion's lawsuits had not been settled as of the current date.

Over time it would become increasingly less desirable to take Aurora Legion to court, not least of all as public opinion turned in favor of the well-intentioned teens who took easily apparent care to avoid collateral damage. So long as the group didn't make any egregious mistakes, they would not receive unpayable bills for their deeds.

As a result, Aurora Legion was free to act even as other heroes hesitated, and so took on more and more villains.

Such as they did on one particular night, shortly after their public debut...

△△△

In one room of Aurora Legion's home base, two teens were locked in an intense and epic duel. One, a dark-skinned boy with short black hair. The other, a light skinned girl with straight, black hair and narrow brown eyes. They both wore domino masks over their faces, black with a purple tint for the boy, blue and yellow for the girl.

Voidspeaker and Chronolock faced one another, each refusing to yield, refusing to even blink.

And so the two teens sat on a couch, eyes glued to the screen ahead, moving their fingers as fast as they could across the controllers in their hands.

"Bro! I am NOT letting you beat me this time!"

"Calm down, it's just a game."

Voidspeaker smirked.

"Then I guess you don't care if I drop this little blue shell, do you?"

Chronolock's eyes narrowed.

"You're dead."

"Calm down, it's just a game. A game that I JUST WON!!! AHAHAHAHAHA!"

"..."

Voidspeaker's eyes widened as he realized what he had just done. Chronolock went dead silent, hands still clutching her controller.

"Um, that was, I mean...i-it's just a game right? A-All fun and games? Right, Chronolock?"

"Rematch."

"Um, I think we should probably get ready. Might have a mission you know?"

"Rematch. Now."

"Um, Pink, a little help?"

"You brought this on yourself, Void."

Pink let out a sigh. She leaned on her elbows over a table further in the room, absently twirling a lock of her hair. She heaved another sigh as she pondered.

Where could he be, she asked herself.

Just then the doors slid open. Pink jumped a little and turned to the door. Her face broke into a wide smile.

"Wonder Knight, there you are! I, ahem, WE have been waiting ages for you!"

"Sorry everyone, the boss lady just pulled me aside. Suit up, looks like she has a mission for us."

Voidspeaker immediately jumped up from the couch.

"Nice timing, bro!"

Wonder Knight raised an eyebrow. Voidspeaker was excited for a mission?

Voidspeaker froze as a hand gripped his shoulder.

Hard.

"This isn't over. We're continuing the moment we get back."

Voidspeaker began to sweat. Wonder Knight turned to Pink Star, who shook her head.

"Don't ask."

△△△

"Bro, you sure there's a villain's here?"

Wonder Knight nodded.

"Boss got a tip they'd be coming in tonight."

The four teens were leaning over the edge of a roof along the oceanfront, binoculars in hand. The sun had already set, and the moon reflected off the water beyond the piers. The team had their eyes fixed on a warehouse in the port. A warehouse that was supposed to be empty.

Voidspeaker shrugged.

"Tips ain't always right, right?"

Chronolock shoved his side.

"Shut up and keep looking."

Voidspeaker gulped down whatever he was going to say next. Wonder Knight shook his head.

"You just had to make her angry before the mission."

"Come on, bro! I said I was sorry, didn't I? Besides it's a perfectly valid…Gah!"

An elbow to the rib was his answer.

"Guys! I think I see someone."

Pink Star pointed to the side of the warehouse. A group of dark figures, carrying boxes. Wonder Knight frowned.

"Suspicious, but we can't go in unless there's a super. Let's get closer and take a look."

△△△

The four teens crept to the wall of the warehouse. Voidspeaker began swirling his hands, creating a small black blanket under the window. Wonder Knight silently nodded to Pink Star, who ducked under the blanket and brought her hands close together.

"I choose you, Owl." She whispered.

A small pink Owl appeared with a small flash of light. Pink Star lifted her hands and let the Owl fly into the warehouse while Voidspeaker dropped his incantation. Pink Star then focused on her visor, where small lights and sparks glittered on the exterior.

"What do you see?"

"There's a bunch of guys in armor and masks, moving boxes around."

"Any supers?"

Pink Star furrowed her brow.

"Hmmm...the guy in the middle is dressed kind of weird and isn't helping with the boxes, but I'm not sure...wait hold on."

"What is it?"

"One of the guys dropped their box. The weirdo is yelling at him, whoa he's wearing some kind of suit with metal wings or something...eek! He just shot some light at the guy!"

Chronolock's eyes narrowed.

"That's a super, let's go."

Chronolock grabbed the edge of the window and hoisted herself inside. Wonder Knight hissed at her.

"Chronolock! Chrono! Wait! We don't have plan...dang it she's gone. Void, follow her and get her back!"

"I-I got it."

Wonder Knight sighed as Voidspeaker climbed into the window. He turned to Pink Star.

"Keep an eye out, I'll try to think of something."

△△△

Inside the warehouse Voidspeaker was quietly floating an inch off the ground, ducking behind boxes and into shadowy corners. He cursed and dropped to the ground as one of the men passed by him, then rolled into the shadow of a stack of boxes. He crawled forward until he caught up with Chronolock, who was peeking out from another stack.

"Chrono! Wait!"

"Took you long enough, let's finish this and go."

"Look I'm sorry! We'll rematch however long after. But right now we need to get back to the others!"

And their vision went white.

Voidspeaker groaned and pushed off the ground with his elbow. The white in his vision and the ringing in his ears slowly began to fade. He looked to the side. Chronolock was lying on her back, also groaning, surrounded by scattered boxes. He shook his head and looked forward.

"Well, well, well, what do we have here?"

Before him stood the weirdo. He wore a gas mask over his face, but with the visor of a night vision headset. He had a fur-lined flight jacket on, along with leather pants. On his back was some sort of metal backpack. The kicker, though, was on his arms: hanging from his arms were polished metal feathers that shimmered in the light as he moved about. He was flanked by a score of armored minions.

This mission was not going well.

"Looks like we got a couple of wannabe heroes, boys. Let's teach them a lesson!"

Voidspeaker grit his teeth and brought his leg up, rising to a kneeling stance. He brought his hands up and began to chant.

The weirdo swung his arms and light flashed off the metal feathers on his arms.

Voidspeaker fell onto his back with a cry as his vision went white again.

"They don't call me the Dazzling Vulture for nothing, you punk. You never should have come here!"

Voidspeaker grimaced. As the effects of the flash faded once more, he found himself surrounded by the masked and armored men. Chronolock was just coming to and shaking her head.

Then the wall exploded.

Voidspeaker ducked his head as pieces of debris went flying. He saw a flash of pink as a mighty, glowing rhinoceros broke through the encirclement, sending masked men flying or scattering out of the way. Wonder Knight leapt from its back and held out his hand. Voidspeaker grabbed onto it, and Wonder Knight pulled him to his feet.

"Thanks bro, I owe you one."

Wonder Knight nodded, then both ducked their heads. There was another flash of light but the glowing rhino leapt in front of them, dulling the blast. Wonder Knight turned to the side and launched a man with a front kick. The man soared through the air, and then smashed a crate with a crash.

"I'll handle these guys! Pink will keep the weirdo distracted, go get Chrono! After that, you two figure out how to bring that guy down!"

Voidspeaker nodded as Wonder Knight turned to catch a fist and then walloped his attacker. Voidspeaker turned and ran towards where Chrono was lying on the ground, breathing heavily and clutching her head.

"Hey! Get up!"

She turned her head up.

"V-Void? I'm sorry, t-this is all my..."

He grabbed her hand and pulled her to her feet.

"Move now, apologize later!"

"Um, y-yeah."

Voidspeaker pointed to where the Dazzling Vulture leapt into the air, a stream of light coming from his metal backpack as he soared out of range of the rhino.

"Head in the game, the other two are keeping them distracted. Wonder wants us to take down that jerk. You up for it?"

Chronolock shook her head a bit, then nodded once and narrowed her eyes.

"Let's get that sucker."

Voidspeaker nodded.

"I'll draw him in, you disable him."

Chronolock nodded and ran behind a stack of crates. Voidspeaker turned back to the front once she was out of sight. The Dazzling Vulture flapped his wings, bright sparks of light floating off them and then accelerating towards the rhino. The rhino roared as each impact caused it to flicker. Void closed his eyes, spread out his hands, and began to chant. He started to float in the air and his robes began to flutter about. Dark orbs grew around his hands and a purple glow surrounded his body. He opened his eyes, which were now glowing with purple light.

The rhino let out a final cry before dissipating into pink sparks. The Dazzling Vulture grinned before turning his attention to Wonder Knight, who currently had six men hanging onto him.

And then he quickly bent backwards as a black beam shot past his face.

Voidspeaker rose into the air, until he was face to face with the Dazzling Vulture. Dazzling Vulture sneered.

"You should've stayed down, kid. You can't handle the Dazzling Vulture!"

Voidspeaker spoke, a deep rumble echoing his voice.

"And you can't handle the void."

Dazzling Vulture let out another flash of light, but Voidspeaker ignored it and shot another beam. Dazzling Vulture grimaced and dropped from the sky, then spread his wings out and swung around. He spread his wings and shot another barrage of sparks towards Voidspeaker's side. Voidspeaker swung his hands into circles, forming black disks that absorbed the blows. He then dropped the disks to resume his attack.

And gasped.

Something slammed into him before he could strike.

Voidspeaker let out a cry as he slammed into a towering pile of crates. The glow faded from his eyes and body, the orbs around his hands shrank and vanished. Before him flew the Dazzling Vulture, hands around the boy's neck as he pushed him into the crates.

"Bad move to block your own vision, kid. That's why amateurs like you shouldn't get involved. You've no idea what you're getting into."

Voidspeaker's mouth curled up, even as a drop of blood dripped from it.

"Right back at you."

Chronolock jumped from the top of the crate pile. She flipped over the two and grabbed onto the Dazzling Vulture's backpack. Dazzling Vulture let go of Voidspeaker and spun around, trying to reach the girl on his back. He then realized he was plummeting towards the ground and tried to direct his light powers into the device on his back.

And then he stopped.

And remained still.

His eyes widened.

His backpack was vibrating in place. No light was coming from it. Nor was it falling, as it was locked into time and place, mid-air.

Which meant now the man was dangling from it like a parachute caught in a tree.

And in front of him rose a boy in black robes and chanting ominously.

"Experience nothingness!"

The Dazzing Vulture's vision dimmed, and then went black.

△△△

The team gathered around the tied up men. Wonder Knight nodded his head, then walked over to the other three.

"Authorities and cleanup are on the way. Good work everyone."

Chronolock kicked at the ground, eyes on her feet.

"Look…um…I'm sorry, everyone. That was incredibly stupid of me."

She gasped as Pink Star suddenly embraced her.

"I'm just glad you're ok!"

Wonder Knight nodded.

"All's well that ends well. Just, don't do it again, yeah?"

Chronolock nodded. Wonder Knight's eyes narrowed and he began to grin.

"Besides, I think someone owes you a rematch."

Chronolock's eyes narrowed.

"That's right."

Voidspeaker backed up.

"Um, hey, bro, we should probably get some sleep, right? Big day and all."

"We'll rematch however long later."

"Ugh, you remember that."

Wonder Knight put his hand on Voidspeaker's shoulder.

"There's energy drinks in the kitchen."

"Not cool, bro!"

The team laughed. As the laughter died down, Pink Star tilted her head.

"But like, what were these guys doing here?"

Wonder Knight nodded and strode over to one the boxes the men had been carrying.

"Let's find out."

He opened the crate.

And blinked.

"Huh?"

Lying in the box was…a bunch of computer chips?

"Why would supers smuggle computer chips?"

Voidspeaker walked up to him, a piece of paper in hand.

"I don't know, bro. But I think I know where we can find out."

The paper was a shipping address.

"Hey team, anyone taking Spanish?"

△△△

And as the team was cleaning up the goons, one masked henchman sat on a small motorboat, speeding through the ocean. Bob heaved a sigh and shook his head.

The meddling kids had nearly ruined everything. He had to send them in the opposite direction of the trail just to buy some time. He would have to call Miguel now and warn him the heroes were incoming.

But he smirked, and placed a hand on top of the box he had in the boat.

Fortunately, this was the last package they needed.

The monster may have been caught...but one of the faceless minions had gotten away with it in the end.

Aurora Legion wouldn't foil his plans today.

AUTHOR'S COMMENTARY: Ah yes, the only thing that can defeat an expert mastermind manipulating the entire world: meddling teenagers! What sort of ingenius and meticulously planned scheme could possibly stop that level of giddy optimism and raging hormones? Anyways! What will the Aurora Legion find at the shipping address? Do any of them speak Spanish? Who won Void and Chrono's rematch? Tune in next time, to find out!

CHAPTER 8 - AURORA LEGION ON THE HUNT

Four teenagers were waiting in the shade of a bell tower, one of them with binoculars in hand. The other three were leaning against the pillars of the tower, trying to fan themselves and hide from the bright noon sun overhead.

"Come on, bro! Why the heck are we waiting?"

Wonder Knight shrugged as he looked through the binoculars.

"The boss lady arranged for some local support, she said to meet them here."

"Come on, they're taking forever! We can take them, I'm dying here!"

Chronolock poked Voidspeaker's side.

"You're the one who decided to wear black robes."

"Hey, you try communing with the Lord of the Abyss just to suggest changes to the uniform!"

Pink Star tilted her head.

"You know, I always wondered about that."

Voidspeaker turned to face her.

"About what?"

"You don't really seem like some crazy cultist."

"Hey, that's stereotyping!"

Chronolock raised an eyebrow.

"Is it really? Weren't you planning some crazy ritual when the Director recruited you?"

Voidspeaker looked over his shoulder to glare at her.

"Hey! That's private! And I never went through with it!"

"But you did get as far as the whole ritual to gain eldritch powers stage?"

"Come on, just because I study the stars for portents of inexorable doom does not mean I'm loopy!"

The whole group took a step back.

"Right..."

Voidspeaker turned to face Chronolock.

"Why are you backing away?! You're the one who tears apart the fabric of reality on a daily basis!"

"But I didn't dance naked in the moonlight to learn how."

"Come on! That was a one-time ritual! I've never done it since and I'm not doing it again!"

Just then, a fifth voice entered the conversation.

"You the kids?"

The group jumped up and turned around. A man appeared on the edge of the tower.

"Whoa..."

"Wow."

"Got to admit, that's pretty nice."

A handsome, muscular man.

Chronolock's face grew red. Pink Star's heated up a bit as well. Even Wonder Knight nodded in admiration.

Icy Falcon had arrived.

Voidspeaker snapped in front of Chronolock's face.

"Hey, his eyes are up there."

Chronolock's gaze didn't move.

"So they are."

"What the heck are you doing?"

"Appreciating."

"Appreciating what?!"

"Art."

Wonder Knight nudged Voidspeaker. Voidspeaker jumped a bit and then turned to the man.

"Um, *hola Señor*..."

"I speak English."

"Oh thank god."

Icy Falcon shook his head and muttered '*gringos*' under his breath. Wonder Knight stepped forward with his hand extended.

"You must be Icy Falcon. We're Aurora Legion. I'm Wonder Knight, this is Pink Star, those two are Voidspeaker and Chronolock."

Icy Falcon nodded and shook his hand.

"Nice to meet you. Where's the target?"

Wonder Knight nodded and walked to the edge with Icy Falcon. He pointed at the building they had been monitoring.

"We tracked them there. Saw a couple of trucks coming in and out, looks like a lot of security? Haven't seen any supers though."

Icy Falcon grimaced.

"Head home, kids."

The team froze. Voidspeaker stepped forward.

"What the crap, bro? We've been dying in this heat all day! We're not just going home!"

Wonder Knight nodded.

"I agree. What exactly is the problem? We came too far to just leave without knowing why."

Icy Falcon sighed, and turned to the group.

"Look, I know this isn't your first mission. You've fought some supers, you've got some wins."

He looked them in the eye.

"But this isn't America, and you don't know this place like I do. In America your villains like to do their own thing. To set themselves apart. To stand above the rabble."

He pointed at the building.

"The guys here? They don't care. See, that's a cartel base you've found. The guys down there are not going to monologue, they're going to put a bullet in your head."

Chronolock frowned and crossed her arms.

"We can handle ourselves."

"I know you can, I saw the news. But I've seen other heroes before. Heroes just like you. And down here?"

Icy Falcon grimaced.

"Heroes end up in ditches."

The four looked at each other. Icy Falcon turned towards the building.

"You did good work, tracking them here. But you don't know what you're getting into. You've been in fights but this is a war. Let the soldiers fight it."

Wonder Knight looked at each of his comrades. One by one, each slowly nodded. He took a step forward.

"We're not backing down. These guys came to our shores, if this is a war we're already in it. Your concern is appreciated, but if you want to help us, then help us win. Because whether with you or not, we're going to do this."

Icy Falcon turned back and stared Wonder Knight down. Wonder Knight met his gaze without flinching or blinking.

They stood.

They stared at each other for a moment.

And another.

Eventually, Icy Falcon dropped his shoulders and let out a sigh.

"Follow my lead. Let me do the talking. I'm not interested in burying any more heroes today."

Aurora Legion gulped as they nodded.

△△△

Aurora Legion kept quiet as they followed Icy Falcon. He led them to a side entrance, quietly incapacitating the guards. They snuck inside, finding a loading area full of boxes and trucks. Workers were packing the trucks while armed men kept watch.

"Come on."

Icy Falcon motioned to them.

And then he stepped out into the open.

Aurora Legion's eyes widened, but they followed the veteran's lead. Icy Falcon came to a stop and let out a cough.

Every person in the room froze and turned to look at him.

"Well, well, well, if it isn't *Señor* Icy Falcon himself! You are bold to come here."

The speaker motioned his hands. The guards stepped forward, guns aimed at Icy Falcon.

"I never thought you'd dare. You know what's going to happen now, right? Are you prepared for open war in the streets?"

"I'm not here to fight you today."

Everyone's eyes widened, Aurora Legion included. The speaker's eyes narrowed.

"Icy Falcon, not here to fight? That's a laugh. What then, *Señor* Falcon? You here to join us? Had enough of the poor life? What else could you possibly be here for?"

Icy Falcon pointed back at Aurora Legion.

"A *gringo* super shipped something here. And now the *gringos* want to know what, and why. And you know what happens when *gringos* get involved, much less *gringo* supers. Give them what they want, and let them fight their war. Then we can go back to fighting ours, on our terms."

The speaker rubbed his chin.

"Let *gringos* fight *gringos*, eh? I can't say I hate it."

The man smiled.

"But there's one thing you didn't consider, *Señor* Falcon."

Falcon encased himself in ice as a blade appeared out of thin air. The blade stopped and the ice shattered. Then an armored man shimmered into being and grabbed Icy Falcon's throat before both of them distorted and vanished.

"You were not the first to team up with the *gringos*. Kill them!"

The guards opened fire at the stunned Aurora Legion. Pink Star screamed.

"Gah!"

Wonder Knight grunted as he wrapped Pink Star in his arms, wincing as the bullets bounced off his back. Voidspeaker looked up from where he crouched, a sweating

Chronolock holding her hands out in front of them both. Vibrating bullets appeared in the air in front of her.

She winced and shouted.

"MOVE!"

Wonder Knight ran, still holding Pink Star behind him. Voidspeaker ran after them, Chronolock walking in step with him. As she moved to the side, the bullets she left behind vanished one by one, holes appearing in the walls and crates behind. The group moved until they were hidden behind a stack of crates, bullets whizzing past and pounding on the other side of the crates. Chronolock fell to the ground panting as Wonder Knight leaned over, hands on his knees.

"What are we going to do, bro?!"

"I don't know! Let me think!"

"Can't you just take them out? You're bulletproof!"

"It still freaking hurts! Can't you make a shield, send the bullets to the void or something?"

"I don't know how to erase matter, bro!"

"Well now's the time to figure it out!"

"Eldritch rituals are NOT something you wing, bro! I could summon a black hole or an elder god if I do it wrong!"

"Then what are we going to do?!"

"I don't know! You're the plan guy!"

"Then shut up and let me think!"

Pink Star stood up. She placed her hands on both the boys' shoulders, and then walked to the edge of the crates.

"Pink?"

"What are you doing?"

She turned and smiled at Wonder Knight.

"You're not afraid of the bullets, or the pain. You're afraid they'll hurt us if you're not here to block, right? If we weren't here, you could stop them."

"That's…"

Wonder Knight looked down, avoiding her gaze. She just kept smiling and nodded at him.

"I will cause a distraction. It will make them stop

shooting. Then you go out there and do what you do best. Chrono can keep us safe."

Wonder Knight looked into her eyes, then down at Chronolock.

"It's too risky. Chrono can't stop them for long."

Pink Star nodded.

"She can't. So you'll need to be quick."

Her smile grew warm.

"I trust you. I know you can do it."

Chronolock groaned.

"Does anyone care if the girl on the ground can do it?"

Voidspeaker gave her a thumbs up.

"I believe in you, Chrono. We're just going to die if you fail, no biggie."

"Shut up, Void."

Pink Star turned back towards the edge of the crate. She extended her hands. Her gauntlets began to glow.

"What are you even going to make? I didn't know you had something bulletproof."

The edge of her mouth curled up as her gauntlets grew too bright to look at.

"I don't, not yet. But it won't matter. Ready, hero?"

Wonder Knight swallowed, then narrowed his eyes and nodded.

"Ready."

"I choose you, Blue Whale."

The world turned pink.

△△△

Icy Falcon looked around as his assailant dropped him and disappeared. He was in a dark room. It seemed empty, but he couldn't see well in the darkness.

But he could hear.

He grimaced. He heard gunshots and shouting all around. Things had gone exactly as he feared. Letting the kids come was a mistake, and not one he was prepared to live with.

Just then, something sharp grazed his cheek.

He narrowed his eyes. If he didn't focus, he wouldn't be around to regret his mistakes. He needed to take care of himself right now. He could worry about the kids once he survived.

He narrowed his gaze. He strained his hearing. He slowed his breath. He didn't move.

A cut appeared on his thigh nonetheless.

He grimaced again.

This was not going well.

He created a thin sphere of ice all around, just a foot away from him. And then grunted as a cut appeared on the back of his right calf.

That confirmed it. He was most likely under attack by some kind of teleportation ability. Icy Falcon let the sphere melt and created a layer of ice right over his skin. He didn't like to do this since it would slow him down too, but he needed a moment to think.

Because he felt like something was off.

He didn't know anyone who could teleport. He had never heard of anyone with that power before. But there was something that bothered him about this situation. Something in the pit of his stomach, something in his pounding heart.

Something he had to confirm.

He dropped the ice armor and gathered the ice to his left fist, encasing it. He then lashed out his fist to the left, without even looking.

Crack!

He hit something.

He turned to the left. He saw an armored man in a mask stumbling back, one hand holding a rapier, the other holding his face. The mask was cracked, and pieces of it began to fall.

Icy Falcon's eyes widened and he took a step back.

The face was one he saw for the first time, covered in

warts, tumors, and burns that seemed to glow with sickly green light. Yet, it was a face he recognized. A face he knew terribly, terribly well.

"El Capa?"

The man grinned as the last pieces of his mask fell.

"Hello *Señor* Falcon. But a slight correction. As you can see, I am no longer El Capa. They call me the Warped Warrior these days."

Icy Falcon's eyes narrowed.

"You died."

The Warped Warrior sneered.

"A word of advice, *Señor* Falcon. If you want to get rid of someone, don't just leave them for dead. You double and triple check. They aren't dead until you see the body with your own two eyes."

Icy Falcon swung his cape forward, launching a barrage of ice shards. The Warped Warrior simply smiled. As the shards approached, the Warped Warrior's body distorted, transparent mirror images jumping out to either side before he vanished entirely. The ice shards shattered harmlessly against the wall.

Icy Falcon let out a grunt as a blade cut his right shoulder.

"It doesn't matter, you're a dead man walking. A bunch of dead *gringo* kids? America won't rest until your entire cartel is burnt to the ground."

Another slash cut his left hip. Icy Falcon spun to the side and let out a blast of freezing wind as the Warped Warrior's laugh echoed.

"Oh you poor, short-sighted fool. You still think this is about cartels? About kilos and profits? No, *Señor* Falcon, I've moved beyond such things. I laugh, even, at how petty and irrelevant I once was. My ambition was so small back then."

Icy Falcon created a ring of ice shards and launched them in all directions. He hit nothing but the walls. Another cut appeared on his left forearm.

"You see, I've been baptized in purifying flames, *Señor*

Falcon. I've been gifted with grand powers, and something more. A glorious purpose, a cause bigger than myself, and true comrades to share it with. A cause that will change the entire world, in a way neither you nor I could ever dream of. And once it does? The entire *world* will belong to us!"

Icy Falcon puffed up his chest and then let out a breath, filling the entire room with snowy gales and daggers of ice. Frost appeared on every surface, snow filled the air. Icy Falcon let out a deep breath that condensed to fog as the winds died down.

And then the Warped Warrior's blade pierced his back.

And the sounds of gunshots fell silent.

The Warped Warrior appeared in front of him, unharmed and with a smile on his face. But he had a cold look in his eyes.

"And the *gringo* kids? Well, I'd say their deaths are on your head, *Señor* Falcon."

The Warped Warrior distorted and vanished. Icy Falcon pulled his arms around his head and encased his body in ice armor once more.

He heard the ice crack.

The blade pierced through his left thigh.

"I thought a lot about our last encounter, *Señor* Falcon, and I've come to realize something. We're two sides of the same coin, you and I."

There was another crack.

The blade pierced through his right bicep. He swung his left fist around, swinging through empty air.

"We both like to leave things unfinished. You see, my problem is that I don't stop. I enjoy it, I realized. I enjoy seeing the pain, the despair. So I prolong the process. I let it go on, even when I know I should stop. And we both know how that ended last time."

Another crack.

The blade pierced through his left foot. He swung his cape with his left hand, barraging the area with ice. The ice shattered on the walls.

"You, on the other hand, stop too early. You never finish the job. And you know why? Because you're a coward. You're afraid. You don't have the stomach for it. You don't have the guts to do what it takes."

Another crack.

The blade pierced his chest. It was just a shallow cut, barely enough to draw blood. Icy Falcon took deep breaths as the remains of his ice armor cracked and shattered, pieces falling to the floor.

"You could have stopped me, you know? But you weren't man enough to do it yourself, to strike the final blow. You just passed it off to someone else. You couldn't even bring yourself to watch. That's why you will never make a difference. Because you will never do what it takes. You can't. Even now, you are hoping for the *gringos* of all people to come and save you, to put a stop to me. All because you are too afraid to do it yourself. And now, children are dead. All because you...are...weak!"

The Warped Warrior appeared before him once more, and took a bow.

"Goodbye, *Señor* Falcon. This will be the last time you see me."

He distorted and vanished once more. Icy Falcon looked to the ground, panting for breath, blood dripping from his countless wounds. He closed his eyes, and slowly opened his mouth.

"You're right. About me, about my problem. And those kids, that's on me."

He gripped his right hand into a bloody fist.

"But you're wrong about yourself. About your problem."

He covered his fist in ice. A voice mocked him from the shadows.

"Oh, do tell, *Señor* Falcon. What then, do you think my problem is?"

Icy Falcon pulled his right arm back, elbow bent, fist

facing forward. He took a deep breath. He started to lunge, extending his right foot out and leaning forward. Then he pulled his left foot back sharply and pivoted around, swinging his torso and his fist around to jab behind him.

And straight into the Warped Warrior's torso.

"You're predictable."

The Warped Warrior's eyes widened as he gasped in pain. Icy Falcon pushed his arm upwards, driving the ice spike up and under the man's rib cage.

"Well...done...Falcon...ha...ha...ha..."

The Warped Warrior's mouth twisted into a sneer.

"But you're...too...late..."

Icy Falcon twisted his fist and the Warped Warrior breathed his last.

△△△

The world turned pink as a glowing whale filled the room. Trucks and crates crashed into the walls and flew out the entrance of the loading dock. Men cried out in shock and pain as they were thrown to the ground.

And in that moment, the gunshots stopped.

Pink Star collapsed to the ground, unconscious.

"Pink!"

Wonder Knight cried before Voidspeaker slapped his shoulder and shouted in his face.

"Go!"

Wonder Knight grit his teeth and ran out from behind the crates. He was short on time, the whale was already dissipating, glowing pink particles floating off of it. Wonder Knight pushed off the ground with all his might, leaping at the nearest man. As the man started to lift himself off the ground, Wonder Knight landed on top of him and quickly punched him in the face, knocking him back to the ground.

Wonder Knight then leapt to the next one, a quick kick sending him spiraling into the dirt. He grunted as a gunshot rang out and a bullet bounced off his shoulder.

One man was firing from a kneeling position, one hand on the ground and the other gripping his gun.

Wonder Knight spun around and grabbed the gun, crushing it in his hand, and then back handed the man into the floor.

On he went through the room, twisting metal and plastic, slamming faces and torsos.

Another, another, and another!

'Go!', he thought to himself.

Move!

Faster!

Faster!

He grit his teeth as a man fired an assault rifle at full auto into his chest. He took one step forward, and then another. He put one foot in front of the other, sucking in through his teeth as the bullets struck him. Finally, he reached forward and twisted the gun's barrel with his left hand while his right pulled back into a fist.

He swung his fist forward, and struck the man's cheek, knocking him to the ground with a heavy blow.

Wonder Knight inhaled, and exhaled. Inhaled, and exhaled.

And then slowly, ever so slowly, he turned back towards the loading dock.

There his team stood, safe and unharmed. Voidspeaker was walking towards him, supporting the two girls as they gasped for breath. He nodded to Wonder Knight. Wonder Knight slowly nodded back, and then collapsed onto his back.

They made it.

△△△

A few minutes later a gust of cool air blew through the entrance. Icy Falcon landed in front of the loading area. His eyes widened.

A bunch of groaning men were tied together on the floor. And around them stood four tired, but unharmed, heroes.

"Icy Falcon! You're alive!"

The kids ran up to him.

"I'm glad to see you all too."

He shook his head to hide the moisture building in his eyes.

He turned to the men on the floor.

"Is that all of them?"

Voidspeaker nodded.

"Pink still has a room or two to check but the building seems empty. We think the fight attracted them all here…or they ran."

Icy Falcon nodded.

"Excellent work. There's more to you than meets the eye. Why don't you four go find what you're looking for?"

Wonder Knight raised an eyebrow and pointed to the men on the floor.

"What about them?"

"I can handle it from here. You didn't come for them, right?"

Wonder Knight paused for a moment, but then nodded. The four nodded and entered the building.

One of the men began to giggle. Icy Falcon raised an eyebrow.

"You think this is funny?"

"Hehehe, ah, yes, it is. We all know how you 'handle' us, *Señor* Falcon. We'll see you again in a month, yes?"

Icy Falcon cracked his knuckles.

"I wouldn't be so sure."

△△△

Wonderknight, Chronolock, and Voidspeaker walked down a staircase, Pink Star having gone ahead. They talked as they walked, and Voidspeaker crossed his arms.

"Seriously, he's cool and all but I don't get what the big deal is."

Chronolock licked her lips.

"He's muscular. Very muscular."

Voidspeaker threw his hands in the air.

"Oh come on, Wonder's muscular. I'm muscular!"

Chronolock just raised an eyebrow. Wonder Knight shook his head and put his hand on Voidspeaker's shoulder.

"Void, let me put it this way. You and I, we're dudes. Icy Falcon, he's a man."

Chronolock nodded, her face slightly flushed.

"A handsome, muscular man."

Voidspeaker grit his teeth at that.

The three then walked into the room where Pink Star was standing. The room was full of half-packed boxes, scattered nails, and shipping labels. She was focused on her visor, a pink hummingbird darting around stacks of crates.

"You find anything, Pink?"

Pink blinked for a second. The hummingbird paused in the air, then picked up a label and brought it to Pink's hand.

"Maybe. Almost everything here is headed to an address in the Americas. Except one."

She handed the paper to Wonder Knight. He rubbed the back of his head, and then looked up at Pink Star.

"Well, you always said you wanted to visit Europe, right?"

△△△

As Aurora Legion moved into the structure, Icy Falcon began carrying the men away to an isolated location. On a tall building across town, two men watched through binoculars. One of them grimaced.

"It seems something happened, this isn't how Icy Falcon operates."

The other man shrugged.

"It was only a matter of time. *Señor* Falcon was trying to fight a war with his hands clean. It was foolish of him, and was never going to work."

The first man raised an eyebrow.

"You're awfully calm."

The second man grinned at him.

"Bob, my friend, who do you think I am? Obviously those are José's men. He was beginning to become a problem, I figured *Señor* Falcon would buy me some time to handle it. But it seems I underestimated *Señor* Falcon, and now I won't have to handle it at all."

Bob just heaved a sigh. He could only hope this wouldn't become a problem later.

At the very least, Aurora Legion was successfully delayed and everything was on schedule now. Even if they found some clues here, he would already be done by the time they arrived.

No matter what these heroes did, the world was about to change. It was…inevitable.

△△△

A plane flew high above the Alps. Convincing parents and school administrators to give Aurora Legion a sudden vacation without explaining their exact activities had been quite the struggle, a tougher fight than even the cartel put up. But the Director of the International League of Superheroes was very resourceful and very persuasive, and so had made it happen.

Snowy winds blew through the sky as the plane approached its destination. The plane turned, and then slowed down. The back ramp began to lower. Two figures leapt off it and into the sky.

One plummeted straight into the snow. The other slowly floated down, as if held by a parachute.

Wonder Knight bent his knees as he landed on the

mountain side, Pink Star held safely in his arms. He let out a grunt, then rose back to standing position. Pink Star gripped his neck hard.

"Are you all right?"

Pink Star nodded.

"I-I'm all right, it was just a little scary."

Her cheeks flushed slightly.

"But...c-could we stay like this, just a moment?"

Wonder Knight nodded.

"Take your time."

Voidspeaker touched down shortly after, the glow around his body fading. He turned his head to Chronolock, who was holding on to his back.

"You need a moment? Take your time."

Chronolock jumped to the ground with a light kick to Voidspeaker's shin.

"If you two are done flirting, can we get to work? It's freezing out here."

Wonder Knight and Pink Star flushed, but Wonder Knight let her down.

"Sorry, let's get to it."

"F-Flirting? W-We definitely weren't f-flirting."

The teens gathered together and trudged up the snowy peak. Eventually they reached an alcove in the mountain. As they peaked over the snow, they saw what they were looking for. There were two large metal doors, hidden by the roof of the cave and leading deeper into the mountain. Wonder Knight looked to Pink Star, who held her hands together in a whisper.

"I choose you, ant."

A little pink ant with wings appeared between her hands and disappeared into the snowy winds. Pink Star focused on the sparks appearing on her visor. She then turned to Voidspeaker and pointed in two directions. Voidspeaker nodded and pointed his fingers in those directions.

"Experience nothingness."

With a whisper, two thin, nearly imperceptible black lines extended out towards two corners of the doors, disabling the cameras Pink Star had discovered. Voidspeaker nodded and the Aurora Legion leapt over the snow bank and rushed to the door. Once there, Wonder Knight stood in front of the door while the other three took up positions on the sides of the entryway. They nodded to Wonder Knight who held up three fingers. He pumped his hand once per second, putting down a finger each time.

On the final pump he grabbed the edges of the door and pulled.

The team winced at the screeching of metal. Wonder Knight grit his teeth and continued to pull until there was an opening large enough for a person. He slipped inside and looked around. The halls were painted white and brightly lit, like the inside of a hospital. They were empty, and quiet.

At least until the alarms started blaring and the lights flashed red, that is.

"Let's go!"

Wonder Knight stepped forward so the rest of Aurora Legion could step inside. They could hear an intercom speaking and boots pounding on the ground. Pink Star held up her hands as the pounding grew, her hands gauntlets glowing bright.

"I choose you, Ankylosaurus!"

A pink dinosaur filled the hallway and began lumbering forward. The team moved in single file behind it, Wonder Knight in front, followed by Pink Star, then Void, with Chronolock bringing up the rear.

They met a squad of men running down the hall, carrying SMGs and assault carbines. The men stopped and lifted their guns, but the ankylosaurus bounded forward with a roar. Men smashed into walls with a crash, their fellows running from the mighty beast. A few fired potshots here and there, but none got past the armored dinosaur. Voidspeaker blinked, his eyes widening at the sight in front of him.

"Dang girl, when did you learn to do that?"
"I watched a documentary and then practiced lots!"
"That's pretty handy."
"Yes well..."
Pink Star glanced at Wonder Knight's back.
"I can't keep letting him save me."

△△△

The group continued their way through the facility. The security forces, armed with nothing but small arms and batons, couldn't deal with a 6-ton armored dinosaur. There were a few close calls and ambushes but with Wonder Knight and Chronolock to stop the bullets and Voidspeaker draining any automated defenses, nothing managed to get through. The group came into a large open area, something like a gymnasium.

And then a bolt of lightning struck the dinosaur, causing it to explode into particles of light.

The team spread out into a combat formation as a bolt of lightning struck the center of the room, a man appearing where it had struck.

He was wearing a...pirate costume?

He had a pirate hat with a skull and lighting bolts instead of cross bones. A metal hook covered his left hand. There was an eye-patch and a rough, red beard on his face. He had a metal peg instead of a right foot.

"Avast ye scurvy dogs! Who goes there?"

Wonder Knight's eyes narrowed.

"Aurora Legion, here to put a stop to a villainous plot. Who are you?"

"I be the Electron Pirate! And ye landlubbers be far from shore now."

Pink Star tilted her head.

"He's...interesting."

Chronolock just groaned.

"Villains are so weird."

Voidspeaker motioned with his hands.

"Bro, are you serious? What do you mean 'far from shore'? We're in the mountains!"

Pink Star shrugged at that.

"I mean, he's technically correct?"

Wonder Knight just put up his fists.

"I don't suppose you'd be willing to surrender?"

The Electron Pirate grabbed his stomach as he let out a laugh.

"Don't be daft ye scalleywags! Expect no quarter, for I won't be giving ye none!"

With that the Electron Pirate turned blue and white and turned into a lightning bolt. The bolt surged forward into the center of the team. Chronolock leapt towards it with her arm stretched out but the bolt shot up towards one of the walls. There appeared the Electron Pirate, standing on the wall like it was solid ground. He thrust his hook into the air, and lightning began to arc from it all over the room. Aurora Legion scattered, jumping to the sides to avoid the barrage.

But not all of them succeeded.

"Gah!"

Voidspeaker let out a cry and fell to the ground, twitching as sparks arced across his robes.

"Void!"

Pink Star cried out. The Electron Pirate grinned and a bolt of lightning shot towards the fallen hero.

And then stopped midair.

Chronolock slid in front of her teammate, her arm outstretched to freeze the lightning. Wonder Knight rolled forward and pulled Voidspeaker out of the way. Then he and Chronolock both leapt to the side as the Electron Pirate appeared between them. He raised his hook again but a pink bull slammed into him, knocking him back across the gymnasium.

Voidspeaker shook his head as he stood on his feet.

"Guh, that freaking hurts, bro!"
Chronolock turned to Wonder Knight.
"We need a plan."
Wonder Knight nodded.
"Yea, I'm thinking. Void, you good?"
The hero just grit his teeth.
"Let me at that stupid pirate."
Wonder Knight nodded at that.
"How wide an area can you cover at once?"
"Depends on how strong you want the drain."
"Can you cover the walls and roof?"
"If you give me enough time, yea. It will barely be a trickle, though."
Wonder Knight nodded.
"That should be enough. Chrono, let's go."
"On it."
A bolt of lightning shot from the ground to the roof and the pink bull scattered into fading particles.
"That hurt you jerks! No more mister nice guy!"
Pink Star tilted her head.
"Hey what happened to your voice?"
Voidspeaker's jaw dropped.
"You can speak normally?!"
The Electron Pirate's eyes widened.
"Huh? Oh, right, uh…I be sending ye bilge rats to Davy Jones' Locker!"
Pink Star shook her head.
"Sorry, it's too late. The effect is ruined"
Voidspeaker nodded.
"You have to commit if you're going to do that, bro."
The Electron Pirate huffed and crossed his arms.
"Well sorry! I didn't decide what the guys started calling me!"
And Chronolock held her forehead.
"Can we please just get on with it?"
"Oh right."

"Sorry."

"My bad."

The Electron Pirate turned blue again and a bolt shot directly into Pink Star. She screamed as she dropped to the floor, convulsing.

"Pink!"

Wonder Knight sprinted forward. The Electron Pirate grinned and pointed his hook at the charging hero.

Thunder surged forward.

And paused mid air.

Chronolock jumped off of Wonder Knight's back, holding the bolt in place. The Electron Pirate frowned as a fist approached his face. He quickly turned blue and shot towards the wall.

Right as the quietly chanting Voidspeaker placed his hands on the ground.

"Experience nothingness!"

Every surface in the room turned black. Chronolock and Wonder Knight winced at the tingling feeling in their feet. The sparks arcing across Pink Star died down.

The Electron Pirate appeared standing on the wall again. His eyes widened.

"Uh oh."

And then he plummeted to the ground.

△△△

The group was walking through the facility after the authorities arrived to take the villain into custody. Voidspeaker was groaning and shaking his head, thinking about the last fight.

"Ugh, I give up! What the heck happened, bro?"

"Didn't you pay attention in Physics?"

Voidspeaker suddenly smiled and gave a thumbs up.

"Master the arcane, disregard the mundane is my motto, bro."

Chronolock rubbed her chin and nodded her head.

"Well that explains your grades."

"Hey!"

Wonder Knight shook his head and chuckled at that.

"Well, he was called the Electron Pirate, right? So I figured he was sticking to walls by stealing electrons and generating a charge between himself and the wall. So what would happen if a counterbalancing energy drain was applied to all the surfaces? Simple, right?"

Voidspeaker just stared blankly.

"Huh?"

Chronolock heaved a sigh.

"Wonder, you have to explain like he's five."

"Not cool, Chrono!"

"You drained his sticky powers."

Voidspeaker went silent. Chronolock grinned and poked his side.

"Better, right?"

Voidspeaker avoided eye contact.

"Shut up."

The three came to a room at the center of the facility. It was some kind of a control center, with lots of desks and computers all facing a one big monitor on the far wall. The monitor was showing a map of Europe and a countdown clock. The clock had a few hours remaining. On the map, a location not too far from them had a glowing red dot over it. Pink Star was sitting in the corner, a hummingbird flying around each of the smaller monitors.

Wonder Knight rubbed his chin as he looked at the map.

"I wonder what they were doing."

Voidspeaker shrugged.

"No idea, bro."

Chronolock raised an eyebrow.

"Why don't you ask the stars?"

"Do you want this to be related to inexorable doom?"

And then they heard Pink scream.

"Pink! What's wrong?!"

The trio ran over to the girl. She was trembling, one hand covering her mouth and the other pointed at one of the monitors. The three turned to the monitor and gasped.

"Void."

"Y-Yeah?"

"Check those stars. Everyone else, look for a landing pad or something, I'll call the Director."

The monitor in question showed the live feed of a workshop in the facility. Inside the workshop was a large metal cone.

With a trefoil painted in yellow on its side.

It was a nuclear warhead.

Wonder Knight slowly glanced up at the clock.

"We only have hours left to stop the Apocalypse."

> AUTHOR'S COMMENTARY: Chrono won the rematch by the way. All 135 of them. And in other news...um...Bob...what exactly are you doing? Blowing up the world is kind of...well, at least we know Icy Falcon going Punisher-mode won't have any consequences? Anyways! Can the Aurora Legion stop the Apocalypse? Will Void be held back this year too? Or have the stars declared their inexorable doom? Tune in next time as the Aurora Legion arc heads towards its ultimate climax!

CHAPTER 9 - THE BEGINNING OF THE END

Bob took a short break, leaning against the wall. He was once again in minion uniform, with body armor and a full helmet. This time there was the picture of a sun with a nuclear trefoil at its center painted on his armor's chest piece. Similarly dressed men and women moved through the room, carrying equipment or typing away at computers.

They were in a nuclear silo, one of the conveniently abandoned locations Bob had identified back in the day.

And inside was a fully operational ICBM, almost prepped and ready for launch.

It had taken some time, arranging for all this. Practically every resource he had at his command was required to make it happen. The manpower from the Eternal Night Sect. Nuclear warheads from the Red Colonel's arsenal. All the smuggling expertise of the cartels. Brand new targeting chips, especially designed by Tanifuji Inc. And of course, a great deal of money and connections, courtesy of Lady Anita and EL Bank.

But now, it was ready. The *pièce de résistance* of Bob's plans. The culmination of all his efforts thus far.

In just a few hours, the world would change forever.

Bob heaved a sigh and rose to his feet.

There was nothing left for him to do.

There was nothing left for him to plan.

The die was cast.

The plan could no longer change, could no longer be

stopped.

All he needed to do now…was finish the work, and hope everything occurred according to his predictions.

He rose back off the wall and stretched his arms. Then he got back to work.

And so it began.

The beginning of the end.

△△△

Aurora Legion sat strapped into the back of a plane. The Director had barely managed to get them in the air in time, having a helicopter fly to the mountain and take them straight to the nearest airport. And now they sat there, wringing their hands, praying they would make it with enough time to stop the end of the world. Pink Star twitched nervously, fidgeting with her hands. She gulped, gripped her hands together, and then looked up.

"W-Wonder Knight, I, um, I have something to tell you."

Wonder Knight looked up at her.

"What is it, Pink?"

She gulped but looked into his eyes and continued on.

"I-I know this isn't the best time, but if…well…um…I might not have another chance. S-So…um…Wonder Knight, I love you!"

Wonder Knight's eyes widened.

"Huh?"

"Please go out with me!"

Wonder Knight looked away.

"Um…that's…"

Tears welled up in Pink Star's eyes.

"Is…is that a no?"

Wonder Knight looked down at the floor.

"…I'm sorry."

The tears started to fall.

"Why?! Is there someone else?! Am I not good enough?!

Please, what can I do?!"

Wonder Knight took a deep breath.

"No, it's not that, it's just…well…"

"What? What is it?!"

"It's…well…I'm…gay."

Pink Star blinked.

"Huh?"

Wonder Knight gripped his hands together.

"I'm sorry, I was waiting to reveal it until…well I guess until everyone acknowledged us as heroes. But…I guess I didn't need to hide it from you all, so…I'm sorry for that."

Wonder Knight suddenly started waving his hands about.

"Oh, and, uh, it's definitely not you, Pink! I definitely care about you, just…not like that. Like, you're a great girl and all and any guy would be lucky to have you but, um, it's not really my thing. If it was…but I'm sorry, it's not."

Pink Star kept blinking as her mind processed the information.

"I-I see, that's, well, um, I'm sorry?"

Wonder Knight shook his head and his hands.

"N-no, it's not your fault. I'm flattered, really."

Pink Star stared into the air for a bit.

"Wait…"

She slowly turned her head.

Voidspeaker shook his head repeatedly.

"No. Definitely not. I am straight. Very straight. We are friends. Just friends."

Wonder Knight stared into the distance.

"Yes…friends…just…friends…"

Chronolock heaved a sigh and waved her hand.

"Yes yes, they're just friends, you're just friends, we're all just friends. Now that that's out of the way, is everyone good for now?"

Voidspeaker started fidgeting.

"A-Actually, Chrono, I've always…"

Chronolock glared at him.

"Quiet."

He looked down at the ground.

"Yes ma'am."

Chronolock exhaled her breath.

"Ok, with that done, CAN WE PLEASE FOCUS ON STOPPING THE APOCALYPSE?!"

The other three looked away sheepishly.

"Oh, yeah"

"Right, we should probably focus."

"It's not really the best time for this."

Chronolock covered her face with both hands.

"We're all going to die."

△△△

Rusted doors creaked on their hinges as Wonder Knight pulled them open. The team crept through the abandoned missile silo. The facility was dark, none of the lights were lit, not a creature stirred. Pink Star summoned a small bird to light the way, but they saw nothing but dust and broken equipment. The team held their breaths as they crept forward, trying not to wince at their own footsteps. Eventually they came to a large open area.

And the world lit up.

The teens shielded their eyes from the sudden, bright lights. They heard something like the air being ripped apart.

"Gah!"

Wonder Knight let out a cry as a beam of sickly green light slammed into his chest, knocking him to the ground. Pink Star and Voidspeaker moved to help him to his feet while Chronolock stepped in front of them, arms at the ready.

"Welcome, little lambs. I'm glad you could join me for this holy moment. The New Dawn approaches quickly."

They were in a large observation area, with a window overlooking the silo on the far wall from them. All around them were cameras and recording equipment, aimed at the missile preparing for launch. To their left was a wall of large monitors behind desk panels full of blinking lights and nobs. In front of them, a large man floated in the air. He wore a preacher's outfit with a yellow radiation symbol painted on the front, and his body glowed with a sickly green light. His exposed face and hands were covered in warts and tumors, some of which glowed green.

Chronolock's eyes narrowed.

"Who are you?"

The man nodded and spread out his hands.

"I am your teacher, your guide. The one who will save this fallen world."

"Bro! You're about to destroy the world!"

The man shook his head.

"I am about to baptize it."

"With nukes?!"

He turned and gazed upon the missile as Wonder Knight stumbled to his feet, Pink and Void supporting him.

"They are not destruction, as everyone fears. They are salvation. I myself was baptized by the holy flame, on that little island in the Pacific so many years ago. It changed me, elevated me, made me something more, something greater. I knew then my purpose. I was to prepare the way, to spread what I had learned, to lead others to the Sacred Light."

Wonder Knight grit his teeth as he stood on his own power.

"You're insane."

The man turned back to them, shaking his head and clicking his tongue.

"Little lambs, have you not seen them yourself? The Dazzling Vulture, the Warped Warrior, the Electron Pirate, all my precious disciples, all fellow recipients of the great gift. They received it with joy and became followers of the Sacred Light, they basked in it and purified their souls as it elevated their bodies. The world is changing, it is growing, and we must grow with it. Are you not the same? Are you not the proof? Why would you hoard these gifts for yourself when we can give them to all?"

Wonder Knight glared at the man.

"Millions of people will die!"

The man clasped his hands together in front of his chest and closed his eyes.

"Millions will be saved. Some of their flesh may fail, but all their souls will be purified, and they will be saved, forever. And those that remain will lead humanity to a glorious future, to our true destiny."

Voidspeaker narrowed his eyes and lifted his hands.

"Bro, I don't think there's any reasoning with him."

Chronolock nodded.

"Convincing coming from you."

"Oh come on! Now?! Really?!"

The man's face dropped, his eyes dropped.

"So you cannot see it? You do not understand? You would give in to impure desire and selfish ambition? You would oppose love and salvation?"

Wonder Knight raised his fists.

"We oppose you."

The man looked down to the ground. He spread his arms, floating higher into the air.

"So be it. Then it is the duty of I, the Atomic Herald, to discipline you, that you might yet see the Light."

He thrust his hand forward and a beam of sickly green light shot into the ground, heading towards the Aurora Legion. All four of them scattered to either side as the beam cut the ground between them. Chronolock and Wonder Knight pivoted and ran towards the Atomic Herald from either side, while Voidspeaker and Pink Star gathered energy into their hands. The Atomic Herald raised his hands, which glowed with their sickly light. Two green beams shot forth.

"Gah!"

"Eek!"

Wonder Knight took another beam straight to the chest.

He flew back and collided into Pink Star, sending both heroes to the floor. Chronolock grunted as she raised her arms, a beam of light vibrating inches from her face.

"I...can't....hold it!"

"Move! Experience nothingness!"

Chronolock leapt to the ground as a black beam shot above her, colliding with the green one. The lights in the room dimmed. The roof tiles began to shake and clatter. Voidspeaker rose into the air, clenching his teeth. Gusts of wind blew about the room as darkness and light attempted to swallow the other.

The Atomic Herald frowned.

"You are one who rejects the light. Who was seduced by darkness. There is no place for such superstition in the New Dawn."

The Atomic Herald brought his other hand to aim at Voidspeaker, adding a second beam to the tug of war. Voidspeaker grunted, sweat dripped from his brow. The green beams grew brighter and brighter, pushing the black beam across the room. The black beam grew thinner and thinner, shorter and shorter.

And then the green beams struck the black sphere covering Voidspeaker's hands, shattering his ritual.

A thundering noise rang through the room as a shockwave rattled the cameras and roof tiles. Voidspeaker flew backwards, bouncing twice on the ground before he rolled to a halt, smoke rising from his robes. He did not stir.

"Void!"

Chronolock leapt through the air. The Atomic Herald clenched his arms for a moment, a flash of light surging forth in all directions. Chronolock let out a cry as she was thrown back.

And then there was a mighty roar, and the earth began to tremble.

The Atomic Herald turned to the window, tears welling up in his eyes.

"It is finally here. It is finally time."

He stretched out a finger. A small beam of light struck a flashing button. The lights turned on. The cameras began to blink red.

△△△

"Good evening and welcome to GNN, all you citizens of planet Earth. I'm your host, Brendan Baird. Today we're going to discuss…"

All across the globe, the television feeds cut with a loud beeping sound, before the Atomic Herald appeared.

"Your salvation. Greetings, all you lost little lambs of the world. Rejoice, for your salvation is at hand! Even as I speak, the missiles are ready. Soon you all shall be baptized by holy fire, soon you all shall see the Sacred Light. Your souls shall be purified and your bodies shall be elevated. You will be confused, you will be afraid, but fear not, little lambs. I, the Atomic Herald, will be here, to guide and shepherd you, and lead you into this New Dawn. Watch now, your salvation approaches!"

And with that, the camera turned, showing the nuclear missile as it launched.

△△△

Chronolock ran where Voidspeaker had fallen. Pink Star was already there, checking his vitals. Wonder Knight had limped over, holding his side.

"We…we're too late…"

Chronolock's eyes narrowed.

"Not yet."

Wonder Knight shook his head, pointing at the missile.

"There's no more time."

Chronolock frowned.

"Then I will stop it. Throw me."

"What?"

"Throw me at the missile! Do it now, idiot!"

Voidspeaker came to as Wonder Knight picked up Chronolock in one arm, a camera in the other. Pink Star's eyes welled up and hugged him.

"Void!"

"W-What's happening?"

Wonder Knight swung his arms, throwing the camera first, and then Chronolock. The hero soared through the air and shielded her face with her arms. The window shattered as the camera struck it ahead of her. She could feel stinging from all over her arms and legs as she passed by the jagged remains of the window but she ignored the pain. She gasped as she hit the platform in the silo area, but she thrust out her arms even before she caught her breath, shouting with all her might.

"GRAAAAAAHHHHHH!!!!!!"

The world grew still.

The roaring stopped.

The missile began vibrating in the air.

The Atomic Herald closed his eyes, a tear falling down his cheek.

"So you cannot be saved. I am sorry little one, but I cannot allow you to delay salvation. May your soul be purified, and find peace."

He raised his hand...

A green light began to glow...

A sickly, glowing beam shot forth...

The beam approached the girl...

She didn't move.

The beam passed the window...

She couldn't.

Wonder Knight opened his mouth to shout...

Pink Star gasped, her eyes starting to water...

Voidspeaker stretched out his hand...

"CHRONO!!!"

She burst into flames.

AUTHOR'S COMMENTARY: ...how will Aurora Legion's tale end? Tune in next time, to find out...

CHAPTER 10 - THE NEW DAWN

There was an explosion of smoke as Chronolock burst into flames, and they saw her no more.

"CHRONO!!!"

Voidspeaker cried out.

He tried to stand.

He tripped, falling face first into the floor.

He grit his teeth and pushed himself up.

He ran towards the window covered in smoke.

Pink Star fell to her knees, tears streaming from her eyes. Wonder Knight's head hung down.

The Atomic Herald clasped his hands and bowed his head.

"May your soul find peace."

And then a ball of fire struck him on the forehead.

Voidspeaker skid to a stop. Pink Star gasped and tapped Wonder Knight's leg. Wonder Knight looked up and his eyes widened. The smoke began to dissipate.

They saw a red mask and cape. Then a red and yellow suit. There were fists covered in fire. Yellow and orange flames painted across a muscular chest.

Captain Hot Devil had arrived.

And Chronolock was lying behind him, still alive and holding the missile in place.

Wonder Knight and Pink Star smiled. Tears dropped from Voidspeaker's eyes.

Captain Hot Devil pulled his arm back for a throw, and lobbed another ball of flame at the Atomic Herald. The Atomic Herald flew backwards into the wall and was covered in smoke and dust. Chronolock grit her teeth, blood dripping from her nose.

"DO! SOMETHING!"

Captain Hot Devil nodded.

"You three take care of the villain. I'll handle this."

He turned to the missile. Aurora Legion nodded at each other and took a formation around the smoke where the Atomic Herald vanished.

A sickly green beam shot from the smoke. Wonder Knight and Voidspeaker dodged to the side while Pink Star stretched out her hands. A pink wolf flashed forward and leapt into the air, meeting the beam. The beam stopped as the wolf exploded into pink shards. The Atomic Herald flew out of the smoke.

"Experience nothingness!"

The Atomic Herald threw up his hands and shot out a beam to catch the incoming void assault, the beams matching each other in the air once more.

And then a boom mic struck him on the forehead with a superpowered swing.

The Atomic Herald let out a cry and threw up his hands. The glow around his body faded as the black beam struck his chest and he fell to the ground. As he tried to stand back up, Wonder Knight appeared before him and sank a fist into his abdomen. He flew back into the wall with a mighty crash, and then sank to the floor against it. He began to raise his hands when a 400-pound, glowing pink gorilla sat on him, holding his arms against the wall.

He looked up in front of him. Wonder Knight stood to the right, arms raised into a boxing stance. To the left floated Voidspeaker, glowing purple and floating in the air. Directly in front of him was Pink Star, arms stretched out and gauntlets pulsing with pink light.

Wonder Knight frowned as he spat out the words.

"Don't. Move."

But the Atomic Herald wasn't looking at them. His eyes

widened.

"No!"

△△△

As the team fought the Herald, Captain Hot Devil surveyed the missile, swearing as Chronolock let out a grunt. There was no time, he'd have to just take the risk and improvise.

"On my signal, let it go."

The girl was in no shape to respond so Captain Hot Devil immediately leapt into action. He jumped into the air, jets of fire shooting from his hand and propelling him upwards. He shot up until he was near the center of the missile and flying towards it. Closer, closer, until he was only inches away.

"NOW!"

The world roared as the missile stopped vibrating and the firing sequence resumed. Captain Hot Devil grabbed onto the missile and grit his teeth. He held on for dear life as the missile flew into the sky.

He held.

He held some more.

Until the trees below grew small.

He closed his eyes and took a breath. He only had one shot at this. He set fire to his fingers, burning a small hole through the metal he was grabbing onto. Then he let go with one hand and pulled it back into a flaming fist. He swung it towards the opening he had made and then let go with his other hand as the fireball shrank into the hole. Then he shot as much fire as he could from his hands, pushing himself away from the missile.

For a few, heart dropping seconds, nothing happened.

And then the sky exploded.

△△△

The team gasped as Captain Hot Devil landed back into the silo. His clothes were burnt and smoking, but the man himself was unharmed. He knelt, picked up Chronolock in his arms, then stepped back into the room.

"Bro, how are you still alive?"

"Hell is hotter."

The room went silent. Captain Hot Devil averted his gaze.

"Uh, anyways, nuclear bombs work very precisely. Explosion like that isn't precise. And I can handle jet fuel."

The Atomic Herald began to giggle, before he broke out into raucous laughter. Pink Star tilted her head.

"Did he finally lose it?"

Voidspeaker shook his head.

"I don't think he ever had it."

Wonder Knight narrowed his eyes.

"What's so funny?"

"What's so funny? You think this is over? You think you can stop the New Dawn? You never had a chance! This is only one of an entire network of silos! Even now, the missiles fly! Salvation cannot be stopped!"

Captain Hot Devil walked over to the wall of monitors and flicked one of the switches.

"I wouldn't be too sure."

The Atomic Herald's eyes widened. His jaw dropped.

"How..how can this be? What is this?"

Each monitor showed the observation room of a different silo.

"I must say, the hospitality of these fellows is quite lacking."

Mr. Dapper Tiger sipped a cup of tea in front of a mound of groaning bodies.

"Tesla Titan reporting, silo is fried."

Tesla Titan gave a salute, surrounded by sparking and smoking machines.

In another monitor Agent Tina was whistling while setting up some small packages in the room. She turned around, and strode to the monitor while tossing a detonator remote.

"Oh hey! Just setting up a little present."

Another room was covered in ice. Icy Falcon gave a nod.

"Assets frozen, justice prevails."

The Atomic Herald's mouth opened and closed.

"This..this is impossible! This cannot be?! What is this?! Who are you all?!"

Captain Hot Devil grinned.

"Why don't you tell him, kids."

Aurora Legion grinned.

"We're the International League of Superheroes!"

The Atomic Herald shut his mouth. He furrowed his brow. He clenched his teeth.

"This isn't over, you hear me?! Even if I am stopped today, salvation will come! The New Dawn cannot be stopped!"

Wonder Knight scoffed.

"Pretty sure it can."

Pink Star nodded.

"Like, we literally just did it."

Voidspeaker chuckled and shook his head.

"It's not cool to be a sore loser, bro."

The Atomic Herald grit his teeth. And slowly pointed a finger at the big red button on the wall, firing a dim beam of light towards it.

The ground shook and all the heroes stumbled. Explosions rang out from all over the facility.

"What was that?!"

Just then there was a flash of sickly green light. The Aurora Legion shielded their eyes. The pink gorilla shattered into shards. The Atomic Herald leapt up and fled from the room. Voidspeaker gripped his fists and started after him.

"Hey! Get back here!"

Captain Hot Devil put a hand on his shoulder.

"No time, kid. This place is coming down, and your friend is still out. We'll deal with him later."

Voidspeaker clenched his teeth but nodded as he glanced at Chronolock, still unconscious in Captain Hot Devil's arms. The Captain nodded at the rest and the heroes ran out of the crumbling silo.

Evil may have escaped to plot again, but the day was saved.

And thanks to the cameras, with the whole world watching...

△△△

"This is my stop."

Captain Hot Devil stood as the plane touched down at a military airfield.

"You aren't coming with us?"

Captain Hot Devil shook his head.

"I have a prior appointment. And I've had my time in the spotlight, today is your win."

Pink Star shook her head.

"That's not true!"

Wonder Knight nodded.

"She's right, we couldn't have done it without you."

Captain Hot Devil gave Aurora Legion a smile.

"The world needs new heroes. I had my time. I'll be around, but it's your turn to carry the torch. And hold your heads up high. We all helped, but it was you four who tracked the Atomic Herald down, who uncovered his plot. You were the only ones still fighting then, the only ones who could. We all owe you. The whole world owes you."

Chronolock slowly shuffled forward, eyes at her feet. She slowly looked up at the Captain.

"Um, thank you, for saving me."

Captain Hot Devil shook his head.

"Just doing my job, kid. You're the one who saved the world."

With that, Captain Hot Devil turned and exited the ramp

of the plane. He walked out towards a car waiting on the runway. The ramp slowly closed, and the plane began to taxi out. The Aurora Legion sat back down and buckled in. Chronolock sat next to Voidspeaker and nudged his side.

"Hey."

Voidspeaker jumped.

"W-What is it?"

"You had something to say to me, right?"

Voidspeaker tilted his head.

"Um…"

Chronolock held her head and sighed.

"Before the mission."

Voidspeaker's eyes widened and then he looked away.

"Oh! Um…I thought you didn't want to hear it."

Chronolock frowned.

"Not before the most important mission of our lives I didn't."

"Right…and…"

"Mission's over now."

Voidspeaker froze, and then his eyes went as wide as they could go.

"Oh…OH! Um…d-do you want to hear it now?"

Chronolock grabbed his chin and pulled him to face her, and then looked him in the eyes.

"Yes."

Voidspeaker gulped and nodded.

"Oh, ok, um, hang on, deep breaths, um here I go…"

Wonder Knight and Pink Star both furrowed their brows, and then shouted at the same time.

""I'M SO JEALOUS!""

△△△

Aurora Legion stepped out of the airport. As soon as they exited the doorway, they stopped and blinked. The entrance was surrounded by flashing lights and screaming crowds.

As they tried to process what was happening, reporters ran forward and jabbed microphones in their faces.

"There they are!"

"It's Aurora Legion!"

"Voidspeaker, how did you get your powers?"

"Wonder Knight, are you and Pink Star dating?"

"How did you stop the missiles?"

"Is Captain Hot Devil training you?"

"Is it true you're actually just students?"

"What exactly is the International League of Superheroes?"

As the teens panicked, a van pulled up to the sidewalk. A woman stepped out and stepped in between the bewildered teens and the reporters.

"That's enough folks, give them some room. I can take any questions you have."

The reporters turned to the newcomer as the teens shuffled into the van.

"Who are you?"

A dark-skinned woman with black, braided hair and wearing a suit and sunglasses stood before them. She reached up and took off her sunglasses, showing her face to the world.

"I'm Londyn Green, director and founder of the International League of Superheroes."

△△△

Back in the remains of the facility, the Atomic Herald panted for breath, taking a second to lean on the wall. He was in a dark, underground tunnel, intermittently lit with incandescent bulbs hanging from the ceiling. It was a long escape tunnel from the silo that hadn't been used since it was built. As he stopped to breathe, his eyes began to water.

Where had he gone wrong?

His plan was perfect. He had been so careful. He had

worked for so long, moving in the shadows, gathering disciples and resources. He had covered his tracks. He hadn't stirred any waters.

So then how did he fail?

Where did this International League of Superheroes come from? How did they track him down?

He clenched his fist. A pulse of green light surged over his body.

He didn't know. He didn't know who they were. He didn't know where they came from. He didn't know how they found him. But he knew one thing.

They would pay for this.

He stood up straight. Long was his path, difficult and uncertain. But it was straight and focused, and he would not stray from it. What did it matter that he failed today? What did it matter that the New Dawn had been delayed? The New Dawn would come, one way or another. He only needed to do his part. The Sacred Light would do the rest.

He was about to resume walking when he paused.

He heard footsteps.

In this emergency escape tunnel which had never been used in all its history.

A tunnel that had been forgotten even by its builders.

And the footsteps were coming from ahead.

He narrowed his eyes, and the glow around his fists grew. He hadn't told anyone about this passage. Not his minions, not his disciples.

Whoever it was was not someone he knew.

The footsteps were light and methodical. But unerring and relentless. There was not a single deviation from the beat. Each step was perfectly in rhythm.

And they were growing louder.

Ever louder.

And then they stopped.

The Atomic Herald could barely make out the silhouette of a figure, still hidden in the shadows between the lights.

There was silence for a moment as both people stood still.
Finally, the Atomic Herald opened his mouth.

"Who's there...?"

And then the tunnel lit up in front of him. The cacophonous roar of automatic fire rang through the hall, coming from two rapidly pulsing lights in front of him. As well as a high-pitched voice.

"DIE DIE DIE! GET SOME GET SOME!!!"

For a minute the barrage continued. Then it cut off abruptly, shell casings clattering on the floor. The smoke cleared as the Atomic Herald held his arms in front of his face, a glowing shield of green light in front of him. He pulled his hands back and then thrust his fists forward, a beam of green light illuminating the dark spots in the hall and slamming into the previously hidden figure.

It was a girl, barely an adult, who was wearing thin silk robes.

And who didn't even blink as she took the beam head on.

The Atomic Herald began to sweat. He grunted and pushed forward again, intensifying the beam.

The girl *yawned*.

More and more the Herald pushed, striking with all his power, but even his strength was not endless and it had been a long day. Soon, he started to breathe heavily. The beam began to fade.

The girl tossed two assault rifles to the ground and began to step forward, reaching into her robes. She pulled out two brass knuckles and slipped them on her hands.

"I got my hopes up when you tanked all that lead but that little light show was kind of disappointing. I hope that's not all you got."

She swung her fists together, a metallic clang as two brass knuckles collided. A blast of wind shot down the hall. The Atomic Herald took a step back.

The girl's mouth curled into a vicious grin.

"Try to entertain me, would ya?"

And so an eternal night fell on the sacred light.

△△△

Londyn Green stood on a pier at night. She leaned on the railing, gazing out at the city skyline. The waves crashed in a soft and steady rhythm. As she did, a person in a hoodie walked up to her. She turned to him and nodded her head.

"Bob."

"Londyn."

She looked back out onto the city. The pair stood in silence for several minutes before Londyn finally spoke.

"Thank you."

Bob shook his head.

"I just gave you the push, and the opportunities. You seized them, and made it happen."

"I see."

There was another minute of silence.

"How did you know?"

"Know what?"

Londyn turned to face him.

"That this would work? The League, the kids, all of it?"

Bob shrugged.

"No one wanted to be the one to act. Now someone else has it handled. They'll complain, they'll stir up a fuss, but deep down, they're glad there's someone to call now."

"That's it?"

"That's it."

Londyn thought for a moment before shaking her head.

"You know, I thought you were crazy when you brought me a bunch of teenagers."

"That was the point."

Londyn raised an eyebrow.

"Oh?"

Bob nodded.

"The world needed them. They needed you. Now, the world needs you too."

The edge of Bob's mouth curled up.

"And they pose questions no one wants to answer, since it's legally inconvenient to let minors save the world. But they can't take down Aurora Legion, not after what they've achieved. So everyone will be careful what questions they ask, for now. Should buy you some time to figure out the rest."

Another minute of silence. Londyn sighed.

"What now, then?"

"Now? Now you do your job, and I do mine."

"Your job went up in flames. Again."

Bob smirked.

"There's always another opening for a faceless minion."

Londyn frowned.

"Are you good with that?"

Bob nodded immediately.

"Yes."

"Why?"

"Because it's necessary."

Londyn looked down at the ground and whispered.

"...But it doesn't have to be you."

She looked up at Bob, then glanced away as she spoke.

"...You know, there's job openings with the League now. I know you have sources. You could do a lot from here. Maybe even more. You don't need to go there yourself."

Bob shook his head.

"Thanks, but this is my place."

"Are you sure?"

Bob waited for Londyn to continue. She looked down at the ground again, furrowing her brow.

"I...No one knows what will happen when a hero reaches a site. And...I don't like the idea that it might be you on the floor next time."

Bob nodded.

"Your concern is appreciated. I'll be careful. Besides, I wouldn't like working at the League."

Londyn frowned at that.

"Why not?"

Bob smiled.

"Because heroes are so annoying."

Bob lifted his hand, and then began to walk away. Londyn watched as he went.

"Will…Will I see you again?"

"If you need to."

Londyn turned back to the city. She took a deep breath.

And then she was alone.

Her phone started to buzz. She took it out, it looked like Director's Assistant Linda was calling her. The edges of her mouth curled up.

Alone, but not adrift. Not anymore.

She pulled out her sunglasses and put them on. She turned, and started walking down the pier.

It was time for Director Green to go to work.

Meanwhile Bob smiled as he walked away.

He had done it.

It had been tough. Thanks to a mix up by an EL Bank clerk, the Atomic Herald's team ended up swapping warehouses with a minor villain and Bob hadn't caught the error until after the tip was passed to Londyn. Aurora Legion had nearly stumbled upon the plot before it was ready. Bob had to quickly improvise to put them back on schedule and they barely stopped the Atomic Herald in time as a result of the detour.

But now, it was done. And the world had changed as a result.

Heroes could no longer operate alone and unilaterally, not unless they could foot a bill for mass collateral damage. They had no choice but to find a patron or retire.

And thanks to the efforts of Aurora Legion and a few tips from a 'well-placed informant', Londyn had now established herself as the only name in the game. The only one who could be trusted to stop villains with acceptable collateral damage. Who could do right by both the heroes and the people they protected.

Others had tried, but there was no one else trusted by all of the public, the ruling powers, and the heroes themselves. So no one could gather the necessary support and resources to make it happen. There had been no one who could solve the problem of supers.

But now, there was.

After all, she had just saved the world in front of every television on Earth. And redeemed the fallen Captain Hot Devil to boot.

In other words...

Soon every serious hero would enroll with the ILS.

The heroes were now contained. They had to do what Londyn said and she had a personal interest in keeping them in line. No hero would be permitted to go around blowing up skyscrapers any longer.

And...there was something more for Bob.

Linda had established a good working relationship with Londyn and demonstrated her competence, so Londyn had been all too happy to bring her onboard as the Director's Assistant. Her second-in-command, the only other person who knew everything to know about the ILS.

Which meant Bob would soon know the location and status of every hero around the world, in real time.

And thanks to EL Bank, he would also be the main source of intel for the ILS for quite a while.

So he could already control when and where the villains appeared.

And now he could control when and where the heroes moved to confront them.

And if he could control those geniuses and supermen, those masterminds and gods? If he could make them dance to his tune, do as he desired?

Bob grinned.

Then he could change the world, however he pleased. Him, a mere mortal, a faceless minion, could now move mountains, and achieve things those *heroes* never could.

And soon, he would do just that.

He had to admit…

He loved it when a plan came together.

Muahahaha behold Bob's evil plan! He killed the Atomic Herald, saving the world from nuclear devastation! And helped found the International League of Superheroes, creating a centralized organization to manage, and deploy superheroes wherever they're needed as well as clean up the damage after! It's so…evil…? Um…Bob, are you sure you're a supervillain? What's that? You never said that? I'm the one who called you that? That's…w-well anyways! What will Bob do now that he controls both the heroes and the villains? Will Londyn ever realize the truth about her friend? Will Xiong Huang ever find a serious fight? Tune in next time, to find out!

SIDE STORY - WHAT IS A HERO?

A young girl, barely a decade old, walked out onto the basketball court and heaved a sighed. Samantha Roberson wasn't sure she even wanted to play today. After all, what was the point of all this? All around her her teammates waved to their families on the bleachers. But not her. She didn't even bother to look.

She knew no one was there.

She didn't blame her parents. Mom came to every game she possibly could, but she had just taken off for Timmy's recital. She was out of time, she couldn't skip any more work. Samantha knew she wanted to come anyways but told her no. She couldn't ask her that. She saw the bags under Mom's eyes. She heard the sobbing when Mom thought everyone was asleep.

Dad…well, Dad was a hero. And not just her hero, everyone's hero. Her daddy saved the day, saved lives. And he was saving lives right now. What was a mere basketball game compared to that? Samantha would smile. She couldn't be prouder of her daddy.

So then why did her chest hurt? Why did her stomach ache? Why was her heart twisted into a knot?

She looked ahead. She tried to focus on the other team. She tried to keep her eyes forward. She tried to get her head in the game.

She tried.
And tried.
No, she told herself.

Don't look.

No one's there.

No one *should* be there.

But she couldn't help herself. She took a quick glance. Just a peek. Just to be sure. And then she would…

Samantha froze.

She blinked.

She rubbed her eyes.

She blinked again.

And then her jaw dropped.

He couldn't be there. He shouldn't be there.

But there he was.

No masks. No capes. Just a pair of jeans and a lame shirt.

Their eyes made contact. He raised his hand and slowly began to wave. She slowly raised hers and waved back.

It was Jim Roberson.

It was Captain Hot Devil.

It was her dad.

Her heart began to pound. She felt something warm rise from her stomach and spread throughout her torso. Her eyes began to moisten.

She shook her head. She turned her eyes forward. The ref was about to toss the ball.

She had a game to win.

∆∆∆

Jim opened the door and let his daughter in. He smiled wryly. She had not stopped talking the entire way home. But he had to admit that was an impressive shot she made.

"Mom!"

The little girl ran to the woman dusting the hallway furniture. Jim watched from the doorway as she recounted the game to her mother.

He took a deep breath.

His wife had been right about many things, but wrong

about one. He loved the glory. He craved the thrill. But that wasn't why he had done what he did.

He acted the way he had because he was afraid.

He was used to the worshiping eyes of adoring crowds who clung to his image. To the sleazy eyes of silver-tongued politicians who craved his fame. To the judgemental eyes of journalists who thought he took it too far. To the jealous eyes of police officers robbed of their day in the light.

But the eyes of his kids, those eyes scared him.

The eyes with no hate, no judgment, no motive. The eyes with infinite faith and trust, that hung on every word he spoke. How could he ever live up to what those eyes saw?

And then, that night happened. The night he ruined everything. Those eyes were filled with fear, longing, and concern.

But without an ounce of judgment or blame.

Something inside him broke that night.

His heart pounded in his chest as he watched his daughter and wife talk. His stomach dropped, his chest curled into a knot. He had failed. He was lacking. He had no idea what to do. He didn't think he could do it even if he knew.

And it scared him how good it had felt to go back. How desperately he had wanted to step into those lights and crowds. Just a little. Just for a bit. Hadn't he done enough today? Couldn't he continue tomorrow?

He took a step forward into the house. He had to.

He wondered if his wife was right. If this family needed him, if they would be better off without him.

But he had realized something that night.

He needed them.

Captain Hot Devil, Jim Roberson, he was many things. But a coward wasn't one of them. He had been given a miraculous second chance. He might waste it. But not for lack of trying.

So he would do whatever he could. Take one step at a time.

He prayed it would be enough.

He stepped forward as his daughter skipped deeper into the house. There stood his wife, dusting away, her back turned to him. He opened his mouth. He closed it. What could he say that he had not already said? What use was there in further begging, further pleading, further apologies, further promises?

"I'm back."

He waited for a moment.

She said not a word. She didn't look at or acknowledge him. Not even a single glance.

Jim dropped his gaze to his feet. He stepped towards the living room, his son was surely working on his homework there.

Then he heard it. A faint whisper. So soft he wasn't sure he had really heard anything at all.

"Welcome home."

He paused. He opened his mouth. He looked behind him. She didn't look at or acknowledge him. Not even a single glance. So he closed his mouth. It wasn't time.

He stepped forward. It was time to greet his son. But now, he kept his gaze up and forward.

He didn't know what he should do.

But he would do whatever he could.

One step at a time.

Because that's what heroes do.

In order for Bob to become the greatest supervillain of all time, he must first defeat the original greatest supervillain of all time. The one that is omnipresent in every hero's tale across every universe. The one who has created countless villains across every reality. He must defeat...bad dads! Anyways! Can the Roberson family find a way forward? Can Captain Hot Devil make up for his mistakes? Can he do what no hero can and be a decent father for once? Tune in next time, to find out!

CHAPTER 11 - THE END OF THE BEGINNING

And so we return to the start of our tale, right after Bob had completed his system of heroes and villains.

On a small island in the middle of the Atlantic stood a mighty fortress of concrete and steel, flanked by air defense towers. Smoke could be seen rising above its walls, explosions and shouts heard even at a distance.

Within the site itself, Aurora Legion rampaged.

Men in black military uniforms fired at them with rifles. Golf-cart sized drone tanks shot fireballs towards them. But neither military might nor technological terrors could stop the super teens.

After all, these were the heroes who saved the world.

It was not long before they cleared the courtyard and entered the large, cylindrical building in the center of the facility. They confronted the Herald of Ashes as he drilled into the Earth, ready to deploy his Geo-Oscillator Bomb.

"The Aurora Legion themselves! Here for humble old me, I am truly flattered! But you are too late! You cannot stop the Herald of Ashes!"

Wonder Knight stepped forward, pointing at the villain ahead.

"It's over, Herald of Ashes! Surrender now!"

The man grinned and spread out his arms. The device behind him quieted and the beam died down. The drill moved out of the way and a glowing, metal sphere lowered from a crane on the roof, positioned right above the giant hole in the ground.

"Over? Yes, it is truly over! My drill has already penetrated deep into the core! Once I drop my Geo-Oscillator into the Earth's interior it will excite the magma across the globe! On every landmass, every continent lava surges will breach the mantle, wherever and whenever I command! And the Herald of Ashes shall rule the world, reshaped in my image! Minions, release the Oscillator!"

And nothing happened.

Silence hung in the air. The Herald of Ashes cleared his throat.

"Ahem, I said, minions! Release the Oscillator!"

Still nothing happened. Aurora Legion exchanged glances with each other. The Herald of Ashes turned his head to glance at the control panel.

"Minions?"

There was nobody there.

"Um, is something supposed to happen?"

"There's no one else here."

"You ok, bro? You might be seeing things."

The Herald of Ashes turned forward, his eyes shrinking into their sockets.

"Oh."

He gulped.

The Herald of Ashes and Wonder Knight both turned and ran for the control panel. The Herald of Ashes threw out a palm shot a ball of lava towards Wonder Knight's chest. Chronolock slid in between them and stopped the ball midair, and a pink kangaroo landed in front of the Herald. It leaned back on its tail and planted both feet on his chest, kicking him to the ground. He raised his hand and summoned the heat.

But nothing happened.

A black beam washed over him, sapping his strength and the very warmth from his body. He could do nothing but cry out as the kangaroo landed on top of him.

"No!"

Wonder Knight smashed the terminal.

"You fool! You activated the Oscillator right here! It will kill us all!"

The device in the center began to vibrate at tremendous speeds. The team stumbled as tremors surged through the floor of the facility. Lava began to bubble up out of the hole in the center of the room.

Wonder Knight blinked several times.

"Um…oops?"

"Let's get out of here!"

Aurora Legion fled the collapsing building. Wonder Knight punched the Herald in the face and then slung him over his shoulder on the way out. The central building went up in flames behind them. They looked around, but strangely all the minions they had battled had disappeared by then, so Aurora Legion escaped with the Herald alone.

And so Aurora Legion saved the day, once again.

△△△

Meanwhile on a boat sailing away from the island sat one of the Herald of Ashes' minions. But not just any minion.

The Faceless Minion himself.

Bob shook his head as another explosion rang out.

"Cutting it real close, aren't you? You just had to show up at the last minute, didn't you? Heroes are so annoying."

Bob took out his cell phone.

"Bob!"

"Markus."

"Did you get it?"

"The Herald's blueprints are secure, I'm sending them to Kanna now. How are we looking on funding?"

"The money's not a problem. You know there's going to be interference though? A lot of people stand to lose a lot of money if this does what you think it will."

"Can't you do something about that?"

"Well I could but I'd have to actually talk with my dad, so no."

"You probably should some day."

"But Boooobbbbb, if I deal with my issues and become emotionally healthy, who will run the bank of Evil?"

"Ivan."

"Ivan? Really Bob? You think he's the type to handle paperwork?"

"Doesn't he already?"

"What, you think I dump my work on him or something?"

"Yes."

"Hahaha you're right. But seriously, my dad's just one player. Takes more than one player to overturn the game."

"Let me think."

"I can't wait to see what you come up with."

Bob took out a notepad and flipped through it, rubbing his chin as he scanned the pages.

"I have an idea."

"That's what I love to hear."

"Approve funding for applicants 151805, 165091, and 173892."

"165091? Seriously? YES! FINALLY! Do you know how long I've been waiting for that one? I was afraid he was going to give up."

"I'm glad you're pleased."

"Come on, Bob, live a little. You can't tell me you're not even a little excited to see *that* go down."

"...I have to make another call."

"Hahaha I knew..."

And then Bob hung up on him and heaved a sigh.

Markus loved to make a mess of things, without any consideration for the people caught in the way. Bob just couldn't get excited over something that was going to hurt a great many people, even if he was the one setting it into motion. Especially then.

But well, there was something that put a smile on his face.

The designs for the Geo-Oscillator bomb were something else. Bob was no engineering supergenius, but if his theory was correct, Kanna could build something with these blueprints that would *truly* revolutionize the world. Something that would steer humanity away from devastation and set it on the path to a bright future.

Which meant it would be resisted by everyone who stood to lose should the status quo change.

So it would take something big to push it through.

But that's why Bob built his system in the first place. To maneuver the gods and the geniuses and let their battles demolish mountains. To change the world as he saw fit.

So it was time to use it.

And first…he needed to get the big one onboard.

ΔΔΔ

Xiong Huang yawned as she leaned back on the couch, eyes on the television in front of her.

Bob was standing behind her, an outsider right in the Eternal Night Sect itself.

She had now worked alongside him for decades, and she *still* hadn't figured him out, not entirely. He hadn't betrayed any sign of cultivation, or greater power, no matter how much she searched or probed. At this point, she was starting to think he *was* mortal after all.

Which meant she didn't really need to keep doing him favors or playing his game. She could turn him down at any time and there was nothing he could do about it. Yes, they had their pact so she wouldn't kill him, and would keep sending him Outer Disciples as requested, but there was no need to interact with him face to face.

And the whole 'pay the debt' thing? Make certain no one would claim the Murderous Bloody Fist had help with her ascension?

Well, a decade or two of overwhelming strength had made her forget all about that. When she could end anyone she wanted, whenever she wanted, with a single punch, what was the point of getting upset over something petty and pointless like that? If it really bothered her, she could go and destroy anyone who she considered to have insulted her. But even that felt more and more like just another chore. She had already conquered the heavens, so why should she care what the ants scrambling on the ground said of her?

In other words, there was no reason to keep entertaining this mortal at all, save the vague and increasingly unlikely possibility he had some great and hidden power.

But she wouldn't admit that. She couldn't. To admit that would be to admit that she, a cultivator of the Ninth Realm who had endured the final tribulation of the heavens and achieved immortality, had been strung along by a *mortal* for decades. To admit that a mere mortal had deceived her father and manipulated him to his death. To admit that he had not only bested her, but every cultivator that struggled over the past millenium.

She still had *some* pride, after all.

And well, he did his best to entertain her. Beating the same disciples and rival sects over and over got old after the first few years. The supers Bob sent her after were generally even weaker but at least it was a change in the routine. Maybe.

Yes, Xiong Huang mostly entertained Bob's requests because she was bored, and it was a habitual reason to get out of the house at this point. And she would admit she was somewhat amused watching the little plots he got up to. Oh how the mortals loved to scramble and dance.

So she was curious as to why Bob would come to her in person, after so many years of just ringing her up whenever he felt like it.

"You came all this way just to ask for more minions? Bob, are you trying to court me or something? Didn't think you were the type to use lame excuses."

Bob shook his head.

"Not the usual deal. I want you to send an Inner Disciple. Maybe even a Core if you can manage it."

Xiong Huang muted the television and turned to Bob. She narrowed her eyes as they stared at each other in silence.

Well, Bob never did fail to surprise her with his sheer audacity. As expected of the man who potentially faced the Ten Slaughters as a *mortal*.

"Wait, you're serious?"

"I'm always serious."

Xiong Huang looked straight into Bob's eyes.

"You want a *real* Eternal Night disciple to kowtow to some mortal kid with delusions of grandeur?"

"Yes."

"Why?"

"Because he needs to succeed."

Xiong Huang held the brow of her nose.

"That's not a simple favor, Bob. There are rules to this, even for me. There will be consequences for that kind of humiliation. And I know you aren't suggesting I do it myself. I'm still disappointed in the last time."

Bob shrugged.

"It's hard finding you good opponents."

She frowned and crossed her arms.

"And who's fault is that?"

"Are you complaining?"

Xiong Huang sighed.

"No, it's just…overwhelming strength is a lot more boring than I thought it would be. But seriously, Bob, I can't just order this without a reason. Well, I could if I wanted to beat the Inners and Cores every day for the next six months, but that would be tedious, so I won't."

Bob took out a package from his pocket. Xiong Huang raised an eyebrow. Bob just nodded, and Xiong Huang took the package, slowly unwrapping it.

Her mouth dropped open.

"What in the heavens is this?!"

Bob smirked at her slightly.

"I trust that will suffice to motivate a volunteer?"

She closed her eyes as a vein bulged on her forehead. This mortal…

"No crap it does. Even I would lick a mortal's boots to get a Thousand Star Ice Heart, if it were the past me at least. By the heavens, where do you find this stuff, Bob?"

Bob simply smiled at her. She heaved a dramatic sigh.

She was an immortal cultivator of the Ninth Realm, and after decades this *mortal* could still get a rise out of her. If he had just used half the stuff he found himself, he'd probably have broken through the heavens by now.

No, he had found the Blazing Dragon Flower too, so he definitely would have.

Which was an even more aggravating thought.

"You're kind of annoying sometimes, you know? Well, whatever. You'll have your volunteers, I can promise you that. But seriously, what is this kid even doing?"

"Changing the world."

AUTHOR'S COMMENTARY: So this chapter and the prologue are a bit special in that they are rewrites of the original reddit prompt response that started this series. Obviously there have been significant changes since I didn't need to drop the entire plot into a single reddit comment and numerous characters have been changed, fleshed out, or didn't exist at all back then.

Still, it's fun for me to see how far this has come. Anyways! What is Bob planning this time? Who is the applicant Markus is excited about? Can Xiong Hung handle the truth that a mortal had her scrambling about for decades? Tune in next time, to find out!

CHAPTER 12 - TO PROTECT THE WORLD FROM DEVASTATION

Once he had gathered all the pieces, Bob got to work. He was currently standing in a small wooden structure with no floor, surrounded by lightly glowing plants. He pulled out his phone and dialed a number.

"Londyn."

"Bob, good to hear from you, you have something for me?"

"Code 23X, Outskirts of Jakarta. Calls himself the Toxic Herald."

Londyn swore through the phone, and then sighed.

"Seriously? Another Herald? I'm starting to believe Voidspeaker is summoning these things. Thanks Bob, I'll get someone on it."

"Anytime."

Bob shook his head as he ended the call. Well, that should keep the ILS busy for a bit. A hero had wandered a bit close to his current location when they weren't supposed to. That happened from time to time, forcing him to keep a spread of villains across the world for emergencies. Even though Londyn and Linda ran a tight ship, most heroes were inherently either free spirits or lone wolves, and so often deviated without informing anyone.

"Heroes are so annoying."

With that, Bob gathered some of the plants into a satchel, and then stood up and left the building, wrapping a scarf around his face. He walked over to where numerous people wrapped up in robes and scarves were mounting horses. Bob strode to the center of the group, where an elephant knelt on the ground, and mounted a black horse nearby.

"There you are, acolyte, we were about to leave without you."

"My apologies, Sentinel, I needed a moment to center myself."

On top of the elephant rode a woman, Vaidehi Dayal, also known as the Sentinel of Harmony. She wore a brown cloak over a simple tan tunic with a brown belt. She had brown skin, brown eyes, and straight, black hair. She wore no makeup or adornments, besides a crown of leaves in her hair. She nodded her head.

"It is perfectly understandable, acolyte. We are about to embark on our great mission, it is only natural to be nervous. What is important is that you are here now. Let us depart, and restore balance to the world."

With that, the Sentinel of Harmony tapped the elephant underneath her and it rose to its feet. Another acolyte blew on a horn, and the thundering hoofs of a thousand horses shook the ground.

The Order of Harmony began their march.

△△△

It was evening time when the Order arrived at their destination, the sun just beginning to set. Before them stood countless pillars and smokestacks rising into the sky. Metal pipes, towering scaffolding, and angular buildings stretched out as far as the eye could see. Hundreds of electric lights illuminated the horizon as the light of the sun faded. Cars and trucks move to and fro, transporting liquid gold.

Before them stood the largest oil refinery in the world, Jamnagar Refinery.

"Halt."

The army came to a stop. The elephant strode forward until it was in the very front, and then turned to face the Order.

"My acolytes, my comrades, thank you for traveling with me today. For over a thousand years our order has devoted ourselves to the care of the Earth. Long have we sought to spread peace and harmony. Long have we maintained the balance. Long have we sat back, striving to do no harm in our vigil. But I have traveled too far and seen too much to ignore the despair in the world any longer. The Earth has lost its balance, its people cry out, the world itself is dying. Our quiet vigil is not enough, not anymore."

She waited a moment as the acolytes murmured, and then continued.

"The only thing necessary for evil to prevail is for good to remain silent. I can sit back no longer, I can remain silent no longer. If not us, then who? Who will speak up for the Earth? Who will speak up for peace? Who will speak up for balance and harmony? I have traveled and listened, and I have heard not one."

She turned half-way and pointed to the industrial sprawl behind her.

"Today we come to Jamnagar, to this monument of short-sighted greed, to say nay. To take our stand. To let it be known that there are still good humans in this world that are willing to fight for the very ground we live upon. And I thank each and every one of you, for having the courage to be one of them."

She turned fully to face the refinery.

"Today, let us go forth, and fight for our world. Let us put an end to the devastation of short-sighted greed and selfishness. Let us restore peace and balance to the Earth."

She turned back and slowly bowed her head, crossing her hands in front of her.

"Remember, we are the ones who fight in the name of peace. Do not be swept up by your passion, righteous though it may be. Do not lash out in anger or aggression. Remain at peace, remember serenity, utilize knowledge, embrace harmony. Show the ignorant and the evil one the error of their ways not by the strength of your arms but by the righteousness of your cause. Let it be known that though evil must be destroyed, that we will not suffer to see good die with it."

She took a deep breath.

"I am one with the Earth."

A thousand voices replied.

""""And the Earth is with me!"""""

The Sentinel of Harmony's eyes shot open.

"Go now. Clear the way. Let none perish who can be saved. Do not strike unless you are struck, do not continue if they are willing to stop. Return to me when it is done, and I will heal this wound in the Earth."

A thousand hoofs thundered towards the refinery.

△△△

Bob and the other acolytes took out wooden staves, pointing them to and fro. Before them stood several refinery workers, hands up, brows sweating, and glancing all over the place.

"MOVE!"

The acolytes shouted. The workers gulped and began to walk away from the refinery. The acolytes brought them to a large crowd, where thousands of workers huddled together in a massive parking lot. All around them acolytes patrolled on horseback.

And then they heard the sirens.

A convoy of police cars and trucks appeared on the road to the refinery, their lights flashing and horns blaring. A few of the heavier vehicles even had machine guns mounted on top. The acolytes gripped their staves tight.

Which is when a voice rang out through the air.

The quiet voice of a woman.

And a deep rumbling voice, as if the very Earth itself spoke out.

"I am one with the Earth, and the Earth is with me."

The Earth trembled in response.

Cracks appeared on the road to the refinery, the ground began to bulge upward. Suddenly roots and branches exploded from underneath, rapidly covering the ground and reaching towards the sky. The lead police car was forced to veer to the side as the convoy came to a halt. Further and further the branches extended out to the sides, forming a wall of leaves and bark that separated the police from the refinery.

"Come not closer, those who would oppose us. Lay down your arms, embrace harmony. We only seek to restore the balance. Those who desire peace shall not be harmed."

The Sentinel of Harmony arrived, no longer riding her elephant but now walking on her own two feet. She nodded to her acolytes and raised her hands. A path opened in the wooden wall. The acolytes began driving the refinery workers through.

A squad of heavily armed police began to march through. The moment they passed the wall the branches came alive. Vines wrapped around weapons and arms, roots tripped feet and legs, branches wrapped around torsos and helmets. The officers were trapped on the sides of the wall. The rest of the police halted their approach, turning instead to accept the incoming workers and usher them past the blockade.

The Sentinel of Harmony turned back towards the refinery.

"Is that all of them, acolyte?"

Bob nodded.

"Yes, Sentinel."

The Sentinel of Harmony nodded. She closed her eyes, and clasped her hands in front of her.

"I am one with the Earth and the Earth is with me."

At first, nothing happened.

"I am one with the Earth and the Earth is with me."

Then there was a slight shift, the air grew still.

"I am one with the Earth **and the Earth is with me.**"

The Sentinel of Harmony's voice took on a quiet echo. There was a tiny tremor in the ground.

""**I am one with the Earth and the Earth is with me.**""

A second voice joined with the Sentinel's, a deep and primal rumble. The trembling of the Earth grew.

""**I am one with the Earth and the Earth is with me.**""

The ground shook violently. The horses began to jump and cry, their riders trying to keep them in check. The police on the other side of the wall had trouble standing, several of them fell to the ground. Though she spoke at the same volume as the start, the Sentinel of Harmony's voice and the second voice echoing it seemed to grow in strength and intensity, until everyone in the area could hear it, no matter how distant. Bob could feel it rumbling within him, stirring his stomach and his chest, causing his heart to pound within him.

""**I AM ONE WITH THE EARTH AND THE EARTH IS WITH ME.**""

It was not a shout, yet it rang in every ear present. It was not a command, yet all bowed to the authority within it. It held no emotion, yet it resonated in every heart. Men and women began to cry. Police lowered their guns, took off their hats, and bowed their heads. All of the acolytes of Harmony clasped their hands together.

There was a moment of silence.

And then the Earth erupted.

Metal groaned and screeched, wires snapped, stone cracked, lights sparked. Roots the size of houses curled from the ground, flipping over buildings and scaffolds. Thousands of vines wrapped around metal pipes and electric lights and obscured them from view. Balls of fire exploded into view before sinking beneath green and brown. Smokestacks crumbled as tree trunks grew from within them.

And then all was silent.

A towering forest now rose above the empty plains.

And no sign remained of the Jamnagar Refinery.

△△△

"Good evening and welcome to GNN, all you citizens of planet Earth. I'm your host, Brendan Baird, bringing you the latest from the day."

"The International League of Superheroes has done it again, foiling a dastardly plot to poison the world's ocean by a nefarious evildoer called the Toxic Herald. The Toxic Herald had nearly completed his plans when he was stopped by a tag team of heroes known as The Gentle Gloom and Dragontooth. In just a moment, we'll meet the courageous heroes responsible for this feat."

"In other news, nonviolent resistance, or eco-terrorism? A group called the Order of Harmony staged a protest at the Jamnagar refinery. The protest seems to have escalated and police were deployed to break up the demonstration, and some rumors say that a super destroyed the entire facility. Yet, there have been no reports of casualties and no eyewitnesses have come forward to tell their story. Just what exactly happened here? GNN goes to the experts to find out."

"All this and more, here tonight on GNN, global news for global viewers."

△△△

Londyn heaved a sigh as she looked over the report. There was a surge in villain activity recently and they were struggling to keep up. Some new heroes had joined them lately but there were only a handful she could trust.

She couldn't pull Aurora Legion out of school every day,

after all.

The door to her office opened up and Linda walked in, carrying a folder full of papers and a pair of coffees.

"Thank you, Linda."

Linda smiled as Londyn took one of the coffees.

"Anytime, Director."

Londyn took a sip and then took a deep breath.

"Ok, hit me with it. What are we looking at."

Linda opened up the folder, then took a deep breath herself.

"Someone called the…"

Londyn crossed her hands and rested her forehead on them.

"…don't say it."

Linda frowned but continued mercilessly.

"…the Herald of Dust."

Londyn groaned.

"Who do we have?"

Linda flipped through her notes.

"Tesla Titan is in the area at the moment."

Londyn shook her head.

"He just finished a mission, he needs a break."

Linda shrugged.

"You know he won't turn you down."

Londyn frowned.

"That's exactly the problem."

Linda smiled at her.

"Well, you know what he'd say. 'Is much easier than Soviet overtime!'"

Londyn stared at Linda for a second, then they both laughed.

"Well, you're right about that. If he says he can handle it, then he can handle it. Try to see if there's anyone we can send for back up."

Linda nodded at that as Londyn heaved another sigh.

"Any word on Jamnagar?"

Linda shook her head.

"Nothing that's not in the news. Just that it was definitely a super, that there were no confirmed casualties, and that the eyewitnesses still refuse to cooperate."

Londyn took a deep breath as she scrolled across a computer at her desk. Finally she sighed and shook her head.

"If that's the case, there's not much we can do. That's a horrific amount of property damage, but with no suspects and no casualties we can't afford to go chasing them down. Let's just hope this isn't the start of something worse..."

△△△

It was a bright and sunny day along the Venezuelan coastline. A peaceful day, perfect for a relaxing day on the beach. But not so at this particular beach.

Wooden ships touched down on the sand. Men and women in robes and scarves disembarked from their boats, running towards the storage cylinders and smokestacks ahead. Everywhere, men and women shouted as robed figures herded refinery workers with wooden staves.

The Order of Harmony had arrived at the Paraguana Refinery Complex.

The Sentinel of Harmony disembarked from her ship, the wood of the bow untwisting into a ramp before her. One of the acolytes came running towards her and bowed at her feet.

"Sentinel."

"Abide in harmony, Acolyte. How goes the preparations?"

"Delayed, Sentinel. The workers are not cooperating. We will need more time to empty the facility."

The Sentinel of Harmony nodded.

"Take your time, acolyte. No good will come from recklessness."

The acolyte bowed once more.

"It shall be done, Sentinel. I am one with the Earth."

"And the Earth is with me."

△△△

Within the facility a line of workers stood facing a line of acolytes. Staves and wrenches waved in the air, voices rose.

"Move! We don't want to hurt you!"

"Then get out of here! Let us do our jobs in peace!"

"Your jobs are destroying the peace! You must leave!"

"You're the ones who destroy things!"

"Defiler!"

"Terrorist!"

"Get over here!"

"Let go of him!"

The acolytes grabbed one of the workers, trying to haul him to the safe zone. The other workers crowded around, grabbing onto their co-worker's shoulders and legs. An acolyte was shoved. A worker was pushed to the ground.

"Let go!"

"Don't you touch me!"

"Get off!"

A fist flew. A wrench caught someone's jaw. A stave collided with a hardhat.

And then a gunshot rang through the facility.

The shouting stopped and everyone grew still. An acolyte fell on his back, a red spot growing on his robes.

Then the screams began.

△△△

The Sentinel of Harmony frowned. She heard shouting growing in the distance, then loud cracks of thunder. Her stomach dropped, and her chest twisted.

Something terrible had happened.

She closed her eyes and took a deep breath. She calmed her heartbeat and slowly exhaled. She centered herself, allowing the ominous premonition to fade from her body.

She opened her eyes, a serene expression on her face.

A group of her acolytes ran down the beach. They carried with them several of their fellows, and laid them at her feet.

"Sentinel…"

"What has happened?"

"The workers, they resisted. They would not move."

"And then?"

"We tried to separate them, to take them one by one."

"And then they shot us!"

One of the acolytes cried out, fists and teeth both clenched.

The Sentinel slowly walked over to him. She took his fist into her hands, and slowly uncurled his fingers. She looked into his eyes. His eyes began to water as his shoulders dropped.

"I am one with the Earth."

All the acolytes joined with her.

""""And the Earth is with me.""""

Wooden branches rose around each of the fallen acolytes, tenderly wrapping them into cocoons. Once completed they slowly sank into the sand.

"Our brethren have become one with the Earth. Do not mourn them, do not miss them, but rejoice for those who have joined with the world."

All the acolytes looked to their feet, and were silent. The Sentinel of Harmony strode up the beach, marching towards the facility. She planted her feet in the ground, she closed her eyes, and she clasped her hands in front of her.

""All you who stand before us, listen now. Hear the will of the Earth.""

She spoke softly, not raising her voice. The echo of the Earth joined with her, carrying her voice across the entire facility.

""We are not your enemy. We wish you no harm. But we cannot allow the devastation of our planet to continue.""

She paused, frowning for a breath moment before regaining her serene expression.

""**Weapons have been drawn. Blood has been spilled. But we will not act in anger. We will forgive.**""

She closed her eyes.

""**Lay down your weapons, for we have none of our own. Let no further blood be shed.**""

She spread out her hands.

""**This monument to greed is at its end. The Earth wills it, the world cries out for it. But you do not have to end with it.**""

She opened her eyes, and looked straight at the facility, her gaze unwavering.

""**Return to your homes. Go now in peace. Embrace your loved ones. Do not let yourself be destroyed in vain. I give you an hour. The Earth would not see any of her children harmed. And neither would I. This monument shall not last the day. I hope that you will.**""

The Sentinel of Harmony turned around and walked back to her acolytes.

"Go, call the others."

"What about the workers, Sentinel?"

"We can do nothing more for them. Their fates are in their own hands now."

△△△

The acolytes lay scattered about the beach. They sat and chatted among themselves, clustered into small groups. Some lay resting, others meditated. The Sentinel of Harmony stood in the sand, eyes closed, unmoving save for her quiet, steady breaths. One of the acolytes glanced around, then up to the Sentinel. Back to the facility, then back to the Sentinel. He took a deep breath, and then opened his mouth.

"Sentinel, it is almost time. None of the workers have moved…"

They heard it before they saw it.

The beating of blades and whirring engines. The Sentinel of Harmony turned towards the sea. Three helicopters approached.

The Sentinel's eyes widened.

The helicopters were too small to carry people.

Which meant they carried something else.

She clasped her hands. She opened her mouth.

She saw flashes of light.

She heard the sound of thunder.

And then the beach erupted.

The Sentinel of Harmony stood still as the helicopters passed overhead, silent save for her quiet, steady breathing. She looked down upon the ground.

She stood in a sea of blood.

All around her lay the bodies of her acolytes. Some were groaning, others crying out, still others screaming in pain. Many more lay silent, unblinking eyes staring at the sky.

She closed her eyes.

She took a deep breath.

But her heart refused to slow.

The knot in her chest would not come undone.

She felt new moisture on her cheeks.

"So…this is their choice…"

She opened her eyes. She knelt to the ground. She reached forward, removing an acolyte's scarf. She lay her palm on the acolyte's cheek.

"Or…was it…mine?"

She closed her eyes, tears streaming down. She slowly withdrew her hand, and stood to her feet. She clasped her hands together.

"I am one with the Earth, and the Earth is with me."

All around her branches and vines grew from the sand. They wrapped around the twisting acolytes, covering their wounds with soft leaves. Those who lay still they wrapped in their embrace.

There were too many cocoons to count.

"I thought…they could change. I thought, we only need to show them the way, and we could bring peace to the Earth."

She opened her eyes, watching as the helicopters swung around and began to approach once more.

"But you've shown me that it's impossible. You will resist. You will cling to your ways. You will march towards devastation."

She took a deep breath. She looked down as the cocoons sank into the sand.

"If we cannot achieve harmony on the Earth, perhaps we will achieve harmony within it? For all return to the Mother's embrace. All become one with the Earth in the end."

She looked up. The helicopters approached. She whispered.

"I am one with the Earth and the Earth is with me."

At first, nothing happened. The beating of helicopter blades grew louder.

"I am one with the Earth **and the Earth is with me.**"

The Sentinel's voice took on a quiet echo. There was a tiny tremor in the sand.

""**I am one with the Earth and the Earth is with me.**""

A second voice joined with The Sentinel of Harmony's, a deep and primal rumble. The trembling of the Earth grew. The helicopters came in range once more.

""**I am one with the Earth and the Earth is with me!**""

The ground shook violently. The sea began to churn. Wooden ships fell apart, their planks twisting into branches that covered the remaining acolytes. The helicopters' noses began to flash once more.

""**I AM ONE WITH THE EARTH AND THE EARTH IS WITH ME!!!**""

As the bullets landed on the beach a massive wave of sand erupted into the sky. The helicopters tilted up and flew back as they tried to avoid the wave.

But they could not avoid the wave of wood growing

within it.

Root, trunks, and branches rolled and tumbled like waves upon the shore. Higher and higher until they blocked the horizon. The helicopters vanished, brief flashes of red and yellow light swallowed by green and brown. And then the wave continued forward.

The Paraguana Refinery Complex vanished from the Earth that day.

Along with everyone inside it.

> *AUTHOR'S COMMENTARY: Ah. Yes. The Sentinel of Harmony. The character who was supposed to be my 'evil Jedi'. Because I thought a Jedi-inspired villain would be fun. So, um, are we having fun yet? Anyways. What will become of the Order of Harmony? How will the world respond? What is Bob planning in all this? Tune in next time to find out.*

CHAPTER 13 - THE FALL OF HARMONY

"Oil prices skyrocketed today as yet another major oil refinery was attacked by the group known as the Order of Harmony. World governments are now classifying the group as a terrorist organization after a super in its ranks destroyed the Paraguana Refinery Complex while it was still in operation. Venezuelan officials have not released an official number but the casualties are estimated to be in the thousands. It is unclear what prompted this change in the group's operation, as previous incidents were notable for their lack of casualties. Due to the clear involvement of a super, law enforcement is now cooperating with the International League of Superheroes to organize a response. Please note that this group is considered extremely dangerous. Please avoid contact and reach out to your local officials should you have any information regarding this threat."

△△△

The Sentinel of Harmony took a deep breath. Her eyes were closed, her hands were held in front of her in a circle with fingers touching. She sat with legs crossed on the ground.

Her heartbeat slowed slightly, but still pounded heavily within her aching chest.

And her stomach refused to settle.

She slowly opened her eyes and frowned, her brow furrowed.

Was this truly the way? Was this the will of the Earth? Must her quest for peace and harmony end in violence and death? Was blood necessary to restore balance?

She closed her eyes once more. She took another deep breath.

She would remain at peace.

Images of broken bodies and unmoving eyes flashed through her mind.

She would remember serenity.

She heard her own voice cry out in pain, the Earth matching her shouts.

She would use her knowledge.

She felt the heat of that day in her chest and stomach, the burning heat overwhelming her mind.

She would embrace harmony.

The Earth killed at her command.

Her eyes shot open. Sweat dripped from her brow. She panted heavily, her heart pounding rapidly. She held a hand up to her chest, holding it over her heart.

She steadied her breathing. She swallowed, forcing down her stomach. She looked ahead.

She stood on a wooded hill overlooking her target. She could see the smoke rising from chimneys. She watched the trucks carrying barrels to and fro.

She saw the Earth dying before her eyes, and a fire lit inside her stomach, spreading heat throughout her body..

She just needed to act one last time. Then they would see. Then they would resist no longer. Just one more time, and this would all be over. They would not continue. They could not continue. One final time, and all this would have meaning. All this death and sacrifice would be worth it. The mission would be complete. The balance would be restored. Harmony would be achieved.

It had to be.

Because she didn't know what she'd do if it wasn't.

She stood to her feet.

She had not restored her balance. She had not mastered her heart. She was not ready.

But she had made her decision.

And she would see it done.

Whatever it took.

△△△

Londyn stood in a room at the top of a tower, the recently purchased headquarters for the ILS. Behind her was a floor to ceiling window, the city stretching out below. Before her was a wall of monitors, each showing a different face. Past the monitors Linda sat at a desk, typing away at a keyboard.

Londyn frowned as she looked at the monitors.

She really wished the authorities had called her in *before* authorizing deadly force. She didn't know which side escalated the situation and Venezuela was well within its rights to protect its territory, but this search would have been much easier beforehand. And now? Now she had to track down a super who could and would take down entire refineries at once, regardless of how many people were killed in the process. Once the door to violence was opened, it was very hard to shut.

But that was wishful thinking. The ILS had been busy at the time, so even if the Venezuelans had called them, events may have played out the same way regardless. And she wasn't sure a single hero could handle someone like this alone.

Which was why the current situation had her on edge.

"Dapper, report."

"Ruwais is clear, I've found no trace of the Order."

"Tina, how's Port Arthur?"

"Quiet, all clear here boss."

"Tesla, anything?"

"Negative, Abadan is clear."

Londyn frowned. The Order of Harmony was tracked down fairly quickly after the big attack. Most of its members were found in hospitals and quickly detained.

But there was no trace of the super.

At this point Londyn had most of her supers and field agents on patrol around major refineries. But if the super was working alone now, there was little chance they could find her before she could strike. And even if they could, any hero who could arrive in time would be alone, and heavily outmatched. So it was unlikely they could prevent an attack even if the ILS was in the area.

Catching the super after though, that was a different story.

Still, having her heroes spread out, alone, and just waiting for people to die was both dangerous and disheartening. But what choice did they have?

Londyn thought back to that day at Kayserling Tower. To the heat of the flames, and the pain as she crashed into the furniture. To the helplessness, as that super tossed her around. To the fear, as she lay at the mercy of a man who didn't spare her a second glance. She grimaced. She pulled out her phone.

She would do better than wait. She had to.

If there was anyone who knew...

And then her phone rang.

Her heart pounded, but she took a deep breath. The director of the ILS could not trust a hope.

"Tell me you have something."

"Not what you want."

Londyn grit her teeth.

"How bad is it?"

"A 23Y in Tokyo."

Londyn swore. Just what she needed right now.

But she couldn't afford to hesitate.

Should she hunt for a potential threat to thousands of lives or respond to a confirmed threat to billions? There wasn't a choice.

"Gloom, you're by Ulsan, right?"

"Seems sooo…"

"Get over to Tokyo on the double. 23Y. Dragontooth, head over as quickly as you can. I'll send you some back up as soon as possible."

"Aight."

"The rest of you stay sharp and call me if you get a hit."

The heroes replied and signed off one by one. Londyn began dialing numbers and shouting commands to Linda.

The Order of Harmony would have to wait. Right now it was time to save the world.

△△△

The Sentinel of Harmony stood on a hill overlooking the refinery. She closed her eyes. She lifted her hands, reaching out towards the facility. She opened her mouth.

"I am one with the Earth…"

△△△

Linda cried out as voices rang through her earpiece.

"Gentle Gloom has located the target and engaged!"

Londyn grimaced. Gloom wasn't one to jump the gun. Which meant he got caught.

"What's the ETA on Dragon?"

"30 minutes out!"

"Tell her she has 15! We're on the clock now!"

△△△

The Sentinel's voice took on a screeching echo. It cracked and distorted. The ground trembled. The birds and beasts fled the area. The branches and bushes around her curled and blackened.

"And the Earth is with me."

△△△

Linda's eyes widened as she listened to the reports.

"10 minutes until Dragon arrives!"

Londyn's eyes narrowed.

"Backup?"

Linda typed frantically at her computer.

"Gray Slayer's en route! Aurora and the Captain are prepping to depart!"

Londyn let out a breath.

The die was cast. She had done all she could. The fate of the world now rested in the hands of her heroes.

△△△

""I am one with the Earth!""

The Sentinel's face twisted. Tears streamed down her cheeks. She clutched her head, pulling on her hair. No mask of serenity remained.

The Earth rumbled. A voice like thunder joined her as she screeched.

△△△

Londyn heaved a sigh. Gloom was still reporting in and Dragontooth was right about to arrive. It looked like they would pull through. Even if they couldn't win alone, with the two of them they could hold out until more reinforcements arrived. The world wouldn't end today and neither would any of her heroes.

She grimaced and turned her attention elsewhere. They had done all they could from here, so their time was better spent elsewhere. She waved at one of her monitors, pulling up the reports from their surveillance teams.

"Any reports on the refineries?"

Linda typed away at her computer and shook her head.

"All teams reporting clear. Same with the heroes."

Londyn paused as she looked through the list of refineries.

"Ulsan, we haven't heard from Ulsan...where's our team in Ulsan?!"

"Um, Gloom was covering Ulsan, Korea branch is understaffed so regular assets took Yeosu instead."

Londyn's eyes widened.

"Gloom never finished his patrol...CONTACT ULSAN AUTHORITIES! GET SOMEONE TO ULSAN NOW!"

△△△

The Sentinel fell to her knees. She threw her head back. She shouted into the sky.

"AND THE EARTH IS WITH ME!!!"

She fell to the ground, sobbing as she curled into a ball.

The ground trembled. The Earth rumbled. The birds took flight. The people stopped working down at the refinery below..

Twisted black branches tore through the ground and rushed over the facility like a wave over the shore.

The Ulsan Refinery vanished.

And the branches kept going into the city beyond...

△△△

A short while later, the Sentinel of Harmony walked among the black and twisted branches, still wrapped around the crumbling remains of a city block. Her eyes stared forward, unmoving, unchanging besides the occasional blink. Her shoulders were hunched over. Her right arm hung limply at her side, her left gripped it.

She didn't know what to do.

She didn't know what to think.

She wasn't thinking at all.

But one foot moved after another. Step, step, step. Why? To what end?

What was her end?

Right now, to move.

To step.

To walk.

To go.

Where?

Somewhere.

Anywhere.

Away from here.

Her heart pounded in her chest. Her stomach boiled. Her mind was clouded, it felt as if she was thinking through a fog. It was…hard…so hard to think. Her eyes barely processed the sights in front of her.

Just…keep walking…she told herself

Just…

Go.

Somewhere.

Anywhere.

And then maybe…

Maybe…she'd find something. Something that could change…this.

Her.

Anything.

Her foot stopped, touching something.

She looked down.

Her eyes widened.

She found something.

A bear. A small toy bear made of cloth. Stuffing was falling from a hole on its neck.

She trembled. Her heart pounded faster and harder. Her vision spun. Her legs gave out.

She fell to her knees.

Her vision went black.

△△△

Bob walked through the twisted branches and broken landscape. The ground was cracked and dark. Black branches twisted through shattered windows and crumbling houses.

He had no expression on his face. He stopped for a second, staring at a broken building. He shook his head.

He kept walking.

He had something left to do.

He kept walking until he heard it. Quiet sobbing. He turned and headed towards the sound.

He found the Sentinel of Harmony curled up on the ground, hugging a torn teddy bear to her chest.

He stepped towards her, and then stopped.

And simply waited.

Eventually, the sobbing died down, and the woman turned her head to face him.

"Acolyte?"

Bob nodded.

"Sentinel."

She shook her head, tears welling up.

"No, not anymore. Not after..."

The tears fell again.

"A-Acolyte...what do I do?"

Bob remained silent.

"I've...what have I done? What do I do? I do not know anymore. I...I can't think. I can't focus. I can't center myself. I...I've tried it all. All the doctrines, all the instructions. I...I failed...I... cannot...the emotions...I cannot find balance. I cannot maintain serenity."

Bob shrugged.

"Then don't."

The woman, Vaidehi Dayal paused.

"Huh?"

"Serenity is overrated. Emotions are a part of you, and right now they're trying to tell you something. You can't control them. So acknowledge them. Set them free. Listen to what they're telling you."

Bob looked her in the eye.

"Then, they won't control you like this."

Tears welled up again and Vaidehi began to cry. No longer quiet sobbing, but loud wailing. Bob walked over and placed a hand on her shoulder. Vaidehi paused for a second.

And then latched onto Bob.

They stood there for a countless moment.

△△△

After a long while, Vaidehi calmed down and the two separated. She wiped her face with her arm.

"Acolyte...what should I do now?"

"What do you mean?"

She heaved a sigh.

"I...the things I've done...what I've become...just...what can I do?"

Bob shrugged.

"What do you want to do?"

"What do I...want to do?"

Vaidehi sat there, blinking, and then lowered her head.

"I do not deserve to answer that."

"And if you did?"

Vaidehi stopped, and thought for a moment.

"I...I would want to atone. Help the people I've hurt. And...I suppose I would want to make the world a better place. I...always did...or so I thought..."

Bob nodded.

"Then do that."

Dayal looked down again.

"How can I? What can I do that would make up for what I've done?"

Bob shrugged.

"You can't. And you'll have to live with that. But that doesn't mean you shouldn't do anything. So do whatever you can."

"Whatever, I can?"

"If you can't do what you should, then do what you can."

Vaidehi furrowed her brow and frowned. Eventually her face relaxed, her expression turned neutral. Her eyes regained some light. She stood up straight.

"I've decided. I will surrender myself for the world to judge. And if they permit me to remain...then we will see."

Bob nodded. Vaidehi looked at him.

"Acolyte...you aren't really an acolyte are you?"

Bob shook his head.

"Then who...are you?"

Bob turned to leave.

"Someone doing what they can."

Vaidehi watched as he walked away.

"Thank you, whoever you are."

As Dayal fell out of view, Bob heaved a sigh. He bent down. There was an ID in the dirt. He picked it up. He looked at it for a moment, then placed it back down and continued on his way.

It was one thing to talk about changing the world, about the sacrifices necessary to do so. It was one thing to talk about the greater good, how all this would eventually lead humanity to a brighter future. It was one thing to manipulate the world through phone calls and plots on paper.

It was another thing entirely to stare the results in the face.

To walk among the devastated city.

To see the Sentinel break down.

To see the lives ruined and destroyed, to hear the people wail, to look into the unblinking eyes.

And he knew...that this was his fault.

Bob stopped walking for a moment and took a deep breath.

Yes...things had gone farther than he thought. Yes, he had *hoped* that the Sentinel of Harmony would stick to her doctrine and spread devastation without blood.

But at the end of the day, he knew that this was a very real possibility. He knew this could happen. He knew it would *probably* happen, if he was truly honest.

He had forged ahead anyway.

So this...this was the result of choices he had personally and intentionally made, knowing it could end like this.

So now he had to ask...

Is this...what he wanted?

Is this the change he envisioned?

Was this the mountain he wanted moved?

Had he not set out to contain the damage?

Had he not set out to prevent this very situation?

Had he not become what he wanted to destroy?

He heaved a sigh.

And then he continued walking.

Like it or not, he was committed now.

Thousands had perished because of his choices.

Thousands more may yet perish.

But could he quit now?

Was it right to balk at the casualties now, after the blow was struck?

Could he face the dead and the broken if he let this all be in vain?

Could he let this all go to waste?

No, no he could not.

He had to continue on.

He had to finish the job.

He had to achieve what he set out to do.

Was it truly worth the cost? Was it truly worth all this?

Bob no longer knew, and it was no longer his place to say.

He had made his decision, and now all he could do was follow through.

The world and the future would judge him.

So he would do what he could.

He would ensure the plan succeeded, and that the payoff was what he originally envisioned. That something good might come from all this pain, whether or not it was worth the cost in the end.

And he would do whatever he could to ensure that the casualties were kept as low as possible.

And that someone was there to help pick up the pieces.

> *AUTHOR'S COMMENTARY: ...yes. The jedi villain was so much fun. So much. Instead a lightsaber fight with a sith hero, we got trauma. Yay. All you characters, stop having serious character arcs! Y'all were supposed to be minor throwaway characters, stop having moments and feelings and stuff! Anyways. What will come of all this? Tune in next time, to find out...*

CHAPTER 14 - THE HEIST

"Tragedy in Ulsan, the Order of Harmony strikes again. Korean officials are reporting thousands of confirmed casualties and rising as first responders comb through the area."

"A super named Vaidehi Dayal was apprehended by the ILS at the scene, and has claimed responsibility for the attacks. Miss Dayal reportedly surrendered without a fight and has indicated full cooperation with the authorities."

"Everyone is asking how this happened, how a super that dangerous went unchecked. Experts point to a recent wave of villains, noting that the ILS was stretched thin attempting to respond to all the various threats at once. The ILS reportedly had heroes patrolling Ulsan just hours before its destruction, but they were redirected to stop the supervillain Lord Elite Merlin in Tokyo. Lord Elite Merlin had a plan to flood the world with global consequences; the analysts are saying Director Green was right to prioritize but point to the lack of local assets as a concern."

"In response to this incident, Director Green has put out a call for recruitment, asking all citizens of the globe to do their part in preventing future tragedies. The ILS is now pushing to recruit more eyes and ears to search for villains, in order to free up their heroes to respond wherever and whenever they're needed. Likewise, there is a new discussion among public officials to mandate ILS registration for all heroes, and several governments are already considering laws to this effect."

"Others are forming public organizations and taking matters into their own hands. The United States has taken the lead here with its announcement of the Bureau of Special Investigations, a brand new law enforcement agency specializing in cases involving supers…"

△△△

In a small cubicle filled with papers, folders, and a small computer sat a man. He was of average size and build, with short brown hair and a well-groomed mustache on his face. He wore a black suit and a blue tie and was currently hunched over a paper on his desk.

His name was Agent Wilson.

Agent Wilson had aged remarkably well, not appearing a day older from his field work in the Eighties. And he was one of the most experienced and successful officers to answer the call, transferring from the CIA to the newly founded BSI.

Agent Wilson reached to his side to grab his cup of coffee and his elbow knocked into a stack of papers, scattering them across the ground. He closed his eyes and heaved a sigh.

Taking the lead in super law enforcement, now that was a funny joke.

Congress had been very excited when they announced the new agency and held long discussions on its name and mandate. They were much less excited when it came time to discuss the budget and office space.

Agent Wilson took a moment to scan the room.

There were a few cubicles and desks jammed into each other, with barely a foot of walking space between them. Papers were stacked high on every desk. There were constantly ringing phones, a single woman with frazzled hair and bags under her eyes attempting to answer them. A grand total of three agents from other agencies, including himself, and one overworked receptionist shared this space, and yet it was still extraordinarily crowded.

Behold America's answer to the super problem.

He took a deep breath and then began picking up the

papers on the floor.

Maybe he should just join the ILS. But that was an idle thought, the ILS was not accepting applications from CIA agents at the time. There had been more than one attempt by government agencies to assert control over the League, so they weren't going to open themselves to that risk. Not yet.

And so here he was, at the 'cutting edge' of super law enforcement.

He took a swig of his coffee as he reviewed the paper in his hand, glancing occasionally at the television hung in the corner of the office.

"Wilson, how's it hanging?"

"Steve, where's Kasey?"

Agent Steve walked up behind him, leaning on his cubicle with a coffee in hand. He was a large man with short, blonde hair and a clean-shaven face. The man also wore a suit like Agent Wilson.

"Ah, our fine Agent Kasey is on a mission of utmost importance!"

Wilson nodded.

"So he's coming in late and grabbing us donuts in exchange?"

Agent Steve grinned.

"That's the CIA for you, you already knew! So what you looking at anyways…oh the Ulsan case? Sorry to say this but the ILS has that covered. Like, you know, any other actually important business."

Wilson shook his head.

"Yeah, I know, it's just…"

"What?"

Wilson had reviewed the details of the different Order of Harmony events. Each and every time, the ILS had been occupied and unable to respond. Certainly, each time there had been a greater threat that had to be dealt with and the ILS made the correct choice. With how many heroes and villains were appearing in the world each day, it was likely just a case of tragic coincidence and insufficient manpower.

But what if it wasn't?

"I can't help but feel like there's something more to this."

Steve raised an eyebrow.

"What, is there something in the case? Villain lady already confessed to everything I thought? Even if she's holding out, higher ups are considering it a closed case."

Wilson shook his head.

"Nothing concrete, it's just, I have a bad feeling about this."

Steve shrugged.

"You're imagining things."

Wilson turned back to the TV and sipped his coffee. On the screen was a recording of Vaidehi Dayal's confession. He narrowed his eyes.

"I guess we'll see."

Well, that was why he had joined the BSI to begin with. From the get-go, Wilson had a hunch. A feeling that there were forces working behind the scenes, forces opposing the work of men like him. That there was a method to the madness, that seemingly random incidents were somehow connected.

That there might be someone behind it all.

He had too many questions. How did the villains keep popping up, how did they keep finding funding and manpower? How did the heroes keep stopping them in the final hour, how were there so few casualties, especially among the villains' employees? And why did the world seem to just sweep it under the rug? How had everyone come to accept that this was the way things were?

And so he went searching for answers.

He had hoped to find something among the CIA...but the CIA was more interested in terrorists than supers. Save for a death squad or two he obviously didn't know anything about. And his bosses hadn't exactly been receptive to 'personal projects'. He had little more than hunches at this stage, so he couldn't get the permission to do anything but speculate. So here he was, at the BSI. Far less resources, far less clout, but a great deal of personal freedom to pursue his own investigations, and an organizational mandate to take on issues beyond the norm.

If there *was* someone behind it all, he was going to find them.

Just then he got a call from the receptionist. He spoke with her for a moment, then sighed and stood up.

It seemed the supers had struck again, and the good citizens were calling on the BSI to respond.

In other words, Mrs. Johnson had left the window open and her flying cat had escaped again.

Agent Wilson shook his head as he went to collect Agent Steve.

He really should join the ILS one of these days.

△△△

Meanwhile, in a dark corner of the world...

There was a small, dimly lit room. In the center of the room was a round table. A single lamp hung over it, the only source of light in the room, illuminating the table and just a bit beyond it. Around the table sat several figures in body armor and masks fashioned from bone and leather.

The secret mastermind behind it all...opened up the message from *his* new boss.

"Ok, we have our orders. We're supposed to steal some oil."

Another of the minions at the table chuckled.

"Looks like we got some liberating to do."

"So what's the target?"

Bob took a deep breath.

"...Freeport."

The chuckling minion went silent.

"...we're robbing Uncle Sam? Of oil?"

Another minion elbowed his side.

"Liberating. He'll understand."

He just held his head.

"...ok. Let's assume the NSA didn't hear that and Seal Team Six isn't on the way to whoop our sorry butts. That's 250 million barrels. How are we supposed to move all that? Bucket brigade across the ocean? We couldn't get enough trucks even if they'd let us drive them in."

Bob looked across the table.

"Chris, you have that part time on the weekend, right?"

△△△

In the middle of the Indian Ocean, a woman rushed along the sea. She had a tall and thin figure with blue hair and glowing blue eyes. She wore a blue pointed witch's hat, a blue cape, and a blue one piece swimming suit. In her hand was a rod of hardened drift wood topped with a gleaming sapphire. Her legs were buried in a surging wave that carried her forward. In front of her stood an abandoned oil platform, covered in rust, barnacles, and condensed salt.

As she approached the platform she lifted the rod above her head with both hands. The wave twisted around her, forming a cyclone of water and mist that propelled her into the air. The spiraling torrent arced straight up and the woman leapt off onto the platform.

"It's over, Dr. Delfino! Surrender!"

In front of her on the platform was a wiry old man. He had scattered white hair that curled this way and that and a pair of swimming goggles over his wrinkled face. He wore an open lab coat over an Aloha shirt and a pair of swimming trunks. On his back was a water tank connected to a hose in his hand.

"You are too late, Aqua Mage! Now that the Super Liquid Intake Compression Kleptomania-nator is ready, the world's oceans shall belong to Dr. Delfino! Muahahahahaha! Minions, activate the SLICK!"

And nothing happened. Dr. Delphino cleared his throat.

"Ahem, I said, minions, activate the SLICK!"

Still nothing happened. Dr. Delfino turned around and glanced around the platform.

"Minions?"

The platform was empty, with no minions in sight. And no sign of the Super Liquid Intake Compression Kleptomania-nator either.

He turned back around. Aqua Mage waved her rod in front of her, forming glowing blue geometric patterns out of light. As she did, water began to gather into dozens of spheres that floated in the air.

Dr. Delphino gulped.

"Um, you wouldn't hurt an old man, would you?"

Jets of water surged forth from the spheres.

Meanwhile on a speedboat driving away from the platform, a minion in scuba gear whistled and spun the steering wheel. In the back of the speedboat were a couple more minions surrounding a cylindrical device covered with a tarp.

△△△

"Ok so we got the SLICK, how are we going to get it inside? One does not simply walk into Uncle Sam's secret stash."

Bob glanced over at Sergei.

"Then we walk under it."

△△△

Sergei and Chris wore hardhats on their heads and blast shields over their faces as they stood in a tunnel, with sweat dripping down their necks. Before them a massive drill on treads ground down the rock and dirt. Sergie looked down at an electronic tablet while Chris held a remote for the drill.

Suddenly Sergei held his hand up. Chris flicked a switch and the drill wound down. He leaned over to take a look at the tablet. On the screen, a green dot now overlapped with a red one.

The two men bumped fists.

△△△

"A drill? Seriously? That's not exactly quiet. They're going to notice, you know?"

Bob shrugged.

"Then we distract them."

The speaker frowned and crossed his arms.

"How?"

"Bombs."

"Bombs?"

Bob nodded.

"Bombs."

△△△

A truck drove up to the entrance of the Bryan Mound facility's loading dock. The watchman kept his eyes on his newspaper as he pointed to a panel.

"ID please."

The driver didn't respond..

The guard shrugged and continued reading his newspaper.

A truck behind them honked.

Finally the guard sighed and looked up.

"ID…please?"

There was no one in the truck, just a camera and a robotic arm taped to the steering wheel.

"What the heck?"

The guard got up out of his station and walked around the truck. There wasn't a soul in sight. Scratching his head he

walked to the back and lifted the door.
And fell back on his butt.

In the back of the truck was a *lot* of bombs.

△△△

"Breaking news folks, the Freeport site of America's Strategic Petroleum Reserve is being evacuated due to a bomb threat! A bomb squad is on site and working to disarm the explosives as we speak. Officials have not yet released a statement but there is widespread speculation that this could be an act of terrorism…or villainy."

△△△

"Ok, so we got underneath and we filled up the SLICK, but doesn't that thing still weigh a ton when it's full? How the heck are we going to move it? It'll go right through a truck!"

Bob glanced up at a man standing off to the side of the room. The only person in the room not wearing armor or even a mask, dressed in thin silk robes instead. Frost crept along the floor around him.

"Senior Brother Wu, could we get an assist?"

Wu Zhengkang's face contorted in rage.

"You dare?! You are courting death asking this honorable young master to act like a common mule!"

The minions all turned to Bob.

"So…"

Bob shrugged.

"He's on board."

△△△

A man wearing silk robes and a scarf wrapped around

his face strode through a tunnel, carrying a large cylindrical device on his shoulder with a single arm. Behind him was an empty salt cavern, a few drops and puddles of black liquid scattered about the stone floor.

"Nice one Wu!"

An armored minion held his hand up high. Senior Brother Wu ignored him. The man looked down and sighed.

A blur flew through the air and hit the man's hand. He slammed into the ground with a shriek.

Senior Brother Wu smirked and continued his stroll.

△△△

"Well ok. We got the oil. Crouching Tiger there can waltz right out with it. Then what? It's still too heavy for a plane or a boat, how are we going to get it across the ocean?"

Bob shrugged.

"Senior Brother Wu can fly."

"...of course he can."

Another minion rubbed her chin.

"Well that's nice and the boss will be happy, but explain how us absolutely, 100% normal people who can't fly are going to escape from Seal Team Six? After we *stole Uncle Sam's oil with a bomb threat.*"

"We don't."

The minions all jumped at that.

"""We don't?!"""

Bob smirked.

"We give them someone else to catch."

△△△

A man hidden in a black cloak approached the normal entrance to the Byron Mound facility. He pulled back his arm, his sleeve falling to reveal wicked black claws with a red shine to them. He swung his hand forward.

Red light tore through the air, cutting through the entrance. The man stepped through the cloud of dust. He tore off his cloak, revealing himself to the world.

His face was scarred and deformed, red light pulsing along his veins. He had black and red protrusions all over his face and torso, reaching all the way down into his black pants. Three wicked black claws were grafted onto his right arm, shimmering red with every pulse of his veins. And in his left hand he held a bag full of bombs.

He spoke with a deep and grating voice.

"Tremble and despair, all ye defilers of the Earth! Your pollution is a sickness to the planet, and I am the cure! Your doom approaches, for the Corrupted Claw has cometh to destroy!"

"FREEZE! DON'T MOVE!"

The Corrupted Claw blinked. In front of him were dozens of police cars and National Guard trucks and several times as many officers and soldiers. All of whom had guns pointed at him. *Lots and lots* of guns.

The Corrupted Claw blinked repeatedly.

"Um, what?"

"DROP THE WEAPON AND PUT YOUR HANDS IN THE AIR!"

△△△

"Ok so we pin it on the super and then we…get…away?"

Bob nodded.

"Yep."

"Just like that?"

"Just like that."

"Won't they like, track us with spy satellites or microchips or something?"

Bob shrugged.

"Probably."

"And?!"
"And we'll be back by then."
Bob let the edge of his mouth rise.
"And then they'll have bigger problems."

△△△

A group of men and women in armored masks stood in an empty warehouse. In front of them was the SLICK laying on the floor, a capacity meter on the side filled to the top with a colored bar that transitioned from red to green. They glanced at each other and nodded.

Handshakes, high fives, and fist bumps were exchanged all around.

Well, all except for Senior Brother Wu, who just scoffed and turned his head in the corner.

△△△

And so every major news outlet began reporting on a single topic...

"A fight broke out at the gas station today..."

"Oil prices are reaching record levels..."

"Blackouts are being reported as power plants shut down across the globe..."

"The government implemented strict rationing today..."

"Mass protests in D.C. demanded the government release its reserves. Government officials have refused to comment..."

"A curfew has been put in place in Shanghai..."

"Just who is responsible for this?"

"Thieves strike across the globe! GNN has confirmed that governments around the world have been robbed of their strategic fossil fuel reserves! Oil, coal, even natural gas are all gone! Combined with the recent destruction of several major oil refineries at the hands of the Order of Harmony, global oil supplies have shrunk dramatically and a full-blown energy crisis is developing as we speak! Who could have done this? How did they accomplish it? What is their ultimate goal? How will the governments and heroes of the world respond? And what will all this mean for you? Tune in tonight as GNN consults the experts on this grave new threat."

△△△

A man and a woman sat at the outdoor table of a cafe, happily chatting away as pedestrians and cars went back and forth. The man stopped and smiled at her. She smiled back, and then glanced down at her drink.

A slight tremor made a ripple in her coffee.
Then another.
And another.
And each was getting stronger.
She looked up.
Her eyes widened.
Her jaw dropped.
A shadow fell over her face as something blocked the sun.
She screamed.

And then a piercing roar shattered the sky...

> *AUTHOR'S COMMENTARY: Ah, that's better. There's the fun! And no one randomly developed a deep character arc this time! What's that? Who's that Agent Wilson guy? Meh, no one important, I'm sure. Anyways! Will the world recover its oil reserves? What do the villains plan to do with all that oil? What did the woman see? Tune in next time, to find out!*

CHAPTER 15 - AN EPOCH'S GRAVE

Men and women in camouflage fatigues and helmets took up positions next to humvees and tanks. Helicopters and jet fighters soared overhead. Police and firefighters directed screaming civilians past the armored blockade. The air was filled with screams, gunfire, explosions, helicopter blades, and smoke. Officers shouted at their men as they ran to join the line.

"GO GO GO! MOVE IT PEOPLE!"

Yet it was all drowned out by primal roars.

The Army took up positions in Times Square, flanked to either side by towering skyscrapers. As the last of the civilians ran past, they were joined by the police officers. They chambered their rounds and took aim with their guns. Pistols, shotguns, assault rifles, grenade launchers, fifty caliber machine guns, anti-tank missile launchers, autocannons, even some of the big boys with 120mm smoothbore cannons attached to 60 tons of pure American freedom and justice.

Ahead of them one of those big boys appeared from the right side of an intersection. The mighty Abrams main battle tank retreated back into the street, its turret still aiming to the right as it turned towards the blockade.

Light and smoke blasted from its cannon as the tank opened fire with a thunderous roar. The Earth trembled with rhythmic steps as the tank fired at some unseen horror.

Then a massive clawed foot came down, smashing through the roof of the tank.

A 10-ton monster stood on the remains of the tank, shattering the air with a primal roar. It stood on two massive legs, a tail like a tree trunk swinging behind it. It had two tiny arms, and one humongous set of jaws filled with sword-like teeth. Its rotting leathery skin had open wounds revealing diseased muscles and pale bones. Empty eye sockets were filled with purple flames as the creature glowed with eldritch power.

The zombie T-Rex had come.

And it brought friends.

Dozens of undead tyrannosaurs marched into the intersection. Their legs were shielded behind a phalanx of triceratops, while countless velociraptors danced and circled between their legs. Lumbering sauropods towered overhead and pterodactyls filled the skies. All of which had rotting skin and purple flames instead of eyes, their bodies lightly glowing with arcane power.

Above the horde an Apache attack chopper floated from behind a skyscraper. Its gun blazed and its rocket pods roared.

And then flew the pterodactyls.

They swarmed over the chopper, its metal blades slicing through their leathery wings. But still they came. They wrapped around the nose and tail of the war machine, pecking with their beaks at armor plates and glass cockpits. The chopper began to sway to the right and left before it spun out of control, crashing into a nearby skyscraper and exploding into a ball of flames.

"LIGHT THEM UP!"

At the command, thunder roared and metallic chimes hit the ground as the entire square lit up in light and smoke. Machine guns buzzed, rockets soared, cannons thundered. Explosions slammed into flesh and asphalt. Velociraptors flew in the air. A triceratops paused as an explosion hit its crest. A tyrannosaurus fell to the ground as tank shells tore through its body. Pterodactyls dropped from the sky like leaves in the fall.

But still they came, the tide of glowing, rotting flesh relentlessly advancing forward.

Closer.

And closer.

The soldiers began to step back. Vehicles began to back up.

But distance continued to shrink.

Until the horde was on top of them.

Humvees flipped as triceratops crashed into them. Tanks were crushed underfoot by sauropods. In the skies above choppers spun out of control and even a burning fighter jet fell from the sky. Raptors swarmed over infantry positions.

The blockade broke.

△△△

"DIE DIE DIE! GET SOME, LOSERS!"

Agent Tina fired her pistols as fast as she could squeeze the triggers. Raptors cried in high pitched squeals as she dropped them to the ground.

But still they came.

"These losers just keep coming!"

A raptor crept up on a car behind her, and then pounced on her back. The other raptors swarmed around her.

She twisted on the ground, pulling out a knife and jabbing it repeatedly into the raptor's neck. She rolled out of the way as the rest of the raptors pounced.

And then she smiled.

A pin-less grenade rolled on the ground where she once laid.

"Later, losers!"

The raptors vanished in an explosion.

Tina stood back up and dusted off her hands when the ground began to tremble. She looked up.

A tyrannosaurus rex marched down the alleyway.

"OH COME ON!"

△△△

Down south in Mexico men in casual clothes lit up the streets. They wielded pistols, shotguns, SMGs, assault rifles, Molotov Cocktails, crowbars, machetes, and even kitchen knives. Anything that could be used as a weapon.

But still the dinosaurs came.

The men grunted as raptors leapt on top of them.

And then an icy wind blew through the streets.

The men pushed off the frozen saurians and stood to their feet as Icy Falcon landed in front of them.

"*Señor* Falcon, great, just what we needed. I don't suppose you're taking a break today?"

The men aimed their guns at the man. Icy Falcon turned down the street where a triceratops knocked aside burning cars.

"Let's put these fossils back on ice."

The man nodded and all the guns turned to the dinosaurs.

"Strange times make strange bedfellows, eh *Señor* Falcon?"

△△△

A green light filled with black spots shot down the street. It slammed into a raptor which crumbled into dust.

There stood a gloomy man. He was thin and wiry, nothing more than pale skin and bones. His messy dark hair covered his eyes. He wore loose black clothes.

He also floated above the ground and appeared vaguely transparent.

"Oh, that's a bother..."

A tyrannosaurus stepped out into the street. Gentle Gloom slowly raised his hand, firing another beam. The tyrannosaurus roared in rage, and began marching towards him.

"DIE!!!!"

A burning comet slammed into its head from above. As the dust cleared a woman came into view. She had long, bushy red hair, brown skin, a smile of sharp fangs, and yellow, reptilian eyes. Two horns curled from the sides of her head. She wore a short orange tank top and a pair of jean shorts, showing off red scales on her arms and legs. She clapped her clawed hands together to wipe off the dust.

"Thanks…Dragontooth."

"There's only one king of the lizards here and that's me! Now get a move on, Gloom! We're missing the party!"

She crouched down and then leapt into the air, clearing a building in a single jump. Gloom gave a yawn and then slowly floated straight through the building's walls.

"Ok…."

△△△

Men and women in black martial arts robes gave out a shout as they charged forward. Ancient blades, curved hook swords, sharp spears, mighty glaives, hefty clubs, and glowing fists met with claws and teeth. Core Disciples soared upon their flying blades as they battled with tyrannosaurs and pterodactyls among the mountain peaks. Inner disciples sang their verses as blasts of qi lit up the sky.

But still they came.

Xiong Huang let out a yawn as she brushed off the dust from the crumbling tyrannosaurus ahead of her. She stretched her arms above her head and turned around.

"Sect leader! Where are you going?!"

"For a nap, maybe some snacks."

"W-What about the invaders?!"

"Meh, I got excited with all that ominous energy flying around, but they're disappointingly weak. You guys can handle it, it'll be good training."

"B-But!"

"I'll be inside. Don't disturb me unless you want to be my next sparring partner. Now clean this place up, it's starting to smell."

"Y-Yes mistress, it shall be done."

△△△

"Void."

"What?!"

"You can be honest."

"What are you talking about?!"

"What did you do?"

"What do you mean?! I haven't done anything!"

Chronolock stood back to back with Voidspeaker. She held a triceratops vibrating in place. Behind her Voidspeaker swept a black beam over a pack of raptors. The corpses fell to the ground and remained still, drained of whatever fell power gave them unlife.

To the side a rotting stegosaurus dueled with a glowing pink one, while Wonder Knight held open the jaws of a tyrannosaurus trying to bite down on him. Wonder Knight nodded as well.

"No, I'm kind of with Chrono today, Void. It's ok. You can tell us. We won't be mad."

"Bro! I! Didn't! Do! Anything!"

Pink Star softly smiled as her stegosaurus smashed its opponent's head.

"It's ok, Void, we still love you."

"Not you too, Pink!"

Voidspeaker swung around as Chronolock let go of the triceratops, draining its life right as it began to move. He grit his teeth.

"Seriously! Why do you all think I did this?!"

Chronolock pointed down the street, where another wave

of dinosaurs approached.

"You're telling me the dino-zombie apocalypse *isn't* the result of eldritch powers?"

"Not *my* eldritch powers!"

Wonder Knight nodded sagely.

"It's ok, Void, we all make mistakes."

"Bro! Seriously!"

Just then a glowing purple sphere shot across the sky towards the approaching horde. Once it landed it shrank into nothingness.

And then a black hole surged into being, pulling the dinosaurs inside of it..

Aurora Legion gasped and shielded their faces as gale force winds blew towards the singularity.

And then the singularity vanished and all was still.

And the horde was gone.

The teens look up and behind them where a helicopter dropped from the sky. A dark skinned woman in a suit and sunglasses leapt from the chopper, her shoes glowing with purple light as she slowly descended through the air. In her hands was a massive cannon, barrel still glowing purple.

Fortunately, a certain former assistant to a supervillain had kept a few of her old boss's designs. Just for a rainy day, of course.

"Director Green!"

Londyn nodded to the teens as she landed, then took off her sunglasses and stared Voidspeaker in the eye.

"Void, be honest. What did you do?"

Voidspeaker clutched his head and groaned.

"Not you too!"

△△△

All around the globe televisions lit up. They displayed a throne made of bones, flanked by wooden torches. A man in black robes sat upon the throne. He had a necklace of teeth and claws and a headdress carved from a saurian skull. His face was hidden by a mask of bone and leather. In one of his hands was a bone staff, tipped with a round piece of amber.

"Greetings, all you *homo sapiens* of the planet Earth. I am sure you are wondering just what has occurred this day. Fear not, I will enlighten you, for all this is my doing."

He spread his arms out, and then pointed to himself.

"I am the Necrosaurus, and I am your conqueror. Your doom."

He paused for a moment before nodding his head.

"And I must thank you, as I could not have done it alone. For it was you who dug into the Earth and pulled from it the greatest riches of all. The necrotic energy of billions of lives cut short, entire epochs of extinction condensed down into packets of deathly power."

The Necrosaurus rose from his throne. His staff and body began to glow with ghostly purple light.

"I have taken this pool of oblivion and harnessed the necrotic energies within to raise my saurian hordes. The same hordes that now conquer your streets and cast down your heroes. As a message, a warning."

The light intensified and wrapped around him, forming a small cyclone of energy.

"When will this come to an end? When will the hordes cease their march?"

The Necrosaurus narrowed his eyes.

"That, dear citizens of Earth, is entirely up to you."

The glowing light around his body died down. He slowly sat back upon his throne.

"When the leaders of the world come before me and offer their surrender. When your heroes and gods swear loyalty to my throne, then we shall have peace. But be warned. Today, my hordes merely stand in your streets, to show you what could happen. Today, they strike only at those who fight back, your armies and your heroes. Today, I permit you to retreat. Today, merely thousands will perish. But what happens tomorrow is up to you."

The Necrosaurus struck his staff on the floor.

"For this is no longer the world of humanity."

The Necrosaurus waited as a tyrannosaurus roared in the background.

"Welcome to...the Jurassic Cemetery."

△△△

And so the world trembled, held hostage by the Necrosaurus and his hordes of zombie dinosaurs. Fortunately, the Necrosaurus had been true to his words. His hordes mainly targeted military and police forces, and did not pursue retreating opponents. And his hordes were animated by fell magic, not some sort of deadly virus, so they responded perfectly to his commands. There were no indiscriminate massacres, the casualty counts stayed in the thousands as promised.

Unfortunately, the militaries of the world were caught entirely off guard. Soldiers and heroes were driven from the major cities, unable to bring their might to bear for fear of hitting the civilians caught in between. The Necrosaurus's hordes now held countless hostages in their grip.

Even if his hordes could be defeated, millions would die in the process.

And so the world's armies and heroes stood helplessly as their leaders wrestled with an impossible choice.

Londyn clenched her fists as she stood before a wall of monitors. In front of her were the faces of the world's leaders. Behind her, smoke was rising from burning skyscrapers and ruined streets.

"And what exactly do you expect us to do, Director? Our people are being held hostage. They're all holed up in population centers, we can't even use the nuclear option. What choice do we have left?"

"I understand that, Mr. President, but we can't just surrender to this madman!"

The President of the United States grimaced.

"I don't see what choice we have."

The other world leaders frowned as well.

"I agree."

"It's foolish to resist, Director."

Londyn crossed her arms.

"Then don't. Just let me handle it, as usual."

"What exactly do you think you can do, Director?"

"What we always do: find this guy and beat him down."

The Prime Minister of England scoffed.

"You think you can stop someone capable of all this? You couldn't even save Ulsan!"

"Not me, Prime Minister, heroes. *All* of them."

The Prime Minister of Japan shook his head.

"It's too risky. If you fail, millions could die."

Londyn shrugged.

"Here we call that Tuesday."

The President of the United States heaved a sigh.

"We've already made a decision, Director. This is not up for discussion."

"And I think it's a stupid decision, so I'm going to ignore it. It's not your choice to make anyways."

All the world leaders raised their eyebrows at that.

"Then tell us, Director, whose choice is it?"

Londyn looked them in the eyes.

"The heroes'. He said he wants them to surrender too. And heroes don't give up without a fight."

The world leaders exchanged glances. Londyn took a deep breath and continued.

"Look, I'm not asking you to do this with us. Go, hide in your bunkers and write your surrender speeches. But at least give us a chance."

"...what do you want?"

"One chance. One shot, with everything we got. Share

your intel if you're feeling bold. We'll save the day or go down swinging. Then, you can surrender all you want."

The world leaders looked at each other once more. The President of the United States closed his eyes and heaved a sigh.

"You have twenty-four hours, Director. Make them count."

The world leaders signed off the call. Londyn closed her eyes and let out a sigh.

Sometimes she missed being just a minion.

And then her phone rang.

"Londyn."

"Please tell me there's not *another* Herald. I really can't deal with anything else today."

"You already have one."

"...do you know something?"

"A location."

Londyn caught herself, sensation from her legs vanishing for a moment as her eyes grew wide.

"Bob, I love you."

"You won't when you arrive."

"...that bad, huh?"

"He makes the Heralds look like street magicians"

Londyn sighed.

"It doesn't matter. We're all in either way. I'll see if I can cook up some contingencies."

"You'll need them."

Londyn nodded.

"That's my job. Thank you, Bob, now we have a chance."

"You're welcome."

"And Bob..."

"Yes?"

"Stay safe out there."

"You too."

The phone clicked. Londyn walked down towards Linda. Linda was staring at her silently. Londyn could see slight trembling and moisture building in her eyes as Linda gripped the tablet in her hands.

"Assemble the League. All of them."

Linda narrowed her eyes, nodded, and rushed out of the room.

Londyn turned to her phone, thinking for a moment, and then punched in a number.

If she did this right, she might have a few more cards to play. Cards she might need.

And thankfully, now she had some time to gather them.

The edge of her mouth curled up.

The President gave her twenty four hours.

And now, that was plenty of time.

All thanks to a faceless minion.

△△△

Londyn stepped into the circular conference room, a remote held in her hand. Countless heroes stood around the room, of all shapes and sizes. She quietly clicked her tongue. There were less than she hoped. But more than she feared. She shook her head.

It would have to do.

The chattering and fidgeting stopped as she stepped to the front of the room.

"Thank you for coming, everyone. We're short on time, so let's get right into it."

"Director, excuse me."

Londyn turned to the man sitting in the front row. He had a golden helmet with fuzzy antennae on the forehead and wore fancy robes more suited to a royal ball than a battlefield.

"Yes, Majestic Moth?"

He frowned, crossing his arms.

"Well, what's the point? What chance do we have against all this?"

Londyn raised an eyebrow. He uncrossed his arms and

waved them around.

"I mean, look around. There's so few of us. Even if we can win on our own, millions of people will die wherever we're not. Wouldn't we save more lives…if we just surrendered?"

The other heroes rose to their feet at that.

"Now see here!"

"You coward!"

"You're out of line!"

Londyn took a deep breath.

"QUIET."

The whole room turned to face her.

"You'd be right…"

Everyone's eyes widened at the Director's words. The edge of Londyn's mouth curled up.

"…if it weren't for one thing. I know where the Necrosaurus is hiding."

Everyone's eyes grew wider. And then narrowed. Someone pounded their fist into their palm. Another started a deep chuckle.

Londyn turned to the wall behind her and pressed her remote. A monitor lit up, showing an aerial view of the Pamir mountains. The view zoomed in on a single mountain, a black spot becoming visible at its peak. Soon the heroes could see a black castle. Some dark figures could be seen moving around it even from this height.

Majestic Moth's mouth gaped.

"How did you even find this?"

She smirked at him.

"I have my ways."

Mr. Dapper Tiger frowned and rubbed his chin.

"You're certain of this?"

Londyn nodded her head.

"He's there."

"Do you have a plan?"

Londyn nodded.

"We can't fight a war of attrition, so we'll use a decoy.

Most of you will drop off onto the neighboring peak, and then assault the castle directly. Meanwhile an infiltration team will enter the castle from behind and go for the big boss himself."

There was silence in the room.

"That's not much of a plan."

"Suicide really."

"What's a small team going to do against this guy?"

Londyn pressed the remote again. The monitor changed to a split screen, showing two different heroes battling the dinosaurs.

"The infiltration team will consist of Aurora Legion, Gentle Gloom, and Dragontooth. As you can see, Gentle Gloom and Voidspeaker's powers seem especially potent against this threat, likely due to them having a similar nature as the Necrosaurus. They will go with the infiltration team, which should give them an edge against the Necrosaurus as well as his monsters."

Majestic Moth frowned.

"Is taking him down even a good idea? What if those monsters go crazy when they lose their leashes? We could end up destroying the world ourselves."

Londyn turned to Voidspeaker.

"Can you explain?"

Voidspeaker jumped at being addressed.

"Oh, uh, me?! Um…I-I guess…"

Chronolock nudged his side. He took a deep breath.

"R-Right, so this is definitely a dark magic ritual, each of those things has the same sort of dark energy flowing through them. And the flow is identical in each one, so it's a constant connection through a single conduit, otherwise there'd be minor fluctuations in the…"

"What does that mean, kid?"

Chronolock shook her head and whispered into his ear.

"In English."

Voidspeaker jumped and swallowed.

"O-Oh...um, right, sorry. S-So, it's like this, we stop the conduit, we stop the magic."

"Which means?"

"Um, all the dinosaurs should drop."

There was a moment of silence as the heroes rubbed their chins and twirled their hair. Finally Icy Falcon spoke up.

"How will they get inside?"

Londyn nodded and pointed to Gentle Gloom.

"We've discovered that Gentle Gloom can possess the dinosaur corpses if they are drained of the Necrosaurus's power and left in good condition. Voidspeaker has been doing that the entire time so there's plenty to choose from. We will have Gentle Gloom possess one of the larger fliers and carry the infiltration team in."

"That will only work until they reach the castle."

"Yes, they will need to move quickly. And we will need to work to keep the Necrosaurus distracted."

Majestic Moth frowned again.

"How do we know he'll go for it? Won't he suspect something if we attack head on?"

Londyn smiled.

"I think he'll go for it."

"Why?"

"Because I'm coming with you."

The heroes glanced at each other and the room filled with murmurs. Londyn nodded her head.

"I know it's not the most elegant plan. There are a lot of unknowns here, and the risk of failure is high. And the risk to your lives is even greater."

Londyn glanced around the room, looking each hero in the eye.

"But this is what we do. This is what we signed up for. When the world faces a threat it cannot comprehend or handle. When all seems lost and failure seems inevitable. When there's no time and little hope. That's when they send us. That's when we stand. Because we can do the things that they can't. We can get it done. We can find a way. And if there's no way, then we can make one."

Londyn paused.

"Because you're heroes. And that's what heroes do."

She turned and walked to the door.

"There's a good chance we won't make it out alive. Each of you should decide for yourself, I won't blame you if you stay behind. But I'm going. If there's even a small chance we can stop this, then I'm going to try. Anyone who's with me, suit up and get to the hanger. We leave in five."

A moment of silence as Londyn left the room.

Wonder Knight stood up.

"I'm going."

Pink Star stood too.

"So am I."

Chronolock stood up and yanked Voidspeaker to his feet.

"Hey!"

"You're part of the plan, you have to go."

"I know! You could've let me stand on my own!"

Captain Hot Devil shook his head.

"You're just kids, you don't know what you're getting into, what it means to go now."

Everyone turned to the man who spoke.

Captain Hot Devil stood and walked up to Wonder Knight, staring him down.

Then he placed a hand on his shoulder.

"That's why I'm coming with you."

He glanced around the room.

"We all are."

One by one the heroes stood.

"Yes we are."

"I'm with you too!"

"Let's get that sucker."

"I never liked *Jurassic Park*!"

Everyone turned to the last person seated. Majestic Moth threw up his hands.

"Ok fine! Fine! I'm going! We're all going! We're all going to die together! There! Happy now?!"

Captain Hot Devil tapped Wonder Knight on the shoulder. Wonder Knight turned back to glance at him, and he nodded.

Wonder Knight turned to the standing heroes.

"International League of Superheroes, move out!"

AUTHOR'S COMMENTARY: This is what Markus was waiting for! At least until SOMEONE decided to wrestle with the realistic consequences of supervillain activity and have an entirely justified emotional breakdown due to tragic deaths and the guilt of murder! But it's ok! We made it! And now the dino-zombie apocalypse has arrived! Tune in next time as we explore Necrosaurus's tragic backstory...wait NO! I reject that! You are NOT taking the dino-zombie apocalypse from me! No family or sympathetic goals for you! Ahem...Can the International League of Superheroes put a stop to the Necrosaurus and his dastardly schemes? Or will the dino-zombie apocalypse conquer the world? Tune in next time, to find out!

CHAPTER 16 - THE BATTLE OF THE JURASSIC CEMETERY

The helicopters touched down on the mountain slope. Londyn disembarked, heroes stepping off helicopters or landing from the sky all around her. She took out her binoculars and looked over the castle on the neighboring slope.

Black stone pierced the sky. The castle was vaguely triangular, with sharp spires reaching up like a bundle of spears. Every angle looked as sharp as a blade, and not a hint of light reflected from the sides. The base was surrounded by a wall covered in spikes and bones.

Around the castle patrolled several sauropods, dozens of theropods, triceratops, and other medium sized dinosaurs, along with countless raptors. Squadrons of pterodactyls patrolled the skies, countless more waiting in roosts among the spires. Londyn grimaced.

Well, this was never going to be easy.

Captain Hot Devil walked up beside her.

"Do you have a plan?"

Londyn shrugged.

"I'm not a tactician. And I doubt anyone knows the proper way to engage zombie dinosaurs."

"Fair enough."

"Be my guest if you have a suggestion."

"...I normally just punch things."

"You'll get your chance."

Captain Hot Devil let his shoulders drop for a second.
"You think they can do it?"
"The kids?"
The Captain nodded.
"Yeah."
Londyn replied immediately.
"Of course."
"Why?"
Londyn frowned.
"Because we need them to."
She turned to the device on her wrist. A green light began to blink. She put her binoculars away and hoisted her grav-cannon.
"Let's get started."

△△△

High up in the sky five people rode on two flying dinosaurs. One had a faint green outline, carrying Dragontooth and Wonder Knight. The other, surrounded with a faint purple glow, carried Voidspeaker, Pink Star, and Chronolock.

Voidspeaker shouted into his mic.
"We're here!"
Chronolock narrowed her eyes at the castle below.
"Looks like it."
Pink Star tilted her head.
"When do we go?"
Wonder Knight answered her.
"Director said she'd give us a signal."
Pink Star glanced around below them.
"What kind of signal?"
Wonder Knight shrugged.
"She didn't say."
Voidspeaker jumped at that.
"Bro! She didn't say?! How are we supposed to…"

The team heard a high pitched whine screeching through the air.

Suddenly a black sphere appeared in front of the castle's gates. The team could see the figures of dinosaurs being pulled into the singularity. The two gate towers began to collapse inwards and vanished.

Chronolock smirked.

"That answer your question?"

Dragontooth grinned and cracked her knuckles.

"Let's go!"

The two fliers began to drop, aiming for the tallest spire. Faster and faster they dropped until the spire was in front of them. Then the fliers spread their wings and flapped until they came to a stop.

Aurora Legion exchanged glances.

"How do we get inside?"

Dragontooth stood up and shouted.

"Grab on!"

Dragontooth leapt from her flier, cracks forming on the wall around her fingers. Wonder Knight followed suit. Once the two were clear Gentle Gloom emerged from the dinosaur, letting it fall lifelessly from the sky. Gentle Gloom let out a yawn and slowly floated towards the wall.

And then bounced off with a zap.

"Ouch...bother...dark magic's flowing through the walls."

Wonder Knight turned to the other flyer.

"Void, can you drain it?"

"Not while flying!"

Chronolock and Pink Star nodded at each other and then at Wonder Knight and Dragontooth, who nodded back. The two girls leapt from the flier, landing on the backs of the other two heroes. Voidspeaker let his flier drop, floating towards the wall on his own power.

"Experience nothingness."

A small beam hit the wall, forming a black circle over top of it.. The Gentle Gloom floated through, shivering as he passed through the draining beam.

A minute later a section of the wall slid up, revealing a window. The heroes nodded and climbed inside...

△△△

Londyn glanced at her wrist. Green light flashed once more.

"At least something's going well."

She ducked as a pterodactyl swooped down over head, barely a foot above her. Once it passed she lifted her gravcannon and fired a small purple bolt. The pterodactyl cried as a purple mist covered its wing, a random collection of chaotic and opposing gravitational forces ripping the wing to shreds.

All around her were snapping teeth and ripping claws. Blasts of light shone about, gunshots rang out. Bestial roars and brave shouts filled the air, along with the smells of dripping blood and rotting flesh.

A flight of pterodactyls approached from above. Gunshots rang out as Agent Tina stepped forward, holding her pistols. Beside her stood a man in a gray coat, a gray broad brimmed hat, and a gray mask. Gray Slayer fired his enchanted magnum with a thunderous roar. The flyers dropped from the sky one by one. A tyrannosaurus roared and charged the pair, but was halted as Majestic Moth filled its vision with sparkling dust. A ball of feathers the size of a rhino slammed into its head as Master Mammoth Owl sent the beast hurtling down the mountain.

The earth rumbled as a wall of triceratops charged across the battlefield. Aqua Mage spun her rod and pointed it towards them, a stream of water dousing each of the beasts. Then Tesla Titan thrust his arm forward, filling the water with lightning. Each of the triceratops crashed to the ground, burnt and smoking. Mr. Dapper Tiger stood back to back with a man with a beautiful samurai kimono and a black ponytail.

Slashes rang out from tiger claws and a golden blade as Master Elegant Katana showcased his name.

Londyn started to charge another gravity bomb when something landed on top of her. A raptor had pounced on her from behind. She twisted and struggled, hands holding snapping jaws mere inches away from her fast.

A burning fist passed by her face.

A burning fist she remembered.

It punched clean through leathery skin as easily as it did wooden walls.

A blast of fire blew away bone and claw as easily as tables and doors.

Captain Hot Devil stood over her once more.

And he extended his hand.

She grabbed it and stood to her feet.

"Are you ok?"

"Fine, thanks."

He looked into her eyes.

She saw concern and relief in his.

She shook her head and picked up her grav-cannon, aiming it at an approaching sauropod.

"No time to rest."

And so the fight went on...

△△△

The infiltration team ran down dark halls. The hallways were made of black stone covered with purple carpets. They were lit by torches of bone, eerie blue flames resting in reptilian skulls. Black and green beams shot out on occasion from the heroes, silencing patrolling raptors before they could react.

The team made good time, virtually unopposed, until they came to two massive doors. They looked around and everyone nodded. Wonder Knight and Dragontooth stood in front of each door while the other four members split to either side of the doorway.

Dragontooth held up her fingers, silently counting down. The doors creaked as the two heroes pushed them open.

Inside was a large circular room with a tall ceiling. It had no adornment or furnishing besides torches on the walls, not even a carpet. But the room needed no decoration, as the object in its center demanded all attention.

There lay a skeletal creature, devoid of all flesh, its pale white bones shining under the blue torchlight. It had a long, thin tail ending in a wicked barb. It had two pairs of legs, tipped with gleaming claws. It had a massive set of jaws with rows of sharp teeth sitting atop a long, agile neck. Large horns curled back from its skull. And it had glowing purple flames illuminating its eye sockets.

Dragontooth grit her teeth and pounded her palm with her fist.

"He's dead. He's so dead!"

And finally, it had a pair of massive, bony wings.

There lay a skeletal dragon.

"Bothersome…"

"Bro, I thought it was only dinosaurs! That's cheating!"

Wonder Knight's eyes widened as the skeletal beast threw back its head. The bones on its neck began to glow purple.

"You have got to be kidding me. EVERYBODY MOVE!"

The heroes scattered as purple flames filled the air.

"Experience nothingness!"

"Please stop…"

Voidspeaker and Gentle Gloom floated into the air above the flames and stretched out their hands.

Two beams, one black as night, the other green with black spots, shot into the dragon's head.

But the dragon kept moving.

Wonder Knight and Chronolock's eyes widened.

"What the heck? What's going on Void?"

"Stop messing around and drain that thing!"

Voidspeaker grit his teeth and poured more power into

his beam.

"I'm trying! It's resisting me!"

"What does that mean?!"

Voidspeaker opened his mouth to answer when a shadow passed over him. The dragon spun around, lashing out its tail. Gentle Gloom's eyes widened.

"Oh bother."

The tail slammed into both heroes. Voidspeaker and Gentle Gloom flew through the air and slammed into the wall.

"GRAAAAHHH!!!!"

Dragontooth leapt through the air with a shout, latching to the dragon's left shoulder with both arms. She planted both feet on the ground and then pulled. There was a terrible creaking sound. The dragon roared and leapt to the side, slamming its body into the wall.

And smashing Dragontooth in between.

The hero groaned and fell to the ground.

The dragon moved to bite her when it was knocked away. A pink triceratops smashed into its side, driving it towards the wall. Wonder Knight ran over and pulled Dragontooth to her feet.

"What do we do?! Our eldritch experts are out!"

Dragontooth's face twisted into a snarl.

"What do you think, kid?! We hit it!"

"That's not a plan! What if it won't go down to fists?!"

"Then we hit it harder!"

With that, Dragontooth pushed off the floor and leapt into the air.

Wonder Knight looked back at his team. Pink Star gave a shrug while Chronolock was holding her head. He heaved a sigh.

"She's the veteran. Chrono, protect those two until they wake up! Pink, let's make sure Dragontooth doesn't die!"

"Okay!"

"On it."

And so the battle raged on…

△△△

Another flight of pterodactyls sped towards the ground.
BAM! BAM! BAM!
Gunshots rang out as Agent Tina fired her guns as fast as she could squeeze the triggers.
The flyer on the left fell from the sky.
"Cha ching, baby!"
BAM! BAM! BAM!
The one on the right spun out of control. Agent Tina grinned.
"I'm so good!"
BAM! BAM! Click.
"Oh sh.."
The pterodactyl swooped past and Agent Tina went flying, bouncing along the ground.
Mr. Dapper Tiger ran on all fours, leaping on top of a triceratops and then pushing off into the sky.
And then a tyrannosaurus's tail slammed him into the ground.
Tesla Titan stepped forward when a whole pack of raptors jumped on him. He tried to swing his arms forward, lightning firing out from his palms, but another pack pounced at his head. The armor suit tipped back and then crashed into the ground.
Londyn grit her teeth and ducked as a raptor pounced over her head, claws brushing past her hair.
"Falcon! We're being overrun, we need air support now!"
She swung her grav-cannon around and fired another bolt as she shouted.
Clouds gathered overhead. Wind began to blow, picking up dust and ashes. Snow began to fall within the gales.
Icy Falcon descended from the sky, his cape held out.
"The dinosaurs give way for an **ICE AGE!**"

With an echoing cry, Icy Falcon spread his cape as far as he could. The frozen winds picked up to gale force speeds and frost grew across rotting flesh. Raptors blew away from heroes on the ground. Theropods bowed their heads to the ground and triceratops tried to dig in with their feet. Pterodactyls went swirling about, at the mercy of the mighty winds. Icy daggers and hail the size of cars descended upon the saurian hordes.

And then a dark shadow passed overhead, crashing into the hero above.

Icy Falcon grunted as he flew from the sky. The wind and the ice died down. The hordes began to move once more.

Icy Falcon found himself twisted with a quetzalcoatlus. The pair soared across the sky, a ball of muscle and leather vying for control.

And the dinosaurs on the ground were free to resume their assault.

Londyn grit her teeth, charging another gravity bomb. She let it soar into the neck of a sauropod, the beast crying as it was crushed by the incredible force.

To her side Captain Hot Devil launched a fireball at a raptor pouncing on Master Elegant Katana, then thrust out his other hand to send a jet of flame at a charging triceratops.

"Director! We can't hold out much longer! We have to fall back!"

Londyn grit her teeth.

"We can't! We have to give them more time!"

"Director!"

Londyn looked to her side.

A massive tail filled her vision.

Londyn cried out as the tail slammed into her and she bounced along the ground.

Finally she came to a stop. She groaned and lifted her head.

Mr. Dapper Tiger let out a roar as he vanished under a pack of raptors.

Master Elegant Katana was knocked to the side by a charging triceratops.

Agent Tina leaned on the Gray Slayer's shoulder as they fired into an approaching horde.

Master Mammoth Owl fell from the sky, covered in pterodactyls.

Aqua Mage fell to the ground as a pachycelphalosaurus smashed through a shield of water.

Tesla Titan let lightning fly as a tyrannosaurus picked him up in its jaws.

Icy Falcon was nowhere to be seen.

A triceratops charged towards Captain Hot Devil's back while he was occupied with a spinosaurus.

They were out of time.

△△△

The dragon twisted its bony neck and bit down on the glowing triceratops. The triceratops let out a cry and vanished into pink sparks. Then Dragontooth flew through the air, smashing her fist into the dragon's head, sending it flying backward. But the dragon pulled back its right arm and swiped forward, sending Dragontooth flying through the air once more.

Wonder Knight ran forward as Dragontooth flew past him. The dragon's neck was glowing once again. Wonder Knight leapt into the sky as the dragon took aim and opened its mouth.

BAM!

Wonder Knight landed an mighty uppercut on the dragon's lower jaw, sending its head shooting towards the roof. A purple light illuminated the room as the purple flames spread across the roof.

As the flames died down, a pink tyrannosaurus thundered through the room, clamping the dragon's neck between its jaws. The dragon cried as it fell backwards, struggling to get its feet under it as the theropod pushed.

And then a wicked barb swung around and pierced the back of the tyrannosaur's head.

The skeletal dragon rose to its feet, ghostly eyes now locked on Pink Star. Its neck began to glow.

Wonder Knight cried and leapt into the air.

The dragon backhanded him into the wall.

And then the beast let out a blast of purple flame.

Dragontooth landed in front of Pink Star and took a deep breath. She opened her mouth and unleashed her own breath.

Red and purple flames clashed in the air with a roar. The room was filled with light and heat.

Then the purple flames stopped midair and began to vibrate, Chronolock standing just underneath.

The dragon let out a cry as it was covered in a red inferno.

Dragontooth shut her mouth, then grabbed Pink Star and leapt to the side so Chronolock could release the purple blaze. As they stood to their feet Wonder Knight came up beside them while a groaning Voidspeaker and Gentle Gloom floated behind.

"What do we do? Nothing we have can stop it!"

Dragontooth frowned.

"Maybe we don't have to."

"What are you saying?"

Dragontooth pointed down the room, where another set of doors was shut.

"You kids make a break for the door."

Voidspeaker's eyes widened.

"Are you crazy?! What about the dragon?!"

Dragontooth pounded her palm with her fist.

"Leave that to me."

Wonder Knight shook his head.

"We should stick together! We can all make a break for it, Chrono can lock it up for a bit."

"No good kid. Last thing we need is to get caught between this thing and the big bad on either side. Get going, we're running out of time. The other heroes down there need us now."

The Gentle Gloom placed a hand on Wonder Knight's shoulder.

"Let it go, she's a bit of a bother when she gets like this. Won't be happy till she wins, it's a dragon thing."

Wonder Knight bit his lip. The Gentle Gloom gave him a smile.

"Don't worry, I'll watch her back. It's not our first rodeo you know?"

Wonder Knight slowly nodded as the dragon strode out of the red blaze.

"Be careful."

Dragontooth let out a grin.

"Just go already, you idiots!"

With that, she leapt towards the dragon.

Aurora Legion nodded to each other and ran for the door as Gentle Gloom fired another beam to cover Dragontooth. Wonder Knight reached the door and pushed with all his might.

"It won't budge!"

Voidspeaker raised his hand and channeled another beam. He furrowed his brow and began to grunt, raising his other hand. His eyes began to glow and he began to chant in indecipherable words.

"EXPERIENCE NOTHINGNESS!"

The black beam grew until the air was humming.

They heard a sound like glass shattering.

And then the doors swung open...

△△△

Londyn groaned as she lifted her head. Heroes were being overwhelmed on the ground. Flying heroes were falling from the sky. There were claws and teeth everywhere. A triceratops was about to run Captain Hot Devil down.

They were out of time.

Londyn groaned and reached for her wrist.

But they weren't out of options.

She pressed a button.

A humming sound thrummed through the air. Pebbles and ashes began to rise all around. The humming grew louder and higher. And then...

There was a sound like thunder.

A wave of purple light passed through the mountains.

Dinosaurs on top of heroes began to float in the air. The charging triceratops smashed into the ground. Pterodactyls and a Quetzalcoatlus fell like rocks from the sky, throwing up dust as they slammed into the ground. Theropods fell over, no longer able to balance on their twin legs. Sauropods cried as their necks crashed to the ground.

The heroes picked themselves up and rose to their feet. Captain Hot Devil turned around and his eyes widened.

"Where...did you get that?"

Back by the landed helicopters, Linda and several technicians typed away at terminals. In front of them, a metal cylinder rested on the ground, a second cylinder held high above it with a metal scaffold. Between the two cylinders floated a silver polyhedron with glowing blue circles on its sides. A fully armed and operational Mass Suppressor now thrummed with power, pulsing with purple light.

Londyn smirked.

"Looks like I'm the sole distributor of the laws of physics now, eh Captain?"

Captain Hot Devil's eyes grew even wider and started to tremble.

"You...you were..."

Londyn stepped forward and picked up her fallen grav-cannon.

"We can reminisce on old times later, Captain. Right now, we have a battle to win and a world to save."

The heroes began to gather behind her. She grinned and charged her gravity cannon once again.

"International League of Superheroes, attack!"

△△△

The Necrosaurus lay back against his throne, hand on his chin as he furrowed his brow. He hummed as he pondered.

"The exaltation of extinction? Nah. The dinosaurs of death? No good. Oh how about this? Ahem, you who grew drunk on the blood of the dinosaurs shall now drown in it. Yes, I like that."

A minion wrapped in black robes worked on the camera and filming equipment in the room.

"Technically sir, it's not really the blood of the dinosaurs. Mostly algae and plants, so not blood at all really. There are even some theories that fossil fuels aren't organic in origin at all."

The Necrosaurus threw a skull at the man.

"Shut up, Carl! Way to take the fun out of everything."

Then they heard a sound like glass shattering.

The doors to the room slammed open and Aurora Legion rushed inside. Wonder Knight pointed his hand at the man sitting on the throne.

"It's over, Necrosaurus! Aurora Legion will put a stop to you, here and now!"

The Necrosaurus grinned.

"Carl, start recording. It's time to show the world what it means to defy the Necrosaurus!"

AUTHOR'S COMMENTARY: Dang it science, why you gotta ruin everything! I just want my necromancer utilizing fossil fuels as a mass dinosaur graveyard but noooooo, we had to go and find out they aren't dinosaurs after all. Next they're going to tell me Pluto's not a planet! Anyways! Can Aurora Legion stop the Necrosaurus once and for all? Will the ILS emerge victorious? Will Dragontooth prove she's the best dragon? Tune in next time to find out!

CHAPTER 17 - SHOWDOWN! AURORA LEGION VS. THE BOSS!

Aurora Legion walked into a large throne room filled with all sorts of cameras and recording equipment. A massive circular formation was carved into the floor, surrounded by skull torches shining with eerie light. Above the circle hung some sort of cylindrical metal device with a colored bar. The bar was about a third filled, colored red and orange. And at the end of the room, sitting on the throne of bones...

The Necrosaurus rose to his feet. Aurora Legion took up formation and cautiously approached. Pink Star's gauntlets began to glow, Voidspeaker began to chant under his breath. As they moved forward, the Necrosaurus pointed his staff at the group and the cameras switched on.

"All you *homo sapiens* of the world, heed me and despair! You who have grown drunk on the blood of the dinosaurs shall now drown in it! Watch now, witness the fate of your so-called heroes and learn what it means to defy me!"

Aurora Legion stared at him with narrowed eyes.

"Technically it's not dinosaur blood. Mostly algae and plants, so not blood at all, really."

Voidspeaker jumped and turned to look at Wonder Knight.

"Wait, bro, it's not?!"

Pink Star nodded.

"Yeah! I heard that too! I learned about it in a

documentary!"

"Wait, Pink, you knew that too?!"

Carl nodded as well and pointed at the heroes.

"See sir, I told you!"

The Necrosaurus scowled.

"Shut up, Carl! I told you not to talk while we're recording! See, look, now you're going to have to edit this out!"

"Uh...sir, you know we're live now, right?"

The Necrosaurus froze.

"Wait, what?"

"I thought you would want it live since it's a battle and all."

"CARL! You need to warn me of these things! We're going to have a nice long chat when we're done here!"

Chronolock just groaned and held her head.

"This idiot is about to conquer the world..."

The Necrosaurus heaved a sigh.

"Hah, whatever, we're improvising now. Welcome, 'Aurora Legion', to the Jurassic Cemetery. Now DIE!"

The Necrosaurus thrust out his free hand and a circle of ghastly purple light appeared on the floor. The amber at the tip of his staff pulsed with orange light, and a pack of zombie raptors rose from the floor.

Wonder Knight's eyes narrowed.

"Let's go, Aurora Legion!"

With that, the heroes leapt into action. Voidspeaker thrust his hands forward.

"Experience nothingness!"

The black beam swept across the raptors.

And nothing happened as they continued rushing forward.

The Necrosaurus cackled and spread his hands.

"Foolish little cultist, did you think I wasn't watching you drain my minions time after time? I've made some special adjustments just for you!"

Wonder Knight began sprinting forward.

"Pink!"

Pink Star lifted her glowing hands.

"Tyrannosaurus Rex, I choose you!"

A pink tyrannosaurus formed into being and shook the hall with a mighty roar. The Necrosaurus frowned.

"Now that's just not fair. Do you know how long I had to work to figure out how to raise dinosaurs? All their bones have been turned into minerals and don't even respond to necromancy any more! I had to figure out how to transmute organic compounds into flesh and THEN I had to locate a source of well-preserved genetic material before I could even START learning how! And now you just wave your magic hands around and suddenly dinosaurs? Seriously! Life is just not fair."

The pink tyrannosaurus thundered forth, grabbing one of the raptors in its jaws. The other raptors surrounded the beast and started to harass its flanks.

The Necrosaurus ducked as a black beam flew past his head.

"Ah, can't drain my minions so you're aiming for me now? Smart. How to fight a necromancer 101 in fact."

His mouth curled into a sneer.

"It's too bad you're weak!"

The Necrosaurus thrust his staff forward. Sharp bones formed in the air and shot towards Voidspeaker. Voidspeaker dropped his chant and hit the ground to avoid the spikes. Then the Necrosaurus whirled around himself and a wall of spikes emerged from the ground. Chronolock leapt back with a grunt while Wonder Knight crossed his arms in front of him.

"GAH!"

The spikes pierced his arms, blood dripping from the wounds. Pink Star's eyes widened.

"Wonder!"

"Heh, I thought you would have known, given you got a cultist friend and all. Those aren't regular bones, they're magic bones. You can't just block them with your hands. Here, try it now."

The Necrosaurus filled the air with spikes and sent them flying at Wonder Knight. The pink tyrannosaurus leapt in front of him, roaring as it was filled with spikes. The dinosaur then exploded into pink sparks.

And the Necrosaurus shook his head, clicking his tongue.

"That was a mistake, little summoner. You should've gone for me while I was aiming elsewhere."

The Necrosaurus pointed his staff at Pink Star. Purple magic circles formed on the ground, surrounding her with zombie raptors.

"And now I will never allow you to form another summon."

Pink Star ducked and weaved as the raptors pounced and bit at her. She just managed to dodge the teeth and claws.

But her gauntlets remained dull, her focus too split to form any more constructs.

The Necrosaurus turned his attention back to Wonder Knight but then his shoulder snapped back. He turned his head. His staff was vibrating in the air, refusing to move. He looked down. Chronolock had crawled forward and was gripping his staff.

"Ah, the little chronomancer! Honestly you are the biggest threat. Not much one can do against someone who rips apart the space-time continuum."

He sneered at her.

"But my staff is just an aid. Every decent magician has a backup plan."

He raised his hand. Bone spikes formed in the air. Chronolock's eyes widened and she rolled to the side, letting go of the staff. She cried out as a spike grazed her thigh.

"EXPERIENCE NOTHINGNESS!"

The Necrosaurus halted a step as a massive black beam struck his chest, causing the room to dim. Voidspeaker floated in the air, winds kicking up his robes around him as he glowed with blackish-purple light. His eyes seemed to burn with power, trails of purple fire coming from the pure black orbs.

"Not bad little cultist, not bad at all. There's just one problem."

The Necrosaurus pointed his staff at the boy.

"Like I said, YOU'RE WEAK!"

A flaming skull flew from the staff and around the beam, exploding in the air. The shockwaves blew Voidspeaker into the ground, trails of smoke coming from his robes.

Voidspeaker slowly turned his head up as the Necrosaurus walked over to him and pointed the staff at his head.

"Word of advice, from one explorer of the dark arts to another. Spend more time studying, less time playing around. Friends are a weakness."

Voidspeaker grinned.

"I wouldn't be so sure about that, bro."

The Necrosaurus turned around.

Wonder Knight flew through the air, his arm pulled back. Blood still dripped from his wounds but he grit his teeth and thrust his arm forward.

And slammed his fist straight into the metal device held on the roof.

Oil flooded the room as the SLICK exploded.

△△△

Londyn breathed heavily. Her arms trembled. She tried to lift her grav-cannon but her arms refused to move any further. So she knelt down on one knee, using the ground to prop the cannon up and aim it forward.

One final grav-bomb roared through the air.

A sauropod screamed and fell over, a massive hole left in its torso as Londyn's final singularity vanished.

It was the last dinosaur.

Londyn let the cannon fall to the ground. She took a few deep breaths, and then lifted her head.

All around her heroes panted for breath, crouched over on their knees or lying on the ground.

And not a single dinosaur stirred.

They made it.

They won.

Londyn's mouth curled into a grin. She felt a cheer welling up inside her stomach. She was about to shout…

And then she heard a crash.

She looked up into the air. A pink quetzalcoatlus flew from the tallest spire of the castle. After a few minutes of flight it landed in front of her, and then vanished.

"Aurora? What happened? Where's Dragon and Gloom?"

The teens sat on the ground, coated in black oil. Voidspeaker took a deep breath.

"We couldn't stop him, he's too powerful, but I think we got his crucible. Should put a stop to his rituals. If we all work together, we should be able to…"

The ground began to tremble. They heard the sound of stone cracking. The top of the castle began to crumble.

A roar pierced the heavens.

Voidspeaker trembled.

"T-That…wasn't…his crucible?"

The roof of the castle crumbled as something massive grew from within it. Something larger than the castle itself, with wings that stretched out and blocked the sky. Londyn saw fierce teeth larger than a man and sharp claws that could spear a whale. The sky was filled with rotting, scaly skin and large curling horns.

It was a zombie dragon the size of a mountain.

The dragon unfurled itself, rising to its full height and spreading out its wings. It threw its head back…

And then it split the sky.

Everyone grabbed their ears and cried out as the mighty

roar assaulted them. A beam of purple light shot into the heavens from the dragon's mouth.

For a terrible minute, the Earth trembled.

The dragon finally closed its mouth and looked down upon the scattered heroes. On its nose stood the Necrosaurus.

"Now you understand the true meaning of the name, Necrosaurus! Behold, my greatest creation! My life's work! Be honored, mighty heroes of Earth! For your deaths shall usher in a new era! For this is the Jurassic Cemetery where the Necrosaurus reigns eternal!"

He sneered at them.

"And once you are gone, the world shall bow before me! And all will know that I! AM! SUPREME!"

The heroes of Earth froze and shivered.

Agent Tina reloaded her guns without a word.

The Icy Falcon frowned and hung his head.

Captain Hot Devil slowly raised his fists, breathing heavily.

Londyn grimaced.

The battle was not going well, it seemed.

> *AUTHOR'S COMMENTARY: Can the ILS resolve this crisis? Who could possible stop the Necrosaurus now? Is this even his final form? Tune in next time, to find out! ...Ok yes Xiong Huang could but she doesn't care and is also busy right now. Don't come between the girl and her shows. Or her snacks. Or anything she happens to want really.*

CHAPTER 18 - THE FIGHT FOR THE WORLD

Londyn heaved a sigh and held her head.

"This is not going to end well."

The Necrosaurus grinned.

"But I am a generous god. Lay down your weapons and bend your knees. Swear fealty to your new ruler and you shall have a place in the new world I will build."

All eyes turned to Londyn. Majestic Moth rushed over to her.

"Director..."

Londyn slowly rose to her feet.

"Director, please. Haven't we done enough? Haven't we fought enough? We gave it our best shot, we gave it everything we had. And we lost. There is no shame in it now. What purpose is there in resisting further? What more can we do?"

Wonder Knight slowly rose to his feet, grinding his teeth.

"We can't just give up!"

Captain Hot Devil grimaced.

"Hate to admit it but he's got a point."

Aurora Legion's eyes widened.

"Captain?"

"Look, I'm a hothead, if there's a ghost of a chance I'll go down swinging...but right now I don't see any chance at all. And there's people who still need us back home."

Londyn closed her eyes. She took a deep breath.

"Yes, there's nothing more you can do..."

Aurora Legion looked to the ground. Voidspeaker grit his teeth and pounded the dirt.

Memories flashed before Londyn's eyes. She remembered lying on the ground. She remembered all her work going up in smoke and flame. She remembered being crushed by the remains of a table, waiting for her death as her betters fought above her.

She opened her eyes.

She made her choice.

"...but I still have cards to play."

And then she pushed a button on her wrist.

Linda nodded and typed away at her terminal, shouting at the other technicians.

The Mass Suppressor let out a piercing screech.

A massive wave of purple light surged forward.

And the dragon crashed into the ground, flattening the castle.

All eyes widened and then turned to Londyn.

"Director?"

Londyn stepped forward, glaring at the dragon ahead of them.

"You all can surrender if you want. Nothing but foolishness to carry on and the world will need you later. Go on, run. But as for me?"

Londyn looked Captain Hot Devil in the eyes.

"I am DONE lying helplessly on the ground while some super being decides my fate."

She turned to the crumbling castle and narrowed her eyes.

"Even if all I can do is put a scratch on these so-called gods, then that's what I'm going to do. It might be pointless. He may conquer the Earth with ease. But he's going to do it over my…dead…body!"

She turned to Majestic Moth.

"Go. The world will always need more heroes. Even when it's ruled by a madman. Especially then."

Majestic Moth looked down and away. He gulped. He whispered in a soft voice.

"Dang it all…"

He stepped to Londyn's side.

"I guess I can't complain when you literally brought a god to his knees."

Captain Hot Devil stepped to her other side.

"If you're standing here now, how can I run?"

Aurora Legion jumped up and ran in front of her.

"We're here too!"

"We aren't going anywhere!"

"I'm taking this jerk down if it's the last thing I do, bro!"

Chronolock just nodded with a frown.

Some gave shouts, others just stood in silence, but ultimately every hero rose and joined the line.

Londyn nodded, and pressed another button on her wrist. It was time to go all in, and put all the cards on the table.

"Then we do it together. All of us."

The International League of Superheroes stood as one.

Just then, a bone lance shot through the air and stabbed into the Mass Suppressor.

A horrific screeching pierced the air and every person clutched their ears.

Cracks appeared all across the silver polyhedron, purple light shining from within them.

Linda's eyes widened and she shouted at the technicians. They all started running in every direction.

A loud cracking sound thundered through the air.

And then a purple shockwave knocked everyone to the ground, kicking up the dust.

The Mass Suppressor was gone.

The dragon rose to the sky. The Necrosaurus snarled.

"You dare to insult ME?! You will die, you will all die! And then everyone will know that THIS WORLD BELONGS TO ME!"

The dragon's neck began to glow.

Purple fire gathered in its neck.

Aqua Mage and Voidspeaker began to chant, magic circles appearing in the air.

Captain Hot Devil lit his fists on fire.

The Icy Falcon spread his cape, cold gales gathering around him.

Agent Tina and the Gray Slayer took aim.

Wonder Knight and Mr. Dapper Tiger gripped their fists.

Pink Stars gauntlets began to glow.

And the edge of Londyn's mouth…curled up.

"I wouldn't say that if I were you."

There was a slight shift, the air grew still.

Soft footsteps touched the ground from a newly landed helicopter.

There was a quiet, soft voice. Barely a whisper.

Yet everyone heard it over the din.

The dragon took a deep breath.

They heard the voice again, just a little louder.

There was a tiny tremor in the ground.

The heroes turned around. Their eyes widened.

"You didn't."

Londyn smirked.

"I did. I told you this is not going to end well."

A second voice joined with the first, a deep and primal rumble.

The card that cost every ounce of political capital Londyn could muster came into play.

The dragon drew back its head.

The ground began to shake. The rocks of the mountain began to crack.

The dragon thrust its head forward and opened its jaw.

The world was drowned in a deafening roar as the air itself was set ablaze by the monster's breath.

But then the sound dimmed and grew silent.

And the world replied.

""I AM ONE WITH THE EARTH, AND THE EARTH IS WITH ME!!!""

There stood the former Sentinel of Harmony, the Destroyer of Ulsan herself, Vaidehi Dayal. Her feet were planted firmly on the ground, her hands were clasped in front of her chest. But her face was no longer masked in serenity or twisted in anguish. Her eyes were narrowed and her mouth frowned as she glared at the dragon ahead.

And the Earth erupted around her.

Roots and branches the size of skyscrapers rolled and twisted from the mountain, passing the heroes and reaching to the sky.

A wave of purple fire collided with a wave of green wood.

The master of death laid claim to the Earth.

And the Earth fought back.

The dragon's mouth closed and the blaze came to an end. Burning branches fell from the sky as purple fire burned.

But still the trees grew, rushing towards their foe.

Massive branches wrapped around the dragon. The dragon roared and swiped its claws, tearing the trees apart. It swung its tail, shattering trunks whole. Vaidehi grunted and began to sweat but her eyes never wavered.

And still the trees grew.

The dragon cried and fired its breath once more. The canopy burned.

But still the trees grew.

They wrapped around the dragon. Wood creaked and groaned as the beast cried. The branches wrapped around its jaws and closed them with a snap.

The dragon grunted and rumbled, but it could move no more.

Branches extended down, forming a ramp in front of the heroes.

"Go! I can hold it, but you must defeat its master! The Earth is with you!"

Londyn nodded and picked up the grav-cannon once

again.

"Let's go!"

All the heroes nodded and let out a shout as they charged up the ramp. The moment they stepped on the wooden path energy surged through their bodies. Their wounds healed, their exhaustion vanished. With another cheer, they surged forth, climbing towards the dragon's head.

The fight for the world entered its final stage.

△△△

Londyn led the International League of Superheroes as they charged up the ramp. They entered on top of the dragon's head, trembling as it tried to move. The Necrosaurus stood there clutching his head.

"No, how can this be? This doesn't make any sense! How is this...what is this...!"

He looked up and saw the approaching heroes. He yelled, he screamed, then he leaned back clutching his head.

"Gah! You know what?! Fine! I'll do it myself!"

He began to float into the air, purple lightning cracking around him. Londyn pointed at him.

"Go!"

Agent Tina and Gray Slayer took aim and opened fire, gunshots ringing through the air. The bullets flew on target, but struck harmlessly on a shield of purple light that appeared as they approached.

The Necrosaurus swung his staff and a hail of bone shards bombarded the heroes. Aqua Mage lifted her staff and a wave of water rose before the heroes. Icy Falcon swung his cape forward and the wave froze. Voidspeaker thrust forward his hands as he chanted and the ice was painted black.

The bone shards pierced through the wave but failed to exit the other side.

The Necrosaurus grit his teeth and slammed his staff

onto the ground. Countless magic circles appeared and zombie raptors charged out of them. But the beasts fell to the ground as Agent Tina and the Gray Slayer gunned them down.

"We got these guys, go get him!"

Mr. Dapper Tiger and the Master Elegant Katana took the vanguard, slashing through the raptors that made it through. The Necrosaurus raised his staff at the charging heroes when a cone of fire enveloped him from above.

"DIE!!!!!"

Dragontooth dropped from the sky like a meteor, covered in flames from her own breath. Gentle Gloom floated from where she had first dropped, raising his hand.

"We made it too...."

A green beam shot down from the ghostly hero, colliding with the purple shield with a screeching sound like metal edges grinding together. The Necrosaurus swore and rushed to the side, flying out of the path of the diving dragon. He swung his staff around to send out a wave of bone shards into the air, forcing the Gentle Gloom to cease his assault. He then turned back to the heroes.

Captain Hot Devil was right in front of him.

The Captain gave a mighty uppercut to the shield, a jet of flame sending the Necrosaurus flying into the sky. The Necrosaurus looked up and saw a shadow. Master Mammoth Owl plunged straight into the shield from above, sending the Necrosaurus hurtling towards the ground. He landed with a crash, slightly dazed despite the protection. And then he was blinded by blue light as the Tesla Titan blanketed the shield with lightning.

"EXPERIENCE NOTHINGNESS!"

A black beam struck the shield as Voidspeaker joined the barrage.

"GET SOME GET SOME!"

"Perish."

More bullets pinged against the shield as Agent Tina and

the Gray Slayer opened fire.

Captain Hot Devil and Dragontooth stepped in sync, one swinging his fist and the other letting out her breath.

Two torrents of flame joined together and then hammered the shield.

Aqua Mage lifted her staff high and a column of water rose above. As it arched back down towards the shield the Icy Falcon flew above a blew a gust of cold wind, transforming the water into a rain of icy spears.

A small crack appeared on the shield.

Majestic Moth swung his glowing wings, sparks of light surging forward in a sparkling beam.

Gentle Gloom raised both his hands, firing two beams that converged into one.

The cracks on the shield grew and began to glow...

And then the shield shattered entirely.

The Necrosaurus flew across the dragon's head, bouncing on the boney ground. When he came to a stop he shook his head and looked up.

Londyn stood in his path, grav-cannon at the ready, the air howling as a purple sphere grew in the barrel. The sphere shot forth. The Necrosaurus's eyes widened and he leapt to the side.

But he couldn't.

A pink pterodactyl flew overhead and a blue-yellow flash shot to the ground. Chronolock landed behind him.

And now his robes vibrated in place.

He tried to move his hand, to point it at the girl. He managed to form a magic circle and fire another bone spike.

But Wonder Knight leapt past and grabbed Chronolock, pulling her out of the way.

The Necrosaurus tried to move as his robes ceased vibrating.

But Londyn's shot landed before he could escape.

The air howled as a black hole exploded into being right on the Necrosaurus's chest, a swirling cloud of dust and debris obscuring him from view.

The heroes surrounded the cloud of smoke as the black hole dissipated.

But as the cloud faded, there was no sign of the villain.

And then someone uttered the cursed words.

"Did we get him?"

Just then a sphere of purple light shot forward from behind them. They heard an explosion in the distance and a cry. They turned to look. Vaidehi bounced along the ground, smoke streaming from her robes. The ground beneath the heroes rumbled.

With a mighty crack the trees shattered.

The dragon began to roar.

Before them there was a flash of purple light. The Necrosaurus reappeared, black mist now filling his clothes instead of flesh. His eyes were now glowing red lights.

"I'll SHOW YOU! I'LL SHOW YOU ALL!!! THIS WORLD IS MINE!"

The Necrosaurus slammed his staff into the dragon, rooting the rod in place. Pale purple light surged across the dragon's skin like streaks of lightning. The ground erupted into clawed, bony hands, grasping at the heroes' legs and holding them in place.

"NOW...DIE!!!"

Dozens of purple magic circles filled the air, glowing with the Necrosaurus's arcane power...

The heroes tried to move but the hands held them in place...

The circles flashed as they activated...

They heard a sound like thunder...

And then a sound like glass shattering as the amber gem broke into pieces.

The bony staff exploded into shards as the Necrosaurus's true crucible was destroyed.

The Necrosaurus clutched at his neck with ghostly hands.

"GRAAAAAAAHHHHHH!!!!!"

A hellish scream pierced the air.

A column of purple light enveloped the necromancer and pierced up into the sky.

And once it had faded…

Empty robes dropped to the ground.

Bone hands ceased their grasping. The heroes freed themselves from the restraints. They crowded around the pile of robes.

"Is it…is it over?"

The ground began to shake. Flakes began floating off of the monster below them. Londyn's eyes widened.

"GET OFF THE DRAGON!"

Some heroes took to the sky, their fellows in their arms. Others leapt for the branches that remained, grabbing hold of whatever they could.

The dragon opened its mouth.

It let out a soft cry.

And then…

The dragon faded into dust.

The heroes blinked at the cloud of drifting ashes.

"What happened?"

Londyn's eyes widened.

"I think…we won."

There was a moment of silence as everyone processed her words.

And then the cheers began.

△△△

The sounds of laughter and sighs filled the air. Heroes clasped each other on the back and recounted the battle. Others climbed onto the helicopters and sat back in their seats, silently closing their eyes to rest. Each celebrated in their own way.

Wonder Knight approached a woman sitting strapped in

a seat, a metal device wrapped around her hands.

"Thank you, for your help."

Vaidehi shook her head.

"Please think nothing of it. It is my purpose to serve."

The rest of Aurora Legion popped over.

"So, are you like, a hero now or what? Or do you have to go to jail again?"

"Void!"

"What, you aren't curious?"

Vaidehi smiled and closed her eyes as she shook her head.

"I do not know what I am anymore. But many lives were lost due to my choices. It is only right that I answer when I am asked. Beyond that, I know only that I must atone."

Londyn walked over and put a hand on Voidspeaker's shoulder.

"Alright kids, that's enough."

She shooed Aurora Legion away, and then turned to face Vaidehi. She crossed her arms and frowned.

"This is only the start, you know?"

Vaidehi nodded.

"I would not have it another way. Nothing can replace the lives I took."

Londyn sighed.

"It's a good start, though. Thank you for helping today. The world was saved, thanks to you."

Vaidehi nodded her head. Londyn stepped away and then the helicopter took off. She took a deep breath and tried to forget the paperwork and politics this would entail.

She turned back towards the rowdy heroes. As she watched over them, Captain Hot Devil came up beside her.

"Hey."

"Hello, Captain."

He rubbed the back of his head.

"Listen, um..."

"Don't worry about it."

Londyn cut him off and turned to face him.

"I was a different person back then, and I think so were you. That part of our lives is over now."

She turned back to the heroes.

"I'd rather focus on what lies ahead."

Captain Hot Devil nodded.

"Still, I want to say I'm sorry. Today was...unlike anything I've ever faced. The helplessness, the despair, I've only ever felt that way one other time. I wouldn't wish that feeling on anyone. So...if I did that to you...then I'm sorry. And twice now, you pulled me out of it. So, I also want to say, thank you."

Londyn turned to face him once more, looking into his eyes. His eyes shook but he held her gaze.

After a moment she extended her hand.

"Apology accepted, Captain."

He took her hand.

"Thank you, Director."

She let out a sigh.

"Then, let's return to the League."

Captain Hot Devil nodded and the pair walked towards the chatting heroes. The Majestic Moth gave Agent Tina a thumbs up.

"Tina! Nice shot there, you really are the best!"

"You know it! But that last one wasn't me."

"Wait, really?"

"I'm too good to steal credit!"

The Majestic Moth turned.

"Then Gray Slayer?"

"...not me."

"Wait, then who made that last shot?"

The edges of Londyn's mouth curled up. She didn't know for sure, but she had a real good guess who might have.

△△△

Up on a neighboring mountain overlooking the

battlefield, two figures were lying down. One was facing the battle, holding a sniper rifle that had robotic arms and a computer attached to it. The other figure was leaning against a rock and yawning.

Bob sat up, packed up the rifle, and then placed it in a metal briefcase.

"All that and it still came down to the wire. Couldn't finish it yourselves, couldn't even get him to stay still, could you? Heroes are so annoying."

Xiong Huang yawned.

"You're the one who's annoying. Brought me all the way out here and I didn't even do anything. Seriously, don't bug me if all it takes is one bullet."

Bob raised an eyebrow.

"That was hardly just a bullet."

Indeed, that one bullet was perhaps the most expensive part of the Red Colonel's arsenal. Made from some extraordinarily rare metal Sergei and Kanna had never seen before, and couldn't even identify.

So of course, the Red Colonel used it to make a bullet. Something to neutralize any sort of defenses, mundane or otherwise, just in case he absolutely needed to terminate one particular target.

Kana had made it extra clear she was *extremely* against even using it, much less wasting it, so she had busted out all of the stops. She applied as much robotic and computer assistance as she could, making a rifle that would guarantee a hit. It was an absolute pain to set up, though, not at all practical. The time and effort required to do so meant it effectively couldn't be moved once deployed. Which was why Bob had to pick the best spot and then just wait to get a clear shot.

But it turned out a bit of machine assistance was just what Bob needed after all.

Of course, Bob hadn't exactly tested this bullet against a necromancer who commanded a world-conquering horde all on his own, so he had also brought the ultimate insurance.

Said insurance shrugged.

"Still could've just given it to one of the mortals. Or let me do it in the first place."

Bob raised an eyebrow.

"You want to be a hero?"

"Eh, maybe if I get *really* bored one day. Sounds annoying though, what's with that whole not killing people who deserve it thing?"

Bob heaved a sigh.

"Being annoying doesn't deserve death."

Xiong Huang shrugged.

"Says you."

Bob crossed his arms.

"Entering your field of vision when you're bored also doesn't."

Xiong Huang rolled her eyes.

"You're starting to sound like a hero now."

Bob froze and went completely silent. Xiong Huang started to grin.

"Oh, you felt that one, didn't you?"

Bob stood up without a word and began to walk down a mountain trail. Xiong Huang followed along, her grin now massive.

"Poor Bob, becoming all goody-good. Maybe even heroic? Wait wait, let me say it this time. 'Heroes are so annoying. So let me make sure they always win and that the villainous Xiong Huang doesn't kill anybody.' Did I get it right?"

Bob closed his eyes. Xiong Huang followed behind, poking his cheek as she teased him.

And at that moment, Bob had a thought.

Villains are so annoying.

△△△

"Good evening, all you denizens of the planet Earth. This is GNN and I'm your host, Brendan Baird, bringing you all the updates you need. Today there is only one thing to discuss: the Necrosaurus and the heroes who put an end to his reign of terror."

"Director Londyn Green personally led a task force of the ILS's finest to confront the Necrosaurus in a battle of epic proportions. While GNN is still investigating all the details of this cataclysmic clash, one thing is certain: the ILS proved victorious in the end. The Necrosaurus's hordes left as abruptly as they arrived, fading into dust with the loss of their dark master."

"For now the world scrambles to pick up the pieces of this brief but destructive dark lord. Scattered armies must be reorganized, broken cities must be repaired, and the loss of the world's strategic fuel reserves remains a heavy blow."

"But for now, the world can breathe a collective sigh of relief. And give a warm thank you to Director Green and the heroes she led for the incredible act of bravery. Some have asked if one organization and one woman have too much power, others have questioned the Director's judgment in the face of unprecedented challenges. But I think she's proven today that she and her League are exactly the heroes this world needs. I know I, for one, will sleep well tonight, knowing Director Green and the ILS are out there, watching over us in the dark. This is GNN's Brendan Baird and I wish you all a good night."

AUTHOR'S COMMENTARY: And so ends the Battle of the Jurassic Cemetery and the Necrosaurus's reign of terror. Farewell, my dino-necromancer, you shall be missed! Anyways! What was the point of all this? What comes next for Bob, Londyn, and the ILS? Tune in next time, to find out!

CHAPTER 19 - TO CHANGE THE WORLD

With that, the Necrosaurus's reign of terror came to a close. The supervillain had taken the world by storm…but for all the chaos he spread his hordes did surprisingly little damage. The casualties were mostly limited to the armed forces that resisted on the first day, but these had been allowed to retreat. In fact, since most militaries don't station their main forces right in the middle of crowded cities, even the armies of the world remained mostly intact. Casualties among the civilian populations were even lower, thankfully.

The world had managed to escape mostly unscathed.

But that is not to say that life went back to normal.

It turned out the greatest damage the Necrosaurus did was draining the world's fuel supplies, consuming the stock of available oil to create his undead hordes. And since the Destroyer of Ulsan, as Vaidehi Dayal was now known, had destroyed the world's largest oil refineries right beforehand, deliveries of new oil had ground to a halt as well. The world entered into a massive energy crisis and supply lines shut down across the globe.

But then, in a miraculous twist of fate, someone presented a solution almost immediately…

ΔΔΔ

"Good afternoon all you citizens of the planet Earth! This is GNN and I'm your host, Brendan Baird. Today we're talking about the only thing on anyone's mind: the supergenius

Kanna Tanifuji and her Tanifuji-Oscillator Engine."

"The CEO and lead inventor of the famed Tanifuji Incorporated announced the engine just a few months ago. The device works by resonating with the geothermal movements of the Earth's own core, producing practically limitless clean energy! And not a moment too soon! The loss of several major refineries at the hands of the Order of Harmony disrupted fuel supplies across the globe and world governments were unable to respond after having their reserves drained by the dastardly Necrosaurus. In fact, the lack of fuel impeded both the efforts to repair the damage done by the Necrosaurus and to rebuild the refineries themselves, leaving the world at a loss on how to move forward."

"Miss Tanifuji's designs proved powerful, cost-efficient, and scalable, all without requiring elaborate infrastructure to implement. As such, governments, companies, and consumers around the globe have all rushed to embrace the Tanifuji-Oscillator Engine. Some are calling it the biggest technological revolution since the steam engine. Many are already calling for Miss Tanifuji to be nominated for a Nobel Prize for this grand contribution to humanity."

"Some critics say the device is too good to be true. They point out accusations that Tanifuji Inc. may have connections to supervillains, and wonder if there are some sort of catch with this wonder device. Miss Tanifuji herself rarely steps into the public view and some claim her silence is a sign of subversion. But I, for one, will sleep soundly tonight, under the warm light for all mankind granted to us by Miss Tanifuji."

"Later tonight, GNN goes to the experts to explore the inner workings of this incredible device. We'll be back after a short message from our sponsors."

$$\triangle\triangle\triangle$$

Bob shut off the television. He heaved a sigh.

He had done it.

Kanna had taken the blueprints of the Herald of Ashes' Geo-Oscillator Bomb and repurposed the weapon into a power source. An almost magical power source that could produce practically endless, fuelless, and clean energy at a dirt-cheap cost. A device that could revolutionize the world economy, drop energy and production costs across the globe, and provide a permanently sustainable future. A warm light for all mankind indeed, as energy might now become the cheapest resource for humanity.

Which, of course, meant it was a huge threat to all existing energy industries, many of which had a great deal of financial and political resources at their disposal. There were entire countries that stood to lose…and so entire countries that might act in opposition.

So he had created a crisis that would force immediate adoption of the device, without any caveats.

He had destroyed the power of the oil industry all in one go, disrupting its viability in the short term. Every country in the world was then forced to choose: adopt the Tanifuji-Oscillator Engine and get things back online overnight, or let their economy grind to a halt and their cities remain damaged until the refineries were rebuilt? All the while falling behind any country that made the other choice?

Or worse, what if a nation that adopted the new power source decided to invade while other countries' militaries remained fuelless and immobile?

After the Necrosaurus held the entire world by the throat, which nation would then choose to remain helpless and stagnant, even for a short period of time?

Almost no amount of bribery or political lobbying could overcome the strategic calculus of the current scenario. At the very least, every sane country in the world wanted its military back up and running as soon as possible, and the logistical advantages of the Tanifuji-Oscillator became immediately apparent once the first vehicles were converted.

And once the corporations saw tanks that never ran out of fuel, they were all too eager to bring those advantages to the private sector. Tanifuji Inc. became perhaps the most important company in the world practically overnight.

And so Bob changed the course of humanity, blowing away any vested interests that might try to interfere.

And as a side benefit, the reputations of Londyn and the ILS had skyrocketed. They had saved the world several times in very short order, including against a villain that had brought all the armies and leaders of Earth to their knees. The ILS was now truly *the* name in the game for heroes. Londyn had become untouchable, every tongue on the planet now sang her praises.

Bob took a deep breath.

But what did it cost?

Thousands of people had perished.

Cities around the world were devastated.

Many lives were broken.

He held his head as remembered the scenes of Ulsan.

As he heard the Sentinel of Harmony's wails.

As he saw the devastation even one day of the Necrosaurus's hordes had wrought.

And this had been the *best* case.

One slip up, one mistake, one miscalculation and things could have been *much* worse. The casualties could have been in the *millions*. Or Londyn, Linda, and the ILS might have perished, all Bob had worked to build and many of his friends gone in a single moment.

So now, after it all was done, Bob had to ask...

Was it worth it?

Did he really need to go this far?

Would the world have refused to embrace the Tanifuji-Oscillator Engine on its own?

Could the fossil fuel industry truly have put a stop to it?

Should he have sat back, let things take their course?

Could he have done something else to push it through, something far less drastic and destructive?

Did he truly have the world's best interests in mind when he made this choice?

But Bob shook his head.

He didn't have an answer for that. He could speculate one way or another, but at the end of the day, the deed was done. The lives had been spent and the future was now secure. Later generations would decide for themselves if all this was worth the cost. He would just have to live with the consequences of his choices, good and bad.

All he could do now…was acknowledge the sheer amount of power at his command. And the risks that came with that. The number of lives he could ruin by design…or by mistake.

All he could do now…was try not to lose his humanity as he sought to guide the world.

All he could do now…was try to be better next time.

Because as much as he hoped otherwise…he had a feeling that his work was not yet done.

△△△

"GNN goes to the experts to explore the inner workings of this incredible device. We'll be back after a short message from our sponsors."

Back in the Bureau of Special Investigations, Agent Wilson stared at the television, rubbing his chin. He turned to look at the paper in his hand and heaved a sigh.

Steve walked over, coffee in hand.

"Why the long face, Wilson?"

Agent Wilson handed him the paper.

"Hm, redacted, classified, redacted, redacted, and redacted. Thrilling read, Wilson. Weren't you CIA? Don't you have some sort of un-redactor glasses or something?"

Agent Wilson shook his head.

"Only the popular agents get those."

"What are you looking at anyways?"

"The Ulsan case."

"This again? Give it up, BSI's never going to touch that one, Wilson."

"I know, but it's strange."

"What is?"

"That case seemed very straightforward and was already highly public. So why are they pulling details now? It makes no sense."

Steve shrugged again.

"Maybe she's got a friend. Or maybe your CIA buddies cut a deal, got her on a suicide squad or something."

"That's just a rumor."

"You sure?"

Wilson glanced away.

"...maybe."

Steven grinned at him.

"For the CIA that means yes."

"...let's just do our jobs."

Steve shrugged again.

"I'll get right to it. I'm sure there's another urgent request to escort a geriatric super across the street. Or maybe another floating kitten stuck in a tree."

Wilson shrugged

"The kitten was pretty cute though."

Steve frowned.

"You didn't get scratched."

"Must be the scary face."

"Ouch. That hurts, Wilson."

Agent Wilson turned to the papers. He sighed and began to put them away. Ulsan. Freeport. The Order of Harmony. The Necrosaurus's reign of terror. No connection. No relation. Just random, isolated incidents.

Yet...they had added up to create a crisis everyone would have thought unthinkable before it happened. A crisis that was then almost immediately resolved by a solution that had *already been in the works*. A turn of events that had created extraordinarily vast profits for the winners and utter devastation for the losers. A massive societal, economic, and technological upheaval conducted almost overnight.

As if it had been planned.

Agent Wilson rubbed his chin as he looked over the redacted report once again...

> AUTHOR'S COMMENTARY: And so concludes the Bob vs. Big Oil arc. Did you know I originally thought this was going to be a filler arc? Just a little taste of Bob's schemery, a little expansion of a line from the OG prompt response, a little break before something more in depth. Funny how things go. Well, anyways! What will Bob do next, now that he's changed the world? Is Agent Wilson imagining things...or has he stumbled upon something big? Tune in next time, to find out!

CHAPTER 20 – AND WHICH DESIRES WILL YOU GIVE ME?

The loading dock of a warehouse was lit by the midday sun from its open garage door. Everywhere men ran and scrambled. Boxes were thrown haphazardly into the backs of pickup trucks and the trunks of sedans. Dollar bills were stuffed into briefcases and thrown into the backseats of cars. Men carrying pistols and SMGs hopped into the trucks and cars, driving off without even buckling their seat belts.

"GO GO GO! Move it! Move it!"

One man ran towards the last truck. A loud crash rang out from the door at the other end of the warehouse.

"Come on Juan!"

"Hurry up! Hurry up!"

"W-Wait for me!"

The doors slammed open.

"GO GO GO!"

The truck began to move.

"WAIT!"

Juan leapt through the air.

He grabbed onto the back of the truck.

The truck drove off.

But then the backdoor fell open.

Juan lost his grip and tumbled to the ground, rolling several times through the courtyard outside of the garage.

The truck was gone.

Juan spit dirt out of his mouth.

He heard footsteps. He turned his head.

Sweat drenched his forehead. He let out a squeal and tried to run.

He stumbled back to the ground.

The footsteps continued to approach.

He trembled, sliding back along the ground, pushing with his arms.

"W-Wait! P-Please!"

His back hit the perimeter wall of the compound. He held up a trembling hand in front of his face.

"P-Please! Have mercy, *Señor* Falcon!"

Sharp ice flew through the air and landed with a thud.

△△△

"Good evening, all you denizens of the planet Earth. This is GNN and I'm your host, Brendan Baird, bringing you all the updates you need. Tonight we're here to discuss the International League of Superheroes and their new and dramatic growth. Let's go to GNN's super-analysts, Lacey Cook and Liam Reynolds. Lacey, Liam, how are you doing tonight?"

"I'm doing great, Brendan."

"Same here."

"Glad to hear that, now let's get to it. Lacey, Liam, what are your thoughts on the ILS?"

"It's wonderful, Brendan. Director Green is doing great things for the world."

"I agree, it's great to see the heroes getting the support they need and the recognition they deserve."

"I think we all can agree that the ILS has made the world a safer place. Now folks, ever since the Battle of the Jurassic Cemetery, the ILS has undergone an incredible expansion. Applicants flood into branch offices in nearly every major city on the planet. What is your opinion on these things?"

"I think it's great and necessary. The more resources the ILS has, the better heroes are going to do."

"Lacey, do you agree?"

"For the most part, Brendan, but I do have some concerns."

"Oh?"

"The world is changing faster than anyone ever predicted, and our laws and societies haven't managed to catch up. The ILS is bridging that gap but I'm worried this is all too much for one organization and one woman to bear. And I'm also concerned that one individual is making all the decisions right now."

"Come on Lacey, if there's anyone who has proved themselves up to the task, it's Director Green."

"Liam, you know there's no one I trust more than Director Green. But it's the principle of the matter. Our society needs to catch up, it needs to stay involved. We need to have discourse, participation. We can't just leave everything to Director Green, that's just not how society works."

"Lacey, would you have any ideas on what that might look like?"

"I want to see the ILS interact with the structures and systems of our world, whether that's individual governments or a multilateral organization. I want to see transparent discussions on policies, procedures, and official lines of communication. If the people are to have a voice, then they need to know what's being discussed. And if we can set up some concrete structures and policies, then Director Green doesn't need to shoulder every emergency on her own. I mean look at this latest crisis. That was nothing short of a war. Yet where were our leaders? Where were our armies? Did they refuse to act, leaving everything to Director Green? Or did the ILS head out without them? And if they did, was it because they couldn't wait, or because they didn't speak in the first place?"

"That's not really fair, Lacey. Are you suggesting Director

Green should have waited? If anything I bet it was the politicians that dragged their feet."

"That's my point though, Liam, we can only speculate what happened. We don't actually know, and now we never will. We don't know what discussions took place or even *if* discussions took place. The ILS ended up acting alone and we don't know why. And I don't think that should be the case going forward."

"Would you suggest the ILS slow down its growth? Perhaps restrict its mandate to a more narrow and specific focus?"

"Not at all, Brendan, the world needs the ILS, that much is clear. And I think the ILS should be as big as it needs to be to do its job, both in manpower and mandate. But I do think we need to clarify what exactly that job is, where the lines should be drawn, and what jobs our society and government should be doing instead."

"Liam, what are your thoughts?"

"I partially agree that the ILS should be more involved in society, but I want to see it the other way around."

"What do you mean by that, Liam?"

"I want to see the ILS receive the authority it's due. Vest Director Green and the heroes with official powers corresponding to the ILS's own internal ranks. Let them make arrests, give them authority to call in additional assets when necessary and coordinate responders. The ILS gets the job done, and they do it well. Let's adapt society to the ILS instead of chaining the ILS to society."

"That's a lot of power for a single, private organization to have, Liam."

"Look Lacey, these days there are kids out there that can destroy tanks with their bare hands. We need the ILS, and we need to avoid constraining them with red tape that no longer conforms to our reality. Let the legal authority match what's already happening on the ground. And if there's anyone who can be trusted with power, it's Director Green."

"But what happens when it's not Director Green in charge anymore?"

"I'm not worried."

"Why not?"

"Because it's the International League of *Superheroes*, so I'm confident that even when Director Green steps down one day, there will be someone there qualified to fill her shoes."

"Well, if there's one thing we all can agree on, it's that the ILS is here to stay. In our society, in our streets, and even in our hearts. We'll continue the discussion on the ILS expansion and how even you at home can get involved after a short message from our sponsors."

△△△

Bob rubbed his chin as he watched the television. He stood up from his seat, walking over to the window with a steaming cup in hand.

It seemed he was suffering from success.

The ILS had grown beyond his wildest expectations. He underestimated the fear and the chaos his plans would spread. Extremists could destroy cities in an instant, a madman could assault the entire world with massive armies out of nowhere. In a world like that, the people were desperate for help, for security, for control.

So it was only natural they latched onto the people fighting back.

The peoples' feelings for the ILS had gone beyond respect or admiration. They were bordering on worship at this point. In the minds of the people, the ILS and Director Green could do no wrong. Londyn could declare herself queen of the world tomorrow and the people would applaud her coronation.

And that was a problem.

Now Bob wanted the ILS to be big, dominant even. And he trusted Londyn with that power and responsibility. She was a former minion once on the receiving end, so she had personal reasons not to let the heroes get out of line. And even if the power and responsibility corrupted her one day, he had Linda right by her side to keep an eye on her, and steer her back on course if necessary.

The problem was that if Londyn and the ILS were untouchable, then their heroes were as well. So as far as the public was concerned, the heroes of the ILS could also do no wrong. And so those heroes would not be held accountable to anyone but Londyn.

And Bob had learned himself that with great power comes great responsibility.

Not because that power comes with any specific obligations…but because every choice made with power comes with greater consequences. He himself had made a choice that seemed good to him at the time and then thousands of people died as a result. In fact, *every* choice he made regarding EL Bank applicants and the ILS could end with massive casualties. He could be said to have murdered thousands, having intentionally taken choices that he knew would end people's lives.

So letting Londyn and the ILS have unlimited power and thus unlimited responsibility was unwise.

Heroes innately had great power. They could end lives and cause mass devastation with even casual applications of their abilities. But what the people didn't realize is that this power did not come with greater wisdom or insight. Heroes were just normal people like everyone else at the end of the day. They made mistakes, they failed, they had errors in judgment. They changed, they got upset, or tired, or angry. They had agendas…and vendettas. They could even break, decide one day that they had enough.

Just like any average person.

But unlike the average person, when that happened to a hero, people could get hurt. A *lot* of people.

So the heroes needed to be restrained, grounded. The

world needed to acknowledge what a hero truly was and the limitations they had.

Because if not...

Well, another incident like the Battle of Kayserling Tower would be inevitable.

It was just then that Bob got a call from Miguel, his associate across the border. It seemed there was a situation brewing down in Mexico...

△△△

On a hot day in Mexico, a group of people stood outside their city's main government building. They were chanting and cheering, waving signs about. Written on their signs were slogans such as 'Stop the killing!' and 'End Corruption'! A reporter stood in front of the crowd, holding her mic out to a teenage girl who had a sign in hand.

"Can you tell me why you are out here today?"

The girl nodded. She had tanned skin with brown hair and brown eyes.

"Because our country has been held hostage for too long! And I am not content to let Icy Falcon fight our battle alone."

"And who are you fighting against?"

The girl narrowed her eyes.

"Who else? The cartels, the drug lords, those men who think they can do whatever they please to whoever they want."

"And what do you hope to accomplish here?"

"To call on our leaders, our politicians, to take a stand. For all of Mexico to take a stand! We cannot allow these men to dictate the future of our country any longer! All across the world, heroes are rising up to throw down villains and killers. So will we be content to let *these* villains and killers run our country? Will we let the Hero of Mexico fight his battles alone? I say no! And so I will do everything I can to fight back, to take back our country!"

With that, the crowd started cheering along with her. The reporter nodded and turned back to the camera, reporting on the protests.

And a nondescript man in sunglasses rubbed his chin as he watched from across the street.

△△△

Constanza Rubio heaved a sigh as she closed the door behind her, wiping the sweat off her brow.

Another day, another protest.

And another day being ignored by all the people that mattered.

She grit her teeth and clenched her fists.

And another day that those *monsters* would continue running amok through the streets, killing whoever they pleased. The police and the politicians would continue to do nothing, continue to take the bribes and then shake down the victims for more.

And innocent people would continue to suffer.

Just like her parents.

She closed her eyes and shook her head.

That's why she needed to fight. That was why she needed to do everything that she could.

But honestly, what did that amount to?

She had no power to take on the cartels directly. Even if she did, what would she accomplish but to expand the violence? Stronger people than her had tried to end this war with force. The government had tried. The army had tried. The *gringos* had tried.

All they achieved was more dead bodies.

And that was why Icy Falcon was the Hero of Mexico. He was the only one who could fight the cartels without sinking to their level. The only one who could put them behind bars. The only one who could make a difference without growing the body count. The only one who could change the terms of the game and bring *real* justice.

The only one who could make their country safer.

But he was alone. And even he could not win a war alone.

Yes, he had the ILS now, but they were only in the superhero business. Supervillains and world-ending threats only. So what about the cartels? The cartels were Mexico's business. And as long as the cartels had no supers, it would stay that way. Icy Falcon could not count on them to fight his war at home.

Icy Falcon needed help.

And Constanza wanted to provide it, more than anything.

But she was just a young girl.

So what could she do but continue to shout at the walls and pray those corrupt jerks would listen? To shout at the people and watch as they ducked their heads and hurried along? To pray for Icy Falcon's success alone in her room, helpless to do anything more?

She held her eyes shut, but could still feel tears growing within them.

It was at that moment that the doorbell rang. Constanza jumped slightly and blinked, shocked out of her thoughts. She shook her head and made her way to the door.

"Coming, coming."

She opened the door to find a delivery driver waiting behind it.

"Constanza Rubio?"

She blinked.

"Um, yes? That's me, can I help you?"

The delivery driver nodded and took out a clipboard and a pen.

"Package for you, please sign here."

Constanza tilted her head.

"Package? From who?"

The driver shrugged.

"Please sign here."

Constanza blinked but took the pen and clipboard and

looked it over. It was a normal package delivery form by all accounts. She decided to sign.

The driver nodded and took the clipboard, and then handed her a small package. He then turned and left without another word.

Constanza just stood watching him leave, then looked down at the package. It had her name and address on it, but no information about a sender or a return address. She shrugged and took it over to the table.

There was a small note card taped to the package, folded in half. She pulled it off and unfolded it.

It read 'A gift from a supporter: the power to change'. Constanza tilted her head at that.

"Well...let's see what this is all about."

She slowly unwrapped the package and gasped.

It was a flower.

The most beautiful flower she had ever seen.

It looked like a rose, only pale blue. It seemed almost transparent, and shimmered as light reflected off the petals. A foggy mist appeared around it, cooling the air nearby.

She felt as if it drew her in. She reached out her hand, more by instinct than thought.

Her finger touched the petal.

And then her vision went white.

△△△

"Good afternoon, all you citizens of the planet Earth! This is GNN and I'm your host, Brendan Baird, bringing global updates for global viewers. Today we have a most disturbing tale: a mystery murder in Mexico! A man was found dead in the courtyard of a warehouse, with no sign of the killer! Even more ominous, authorities did not find a weapon and could not identify the nature of his wounds, or what caused them."

"The warehouse was suspected to have connections with drug cartels, and so the Mexican authorities are treating this as another instance of cartel violence. But GNN's own investigations found little sign that the warehouse was assaulted by a rival cartel. Eyewitnesses did not see anyone enter the warehouse, only the occupants fleeing in a panic, so our analysts say it is too early to identify a suspect."

"What do you think folks, is this just another bloody page in the tragedy of drug violence? Or is this the sign of a terrifying new player? Stay with us as GNN consults the experts, to find out! Now for a quick word from our sponsors."

△△△

A teenage boy walked down into an empty alleyway. He had short brown hair, lighter tanned skin, and brown eyes. He was of average build for a boy his age, wearing a simple t-shirt and shorts.

This was Antonio Miralles, Constanza Rubio's childhood friend and current roommate.

He was just on his way back from a part-time job when someone stepped into the alley in front of him.

Antonio tensed. The figure wore jeans and a hoodie, their hood pulled up despite the heat. Sunglasses and a mask hid their face as they approached the boy. Antonio grimaced.

"W-Who are you?"

And then he heard a girl's voice reply.

"Antonio, it's me."

His eyes widened.

"Constanza? What's going on? What's with the getup?"

Constanza held up a gloved finger to the mask and whispered to him.

"There's...something I have to show you."

Constanza glanced back over her shoulder at the entrance to the alley, then removed her sunglasses and mask.

Antonio gaped.

"Whoa! What happened to your hair?! And your eyes?!"

"Shhh! Keep it down, Antonio!"

Her hair was now pure white and her eyes a pale blue. Antonio blinked.

"Just, what happened?"

"I don't know! I got this weird flower in the mail and..."

Antonio stared at her with narrowed eyes.

"Constanza..."

She bopped his head with a gloved fist.

"You're a jerk, Antonio! You KNOW I would never! I've never seen this flower before and all I did was touch it!"

Antonio nodded. Constanza had more reasons to hate narcotics than most. She had lost her parents at a young age, bystanders in the wrong place at the wrong time. Antonio's family had taken the girl in...but Constanza had never forgotten or forgiven that incident. If she had even the slightest hint she was handed a narcotic, she would have burned it.

So this had to be something else.

Besides, he didn't know of any drugs that could change eyes from brown to blue.

"Then what happened?"

"I don't know! There was a flash of light and then I was lying on the floor and the flower was gone! And when I looked in the mirror I saw this!"

Antonio shrugged, tilting his head.

"I mean, that's really weird, but I don't see why you're raising all this fuss. Just tell people you dyed your hair. Eyes will be harder but you can just say it's contacts or something."

Constanza smirked at him, and then silently removed one of her gloves. She placed her hand on the nearby wall. Antonio's eyes widened.

Ice crystals started to grow along the wall.

"Do you get it now?"

Antonio stammered.

"Constanza...you're..."

She grinned at him.

"I'm a super now."

Antonio's mouth gaped open.

"Wow...that's..."

Constanza looked at the frost at the wall and then at her hand.

Her eyes narrowed.

"I'm like Icy Falcon now..."

Those words, barely a whisper, shook Antonio out of his stupor.

His eyes started to tremble as he saw Constanza smile.

He knew that look.

And he knew her.

So he knew exactly what she was thinking.

"Constanza...just wait a moment, ok? Let's think carefully about what to do next."

She clenched her hand into a fist.

"Oh, I'm thinking. Just imagine, all the things I could do now..."

Antonio gulped. That's exactly what he was afraid of. His mind raced.

"Well, what can you do now, exactly?"

Constanza paused and blinked.

"Hm? What do you mean?"

Antonio nodded and crossed his arms, jumping on the chance.

"You made some frost, yes, but do you know what you're actually capable of?"

She looked at him for a moment before looking down.

"Oh...um...I came straight here."

Antonio nodded.

"Well then, you should at least test things out for yourself, BEFORE you do anything, right?"

Constanza nodded.

"Yeah, that's right."

She covered her hair and face again, and then started

walking out of the alley.

"Wait, where are you going, Constanza?"

"What do you mean, we just talked about it? I'm going to go test my powers!"

Antonio jumped.

"Wait, right now?!"

"Um, yeah? Why not?"

"That's…"

Antonio heaved a sigh and shook his head. There was no helping it now.

All he could do was hope Constanza would be reasonable.

△△△

Antonio and Constanza stood in the middle of an empty warehouse. There were holes in the roof, and rust grew along the metal panels. Some of the windows were shattered, and the boxes inside had black and green streaks along their sides.

Antonio heaved a sigh and crossed his arms. Well, time to see what they were dealing with.

Constanza pulled down her hood, mask, and glasses, then removed her gloves. She held out her hand, fingers open and palm facing forward.

Antonio raised an eyebrow.

"Um, is something supposed to happen?"

Constanza pulled her hand back and then pushed it forward once more. She tried it three quick times in succession. She tried with both arms, and then waved her hands around while holding her arms out.

"Um, is that the right way to do it?"

She frowned.

"I don't know! I've never had superpowers before!"

Antonio rubbed his chin and tilted his head for a second.

"Maybe it's a different motion? Try something different?"

Constanza nodded. She curled her hand into a fist and

swung it forward.

Nothing happened.

So Constanza tried everything she could think of. Jabs, swings, uppercuts, haymakers. Front kicks, roundhouse kicks, back kicks, leaping kicks. Baseball throws. Basketball throws. Soccer kicks. Finger guns. Jumping jacks. Twirls. Pirouettes.

Antonio heaved a sigh of relief.

If all she had was a lower body temperature, then he wouldn't have to convince her at all.

Constanza slouched over, breathing heavily.

"How about pushups? Situps? Squats? A ten kilometer run?"

She just glared at him. Antonio waved his hands in front of him.

"Ok, ok, no more motions. Maybe it's voice activated?"

"What should I say?"

"How should I know? Just say whatever comes to mind!"

Constanza crossed her arms.

"You're no help."

Antonio just shrugged.

"You're the one who doesn't know how to use her own powers."

"I just got them!"

"Well maybe try think of something related to them?"

"...ok."

Constanza took a deep breath and closed her eyes. Antonio just watched her think in silence.

Suddenly Constanza's eyes shot open.

Antonio watched her closely, leaning forward a bit. He was curious as to what she had come up with.

She pulled her right arm back by her side, curling her fingers into a fist. She brought up her arm behind her, elbow angled forward so her fist was parallel to the ground. She knelt down, right knee on the ground, left knee at a ninety degree angle. She began to shake her fist, curling her arm up.

"Falcooooon...PUNCH!"

She pushed off with her right leg, swinging her body and thrusting her fist forward with all her might.

Nothing happened.

There was a moment of silence.

Antonio started to grin.

He was never more thankful for that console his father sent them than in that moment.

Constanza slowly covered her bright red face with both her hands.

"You..."

"Don't say anything."

"So that..."

"Don't. Say. Anything."

Antonio just chuckled. A high-pitched whine eeked out of Constanza.

A few minutes later...

"FREEZE! Ice, on! Winter has come! Ice, activate! Let it go! Cold! Cool down! Frost! Blizzard! Blizzaga! Cone of cold! Falcon ice!"

Antonio leaned back against a wall while Constanza knelt in a corner, her face hidden behind her hands.

He heaved one last sigh of relief. It seemed Constanza wouldn't run off to fight the cartels after all. He stood up and walked over to her.

"Let's go home for today, Constanza."

She didn't respond.

"Hey, you can try again tomorrow, yeah?"

"...you go ahead."

"Constanza..."

A small piece of ice dropped against the ground...from her face. Antonio froze.

"...are you alright?"

She buried her head in her arms with her legs pulled to her chest.

"...I'm sorry. It's just...each and every day, I try and I try.

Each and every day, I shout and I beg. And each and every day, nothing ever happens. Those jerks in the government don't care. They'll never listen to us. And the real monsters? I call them out in the streets and they don't even care enough to stop me. I mean nothing to them. I can't do a single thing that matters."

Antonio hung his head. Right, the protest was today. Constanza...never felt great after those.

"So...when it happened...I thought maybe I could do something. Maybe I could actually make a difference for once. So I got my hopes up. But...I still can't do anything. At all. I got these powers and I can't even use them! I'm...I'm..."

Antonio took a deep breath.

He had lost family too, though not to the violence. His mother fell ill a few years ago. And his father was a migrant worker, away across the border trying to keep them afloat. He knew what loss and loneliness felt like.

And so he was terrified that he might lose Constanza one day, with her foolish crusade. He hated the idea of her being in harm's way, of her attracting real attention from the cartels one day.

But he also hated when she felt hopeless like this. When all the loss and injustice she had faced came crashing down all at once and he couldn't do a thing about it.

But today...maybe he could. If he was willing to take the risk.

So he rubbed his chin and thought as hard as he could. And then he took a deep breath, trying to calm his beating heart.

Well...he'd see what he could do and what she could do. If it turns out she *could* do something, he could always try to talk her down later. Maybe convince her to join the ILS instead of running off into the streets?

But first things first.

"Have you felt anything different since it happened?"

Constanza paused, and glanced up at him.

"Huh?"

"Like, does anything feel different? About your body? Or inside you? Maybe you should focus on that?"

Constanza dropped her hands and tilted her head. She felt...cooler? Maybe? She wasn't sure, so she sat there for a moment. She took a deep breath and closed her eyes.

She focused inward on her body. She focused on her legs, then her waist. Then her stomach, then her torso. Up to her arms, and then to the top of her head. She searched for anything that felt different, anything out of place.

And then she felt something.

She felt it more with her heart than her body. More out of instinct than knowledge. She didn't know what it was. She couldn't even describe it. But somehow, she knew it was there, flowing through her. Almost like a cool mist, a foggy cloud idling within her.

She reached out to the cloud, focusing on its location in her body. It dispersed. She frowned, and searched once more and found it again. She jumped at it. It dispersed again. She found it once more, in her stomach this time. This time, she reached out slowly, gently.

She felt something connect. The cloud jumped and then sat still.

As if it was waiting.

Slowly, ever so slowly, she encouraged the cloud to move. From the pit of her stomach up to her chest, from her chest to her shoulder, then down her arms to the tips of her fingers.

She slowly raised her hand, fingers held out and forward.

The cloud shot forward from her fingers...

And out into the air.

"Whoa!"

Constanza opened her eyes. A cone of fog drifted in front of her, passing mere inches from where Antonio stood. He rubbed his arms while walking over to her, his teeth clattering.

"A-A little warning next time?!"

"S-Sorry."

The two just stared at each other for a moment.

Constanza's eyes widened.

Moisture built in her eyes and a smile grew on her face.

She leapt up and wrapped Antonio in a hug as she cheered.

Antonio stood completely still for a moment before smiling wryly. He heaved a sigh as he patted her on the back.

It looked like he had a lot of convincing to do after all. But for now…he would let himself be happy for her.

△△△

Bob stood on the roof of a building near the warehouse. He had a pair of binoculars in his hand and a mask on his face.

He watched as foggy clouds blasted around and streaks of blue and white appeared on floors and crates. He rubbed his chin. And then he heaved a sigh.

He pulled out his phone and made a call.

"Miguel."

"Bob! It's good to hear from you. Any progress on your plan?"

"Maybe. But I have a favor to ask."

"Of course! Anything for you, Bob."

After the conversation Bob hung up the phone. He put away both the phone and the binoculars and started to walk away.

His face was curled into a frown.

If he was honest, he didn't like this plan.

But events were forcing his hand.

He heaved another sigh.

"Heroes are so…annoying."

AUTHOR'S COMMENTARY: ...I couldn't resist. And neither could Constanza. I mean, can you even have a hero named Falcon and NOT have a Falcon Punch at some point? Anyways! Will Constanza learn to use her new powers? Can she endure the new addition to her dark history? Will she master the Falcon Punch? And what is Bob planning now? Tune in next time, to find out!

CHAPTER 21 - A HERO'S DEBUT

Constanza stood in the warehouse once more and took a deep breath. She felt her power stir within her once again. She pulled on it, willing it to grow stronger.

Then she thrust her left hand forward, firing a blast of cold fog.

And then she repeated the motion with her right hand.

And then again with her left.

One after another, cones of frost surged from her hand, blowing away tin cans set up on a box.

She exhaled her breath and shivered, her breath condensing into fog.

She looked up.

All the cans had been blown across the warehouse and the box was now covered in frost.

She grinned and clenched her fist.

She was making progress.

She was no Icy Falcon just yet…but she wouldn't want to be on the receiving end of one of those cones.

She was no longer defenseless.

She was no longer helpless.

Which meant that soon…she would no longer be stuck shouting uselessly at uncaring and corrupt politicians.

Soon…she would have the power to change things, all on her own.

She gripped her fist tighter.

Soon…she could create a country where little girls didn't lose their parents.

△△△

A bit later Constanza was resting at home, watching the television as she ate something. Antonio came through the door, holding a stack of papers in his hand. Constanza raised an eyebrow.

"Hi Antonio, what've you got there?"

Antonio nodded and walked over to her.

"Hey Constanza, I just stopped by the new ILS branch office."

Constanza frowned. She put down her food and crossed her arms.

"This again, Antonio? I already told you, I'm not applying for the ILS."

Antonio heaved a sigh.

"Constanza, just listen, ok? Look, the ILS is starting a training program for new heroes. They can help you learn to use these powers, get you some support. You can even get paid for it, look!"

Constanza shook her head.

"I'm not interested in going to America and fighting supervillains, Antonio."

Antonio frowned.

"Neither is Icy Falcon, and he's a part of the ILS. You don't have to go anywhere, Constanza."

"You're right. I don't."

Antonio clenched his teeth.

"Why are you so against it, Constanza? You could do a lot of good there!"

She stood up and faced him, eye to eye.

"Because the ILS is up there, in the sky, facing down the big bads that threaten the entire world. But they don't care about what's happening down here, Antonio. They don't care about drugs and cartels. My place is right here, down in Mexico, fighting Mexico's real villains. I can't do that up there with the *gringos*."

"You're going to get yourself killed, Constanza! At least go learn *how* to fight! The ILS can teach you that."

Constanza glared at him.

"Admit it, you're just trying to keep me away. You're trying to stop me."

Antonio shouted back at her.

"I'm trying to *save* you, Constanza! Just because you can freeze a room now doesn't mean you're ready to take on the cartels! We both know what they're capable of!"

Constanza went dead silent, clenching her fists. Antonio froze, and then lowered his head.

"I'm sorry...I didn't mean..."

"...that's why, Antonio. It's *because* I know exactly what they're capable of, what they're *already doing*, that I refuse to let it go on any longer."

Antonio went silent as she turned away from him. After standing there for a moment, finally he heaved a sigh. He spoke in a soft voice.

"...I just...I don't want to lose you too, Constanza."

She didn't respond...but her face softened. She took a deep breath.

And then she paused.

After a second Antonio turned to look in the direction she was facing, at the television.

A super was rampaging through their local marketplace.

He froze...and then his eyes widened as he turned back to Constanza.

"Constanza, I know what you're thinking."

She rushed to her desk, grabbing a handmade mask. Antonio rushed after her as she stepped towards the door.

"Well, you wanted me to fight supervillains, right Antonio?"

"Constanza, wait!"

△△△

Screams filled the air as people rushed from the marketplace. Stands were knocked over, fruits rolled along the floor, and pieces of meat flew through the air.

In the center was a massive, obese man, a giant boulder of flesh. He had on a white apron with red and orange stains all over with a sailor hat far too small for his massive head. He laughed as he swung and hacked at pieces of meat with a rusty butcher's knife.

"Muahahahahaha! All your meat belongs to me! For I am...Captain Repulsive Butcher!"

Two teens hid in the shadow of a stall further down, conversing in hushed whispers.

"Constanza, wait! Just, just think about this for a moment."

Constanza's eyes narrowed.

"I've thought about it. I'm going, Antonio. I'm not going to let anyone terrorize our country, not anymore."

"There are better ways to start than taking on a super!"

But Constanza wasn't listening anymore. She took one final breath and then stepped out into the open, putting on a light blue mask over her eyes.

Captain Repulsive Butcher halted his rampage and turned his head towards the quiet footsteps approaching.

"Who the heck are you?"

She lifted her hand and pointed at the man, who suddenly seemed much larger than before. She winced as her arm trembled, adrenaline coursing through her.

"S-Sto...ouch..."

She bit her lip.

She held her lip for a second and then took a deep breath.

"S-Stop your criminal ways, evildoer! Or the I-Icy Swallow will put you on i-ice!"

Yes, Constanza had no intention of joining the ILS...but

not because she disagreed with their methods. In fact, that was the point for Constanza. She always said she wanted justice, not vengeance. She wanted to end drug violence, not add to it.

That was why she looked up to Icy Falcon.

That was why she, too, wanted to become a hero for Mexico.

Which is also how she chose her name.

And what was the response?

A moment of silence.

And then Captain Repulsive Butcher clutched his stomach and threw his head back in raucous laughter.

"BWAHAHAHAHA! I-Icy Swallow! BWAHAHAHA I can't, I can't!"

Icy Swallow's face flushed red.

"Ahahaha, ahhhh, that was a good one. Thanks girlie, I needed that."

He waved his hand in a shooing motion.

"Now run along. This is no place for a Falcon fangirl."

Icy Swallow clenched her fists.

"Don't ignore me! I'm the one who's going to change things in this country!"

Captain Repulsive Butcher's face was still twisted in a smile, but his eyes grew sharp.

"Are you now? You have no idea what you're doing, do you? Go home kid, while I'm still in a good mood."

Icy Swallow grit her teeth. She felt the power welling up inside of her and pulled on it with all her might.

She had been helpless and ignored long enough. But now?

Now she had the power to make people listen.

"Don't mock me! You're going to stop! Right! Now!"

She thrust her hand and upper body forward. A massive blast of cold fog flew from her hands, sending fruits and chairs tumbling forward. Captain Repulsive Butcher disappeared as the blast collided into him.

Icy Swallow leaned over and breathed heavily.

"D-Did I get him?"

"Constanza!"

"Antonio! Use my hero name!"

"Watch out!"

She spun around. There was a massive shadow in the fog. And the back of a giant hand rapidly approached her.

"Constanza!"

Constanza let out a cry as she soared through the air, crashing into one of the stalls. She groaned and tried to lift her body, then cried and fell back down as she scraped her arm on a jagged piece of wood.

And then she heard heavy footsteps.

Her eyes widened as the massive shadow stepped out of the fog.

It was Captain Repulsive Butcher.

And he was no longer laughing.

"Well well well, looks like you're a little super after all. A little Icy Falcon wannabe. Well I've got news for you girlie."

She began to tremble as he approached the broken stand. She tried to move but she could hardly feel her body anymore. She reached for her power but it eluded her frantic grasp.

"This isn't a game. This isn't a fairy tale. This is a place for men and monsters. Kids like you?"

His face curled into a twisted grin. He raised his cleaver.

"Kids like you just get hurt."

He brought the cleaver down.

"Constanza!"

She shut her eyes and let out a scream.

But the cleaver never landed. Antonio's eyes widened.

The clever was frozen in ice.

"A butcher like you belongs in cold storage."

A snowy gale blew the massive butcher back. He stumbled and then fell to the ground with a mighty crash.

And someone else flew into the broken marketplace.

Icy Falcon landed in front of the fallen girl. He pulled

his cape back and swung it forward. Ice covered Captain Repulsive Butcher all the way up to his neck. The Icy Falcon then turned around to the fallen girl.

Her eyes were as wide as they could go. She trembled now, for a different reason.

"I-Icy...Icy Falcon...i-it's you...you're here..."

Icy Falcon lifted an eyebrow.

"Who are you?"

△△△

Constanza sat on a chair, a blanket wrapped around her and Antonio's hand on her shoulder. In the distance, police and ILS personnel moved a restrained Captain Repulsive Butcher into the back of a large truck. Icy Falcon stood on guard, his arms crossed.

Constanza sighed.

"You ok?"

"...I was useless."

Antonio frowned.

"That's not true."

"Isn't it?"

Tears welled up in her eyes.

"What was I even doing? I just went out there and talked crap. And then I was down on the ground. If Icy Falcon hadn't come in time, I'd...I'd..."

She covered her face in her hands.

She had been granted great power. She was super now.

And yet...

She was still a helpless little girl, unable to do anything.

Just then, she heard footsteps approaching.

"You ok, kid?"

She looked up and gasped.

Icy Falcon stood before her.

Her cheeks took on a light pink.

"U-Um, I'm ok, thank you for saving me."

Icy Falcon nodded. Then his eyes narrowed.

"Good. Now, go home, kid."

Her eyes widened.

"*Señor* Falcon?"

Icy Falcon sighed.

"Look, it was brave of you to step out there. But it didn't go like you thought, right kid? Just because you're special doesn't mean you're ready to fight. This isn't a game. It's a war. So it's not enough to be special. If you're not a soldier, you're just going to get hurt."

Constanza bit her lip and looked to the ground. Icy Falcon let out another sigh and turned to walk away.

Constanza clenched her fists and stood up after he took a few steps.

"Then teach me!"

Icy Falcon stopped and glanced back over his shoulder.

"Teach me how to fight! Teach me how to be a hero!"

Icy Falcon shook his head, speaking in a soft voice.

"I'm no hero, kid."

"Yes you are!"

Icy Falcon paused, and then turned to face the girl.

"We can't do anything! Us normal people just hide in our homes every single day! Villains, gangs, monsters, all of it! We just hide under our beds and hope it goes away! And no one does anything! The government, the police, no one cares about us down here! We suffer and we die and we can't do anything about it!"

She looked into his eyes with a glare.

"Except you! You're the one who stands up for us! You're the one who's fighting back! You're Icy Falcon! The Hope of Mexico! You stopped El Capa! You fought the Necrosaurus! You're the only one who gives us hope!"

Constanza grit her teeth.

"So I'm not going home! You said this is a war? We know! Everyone in Mexico knows! We're all a part of it already! So I'm not going to go back home and cower under my bed! Not when I finally have the chance to do something about it!"

Constanza slouched over, breathing heavily.

But her eyes never wavered from Icy Falcon's gaze.

He looked into those eyes.

Those eyes he had seen before.

Time and time again.

He slouched his shoulders and heaved a sigh.

"You don't know what this war is like, kid, not really."

Her eyes still didn't waver.

"Yes, I do. I've been in this war since I was six years old. I know *exactly* what it's like. That's why I'm going to stop it, whatever it takes."

Icy Falcon looked into her eyes for a minute longer, then heaved a massive sigh.

"...fine."

Constanza took a step back.

"Huh?"

"Come with me, kid."

Constanza blinked.

"You mean...?"

He nodded his head.

"I'll show you a thing or two, hopefully teach you how not to die."

His eyes narrowed.

"But you do what I say. And you don't get involved in *anything* I tell you not to. Understand?"

Her face broke out in a massive smile and she nodded over and over.

"Yes! I understand! Thank you!"

Icy Falcon sighed once more as the girl ran over and hugged her friend.

He had heard this story before.

He knew how it ended.

But he also knew those eyes.

She wouldn't stop, no matter what he chose to do. And without him, she would get herself killed within the month, possibly her family with her.

So the only thing he could do was pray that this time would be different.

But maybe it would.

He hadn't thought much of Aurora Legion at first either, they seemed like a bunch of naive *gringo* kids who thought they were on an adventure. But they had proven themselves. They survived against the cartels…and worse…even when he had screwed up and put them in harm's way.

So maybe…just maybe…if he did this right…if he focused her on the the supers instead of the cartels…maybe she could become like them too.

Maybe heroes *could* rise in Mexico after all.

△△△

The sun beat down overhead. Constanza gasped for breath. She blinked as the sweat stung her eyes and her hair stuck to her face and neck. Her legs burned, her lungs screamed, every muscle in her body felt like jelly.

And then she heard the merciless voice.

"Again."

Constanza gulped but pushed off the ground once more. She put one leg in front of the other. She ran one step at a time. She fixed her eyes on a post just a few meters ahead, trying to think of nothing but reaching it.

Then repeated the process with a rock in the distance.

And then a tree.

So on and so forth she stumbled onward, willing herself just to reach the next goal.

Until finally, she passed her starting point once more.

Constanza dropped to the ground as she passed her mentor, breathing heavily.

"Again."

She screamed in her heart. She opened her mouth, but the

dust made her cough.

And after another lap...

Icy Falcon handed her a bottle of water. She accepted it and tanked it down without a word.

"W-Wha...What..."

"What does running have to do with hero work?"

Constanza nodded her trembling head.

"Stamina. Strength is irrelevant if you can't last through the fight. Winning is irrelevant if the target escapes and you're too tired to chase. Now, again."

Constanza closed her eyes and grit her teeth.

But she rose to her feet once more.

△△△

Constanza let out a cry as a fist hit her cheek, sending her sprawling on the ground.

"Get up."

Icy Falcon pounded his palm with his fist.

"Villains won't wait for you. Neither will I."

Constanza rolled to the side as a foot stomped by her head and jumped to her feet. She swayed from side to side but held her hands in front of her.

"Come."

She charged with a shout.

△△△

Constanza grunted as she held her hands out in front of her, palms spread apart and facing each other. Two clouds of fog sprayed from each palm, ice starting to form where they collided. This way and that the ice crystals grew, until a deformed spike floated between her hands. Constanza grit her teeth and flung her hands forward, the spike followed suit and shot forward.

And missed entirely, landing nowhere close to the target,

much less the bullseye painted on it.

"Again."

△△△

Icy Falcon lit a burner can, and then placed it under a pot of water. He waited until the water began to boil.

"You can't fight near civilians if you don't have control. Cool the water, but don't put out the fire. Do it until you can keep the water liquid."

Constanza nodded and closed her eyes. She held out her hands and took a deep breath. She called upon her power.

She tried to control her power.

She pulled just a bit.

Just a strand.

Just a little.

She started to sweat as she struggled to hold onto the tiny wisp of power. She grunted. She grit her teeth.

She gently pushed her hand forward…

And then she heard a clang.

She opened her eyes. The fire was out. The pot was on the ground. And a cone of ice covered the ground in front of her.

She grimaced.

That was…a *bit* more than she intended.

Icy Falcon relit the can and placed another pot above it.

"Again."

△△△

Constanza screamed as an icicle cut her cheek. She dropped to her knees, the wall of ice in front of her collapsing into shards.

"Villains won't let you concentrate. If you can't handle pain, then give up now. Again."

Constanza grit her teeth and held out her hands. She began building up the ice wall as she had been taught.

The ice spikes shot towards her once more.

△△△

And then after some time...

△△△

Constanza flew across the ground. One leg after another pushed off and sent her soaring across her route. She flew past the Icy Falcon, not pausing to hear him talk. Another lap awaited.

△△△

Constanza held out her palm. Five icicles grew in the air, each perfectly straight and sharp. She swung her palm down so that her fingers were facing forward. Five icicles shot forward and hit the center of five targets. Constanza took off running and leapt into the air. She spun to her side and thrust out her hand once more. An icicle shot towards a swinging target.

It landed dead center.

△△△

Constanza held her hands to the left and right of her. Two pots of water sat over campfires. Inside were two pools of water, completely still. Not a bubble rose, not a single ice crystal formed in either.

△△△

Constanza grunted as sharp ice cut her cheek. A whip lashed her back. A gale force wind knocked her off her feet.

But still her wall held.

In fact, both of the ice walls on either side of her held, no matter what pain she felt.

△△△

Constanza leapt back as a leg passed by her stomach. She stepped in and ducked to the left as a fist flew past her face. She jabbed into her opponent's abdomen and then stepped back to avoid the countering haymaker. She picked up her foot and sent it forward, placing it right on her opponent's torso. The Icy Falcon took a step back from the front kick. He held up a hand.

He heaved a sigh.

Then he nodded at Constanza.

"You're ready."

△△△

Constanza was sitting at home, tossing a ball of ice in the air. Antonio was watching her with a frown on his face, before he heaved a sigh and walked over to her.

"Constanza."

She glanced over to him.

"What is it, Antonio?"

He took a deep breath.

"I found a new job, I'm starting next week."

Constanza tilted her head.

"What do you mean, I thought you liked it at the grocer?"

Antonio took a deep breath.

"Well, I figure you'll probably be taking less shifts from now on, right? I found something that pays better, there's some new research foundation paying good money for interns. Should cover us, give you some more free time."

Constanza's eyes went wide.

"Antonio...you..."

He gave her a wry smile as he rubbed the back of his head.

"...I still don't like this. I don't like the idea of you being out there. But...I know how much it means to you, and if there's anyone who can keep you safe, it's Icy Falcon. I know I can't do anything for you out there...so I'll do what I can to support you here. Just...just promise me you'll be safe, ok?"

Constanza's eyes watered but she shook her head to clear them. Then she stood up and hugged Antonio.

"...thank you. I'll be careful."

Antonio nodded silently.

Just then, Constanza's phone began to buzz. She glanced at Antonio and he nodded, cracking a smile at her.

"Go be a hero, Icy Swallow."

She smiled bashfully at that and then answered the phone.

"This is Constanza."

"Marketplace, meet me at the west entrance. Don't be late."

Constanza grinned as she put away her phone.

It was finally time to make a difference.

△△△

Screams filled the air and fleeing people flooded the street. Something crashed into a fruit stall and began feasting. It had a large round black shell, short, stubby limbs, and a rodent-like face.

It was an armadillo.

And it was the size of a car, with a shell made of metal.

The giant armadillo gorged upon the fallen fruit, ignoring the scattering crowds.

Suddenly something cold slammed into its face. It let out a cry and stumbled back.

"Who dares to defy the Iron Armadillo?!"

A girl stepped out into the street. She wore a blue hawk mask, a dark blue cape, and a light blue dress. She had a pair of blue boots underneath. She placed one hand on her hip and pointed the other at the Iron Armadillo, turning to the side.

"Surrender now, evildoer! The Icy Swallow is freezing your career!"

The Iron Armadillo laughed.

"You will try, you Falcon wanna-be!"

The Iron Armadillo curled up into a ball and began rolling forward. The Earth rumbled as the thousand pound iron mass trampled the stalls and fruits in its path. Icy Swallow leapt to the side, the ball passing her by. She swung out her palm.

Ice spikes flew through the air and found their mark.

But they shattered harmlessly on the villain's shell.

"My shell can stop bullets! You'll need more than that weak Falcon imitation to stop me!"

The Iron Armadillo leapt into the air and curled up into a ball. Icy Swallow dropped her barrage and dodged once more, the iron mass cracking the ground where she once stood. The Iron Armadillo spun about as he uncurled.

And his tail caught Icy Swallow's head.

She let out a cry as she flew through the air, landing into the wreckage of a stall. The Iron Armadillo grinned and curled up once more.

He spun about once in place and surged forth.

The ground shook.

A spectator screamed.

Icy Swallow lay still on the stall.

And the edge of her mouth curled up.

She spun onto her stomach and used both her arms and legs to push herself out of the way. She managed to clear the incoming mass a mere second before it flattened the stall.

And then it kept going.

The rolling armadillo swayed side to side as it careened forward.

The ground underneath it was a solid path of ice that reflected the sun.

Faster and faster the armadillo slid, unable to stop.

Until it slammed straight into the mighty oak at the center of the marketplace.

The armadillo uncurled, head on the ground and tail in the air, eyes spinning. Icy Swallow slid gracefully along the frozen path and placed her palm on the armadillo's stomach. Ice grew from her hand until a block of ice wrapped around the tree, the torso of the Armadillo stuck inside of it.

She let out a breath and let her shoulders drop.

And then she heard a thud behind her.

Icy Falcon landed there and crossed his arms. He nodded. "Good work."

Icy Swallow clenched her fist.

She had done it.

She was finally ready.

She could finally join the fight for Mexico.

△△△

Agent Wilson yawned and leaned back in his chair at the BSI. He glanced at the computer screen before him.

His resume was done, his references contacted, and his application filled out.

He just had to write that dang cover letter.

He had hoped that the BSI might get some funding as the United States tried to assert itself in the hero sphere. Or that the government would at least prop it up as a publicity stunt. Or perhaps the other way around, that the US would let it flounder in public but offer some special intel and resources behind the scenes, use it to trial new ways to deal with supers.

But the government had done, well, nothing. Clearly they never had any plans besides 'form a new agency'.

So the only thing the BSI was good for was acquiring 'relevant experience' to apply for the ILS, which fortunately had grown enough to handle former CIA agents in its ranks.

And so it was time to go. There wasn't much more he could do here, for himself or for anyone else.

He grimaced as he glanced at the blank cover letter in front of him. Now he just had to figure out how exactly he should word 'I'm jumping ship because the BSI is useless'? Something about heroes and justice? Crush on Director Green's bravery and leadership? Just say 'I'm CIA and it's classified'?

Steve walked up to his desk.

"Pack your bags, Wilson, we're going on a trip."

Wilson yawned again.

"What, another lost super-cat, Steve? Take Kasey with you, I'm kind of busy."

"He's out for donuts again, and said he doesn't feel like flying economy. So finish your application later, this time is serious."

Wilson raised an eyebrow.

"Serious? Who gives the BSI a serious call?"

"The DEA apparently."

Wilson blinked.

"The DEA? What the heck is the DEA calling us for?"

Steve tossed him a folder. Wilson quickly scanned through the pages.

"Some sort of super drug?"

Steve nodded.

"And apparently a super's been murdering cartel guys. No one's been able to stop or catch him. Can't even ID the guy. DEA requested we head down to Mexico to support in our 'area of expertise'."

Wilson raised an eyebrow.

"And what exactly does the DEA expect the two of us to do about it?"

Steve shrugged.

"Official story or honest opinion?"

"I was CIA, I wrote the official story."

Steve shook his head.

"Supers in a cartel war? New magic drugs? DEA don't want none of that, so they'll hand it to us and shrug when we fail. Then they'll use our failure to push for extra funding, or maybe even a super of their own."

Wilson sighed.

"Figured as much. So why are we going?"

Steve gave a wry grin.

"Don't you want to try and do something as the BSI? One last hurrah, get the blood pumping a bit, and then stop by the ILS recruiter on the way home. Who knows, maybe we get to run from a super and write it down as a relevant experience."

Wilson smiled and shrugged. Well, it *was* a chance to grab some classified intel from another agency, the kind of chance he had been looking for. He might as well take it and see if he could get *something* out of the time he spent here.

"I was never any good at cover letters anyways."

AUTHOR'S COMMENTARY: Because what action adventure story is complete without a training montage? And oh, hey! That Agent Wilson guy is doing something after all! Anyways! Will the Icy Swallow take her place among the pantheon of heroes? Will the BSI get to do anything? Will Agents Wilson and Steve land interviews with the ILS? Tune in next time, to find out!

CHAPTER 22 - ESCALATION

Pedestrians screamed and ran to the side as a monster landed on the road. It had two large, long feet and a massive, several hundred pound body. The body was covered in short green fur and two long ears poked out from the top of its head.

The Viridian Rabbit was on the move.

In her paws was a briefcase full of banknotes, a few of which fell out and floated on the wind. She leaped up into the air, jumping past a full block in a single bound.

"Ahahahaha! Catch me if you can! No falcon's outrunning this rabbit!"

Behind her a gust of cool wind blew through the streets, kicking up dust and falling banknotes. Icy Falcon soared through the air with his cape spread wide.

The Viridian Rabbit landed dead center in an intersection and took off to the right. Cars blared their horns as they swerved out of the way and tried to brake. Icy Falcon banked the turn and spoke into his earpiece.

"She's heading to you, get ready."

The Viridian Rabbit grinned as Icy Falcon turned the corner. She kicked a nearby fire hydrant, sending a spray of water into the air, then jumped onto a parked car, leaving two massive footprints in the metal hull. She then leapt with all her might…

Sideways into an alley.

She hid behind a dumpster, ears raised and at the ready. The edge of her mouth curled up.

Icy Falcon flew past, heading down the street.

"Hehehe, not much of a hunter after all, were you *Señor*

Falcon? I'm a little disappointed with how easy that was, given your reputation and all."

Suddenly Viridian Rabbit felt a chill down her spine. Where was this ominous premonition coming from?

Then she realized it wasn't a premonition at all! The chill was actually on her spine!

She whipped her head around. Behind her stood the Icy Swallow, a big grin on her face and arms stretched out. Ice had already begun to grow on the rabbit's back.

"Hehehe, not much of an escape after all, eh Viridian Rabbit?"

"Screw you!"

Viridian Rabbit leapt with all her might. The ice slowed her down so much she didn't even clear the alley, but she managed to get out of range of the girl in blue. She turned her head around and stuck her tongue out at Icy Swallow.

"Hah, get lost you stupid hero! Remember this as the day you almost caught the Viridian Rabbit!"

She turned forward to run out of the alley.

And ran headlong into a wall of ice.

Icy Falcon landed on top of the wall.

"Remember this as the day you almost escaped."

A few minutes later the authorities were packing the Viridian Rabbit into a large truck. Icy Falcon frowned.

This was the fifth public attack by a super within a week. And all the short-sighted kind, the ones that just ran out and rampaged with no minions and little plan. Something was up, there shouldn't be this many small timers this often in this small of an area. But what could be the cause?

"We did it, *Señor* Falcon!"

Icy Swallow ran up to him, stars in her eyes. Icy Falcon almost felt the edge of his mouth curl before he shook his head and frowned. The girl was growing more and more confident and more and more enthusiastic with each mission. Perhaps dangerously so.

"Good work, kid. Go home and get some rest for now."

But life would teach her that soon enough. And what he said was true, she was focused and determined and her efforts were paying off in the field. She didn't need him to damper her spirits just yet.

"Are you sure? Weren't we going to patrol the next neighborhood?"

"It's fine, your friend is starting a new job soon right? You should spend some time with him while you both still can."

She bit her lip and hung her head. Icy Falcon patted her shoulder.

"Go on. There's always more work, there's not always time for friends. Cherish the people you have."

Icy Swallow slowly nodded her head.

"Um, ok, thank you, *Señor* Falcon, sir. I'll see you again soon!"

Icy Falcon let out a sigh as she ran off.

Kids like her shouldn't be fighting crime, she should be off having fun.

For as long as she still had people to have fun with.

△△△

Agents Wilson and Steve stepped into a crowded DEA office down in Mexico. Agents were walking back and forth, speaking on phones, or working at desks covered in stacks of paper. The two BSI agents looked at each, shrugged, and walked towards a door that seemed important.

A few knocks later and they were ushered inside.

"Agent Wilson, and this is Agent Steve, BSI."

The man at the desk stood up and shook their hands.

"Nathan, head of this bureau. Go ahead and take a seat."

He heaved a sigh as he sat back down. Steve spoke first.

"Why the long face?"

"Pardon me but when I asked DC for backup, I was hoping to get some."

"Ouch."

Wilson shrugged.

"You could always call the ILS."

Nathan grimaced.

"If it were up to me I would have."

"Then why didn't you?"

Nathan heaved another sigh.

"Honestly neither Mexico City or DC wants either of these solved."

Agents Wilson and Steven exchanged glances.

"Well, we suspected as much when they called us, but that bad huh?"

Nathan handed them one file.

"As far as the *Federales* are concerned, a killer targeting cartel guys might as well be an angel from above. They've been...less than enthusiastic in their investigations."

Steve gave a shrug.

"Might have a point, you have a different take?"

Nathan grimaced again.

"Whoever it is is a dangerous new player. What happens if they succeed? Will they stop at cartel guys? And the cartels aren't going to just lay down and die either. I think however this goes down, we're going to end up with something far worse."

The two BSI agents rubbed their chins and then slowly nodded.

"Makes sense, heard there are some new drugs as well?"

Nathan nodded and handed them a second file.

"We're still not sure about this...but if we're right..."

He took a deep breath.

"There's something out there that can mutate people. Turn them into monsters."

Steve raised an eyebrow.

"Really? Sounds like a fairy tale to me. Some politician trying to cover up some villain friends maybe?"

Nathan nodded.

"We thought so too, but super attacks are on the rise here.

New guys with no record or history. And a similar one just occurred in Miami, known cartel associates were involved."

Steve frowned.

"If that's true then where's the ILS? Shouldn't there be some sort of super-DEA task force by now?"

Wilson shrugged.

"That one's easy. If there is a drug that can turn people into supers, even monstrous supers, the last thing anyone in charge would want is for the ILS to get it."

Nathan nodded again.

"Neither Mexico City nor DC has been…helpful regarding this case. And there's a cartel they've been obstructing for, even more than normal. Which makes me think this is more than the usual corruption."

He stared the two BSI agents in the eye.

"And now that you've arrived, I'm almost certain something's up."

"Again, ouch."

"Fair enough."

Nathan sighed.

"Well, we're not going to get anywhere talking about conspiracies. As long as you boys are here, might as well take a look. We'll get you some desks and whatever we managed to scrounge on this. Either of you speak Spanish?"

"Wilson, you were stationed abroad right?"

"In Eastern Europe."

"Let me know whenever you're going out, I'll try to get you a translator if I can."

The BSI agents nodded and stood up. Steven turned to Wilson as they exited the office.

"You want the super serial killer, or the magic drugs?"

"I'll take the super."

Steven raised an eyebrow.

"Really? The CIA didn't ask you to cut them in on the goods?"

"You think they'd wait for me to get here?"

"Ah, right."

Wilson shook his head.

"No it's just…"

He opened up the killer file and took out a picture of one of the victims.

"…there's something familiar about this."

△△△

Bob heaved a sigh as he watched the news.

Icy Falcon had taken the young girl under his wing, and she had successfully debuted as a hero. The two were now working together, tackling a 'coincidental' surge of villains side by side.

Which meant…it was time for the next phase of the plan.

Bob heaved another sigh.

This was his last chance to change his mind. Once he made this call he would hit the point of no return. If he wanted to back out, to change his plans, he had to do it now. If he didn't want things to end how he thought they would, he had to come up with something else before he picked up the phone…

Bob picked up the phone and dialed the number.

This was necessary. He truly believed that, this time. So there was no point in wavering now.

He would follow through, whatever happened.

He made the call…

△△△

Icy Falcon and Icy Swallow stood on a rooftop, surveying a busy street below.

"Um, *Señor* Falcon, what are we here for? I don't see any supers anywhere near here. Everything seems normal."

Icy Falcon shrugged.

"That's a good thing, kid. The ILS got a tip that a super

attack might happen here. If we managed to arrive early we can stop it before there's much damage."

"What if nothing happens?"

"Even better."

Icy Swallow frowned as she continued to survey the street.

"I don't see anything, other than a couple junkies in that alley over there."

Icy Falcon's eyes narrowed.

"Which alley?"

"Oh, that one over there, by the bank."

Icy Falcon took a look. A couple of figures in the alley, small lights popping up near their faces. Nothing out of the ordinary...

Icy Falcon focused in.

One of the guys was twitching. He fell to the ground.

"Whoa, what's going on down there?! I think he's having a seizure!"

Icy Falcon held up his arm in front of Icy Swallow.

"Stay here. I'll check it out."

Icy Falcon spread his cape and flew over to the building near the alley. He peered over the edge. As the girl had thought, the man was frothing at the mouth and convulsing. He frowned and pulled out his phone. He was no medic.

And then the man's shoulder began to bulge.

And grow.

And then his other as well.

Soon all his muscles were pulsing, bulging up and then shrinking down, over and over. The man got on all fours, and then stood to his feet. He threw his head and arms back, shouting into the sky. His shirt began to rip apart. The other people in the alley began to back away, one falling onto his bottom.

The man let out a massive roar. His arms gave a final pulse and then began expanding and extending, taking on a red tone.

And a pincer-like shape.

The man's torso followed. Soon his entire body was covered in red chitin, ending in two huge pincers. Even his head changed, gaining a chitin helmet and eyes extending upon stalks. The man turned his head to his right arm, clacking the pincer there, and then to his left, clacking again. Soon he began to laugh.

"Red Lobster? The Mighty Crab? Captain Pincerhand? Crablante? Ah whatever, I'll figure it out later."

He turned to the wall of the bank beside him. He made a grin.

"First things first, I got a withdrawal to make."

Icy Falcon grimaced.

This was bad.

Not the monster, the kid could handle this guy on her own. But rather, the implication.

A man turned into a monster while smoking.

So there was a strong implication the smoke had something to do with it. And if that was true...

Then the cartels had branched out into supers.

No, they had gone beyond that.

They had a way to make supers of their own.

Icy Falcon had to figure out exactly what just happened, right now.

Just then, Icy Swallow's voice came in through his earpiece.

"*Señor* Falcon! What's going on?!"

"Take the crab."

"What about you? What are you going to do?"

"Catch his friends."

With that the earpiece went silent. Icy Swallow gulped. This was not her first villain, but it was the first time Icy Falcon wouldn't be watching her back.

She winced as the crab-man smashed straight through a solid wall. She frowned, and nodded once.

This was her job now.

This was her chance to start making a real difference.

To assist Icy Falcon in his fight.

To prove once and for all she had the power to change this country.

She narrowed her eyes.

She would not fail this time.

She leaned over the edge of the building and thrust her hands out. Cold fog plummeted down the side of the wall, leaving behind a pillar of ice. She stepped onto it and then deconstructed the pillar from the top down, dropping herself onto the street. She thrust out her palm again, sending a ball of snow into the shoulder of the mutated man.

"Stop now, evildoer! Or this Icy Swallow will make you a snow crab!"

She winced as the words left her mouth.

She really really hoped no one was listening to her.

The crab man turned around and stepped into the street.

"Well well well, if it isn't the little mini-Falcon. Where's your chaperon, little girl?"

He snapped his pincers together with a loud clack. She just scoffed at him.

"Somewhere *actually* important. I'm more than enough for a small fry like you."

The man's face twisted into a snarl.

"Don't you look down on me!"

He leapt off the ground and ran into the street. Icy Swallow raised both her hands, launching balls of ice at the charging hulk. The ice shattered on the red chitin.

"That won't work on me anymore!"

The man pulled back his left pincer and thrust it forward. Ice Swallow ducked underneath and then lifted her hands, sending a wall of ice shooting towards the sky. The wall caught the crab man on the chin, sending him stumbling back. He let out a growl and grabbed a parked car, hurling it at the girl. Icy Swallow dove to the side as the car smashed into the street.

She looked up to see the man charging at her, shoulder tucked down and facing her. She placed her hands on the ground, ice freezing the ground in front of her and racing towards the man's legs. The ice began to climb up his shoes but broke as he stepped forward. Still, he began to slip on the frozen ground and Icy Swallow was able to dodge once more.

She grimaced as the man plunged into a car, shattering the window. Ice wasn't working, the man's shell was too tough, and he wouldn't stay still and let her encase him. What else could she try?

The man stood back up and shook his head, then started to lumber towards her once more.

She held up her hand and let out a blast of chilly fog.

The man took a second to wave the fog from his face and then continued his march.

She sent another blast at him. He scowled.

"Stop that!"

He ran towards her, swinging his pincer in a wide arc. She ducked under and shot another blast. He tried to kick her but she moved to the side. She shot another blast.

She dodged, then blasted him. Dodged, then blasted him. Over and over, she repeated the same attack. The pincer caught the tips of her hair but she managed to evade its grasp. She continued her assault

"Stay, still, you little…!"

The man swung and swung and swung some more.

But he began to slow down.

One swing moved a little slower. A kick was a few seconds later. The man was breathing heavily, and started to shiver. Icy Swallow kept up the barrage, keeping him veiled in cold fog.

"Ugh, so…cold…feeling……sleepy……"

The man's eyes drifted shut.

And then he fell to the ground with a crash.

△△△

Agent Wilson heaved a sigh.

This investigation was not going well.

The reports listed bare-bones autopsies, with corpses cremated if not lost entirely. There was not a single eyewitness account or camera recording on file. So he had no clues, no potential motives, no weapons. He didn't even have a fresh crime scene to visit, as the attacks had died down lately.

Sometimes he missed the KGB. At least he knew who he was looking for back then. And why.

Agent Steve looked up from the paper he was reading at the nearby desk.

"Sounds like it's going great, Wilson."

Wilson shrugged.

"Redacted CIA docs give more details than these reports, how about you?"

Steve shrugged.

"About the same. Someone's keeping a real tight lid on things."

Wilson nodded and glanced up at the TV in the room.

"Breaking news folks! We have word of another super attack! Icy Falcon and his prodigy Icy Swallow are already on the scene and engaged with the super in question."

Wilson raised an eyebrow.

"Since when does Icy Falcon have a sidekick? I thought that guy worked alone most of the time."

Steve shrugged as he glanced at the TV as well.

"She started showing up about two weeks ago or so. Maybe the League introduced them or something."

"Super-interns?"

"Getting paid in exposure and experience most likely."

Wilson's eyes narrowed as he watched Icy Swallow launch a barrage of ice at the rampaging crab person.

And then his eyes widened.

He looked back to a photo of one of the mystery killer's victims and the relevant autopsy report.

"...crap."

Steve looked back over at him

"What is it?"

Wilson took a breath.

"I know what this body reminds me of now. Something of a KGB special for winter assassinations. Fill a mold with water, throw it outside, make some spikes out of ice. Stab a guy indoors, then the ice melts away. No fingerprints, no weapon, no clues. This one is messier but the wound looks similar and what details the autopsy does have match up."

Steve frowned.

"That's pretty messed up you know?"

Wilson shrugged.

"Just stabbing someone's tame for the KGB."

Steve started shaking his head repeatedly.

"Ah, nope, that's classified Wilson. Can't tell those horrific stories to my poor, innocent, civilian ears."

Wilson raised an eyebrow.

"Weren't you on homicides for the FBI?"

"I was hoping supers would be a bit neater."

"...I guess me too."

Steve heaved a sigh.

"Well that's a wonderful, gruesome story, Wilson, but I don't see how it's relevant. In case you forgot, we're in Mexico, so I don't think anyone's carrying icicle shanks around."

Wilson lifted a finger and pointed to the television.

"I can think of two."

Steve's eyes widened.

"...No way...that can't be."

Wilson took a look at his papers.

"Attacks died down recently...right before she showed up. As if someone was taking a break from the cartels..."

Steve shook his head.

"You're out of your mind Wilson. This is Icy Falcon we're talking about. Founding ILS member, helped defeat the Atomic Herald and the Necrosaurus, ring any bells? Even if that insane hunch is right, nothing good would come of it. That's not just a hero, that's *the* Hero of Mexico himself. He's more likely to get elected *el presidente* than incarcerated."

Wilson heaved a sigh.

He really missed the KGB.

△△△

One of the crab-man's friends sprinted down a dark alleyway, sweat drenching his brow. He breathed heavily as he stumbled forward. He glanced behind him.

And then ran headlong into a wall.

A wall of ice which hadn't been there before.

As he backed himself away from the wall he heard a thud behind him. He slowly turned his head.

Icy Falcon stood behind him, his arms crossed and a frown on his face.

"*S-Señor* Falcon, what are you doing here? S-Shouldn't you be dealing with that monster?"

"Already handled. I have questions for you."

The man scooted until his back hit a wall and raised his hands in front of him.

"M-Me? W-What could you possibly need me for, *Señor* Falc…"

A spike of ice cracked the wall next to his face.

"I saw you in the alley. You and your buddies were having a smoke. Then one of them turned into that. I want to know how."

"I-I don't know what you mean, *Señor* Falcon. He just came out of nowhere, how am I supposed to know what happened?"

The man screamed as ice filled his vision and shut his

eyes. He trembled, his heart pounded. But he didn't feel any pain.

Slowly, slowly he opened his eyes. A spike of ice hung in the air, almost touching his eye. He whimpered.

"Last. Chance."

"Ok Ok! I'll talk!"

The man scrambled to reach inside his pockets, pulling out a bulb.

"I don't really know, honest! They just gave us these with our usual purchase, said it was a sample of something new! Juan was the first to try it! We had no idea..."

The man shrieked as Icy Falcon took a step closer.

"...O-Ok, they said...it might give us something special...if we were lucky. Just a high if we weren't. B-But we didn't mean any harm! Just, who doesn't want to be a super?! P-Please, we won't do it again."

Icy Falcon held out his hand. The man lifted a trembling arm and placed the bulb in it. Icy Falcon looked it over. A normal Adranis bulb by the color and structure.

But it occasionally shimmered with a faint, green-yellow glow.

His worst nightmare had been confirmed.

"Who gave this to you?"

The man trembled and shook his head.

"Who. Gave. It. To. You?"

The man shook his head again.

"*Señor* Falcon, you know how it goes! They'll kill me if I talk!"

The man squealed as a small cut appeared on his cheek. Icy Falcon lifted a hand, covered in an icy spike.

"And you think I won't if you don't?"

△△△

Icy Falcon stood on a rooftop. Icy Swallow rose up on an ice pillar, stepping onto the roof.

"I got him, *Señor* Falcon, sir! This street is safe now!"

Icy Falcon's eyes were closed, and he let out a sigh.

"Good work kid."

He turned and opened his eyes, looking into hers.

"Now go home."

She tilted her head.

"Don't we need to chase the other guys? Or did you get them all already?"

Icy Falcon shook his head.

"You're going to take a week off."

Icy Swallow blinked.

"What…What do you mean?"

"I have something to do. It's too dangerous this time. I'll call you when it's done."

Icy Swallow paused, then frowned.

"So is fighting supers! This is what you trained me for, isn't it? If I can't help you when it matters, then what's the point?"

Icy Falcon sighed once more.

"Look, kid, this just got a lot more complicated. The cartels are involved. And you know what that means, don't you?"

The girl's eyes widened, but then narrowed as she gripped her fist.

"Then I'm definitely going."

"Wake up, kid."

She took a step back. Icy Falcon glared at her.

"It's one thing to play with supers. It's another thing to declare war on the cartels. They're not just going to wait for you to come lock them up. They're going to go after you. They're going to go after your home, your friends, your family. You know what they're capable of, what they're going to do if you get involved. So you're not going to."

But Icy Swallow held her ground, clenching her fists.

"I know that. I already know exactly what they're capable of. They gunned down my parents when I was just a little girl! It wasn't even on purpose, they were just in the wrong place at the wrong time! That's why I'm here, that's why I'm doing this! I am NOT going to let them do that anymore, to anyone else!"

Icy Falcon paused as she shouted at him. He cursed in his mind.

Right now, he really wished she *was* just a naive girl idolizing heroes. He should not have equated her with Aurora Legion.

He knew she was driven, but he didn't know she already had blood to settle. Not a vendetta like this. He had seen it before. She wouldn't back down. She wouldn't just go home. He had tried that with others like her. Trying to keep them out of it hadn't worked before. It wouldn't work with her either.

Especially now, after he had given her the power and the confidence to fight.

If he didn't satisfy her need to strike back, she would end up getting herself involved, one way or another. She wouldn't rest until she was in the fight.

He couldn't stop her from getting involved at this point. So he'd have to try to limit her involvement instead.

His eyes narrowed at her.

"...I see. But you're still not ready for this fight, and you are NOT joining it until I'm satisfied you are. So here's what's going to happen. You can come, and you can help. But you do NOT get involved, no matter what. You stay outside, you watch the perimeter, and you keep your head down. If and when they run, you tail them, *quietly*, and let me know where they go. You do NOT engage under ANY circumstances, am I clear?"

She frowned...but she slowly nodded. Icy Falcon sighed.

"Remember, you do as I say. If you don't, we're done. Do you understand?"

She looked down and away, but she replied in the end.

"...I understand."

Icy Falcon heaved another sigh.
"...then follow me, and stay quiet."

AUTHOR'S COMMENTARY: Rest in Prison, crab man, we will never forget your villain name! Mostly because you and I never decided on one. In other news, super drugs huh? Well, I'm sure this will go super well. Anyways! Can the Icy Falcon and Icy Swallow stop this latest threat? Can Icy Falcon keep Icy Swallow from getting involved? Can Agent Wilson do anything about his shocking theory? Tune in next time, to find out!

CHAPTER 23 - BLOOD

There was a building at the corner of a busy intersection. The front door was swinging open with frost on its hinges. Inside the building furniture was knocked over, carpets were ripped to shreds, and television screens were shattered and sparking. And the entire room was covered in snow and ice.

Up on the second floor, men groaned and shivered, their torsos and limbs encased in blocks of ice. And a shirtless man in a cape stood near the window, walking past it and then out of view of the street. One of his hands was encased in an icy spike. The other hand held a man's neck. The man coughed as Icy Falcon slammed him into a wall.

"I don't know what you're talking about, *Señor* Falcon. Surely you know we of all people don't give out free samples."

Icy Falcon swung his fist. A man on the floor cried as an icicle pierced his thigh. The man in his hand widened his eyes, but then he shook his head and started to chuckle.

"Oh come on now, *Señor* Falcon, you really should have expected this. It was only a matter of time before we got supers of our own. Did you expect that we would just let you kill us all?"

Icy Falcon held his ice encased fist up to the man's jaw, poking his chin with the tip.

"I don't know, will you?"

The man gulped and glanced around the room.

"Ok, ok fine. Let us live, and I'll give you our supplier."

The man began to talk. Icy Falcon's eyes and fist didn't move a single millimeter until the man was done.

But he was so focused on what the man told him that he

didn't notice the man's phone vibrate...

△△△

Icy Swallow stood on the roof of a neighboring building, watching the streets in front and the alley to the side of the target. Icy Falcon had stormed inside, and she had just seen him in the second floor window. His fist had been covered in ice, so he was clearly fighting someone.

Alone.

Icy Swallow grit her teeth and furrowed her brow. She had not done all this, come all this way just to be left behind at the crucial moment. She had not come to sit and watch as Icy Falcon fought alone, just like she had before, when she was still helpless.

She took a deep breath and slowly exhaled it, forcing herself to unclench her fists.

Icy Falcon had spoken. And he had fought the cartels for decades now. If he said she wasn't ready, then she had no choice but to accept his verdict.

But he had agreed to let her come, so she would be satisfied with that. She remained a part of this fight, even if she couldn't be in the thick of it. And so, she would play her role to perfection. She wouldn't let a single one of these *monsters* escape unnoticed.

She was just looking over the alleyway when a group of cars pulled up across the street. A group of men got out of the cars.

They were holding guns.

Icy Swallow turned to look at the street and gasped.

The men were taking aim at the structure.

Right towards the window where Icy Falcon had last been visible.

She shouted into her mic as the men shouted in the streets.

"FALCON! YOU HAVE INCOMING!"

"LIGHT IT UP!"

The men opened fire, shattering the windows and chipping the walls of the structure. Icy Swallow ducked her head down behind the edge of the roof, reinforcing it with a wall of ice.

And then she heard a scream.

She glanced over the edge.

Her eyes widened.

Time slowed to a crawl.

There, caught between the men and the structure, was a woman and her young son. She was crouched behind a parked car, desperately holding her son in her arms, trying to shield him from stray bullets.

The cartel guys didn't see her. If they did, they didn't care.

And then the bullet holes started to move across the walls, as the men began sweeping their aim across the building, trying to ensure they would hit anyone inside.

Which meant they would hit anyone outside as well.

Images flashed before Icy Swallow's eyes.

She saw bloody torsos.

Unblinking eyes.

And a young girl, wailing as she clung to her parents' bodies.

Her body moved before her mind.

The next thing Icy Swallow knew she was falling from the building, a slide of ice forming underneath her feet. Her hand thrust forward, a blast of cold fog streaming from it.

Bullet holes appeared on the wall, kicking up the dust. With every moment, they inched closer and closer to the car the civilians were crouched behind…

And then the men's guns swept across the car.

The woman screamed and hugged her son tight, shutting her eyes as she shielded him with her body.

But…she didn't feel any pain.

And the bullets sounded like they were striking something hard.

The woman opened her eyes and gasped.

Icy Swallow was standing over her, her teeth clenched and her hands thrust out in front of her. A huge wall of ice now covered the car, bullets hanging inside of it where they stopped. The woman's eyes widened.

"GO!"

Icy Swallow's shout shook the woman out of her shock. She grabbed her son and ran with all her might. The wall extended to cover her, and the woman was able to round a corner, clearing the line of fire.

"She's with Falcon, take her down!"

The men resumed their fire, bullets striking the wall of ice.

But Icy Swallow stood firm, the bullets unable to penetrate through her defenses.

And as the woman exited the street, Icy Swallow turned her head to face the men.

Her heart pounded.

Heat coursed through her body, cutting through the cold and lighting a fire in her stomach.

Her face twisted into a snarl.

The wind picked up and lifted her hair.

Dust and snow began to twirl around her.

Ice crept out along the ground beneath her feet.

Cold fog surrounded her hands.

Her breath condensed.

Her eyes began to shine with blue light.

"You...you *monsters.* Your rampage through this country ends today!"

She pushed her hands forward. The wall of ice began sliding forward, grinding the street underneath. The men kept firing but were forced to jump out of the way as the wall crashed in their cars. They rose to their feet but Icy Swallow thrust her left hand forward, and a mighty cone of cold air blasted, flipping another car over. With her right hand, she formed another wall in front of her, blocking the bullets as the men resumed firing.

And she began to step forward. She formed icicles in the sky above her wall, and sent them whizzing forward, striking into the ground around the men as they dodged. She launched another blast of cold air, freezing the guns in the men's hands, and then trapping their feet in blocks of ice. She grit her teeth as she marched towards them.

But she didn't notice as one man crawled out from underneath one of the cars she flipped, blood dripping from his forehead. His arm shook as he extended it forward, a pistol in hand.

He squeezed the trigger.

The sound of a gunshot rang through the street.

Icy Swallow stopped moving.

A shell casing hit the ground.

Time stood still.

Her eyes widened.

She slowly looked down.

A red spot appeared on her side, growing around a hole in her clothes.

She fell to the ground.

Everything started to grow quiet.

She faintly heard someone shout behind her.

"NO!"

She heard windows shatter.

A cold gale blew overhead, stirring up the streets.

She heard men shout.

She heard guns fire.

She heard men cry.

She heard wet thuds.

She heard men scream.

She grit her teeth and focused on her wound. Ice began to grow on her side. A small bullet dropped from her body, pushed out by ice that grew and covered the injury.

She gasped.

She coughed.

And then she groaned, lifting her head.

Her eyes widened.

Blood filled the streets.

All around her were dead men, spikes of ice piercing through them.

Icy Falcon now stood over the man who had shot her, crushing the man's hand with his boot.

He had a huge spike of ice covering his fist.

The man was crying.

"N-No, please! Have mercy!"

Icy Swallow opened her mouth.

"F-Falcon…"

Icy Falcon swung his fist down.

Icy Swallow winced.

The man went silent.

Icy Falcon slowly rose to his feet. He turned to face her, blood still splattered on him in places. His eyes widened as he saw her. He glanced to her side, exhaling his breath as he saw the ice there.

Then he shook his head and narrowed his eyes at her.

"Go home. Stay there. You're done."

"F-Falcon…"

He turned away from her.

"This is war. This is not a place for children. This is not a place for heroes."

Moisture built in her eyes.

"It's a place for soldiers."

And with that, he took off into the air.

Icy Swallow reached for him but she couldn't stand to her feet.

She fell back.

She lay on the ground.

And then her tears burst forth.

△△△

Bob heaved a sigh as he watched in the distance.

The paramedics were already on the way. Good ones, already paid ahead of time. From what he saw, the girl should survive.

The match was lit.

Now to toss it into the powder keg…and then try to contain the damage.

Bob heaved another sigh.

And then he began uploading the film on his camera…

△△△

On the second floor of a building, men ran up the stairs, grabbing handguns and shotguns. They slammed the double doors closed, knocking over tables and dressers to form a makeshift barricade. The men then ran to the center of the room, taking cover behind couches and tables on their sides. Sweat dripped down their faces. One of them gulped.

Beyond the doors were shouts and thuds. A gunshot rang out, and then a man cried in pain. The wind howled, rattling the doors, as if a storm grew within the building itself. They heard a final thudding sound.

And then all went silent.

The men held their breaths, pointing their guns at the door with trembling hands.

Footsteps broke the silence.

Thud.

Thud.

Thud.

Thud.

They grew louder…and then stopped.

BANG!

Something hit the door.

A man yelled in the back.

The room lit up with smoke and light as all the men opened fire.

The door was filled with holes and splinters.

Shell casings clattered to the floor. Men gasped for breath as the smoke lingered in the air.

And then the wall to their side exploded.

A boulder of ice smashed through the room, crushing furniture and legs. Guns spun towards the hole in the wall when a volley of sharp, cold daggers sped through the room. Men cried as blood filled the air. A blast of wind and snow knocked the men to the ground.

They groaned and tried to stand to their feet. They lifted their heads.

A howling white vortex spun through a large hole in the wall.

It surged forward.

A layer of ice covered the entire room and all the furniture inside it.

And all the men along with it.

△△△

"Breaking news: Icy Falcon battles cartels in the streets, with deadly results!"

△△△

A car had ice covering its wheels. There was a jagged hole in its windshield, surrounded by blood...

△△△

"Let's take a look at footage straight from the scene. Viewers please be advised, the following images may be disturbing."

△△△

At another building, broken doors fell off their hinges. A body leaned over a broken window. Red blood and melted ice mixed on the floor...

△△△

"Neither Mexican authorities nor the ILS have released any statements or responded to any requests for comments. Questions remain on whether this was an arrest gone wrong, an act of self-defense, or a brutal killing."

△△△

On the side of the road in the dead of night there was a ditch. A ditch filled with 6-foot blocks of ice...

△△△

"I have to ask, why is it that this man is allowed to commit murder in public and just...get away with it? What separates him from the cartels?"

"I'd say the fault lies with the cartels. If you're going to shoot first, you should expect people to shoot back. Icy Falcon did nothing wrong as far as I'm concerned."

△△△

A bar was heavily damaged, its neon sign now broken and sparking. A police chief lay among the bodies scattered across the booths inside...

△△△

"Further investigations reveal Icy Falcon's mentee Icy Swallow was on the scene and injured during the battle. Should Icy Falcon have assaulted the cartels with a young girl in tow? Was this mission too risky?"

△△△

At a restaurant in a high-class hotel, a glacier stood around a table where the mayor sat. He was locked inside the glacier, his face frozen in a scream.

△△△

"Icy Falcon is a hero. We all know what the cartels do. They deserved it, one hundred percent."

"I, I don't know. I look up to Icy Falcon, he's our hero. I'll stand behind him, whatever he did. I have to."

"I thought he was different. That he was better. But in the end it's just more of the same. Just another killer in our streets."

△△△

Londyn stood in her office, holding a phone by her head. She was frowning, heavily.

"Look, Falcon, you need to tone it down. You're going too far. I get you had a good reason, but killing men in the streets wasn't the right way to go about it."

"It is in war."

Londyn held the brow of her nose with her free hand.

"Look, things aren't too far gone yet, Falcon. I'm not asking you to stop, just, lay low for a bit. Come in, talk with us. Maybe we can find a better way, get you some support.

You don't need to do this on your own, let us help you."

"This is not your war, Director. This is not the League's fight, it's Mexico's. Don't interfere."

"Falcon, wait…"

Icy Falcon hung up the call.

Londyn heaved a heavy sigh. Linda walked up behind her, a concerned look in her eye.

"Director, what are we going to do?"

Londyn heaved a sigh and turned to the other person in the room. He was a man in a suit with neat hair just starting to gray.

This was Edward Carter.

Once Londyn's political liaison during her minion days, Edward Carter now took on a new role as the Vice-Director of the ILS. With how quickly and dramatically the ILS was expanding, Londyn needed a bit of help at the top level. So she had brought in her old contact to help her manage the political side of things.

A side of things that wasn't going particularly well, as Vice-Director Carter heaved a sigh.

"Mexico City hasn't even pressed charges yet, much less called for an arrest, so they won't take kindly to us getting involved. And technically, he's right. The ILS has no business getting involved with drug cartels, so eyebrows will be raised if we unilaterally step into law enforcement. Which means until a super shows up or the authorities ask for our help, there's not much we can do, not if you want to keep them playing ball, Director."

Londyn heaved another sigh and turned back to Linda.

"Have our people keep investigating that rumored new drug. Vice-Director, handle the clean up for that situation in Ethiopia. I'll talk with Mexico City personally, I want us ready to act the moment we can."

"Yes Director."

"I'm on it."

△△△

Back in the DEA office, a whole bureau of agents stood in silence in front of the television. Steve stared blankly.

"Well, Wilson, looks like you weren't crazy after all."

Wilson heaved a sigh.

"Kind of wish I was."

"So what now?"

"I'm not sure…"

Agent Wilson turned to look at the Bureau chief, Nathan. Nathan sighed, and shook his head.

"…it doesn't much matter. Even that's not enough for Mexico City to change their tune. Or rather, they're scared of ending up on Falcon's list. I'm not even sure if they should, we have plenty of enemies without adding a superhero to the list. Speaking of which, time to get back to work everyone."

Steve turned to Wilson.

"So what are you going to do now?"

Wilson shrugged.

"My job, what else?"

Steve raised an eyebrow.

"Seriously? You're going to investigate Mexico's Hero?"

Wilson sighed.

"That, that out there? That wasn't justice, it was vengeance. Falcon's getting more sloppy, more emotional, more brutal. I've seen what happens to good men who spent too long in the field, how it changed them. Trust me, nothing good is going to come from letting this go on, for anyone. Besides…"

"Besides…?"

"However this goes down, however this ends, we need to understand the Icy Falcon. Not just the cape and the powers, but the man underneath."

Wilson sat down on his desk. Arranged across it were numerous clippings from old newspapers, and a map.

"I just hope I have enough time."

△△△

Icy Falcon stood on a rooftop at night, a pair of binoculars in hand. He was watching a building on the outskirts of town, hidden on the other side of a large hill.

He already knew what was inside. A major cartel warehouse, the loss of which would be a heavy blow.

But he wasn't here for them. Not tonight.

His heart began to pound as he waited. He could feel his chest tie into a knot.

Memories flashed through his mind unprompted.

The sound of gunshots ran through his head.

He saw a shocked face and dripping blood.

He heard a tear-filled wail.

He narrowed his eyes and took a deep breath, pushing his churning stomach down.

It didn't matter. What mattered was the war. Finishing this fight.

Mexico had no heroes. Mexico needed no heroes.

It needed soldiers.

It cried out for justice. For vengeance.

And he would deliver it.

Whatever he needed to do.

There, finally, two lights appeared in the distance, driving along the dusty road. A truck approached in the night, heading to the back lot of the cartel's warehouse. Icy Falcon kept his eyes on it.

The truck came to a stop and the back opened up. Men exited the rear, carrying boxes and crates.

They weren't cartel guys in casual clothes.

They weren't dirty cops in uniform.

They were armored men with fully enclosed helmets.

Icy Falcon furrowed his brow.

This was it.

The villain behind the super drugs.

Icy Falcon waited as the truck was unloaded and closed. The headlights came on, and the truck began to move. Icy Falcon spread his wings, using the faintest gust possible to carry himself through the sky. He stalked the truck as it drove down the empty road, careful to stay away from the light of the moon.

Finally, the one behind all this.

The source of the new drugs.

And the last weapon the cartels had to stop him.

Soon, he would end this threat at the source.

And then the cartels would be helpless before him.

And he would cut them down.

One, by, one.

△△△

Agent Wilson sighed and held his head with both his hands. It was late at night at the DEA office, Steve and the DEA agents had already gone home. Wilson was taking a break, watching the news. There was more and more blood. More and more killings. And still the authorities did nothing. Still he had nothing but what he could scrounge on his own, in a country he couldn't even speak the language of. Didn't they see what was happening? Didn't they see how this was going to end?

Agent Wilson sighed again.

Even if they did, still they wouldn't act. How could they? The Falcon's prey was no longer limited to the criminals themselves. Informants, dirty cops, even corrupt politicians had fallen by his hands. Anyone who stood up against him might find themselves next on his list.

And the ones with the courage to stand up anyways would sing his praises instead.

He thought of calling the ILS. Director Green couldn't be happy with what was going on. But what was the point? The

ILS wasn't going to let a government agent tell them how to handle one of their top heroes. And, well, if the ILS was willing and able to do something, it would have already been done.

So that left him. One federal agent in a country not his own, with no resources and no backup, investigating the most popular and powerful man in the nation. For a crime no one considered a crime, with nothing but a gut feeling to convince them that they should be worried.

He sighed and turned to the paper on his desk, giving it one last look.

This was it.

The end of the trail.

The earliest known appearance of Icy Falcon.

And still no clues to who he was or where he came from.

Wilson stood from his seat and walked out of the room.

Still, he wasn't going to give up just yet. If he couldn't figure this out...there was no way he'd figure any of the other mysteries he was interested in. At least he *had* a trail this time, which was much more than the raw gut feeling that drove him on the other cases.

So...whether he was too late or not...whether anyone in the country wanted him to or not...he was going to go as far as he could, and see where the trail led...

> *AUTHOR'S COMMENTARY: ...this is not my favorite chapter. Anyways. Who is behind the mystery drugs? What will be the results of Icy Falcon's crusade? What will become of Icy Swallow? Can Agent Wilson do anything about all this? Tune in next time, to find out...*

CHAPTER 24 - WAR NEVER CHANGES

The truck entered a small suburban area and pulled into the lot of a warehouse. Icy Falcon swung around several times, making notes of entrances and probable escape routes. Once he was satisfied, he dove straight for the garage area.

The minions in the area had but a moment to turn his way before icy spikes shattered on their skulls. They fell to the ground, though their armor kept them alive. A quick blast of snowy wind covered them, encasing them in ice before they could rise.

Icy Falcon strode into the still open garage door, freezing the wheels and engines of every vehicle he could find. He then turned to the door leading into the compound.

The outside of the building hardly warranted attention. It had the same bricks, wood, and metal most buildings in the area were constructed from. Its walls were rough and dirty and there was graffiti all over. Dust coated the walls and the roof, the windows were fogged and dirty. The metal parts had started to rust, what paint remained was cracked and peeling.

The inside could not be more different.

There were spotless, sterile tile floors and walls, all colored white. The facility was lit by bright, fluorescent lights. There were automatic glass doors, allowing for movement without touching the handles.

It looked more like the inside of a hospital than an aging warehouse.

Icy Falcon frowned and narrowed his eyes.

This was it.

At first he crept along the walls, freezing over any camera he saw and listening for the thud of boots.

But the facility was quiet and empty.

His eyes narrowed further and he started to run.

He heard no alarms. He saw no guards. He encountered no patrols. He didn't find defenses of any kind. That meant one of two things.

One, these were rank amateurs who had no idea what they were doing.

Or two, they already knew he was here and were already halfway out the door.

Faster and faster he moved until he was sprinting at full speed. Eventually he came to a large double door. He spared a moment to catch his breath, then he pushed the doors open.

He found himself in a large, dark room. There were large vats, some empty, others filled with a bright green liquid. There were tables where he could make out the form of faintly shimmering Adranis bulbs, surrounded by machinery, tools, and scientific instruments he could not identify in the dark. In the corner were barrels of toxic waste.

And then he was blinded by light.

As he shielded his face he heard the voice of an old man. He looked around the room as the glare began to fade. There, up on an elevated platform and surrounded by recording equipment, was an old man in a lab coat. He was bald, his skull covered in some sort of scarring, and he was facing one of the cameras. He glanced behind at Icy Falcon, and then turned around with a big grin on his face.

"Icy Falcon! Welcome, welcome! I am humbled that one such as you would visit my humble abode! Come, come, take a look at the work of Professor Mutant!"

Icy Falcon gripped his fists.

"Your work ends today."

"Not so, Mr. Falcon. For science, science never sleeps!

Never dies! And I am in the midst of the greatest breakthrough of our generation!"

Icy Falcon narrowed his eyes.

"And what is that?"

"I'm glad you asked! While that charlatan Tanifuji plays around with a campfire, I have unlocked the fundamental truth of humanity! No longer shall we be at the whims of fate and evolution, no longer a random cosmic fluke in an uncaring universe! For I have mastered evolution itself! No longer chaotic and random, but beautiful and with purpose! Behold!"

Professor Mutant pressed a button on a remote. One of the vats ahead of Icy Falcon began to drain its liquid, revealing the form inside.

Inside was a hulking beast of a man, standing twice as tall as Icy Falcon. He had rippling and bulging muscles, with hands larger than his head. A coat of brown fur covered the man from head to toe, revealing only his face and hands.

Icy Falcon gripped his fists tighter.

"So you're the one responsible for the super drug after all."

Professor Mutant shook his head.

"Drug is such a paltry term for my work, Mr. Falcon! This is no mere narcotic, nothing more than a fleeting moment of juvenile pleasure. This, this is the cure! The solution! An end to weakness, to sickness, to the death of humanity at the hands of uncaring gods and an indifferent universe!"

He pressed another button. The vat began to hum and vibrate.

"I must thank you, Mr. Falcon, for volunteering today. Live combat tests with natural supers are a major gap in my data."

The man in the vat opened his eyes.

He snarled.

Then he let out a mighty roar, and then smashed straight through the glass.

Icy Falcon simply raised his hand and the beast was obscured in a mighty, cone-shaped blast of snowy wind.

"Testing finished."

Icy Falcon took a step forward.

And then a furry fist slammed into his face.

Icy Falcon bounced once on the ground before righting himself, a gust of wind slowing his speed. The beast was bounding towards him, winding up another punch. Icy Falcon quickly leapt to the side, the man's fist crashing into an empty vat behind him.

Professor Mutant chuckled.

"I think you'll find my Feverish Nephilim to be quite the hurdle, Mr. Falcon. After all, he was specifically developed with you in mind! For the record, I have no personal quarrel with you, in fact I find such emotional vendettas quite the inefficient allocation of effort. But it was somewhat refreshing to have a specific goal in mind, a great challenge to overcome. So I must admit, I've been greatly anticipating seeing you clash!"

Icy Falcon lifted his cape as he leapt to the side, shooting a barrage of ice spikes. But as the spikes approached Feverish Nephilim, the air around him shimmered. The spikes began to melt mid-flight, with barely a needle landing on target.

"Impressive, is it not? His sweat glands have been replaced with specialized vent organs that can heat his surroundings to quite the temperature. Combined with his dense fur and naturally armored skin, and I think you'll find even your ice cannot leave a scratch on him, Mr. Falcon!"

"We'll see about that."

Icy Falcon drew his arms up and then dropped to the ground, slamming his hands on the floor in front of him. A thin layer of ice shot from his hands along the floor, forming a line along the floor between Icy Falcon and Feverish Nephilim.

And once the ice reached within a few feet of the man...

A glacier exploded into being with a loud crackle,

encasing Feverish Nephilim in several feet of ice all around. The man stood still, his face locked into a vicious snarl. Icy Falcon let out a breath that condensed midair.

And then he heard a cracking noise.

A small crack formed on the edge of the glacier.

And then another.

Another crack formed.

And the noise grew louder...

The cracks joined together and spidered across the icy structure.

And then with a mighty crack and a thunderous roar Feverish Nephilim broke free from the glacier, leaping forward. The ground rumbled as he landed, the super himself dropping his shoulders and breathing heavily.

But never once taking his eyes off Icy Falcon.

Icy Falcon grimaced and flapped his cape, launching into the air. He banked hard and swung towards Professor Mutant.

Feverish Nephilim took a deep breath and let out a roar towards Icy Falcon. The air shimmered along the path of the shout. When the shimmering air met Icy Falcon he tumbled to the side and dropped from the air.

"Hehehe, you didn't think I wouldn't account for your mobility, would you Mr. Falcon? It is quite literally in your name after all."

Icy Falcon winced as he slammed into the ground. He barely had time to roll out of the way as two fists slammed upon his landing position. He stumbled to his feet, leaning back as a fist swung by his face, fur brushing the tip of his nose. He leapt back, flapping his cape for a gust of wind, and then rolled along the ground when the shimmering air disrupted him once again. He stood up just in time to see Feverish Nephilim charging straight towards him. He barely leapt to the side as the man slammed into a pillar of metal pipes, the metal bending and snapping with a crunch.

Professor Mutant tapped upon his tablet as he watched

the battle unfold. Icy Falcon dove this way and that, time and time again avoiding being flattened against a wall or a pillar by the skin of his teeth. Icy Falcon launched a large spike, and Feverish Nephilim grabbed it out of the air. Icy Falcon sent out a gust of cold air, and Feverish Nephilim's fur parted it like a rock in the waves. Icy Falcon froze the ground, and Feverish Nephilim's wide and rough feet gripped on it as easily as pavement.

Nothing Icy Falcon did had any effect.

And with each movement he was getting slower, fatigue starting to set in.

Professor Mutant's face broke into a wide grin.

△△△

Constanza was lying in her bed, her face buried into her pillow. Quiet sobs could be heard coming from the room.

She had only returned from the hospital a few hours ago. The doctors had praised her quick thinking, but there was more to her recovery than removing the bullet. No one had expected the wound to heal that quickly, not even her. She could still feel the cloud of cold hanging around the wound, her insides tickling as her power donated energy to her cells.

She was going to be fine.

Physically that is.

Beyond that she didn't know what to think. She barely even could think. A fog hung over her mind as a knot constricted in her chest. Anytime she thought, anytime she remembered what happened, the dam would burst forth and fill her eyes with water.

Why did things turn out like this?

She finally gained the power to help. She finally gained the power to fight back, to make a difference. She finally had the chance to change things.

And things had changed.

But not like she had ever imagined.

Icy Falcon wasn't just the Hero of Mexico because of his power, or his bravery. He was the Hero of Mexico because he was *better*. He was the only one who could wade into the muck of the drug war and yet stay above it. He was the only one who could stop the violence without expanding it. He was the only one who gave them any hope that one day, the situation might change.

And now that dream was dead.

Icy Falcon, like so many others, had been pulled into the cycle of violence and blood.

And it was all her fault.

If she had been more careful…

If she had paid more attention…

If she hadn't lost herself in that moment…

If she had just listened…

She thought she, too, could be better. That she could fight back without falling in. That she could achieve justice for her parents without sinking to the level of those scumbags.

But she was wrong.

When she thought of that moment, her stomach still boiled. Her hands trembled. She still wanted to rip those monsters apart. A part of her was *happy* when she saw Icy Falcon end their lives.

In the end, she wasn't better. She was a killer, just like them. She lost herself to her rage, she wanted their blood. She didn't seek justice. She sought vengeance.

And because of that, she had gone too far. Saving the woman and child was one thing. Attacking the men was another. And losing awareness of her surroundings in a fit of rage was simply unacceptable.

And because of that, now Icy Falcon was a killer too.

And then she heard a knock on the door.

She ignored it. Antonio could let himself in, and anyone else could wait.

The knocking continued.

She heaved a sigh.

But she stood up.

She slowly walked to the door. She let out another sigh and opened it up.

There was no one there.

She looked around. There was no one even in the area. She felt a scream building in her chest.

And then she looked down.

A plain white envelope sat in front of the door.

It was addressed to her.

She picked it up. She gulped. Just what could this be?

She opened it up.

Inside was a letter and nothing else. Written on it was a single line and an address.

And as she read the words, her heart dropped to her stomach, and began to pound in her chest.

Your friend is in danger.

Who sent this to her? What did they mean? Why did they send it?

But...

She felt something. Something in the pit of her stomach, in the back of her mind.

It told her that the warning was true.

Her legs leapt into motion the moment that thought passed her mind. She barely remembered to grab her mask and a wad of cash before she flew out the door, screaming at the first taxi she saw.

She had to get there.

Nothing else mattered.

She couldn't lose anything else tonight.

ΔΔΔ

Icy Falcon's shoulders moved up and down, his mouth hung open as he took deep breaths. Cool sweat dripped down his brow, his arms and legs were trembling. He looked up at the beast ahead of him.

Feverish Nephilim was unscathed.

There was not a scratch on his fur, not a spot of blood. He was breathing a little heavy but even now his breaths quieted down.

The situation wasn't great.

On the platform above, Professor Mutant scribbled away at his tablet, finishing it off with a final tap.

"Well, Mr. Falcon, this has been a pleasure. This experiment has been most enlightening, the data gathered tonight will push my research to new heights. But all good things must come to an end, no?"

He pressed a button and Feverish Nephilim stood still.

"As I said though, I have no personal quarrel with you. In light of your contributions to my research, I am willing to let bygones be bygones. Or perhaps we could come to a more fruitful arrangement? Everyone has room for improvement, even someone as impressive as yourself, no?"

Icy Falcon took a deep breath, trying to steady his breathing. He wiped the sweat from his brow and glared at the villain.

"This ends today."

Professor Mutant let out a sigh, shaking his head.

"I had not thought you one to be swept by emotion, Mr. Falcon. But so be it then."

Professor Mutant pressed another button. Feverish Nephilim resumed his approach. Icy Falcon gripped his hands into fists and raised them in front of him.

Feverish Nephilim let out a roar and lowered his head, charging for a mighty tackle.

Icy Falcon shuffled his feet, entering a more secure footing.

The ground rumbled as the beast approached.

This time, Icy Falcon didn't bother with ice.

Feverish Nephilim was nearly on top of him.

Icy Falcon put his weight onto his legs, bending his knees.

And then he leapt to the side at the last second.

CLANG!

Feverish Nephilim slammed headfirst into a metal pillar, and lay still for a moment. Professor Mutant shook his head and chuckled.

"Very clever, Mr. Falcon. But it only delays the inevitable. You still cannot harm my Feverish Nephilim with your powers."

Icy Falcon raised his hand, his palm facing forward.

"I don't need to."

With a grunt, he shot the largest spike of ice he could still make.

Right at the last undamaged pillar.

The metal across the facility groaned and the overhead platforms swayed, Professor Mutant latched onto the railing and clung to it with all his might.

The upper platforms fell to the ground with a mighty crash, crushing everything underneath.

As the dust settled, Professor Mutant groaned. He tried to lean up but winced as sharp pain shot through his back. Ahead of him, Feverish Nephilim lay on the ground, his head peeking out of a pile of rubble.

And then Professor Mutant heard footsteps approaching.

Icy Falcon strode into view, a jagged piece of metal in hand. He walked over to where Feverish Nephilim lay, the large man still unconscious. Icy Falcon raised his hands.

Professor Mutant winced as the jagged edge plunged into Feverish Nephilim's head.

"That…"

Professor Mutant coughed some dust out of his mouth.

"That was excessive, Mr. Falcon. He was no longer a threat to you. There was no reason for such brutality."

Icy Falcon turned towards him, striding forward.

"You claim to do science, yet you participate in a war."

An icy spike filled Icy Falcon's right hand. Professor Mutant sighed and closed his eyes.

"I see. I seem to have misjudged you, Mr. Falcon."

Icy Falcon raised an eyebrow.

"You seem awfully calm."

Professor Mutant shrugged.

"I am going to die now, that much is clear. But I am a scientist, not a soldier. I care not for victory or defeat, my only goal was progress. I stand on the shoulders of giants, Mr. Falcon, and now? Giants shall stand on mine. My work shall change the world, incomplete or not. Though my life shall end, my legacy will endure forever. My only regret is that I shall not see it finished."

Icy Falcon's eyes narrowed.

"No."

He stepped forward.

"I am going to kill every last person in this facility, destroy every last computer, and shred every piece of paper. Nothing will remain when I am done. Your work dies with you."

Professor Mutant's eyes widened.

"Y-You can't! I-I know you are angry, but even you must see the value of my work! We can eliminate all disease, we can make humanity immortal! P-Please, I beg you, give it to the ILS, or to a non-profit, or something. Take it out of the wrong hands, keep it for yourself if you must. But don't let humanity suffer for our differences!"

Icy Falcon continued to step forward.

"P-Please, Mr. Falcon. Even you must see that there is no good in the destruction of knowledge. This, this is not justice. This is madness!"

Icy Falcon raised his hand.

"This…is war."

The ice shot forth.

△△△

Antonio sighed as he stared at the computer. His nose itched something fierce. But company policy was clear, these hazmat suits were to be worn at all times on the premises.

Antonio hadn't actually seen anything hazardous but he wasn't going to take chances with that.

He typed away, entering in some data and stifled a yawn.

Don't get him wrong, this was a great job. The pay was amazing and the hours weren't too bad. He would always be thankful to his employer, working in a fancy medical research facility like this was something he hadn't even dreamed of.

But well, entering numbers he didn't understand into sheets he didn't understand got boring after a while.

Something reached his ears. He couldn't make it out, but it sounded like muffled voices and soft thuds. And something like the wind blowing? Antonio, curious and perhaps desperate for a break, looked up, straining his ears to catch whatever was going on. But the noises stopped as soon as they started, all Antonio could hear was the soft steps of someone walking down the hall outside.

Suddenly the door slammed open. Antonio dropped to the ground, his coworkers screaming all around him. Something slammed into the computer overhead, sending sparks and shards of metal flying over him. Antonio whimpered and crawled under the desks. He nearly jumped as something landed in front of him.

It was a body.

Antonio's heart raced and he closed his eyes. He crawled on top of the obstacle, desperately trying not to think of what it was.

Then a blast of wind sent him flying through the air.

He cried out as he slammed into the wall, sliding down until he was leaning against it. The eyepieces of his mask were cracked and fogged, so he pulled it off.

And his eyes widened.

"Icy...Falcon?"

Icy Falcon was surrounded by a vortex of wind and hail, smashing every computer in the room.

And sending icicles into the skulls of Antonio's

coworkers.

Icy Falcon turned to him. Antonio let out a scream. Icy Falcon lifted his hand...

"NO!"

Antonio heard another scream join his own.

Ice soared towards him.

Something passed in front of his eyes.

Blood flew through the air.

Antonio's eyes widened.

Icy Falcon's did too.

A thin wall of ice hung over Antonio, ice spikes were pierced through it.

Antonio lay against the wall, trembling in fear and shock.

Constanza had jumped on top of him, blood now dripping from the wounds on her back.

"I...won't...let you..."

"Constanza? Constanza!"

Icy Falcon took a step back.

Images flashed before his eyes.

A girl with white hair and a blue dress known as Icy Swallow, her eyes widened as her side bled.

A man with a wide grin on his face called the Red Hawk, the last time he was ever seen.

A boy with red hair who named himself Fiery Falcon, his broken body laying on the side of the road.

A woman with sharp eyes and straight black hair who the people called Nightbolt, her eyes closed as she breathed her last.

An old man in his favorite car, now a burning metal husk across the street. Icy Falcon never got his name in the many times they spoke.

And a girl. Just a bit older than he was at the time. Not someone anyone would know. She had tears in her eyes but had a smile on her face as she lay on top of him. Blood streamed down the side of her head. She uttered a faint whisper he barely could hear.

"Please...live..."

Icy Falcon's eyes shook. He stared down at his hands. He stared up again.

"Constanza! Talk to me! CONSTANZA!"

Icy Falcon fled.

△△△

Bob sat in a plain van a block over. He was staring at a wall of monitors connected to security cameras from the facility. He focused on one in particular, a blinking red light in the corner of the screen. He closed his eyes and let out a deep sigh.

He shook his head.

He hit a key and stopped the recording.

He moved the mouse.

He clicked 'upload'.

He leaned back in his chair.

He took out a flask.

"Heroes...are so...annoying..."

Paramedics were already on the way. It was out of his hands at this point.

He let out another sigh and then took a drink.

△△△

On the television, Brendan Baird heaved a sigh. He took a deep breath before he started to speak.

"...breaking news folks, Icy Falcon and his protege Icy Swallow had a falling-out that turned violent just last night. GNN is still investigating the details, all we know at present is that Icy Swallow was taken to the hospital in critical condition and Icy Falcon has not been seen since. We suspect the facility where the fight occurred was in use by a supervillain and that the two heroes disagreed on the treatment of the workers there. GNN has discovered footage from the scene that was posted to the web, please be advised that the following scenes may be disturbing."

> AUTHOR'S COMMENTARY: ...this is also not my favorite chapter. Anyways. How shall the tale of the Icy Falcon and the Icy Swallow conclude? Tune in next time, to find out...

CHAPTER 25 - THE CAPTAIN AND THE FALCON

"Icy Swallow remains in critical condition, doctors continue working to save her life."

"We have confirmation the location was a supervillain hideout, but questions still remain on the fateful showdown."

"Icy Falcon has not been seen since. Director Green has not confirmed if the ILS has been able to contact him."

"All Mexico holds its breath as we ask, how did it come to this?"

"What was Icy Swallow doing? That was a supervillain base for crying out loud! No one good works there. It was just naive to stick her neck out for someone like that."

"No matter what, Swallow is just a kid, and Falcon was her mentor. He should not have let her get hurt, least of all by his own hand."

"Did you hear what's been happening? Super-drugs in the streets, superpowered cartels? I don't care what happened, Icy Falcon needed to stop them. No matter what."

"I feel for Icy Falcon, I really do. But he stooped down to the cartel's level. What makes him any different from them? It's not the drugs that ruin things, it's the violence in the streets. And that's exactly what happened here."

"Why didn't someone do something? Anything? About Falcon, about the cartels, about all of this? Shouldn't the government have stopped them? Where was the ILS? Shouldn't someone have stepped in sooner?"

"Should any of us be surprised? Icy Falcon has been killing

his way through this country for months. He killed a mayor for goodness sake! Oh they say the man was dirty but where was the proof? Are we really shocked now that someone like Swallow got caught in the crossfire?"

"Just...what is happening to this country? If this is our hero, then...just...where do we find our hope?"

"The Mexican authorities have reluctantly put out a call for Icy Falcon's arrest. No matter what happened, it seems there is a consensus that things have gone too far and Icy Falcon must give an account for his actions. Director Green has signaled that the ILS will cooperate in the investigation and, if necessary, the arrest."

△△△

Agent Wilson sat down at the table in a library, sweat dripping down his brow. There were nothing but old, rickety fans to ward off the heat. But he supposed he was lucky that a town like this even had a library.

He dropped a stack of old newspapers in front of his comrade. The brown skinned man rolled his eyes.

"Look, *señor*, do you even know what you're looking for? Nothing here you can't find in the city."

Wilson sighed and pulled out a wad of cash.

"Why don't you get us both something to drink?"

The man looked at him for a moment, then shrugged and took the cash, standing up and exiting the building.

Wilson shook his head.

What was he looking for, indeed?

Icy Falcon was a ghost. No one had seen heads or tails of him since that night. If they were even looking, that is. Oh, the ILS was on it, but the DEA didn't like changing focus. They just kept to the cartels with the excuse that Falcon would hit them again soon. The *federales*, well, even now they still weren't sure which side they fell on.

Wilson let out a sigh. He couldn't help but wonder if this

had any meaning. Clearly he was late, very very late. For a man with a lot of time on his hands, he sure ran out of it quickly.

Wilson began perusing the newspapers, just glancing at the photos since he couldn't read the words without his trusty assistant. The effort might be meaningless. It might be a waste of time. But if nothing else, it wouldn't be because he didn't try. He would see this through to the best of his ability.

And then he saw something.

The edge of his mouth curled up as he exhaled his breath.

"Looks like I found you."

There, in the corner of one of the pictures, was a little boy. He looked just like any other boy from a poor town in Mexico.

Except for his pure white hair.

△△△

Captain Hot Devil walked into the top office of ILS Tower as the elevator doors opened up. Director Green finished up a call as he entered.

"Hello, Director."

"Hello, Captain."

"What's the job this time?"

Director Green let out a sigh.

"...I need you to bring him in."

Captain Hot Devil raised an eyebrow.

"That's a tough ask. It's his home turf and I don't even speak Spanish. I won't be of much help."

Director Green shook her head.

"Local assets are already working to find him. I just need you there when he's found."

Captain Hot Devil heaved a sigh.

"...are you sure about this?"

"...I'm not sure about any of this. But he's gone too far, we can't let it go on any longer. And there's the question of the girl too..."

She sighed again.

"Look, try to talk to him. If anyone can reach him, it'll be you."

Captain Hot Devil groaned at that.

"...I'll try. But if I can't?"

She looked him in the eye.

"Then you're the best one to have there. He has to come in. No matter what."

Captain Hot Devil closed his eyes, sighing one more time.

"...all right. I'll leave immediately."

Director Green gave him a nod.

"I'm counting on you."

△△△

Captain Hot Devil arrived at the local ILS branch. Every which way ILS agents and employees ran about, searching papers, typing on computers, and answering phones. The Captain weaved around the bunch, careful not to get in anyone's way as he walked towards the branch leader.

"Ah, Captain Hot Devil, I'm Branch Director Chavez, glad you could make it. How was your trip?"

"Fine, you find anything yet?"

Chavez shook his head.

"We're coordinating with the DEA, got some eyes on the major known and suspected cartel bases. Next time he strikes, we'll know."

Captain Hot Devil grimaced. Just waiting for an attack didn't sit right with him. But he wasn't exactly the world's best detective, so what else could he do? Icy Falcon had ditched his ILS phone, and with it the only way for the ILS to track him directly. He always appreciated the ILS's support for hero privacy beforehand, but now the downsides of that policy were all too apparent.

"Sir?"

Another ILS staff member walked up to the pair.

"We have someone on the line. Says he's from BSI and he has a lead."

The Captain raised an eyebrow.

"BSI? What are they doing down here?"

Chavez shrugged.

"Guess they must've been sent to assist the DEA. Can't imagine what they found that we missed."

This time the Captain shrugged.

"A lead's a lead."

"That's true, I'll put it on speaker for you."

"This is ILS Branch Director Chavez."

"This is Agent Wilson, BSI."

"Hello Agent Wilson, heard you got something for us?"

"I think I know where he could be: town of Ciérón"

Chavez nodded to another staff member. Ciérón appeared on a large monitor in the room, relevant information popping up on the side. Chavez frowned.

"I'm not sure where you're coming from, Agent Wilson. Small town in the middle of nowhere, looks like even the cartels forgot it. Why would Icy Falcon go there?"

"He's from there, sir."

Chavez paused for a moment.

"You sure?"

"Positive. And I think he has people buried there too."

Captain Hot Devil nodded.

"I'll head over."

Chavez put the phone on mute.

"You sure? I'm not sure he'd be there even if Agent Wilson is correct. We can send someone to check it out first."

Captain Hot Devil shrugged.

"Just a feeling. Besides, I'll only be getting in your way here. Might as well check it out instead of breathing down your people's necks."

Chavez nodded.

"Agent Wilson, ILS is enroute. Thanks for the tip."

"Happy to help, I'll meet you there."

Chavez hung up the phone and nodded to the Captain as he turned to leave.

"We'll call you if there's any developments."

"Same."

△△△

A bit later, Captain Hot Devil arrived at Ciérón. Agent Wilson was waiting for him by the entrance to the town. He stepped out of the car and shook the agent's hand.

"Is he here?"

Wilson shrugged.

"Just got here, myself. Cemetery's that way, I'm betting that's where he'll be"

"I see."

The pair began to walk in the direction Wilson had pointed. When they arrived at the cemetery, they saw him.

Icy Falcon, standing over a simple, time-worn grave.

"Nice work, Agent Wilson."

Wilson nodded.

"I'll call for backup, you going in right away?"

Captain Hot Devil nodded.

"He deserves a chance to talk."

△△△

Icy Falcon stood motionless, staring down at the grave. Captain Hot Devil walked up behind him at a casual pace. Icy Falcon spoke without moving his head.

"Captain."

"Falcon."

The two stood in silence for a bit.

"Are you here to bring me in?"

"I am."

"I see."

There was another moment of silence.

"So even the ILS wants to stop me now."

Captain Hot Devil frowned as he thought back to the past.

"Sometimes we need someone to stop us."

Icy Falcon closed his eyes.

"...it's the cartels who need to be stopped."

"No arguments here, but there are still lines you shouldn't cross. Trust me, I know that better than anyone."

"This is war, Captain. My war, Mexico's war. If not me, then who?"

Captain Hot Devil dropped his shoulders as he let out a sigh.

"Look Falcon, I once thought that too. These sons of guns need to be stopped. And we're the ones to stop them, whatever it takes. And, well, you know how it ended for me. I got so focused on the fight I forgot what was around me, and a lot of people got hurt who didn't need to. Our fight, it needs to be fought. But when we start hitting innocents in the crossfire, well, sometimes to move forward you need to take a step back."

Icy Falcon did not respond for a moment. He then began to clench his fists.

"...I can't stop. Not now. I need to do this. I need to win. For Mexico."

"...I think there's someone else who needs you right now. You come in with me, you'll have at least one more chance to talk."

Icy Falcon went silent at that. Captain Hot Devil nodded.

"She's alive. It's still up in the air but we think she's going to make it. And she'll need to talk to you. She deserves to talk to you."

Icy Falcon didn't respond at first. He frowned, and clenched his fists tighter. Eventually, he shook his head.

"...she's better off staying out of this. Staying away from me. Everyone is."

Captain Hot Devil sighed once more.

"You know I can't just let you go?"

Icy Falcon turned around, looking Captain Hot Devil in the eye.

"And you're going to stop me?"

Captain Hot Devil nodded, then glanced at the gravestone behind Icy Falcon.

"Yes, but not here."

Icy Falcon took a deep breath and nodded once.

Then the two heroes walked to the outskirts of town...

△△△

Captain Hot Devil and Icy Falcon stood in an empty desert, staring each other down. The sun shone down on them, a gust of wind blew a spiral of dust between them.

Without a word they leapt at each other, both their fists pulled back. Icy Falcon swung first, Captain Hot Devil leaned to the side and countered. Icy Falcon blocked with his left and jabbed his right into Captain Hot Devil's side. Captain Hot Devil answered with a swing that caught Icy Falcon's jaw.

They traded blows for a minute before stepping back as if in sync.

Ice covered over two fists.

Flames blazed around two more.

They stepped back in and resumed the barrage, this time careful to catch fists with hands instead of faces. Flame met ice as fists collided over and over, a storm of bright red and shimmering blue.

Icy Falcon flew back, holding his cape wide to catch a gust of wind. He swung it forward, a barrage of ice flying out. Captain Hot Devil rolled to the side and swung his hand, a fireball burning across the sky. Icy Falcon spun around the ball and launched his counter.

Balls of fire met spikes of ice. Puffs of steam formed as they collided until both men were obscured by the mist.

Captain Hot Devil grimaced as a wall of icy spikes flew from the mist. He thrust both his hands forward, a wave of fire surging forth. The spikes shrunk and vanished into thin air as the wave collided into the mist.

Icy Falcon leapt above the burning wave, taking to the skies as the wind wrapped around him. He swung his left arm, ice raining from the sky as he did. Captain Hot Devil ran to the side, a trail of icy spikes following behind him. He leapt and rolled. As he came out of the roll he held his fists down, jets of fire streaming from them, and launched into the air.

The winds howled and intensified around the Icy Falcon. Captain Hot Devil was knocked to the side, sent spinning through the air. He surged backward with a jet of flame from his feet, then righted himself with flames from his hands.

"Stand down, Captain. You can't stop me."

"I can't do that, Falcon. You aren't leaving until you beat me."

Icy Falcon frowned. The winds around him howled and surged to gale force speed. Icy Falcon was shrouded in white as the vortex filled up with snow and hail. Captain Hot Devil let out a sigh.

"You can reach him, she said. You're the best one to have there, she said."

Captain Hot Devil wrapped himself in flames as a storm of wind and hail tore through the air. He let himself drop under the barrage of ice and then shot up at an angle towards the whirling vortex. He stopped his own movement as he collided with the wall of wind, allowing the gales to blow him around. He grit his teeth as chunks of ice pierced through his flames, leaving cuts and bruises all over his body.

He held on, spinning around the vortex.

His stomach began to churn.

More and more cuts appeared, his flames started to flicker.

He waited for his moment..

And then...

He found his timing.

He poured all his power into his feet, rocketing into the

sky. He left behind a ball of flame that continued to spin around the vortex as he launched straight towards the sun. He then cut off the flames around his body. He hung in the air, looking down upon the vortex. Wind and ice tore through the ball of fire until it flickered and died down.

And then the winds died down too.

Icy Falcon looked towards the ground, searching for his opponent.

Captain Hot Devil pulled back his fist as he began to fall, relying only on gravity to move.

Icy Falcon didn't see him.

And then his fist collided with Icy Falcon's cheek.

Both men plunged from the air.

Wind and flame barely slowed their descents as they slammed into the ground.

Captain Hot Devil groaned. Every inch of his body ached. Several parts more than ached.

But he leaned on his hands, pulled his legs under him, and began to stand on shaky feet.

He took deep breaths as he looked in front of him. Icy Falcon stood, slouched over and breathing heavily. He lifted his hand. Wind and snow began to swirl around it.

Captain Hot Devil swore under his breath as he lifted his own, his flame beginning to build once more.

The wind howled.

The fire raged.

The air began to freeze.

The air began to shimmer.

A blast of ice shot forward. A glacier grew in the desert.

A jet of fire ignited the air. A small column of red was swallowed by a sea of white and blue.

Icy Falcon panted for breath as he stared at the glacier in front of him.

It was over, he thought.

And then a red circle appeared on the ice in front of him.

A blast of smoke and shards of ice knocked him to the

ground. He shook his head and looked up.

Captain Hot Devil was standing over him, still shivering from the bits of ice stuck to his body but with flames coating his fists. Icy Falcon started to rise.

And then fell onto his back.

He stared at the sky as he took deep breaths.

Suddenly his arms felt heavy.

His legs refused to move.

His chest curled into an even tighter knot.

His vision spun and blurred.

He closed his eyes.

It was hard to think.

He was tired.

More tired than he had ever felt before.

He let out a deep breath as something wet fell down his cheek.

He had lost.

△△△

Captain Hot Devil sat on a low stone wall and watched as ILS agents loaded Icy Falcon into the back of a van, strapped down to a stretcher with medics at his side. Agent Wilson walked up to him and held out a bottle of water. The Captain took it with a nod and tanked it down.

"That was impressive."

Captain Hot Devil rolled his right shoulder and winced.

"That was painful."

Wilson watched as the doors of the van closed.

"You don't need to go with them? I'd think you'd need more than a couple straps to hold him down."

Captain Hot Devil shook his head.

"I'm sure the Director has some tricks up her sleeve. But it doesn't matter either way."

Wilson waited as Captain Hot Devil took a breath.

"...I shouldn't have beat him. Not if he wanted to win. Not

at his peak. But I saw the look in his eyes. He was already beat. He just hadn't realized it yet."

Wilson nodded.

"War wears down the best of us."

Captain Hot Devil nodded and stood with a sigh.

"Thank you for your help, Agent Wilson. It was thanks to you I had a chance to talk with him."

Wilson shook his hand.

"Anytime Captain. What will you do now?"

Captain Hot Devil began to walk.

"The ILS still has some business here."

△△△

Constanza leaned back into the raised hospital bed. She had her head turned, staring out the window. There was no expression on her face, no words in her mouth.

Right now, she had no idea what to think.

And then there was a knock at the door.

Constanza tilted her head. Antonio had gone to buy them some food and the nurse had just left, so who could it be?

She answered in a soft voice.

"Come in."

She gasped as her guest walked into the room.

"C-Captain Hot Devil?"

Captain Hot Devil nodded, and then smiled softly at her.

"Hey kid, glad to see you made it."

Her eyes widened.

"What are you doing here?"

The Captain frowned slightly, and then gave a sad smile.

"I'm here to apologize to you on behalf of the League and of Director Green."

Constanza's eyes widened even further.

"Apologize? To me? What for?"

The Captain let out a sigh.

"We can't help but feel responsible. There should have

been something we could've done. And in any case we should have reached out to you sooner."

Constanza shook her head.

"N-No, that's not true. I chose not to contact the League, so I don't blame you. I-If anything it's my fault. It's...my..."

Constanza turned back to the window. Captain Hot Devil waited in silence for a minute.

"...you ok, kid?"

She shut her eyes tight, but the tears still welled up.

"It...it's all my fault. If I hadn't...Icy Falcon...he wouldn't have..."

She covered her face.

And then she felt a hand on her shoulder.

"Look at me kid."

She let her hands drop and opened her eyes. Captain Hot Devil looked her in the eye as he spoke.

"It was NOT your fault. You did great work, and you were incredibly brave. Falcon's choices were his own. Don't blame yourself for any of this."

Her tears began to fall.

"It's just...h-he was my hero, you know? I looked up to him, w-we all did. He was the one who gave me hope. H-He was everything I wished I could be. S-So when he agree to train me...I thought I could help him, that I could finally change things. But then...I messed up...and now...everything has gotten worse and I just, I can't help but think it would have been better if I never got these powers. I don't deserve them."

The girl's shoulders trembled as she began to sob. Captain Hot Devil sighed once more.

"Look, kid, that's the thing. Falcon, me, us, heroes, we're all just people. People look up to us, put us on a pedestal, but at the end of the day we're no different from anyone else. We try our best, we try to do good, but it doesn't always work out. Sometimes we fail, sometimes we make mistakes, and sometimes we get messed up by what's going on around us."

He patted the girl on the shoulder.

"But that's all we can do, one step forward. Own our mistakes and try to be better next time. And Falcon, he was a hero. He was the man you looked up to, someone trying to do some good. But he's also just a man, and this time he took things too far. Even if you made a mistake, he did too, and his mistakes were his alone. And you were the one who ultimately paid the price for that. And well...things might never go back to the way they were before, for you or for him. This job is a lot messier than everyone realizes...so we have to just press on and do our best."

Captain Hot Devil gave a soft smile.

"And who knows, maybe there's still hope for him. I think he knows what he did. It might take him some time, but if there was a way back for me then maybe there's a way back for him too. And you better believe that if the two of us can move past our mistakes, then you can move past anything you did as well. You haven't even blown up a skyscraper yet, you know?"

Captain Hot Devil took a phone out of his pocket and placed it in Constanza's hand.

"And we want you to know that you're not alone, not anymore. The League will be there for you. If you need anything, even if you just want to talk, feel free to give us a call. And, if this is still the life you want for yourself, there's a place for you there too."

Constanza took the phone and gave a silent nod. The Captain rose to his feet.

"I know this is a lot to deal with. I'll be in the country for a while longer, so I'll check back in with you again, if that's all right."

Constanza looked up at him.

"What will you be doing?"

Captain Hot Devil narrowed his eyes, the edge of his mouth curling up slightly.

"Oh, just visiting some of Falcon's friends."

With that, Captain Hot Devil left the room. Constanza stared at the phone in her hand.

She closed her eyes.

After everything, after all she did, after all that had happened...

What...should she do?

She thought of the ILS...

She thought of Icy Falcon...

Tears streamed down her face once more.

But as she sobbed, her mind continued to work. Soon... she decided what to do.

△△△

The doors slammed open. Men pulled out their handguns and revolvers.

Captain Hot Devil strode through the door.

One of the men laughed and raised his hand. The others lowered their weapons.

"Ah, Captain Hot Devil himself! What does a *gringo* hero have to do with our humble business?"

Captain Hot Devil waved his hand. Jets of fire shot through the air, wrapping themselves around the guns and melting the barrels shut. The men in the room cried out and dropped the weapons. The leader stepped back.

"W-What are you doing? The ILS can't just hurt civilians like us!"

Captain Hot Devil strode forth and grabbed the speaker by the collar, lifting him into the air. Behind him, armed ILS and DEA agents rushed into the room, securing the other men.

"The ILS doesn't. But you're not a civilian anymore. You worked with a supervillain, spread super drugs into the streets. So you see, this isn't the ILS getting involved in your business. *You* stepped into ours."

Captain Hot Devil raised his fist. The man gulped at first, but then started to chuckle.

"Nice try, but you can't threaten me, Captain Hot Devil. A *gringo* hero beating down us regular *chicos*? That'll be all over the news, no matter what you say we've done."

The Captain's fist burst into flame, the man's eyes drawn to it.

"You know who I am, right?"

The man turned to him and nodded.

"Then you know I blew up a skyscraper in *downtown New York*."

He brought his fist closer, the man starting to sweat from the heat. The Captain stared into his eyes.

"So what do you think I'll do to you? Especially after what you did to some of our own?"

The man began to tremble as Captain Hot Devil brought his fist closer.

"Start. Talking."

> AUTHOR'S COMMENTARY: Did I plan the Captain / Falcon reference when I first made these characters all the way back in the first few chapters? Yes. Absolutely. It was all my master plan. Because I ~~pulled names from a random name generator and then wung it~~ spent a lot of time and effort developing unique and original characters with fully planned arcs, obviously. Anyways! What shall be the final conclusion of these things? What was the point of all this? What is the next step in the author's ~~definitely not improvised~~ ultimate master plan? Tune in next time, to find out!

CHAPTER 26 - THE END OF WINTER, THE START OF SPRING

Agent Wilson heaved a sigh as he returned to the BSI. He had been strongly commended, brought before the cameras. Even shook hands with a Senator. The BSI had been a 'stunning success' they said. Helped bring in a rogue hero, even! The Senator, who had been one of the ones to propose BSI in the first place, was playing up Wilson's 'victory' for all it was worth.

Not that anyone was expanding the BSI's budget, of course.

But Agent Wilson had left feeling unsatisfied. Yes, he had helped track down Icy Falcon. Yes, he solved the mystery murders going on down there.

But he still felt like there was something they all had missed.

Well, there wasn't much more he could do in any case. He had no evidence or ideas on what that gut feeling even was. And all the other loose ends were being wrapped up. The ILS was taking down the cartel in question and the DEA had thanked him and sent him packing.

So he'd just try to play up this victory as much as he could, see if he could gain access to a few more reports.

Maybe if he had a bit more intel, he could identify if he was just imagining things.

Or if there really was more going on in this world than anybody saw.

He heaved another sigh as the BSI receptionist called him. The cat had gone missing again.

Well, he'd stick it out at the BSI, for just a little longer...

△△△

And so the ILS and Captain Hot Devil rampaged through Mexico, tearing through the cartels and tracking down every last trace of Professor Mutant's work. Mexico City wasn't the most comfortable with the situation, but as both heroes and villains had gotten involved the ILS had a clear reason to act.

So now Director Green stood in her office, her phone in hand, listening to Captain Hot Devil reporting on the other end.

"The warehouse is secure. We found one of the special bulbs, but otherwise it was all normal stuff."

Londyn nodded.

"Our intel says that's the last of them. Once you've wrapped up you can head on home."

"Got it, I'll check in with the kid one more time on my way back."

"Thank you."

"No problem."

Londyn hung up the phone and let out a sigh. She walked over to Linda.

"Transfer our intel over to the *federales* and the DEA, and let them know we're pulling out now."

Linda frowned.

"Is that all right, Director? Are you sure you want to end it here?"

Londyn crossed her arms.

"We've destroyed an entire cartel at this point, and the super-drugs are accounted for. This is no longer the ILS's fight. But between Icy Falcon and ourselves, the cartels should stay quiet for a bit, the smart ones at least. We bought them some time and some quiet, the rest is up to Mexico.

Speaking of our fight, how are we looking?"

Linda nodded and typed into her computer.

"I have the files you requested, as well as your schedule for the hearings."

Londyn let out another sigh. Now came the hard part.

△△△

"Good evening, all you denizens of the planet Earth. This is GNN and I'm your host, Brendan Baird, bringing you all the updates you need. Tonight we are here to discuss the latest developments on the now infamous Icy Falcon question."

"The man himself still remains in ILS custody, as it is clear sending him to a Mexican prison is a recipe for disaster. Yet, the international community could not let this case remain in the ILS's house. Mexican authorities were long at a loss on how to approach the case, but the deaths of Mexican politicians and police officers at Icy Falcon's hand made this a question of Mexico's sovereignty and national security."

"But the global community *has* decided that something must be done to prevent future cases such as this one. And after countless public hearings and closed-door discussions, it seems the United Nations and the International League of Superheroes have reached an agreement. The UN released a resolution tilted the Code of Conduct for Extra-Normal Actors, which has been approved by both the General Assembly and the Security Council as well as signed by Director Green."

"While the international community could not agree on the situations that justify a response by supers, or even the fundamental definition of a hero, the Code does outline some red lines that will determine when a hero has gone rogue and the consequences of such infractions. Conversely, the Code also identifies specific scenarios where organizations such as the ILS are empowered to protect one of their members, including from certain non-super threats, and the actions they are permitted to take in order to do so. The Code thus both sets a limit on hero activity while also officially sanctioning ILS action, the first time either has been officially coded into law. The hope is that such safeguards will prevent future cases like the one with Icy Falcon and Icy Swallow, where neither the local government nor the ILS were certain when, how, or even if they should intervene."

"The Code is now in the hands of individual governing bodies, as each nation moves to ratify it for themselves. As only a handful of nations voted against or abstained from supporting the Code, it is expected that most of the world will sign it into law with only minor adjustments. As for the ILS, Director Green has laid out revisions to the ILS's internal structure and rules in order to comply with this new standard. She will be discussing the exact details of these changes within the ILS, but all the heroes interviewed by GNN indicated they will defer to the Director's judgment."

"As for Icy Falcon, with the Code now in place to prevent future occurrences, Mexican authorities and Director Green were able to come to an agreement. Icy Falcon shall receive several years in confinement, specifically for the vigilante killings of Mexican government and police officials and for the assault on Icy Swallow. The rest of the charges against him were dropped due to the murky legal status of violence between a super and a criminal organization as well as in light of his overall contributions to Mexico and the world. He has also been suspended from the ILS, which will only be lifted upon review and will last at minimum for the duration of his incarceration. Given that the majority of his victims had connections to current inmates of the Mexican prison system, he will remain in ILS custody for this time period, with Mexican authorities possessing the right to inspect his condition at any time."

"For more on this story, join us later tonight as GNN consults the experts on what this might mean for heroes, for the world, and for you. And now for a quick word from our sponsors."

△△△

Bob leaned back in his chair as the channel transitioned to commercial break. He let out a sigh. He did what he had to, and he believed it this time. The ILS was growing too powerful, too popular, and all too quickly. People were putting its heroes up on pedestals, treating them as gods and icons rather than people.

Even Bob would admit that this world needed heroes. So they cannot be stopped or held back, but they needed to at least be held in check. The world needed a reminder how human and vulnerable their heroes really were...and now Icy Falcon had given it to them. And thanks to that, the world had sat down, and agreed on the Code, a standard to which heros would now be held.

And Icy Falcon had become a ticking time bomb after his last fight with El Capa. He had become judge, jury, and executioner. He broke his own code, crossed a line he held for decades. He was not a killer, like Bob or Xiong Huang or even some of the heroes with military backgrounds like Agent Tina and Tesla Titan, people who could do what they needed to do and still remain who they were. He was a good man who defied his own morals, and so started to lose who he was. A man like that fell down a slippery slope, found himself justifying more and more compromises in the name of his mission. It was only a matter of time before everything blew up in his face. And possibly in Londyn's too.

So Bob had tossed a match into it, to light the powder keg before it hit critical mass. He found Constanza, a girl as desperate to fight as Icy Falcon was to win, and then used the super-drugs to draw them both together, knowing it would likely end badly. And then when the time was right, he had Miguel pass the drugs into the street, setting Icy Falcon on a crusade that would catch Constanza in the crossfire. And then he made sure the world knew of Icy Falcon's deeds...and the casualties that resulted.

And so he gave Londyn a house fire instead of a blazing firestorm, right when her political power was at its peak. And he reminded the world just how human the heroes really were, the good and the bad.

And it worked.

The Code restricted hero behavior, but also officially sanctioned hero activity and the ILS for the first time. It was simultaneously a significant victory and a significant compromise for both Londyn and the governments of the world. It had been the best time to hold such talks, after the ILS's stunning victories and Icy Falcon's shocking fall, when both sides held decent leverage and could meet as equals. And now the world acknowledged both the potential of heroes and the risks, and so encoded this new community into laws that would balance both.

And it was even the best case scenario. Icy Falcon had been apprehended by the ILS, possibly before he was completely irredeemable. Constanza had survived both her battle with the cartels and her wounds from Icy Falcon. Miguel's organization had survived as well, as he had carefully quarantined the groups working with Professor Mutant. And now he owed Bob yet another favor.

But all that said, it was not pleasant watching children go to war. Especially not by his own design.

Part of him had hoped that this plan would fail. That Icy Falcon wouldn't explode in the end. That the girl would bring him back and he would reign himself in. That things would end well for them both. Even though he knew the chances were slim.

But for better or for worse, events had transpired according to his predictions. According to his design.

So now all he could do was live with the consequences of his plan, and hope that Londyn might be able to help the wounded heroes.

And speaking of the consequences of his plan...

Suddenly the door slammed open. Bob barely had time to turn his head before he found himself floating in the air.

"You are going to tell me *everything*."

Bob raised an eyebrow as Xiong Huang held him up by his collar.

"About what?"

"Don't play dumb! I watched that girl's interview, the one where she explains where she got her powers. She described things in *exact* detail. And there's only one person in this entire world who would give a Thousand Star Ice Heart to a brat who doesn't even cultivate!"

Bob tilted his head.

"And? Why does that matter to you?"

Xiong Huang's face twisted in a snarl.

"It changes everything, Bob! Fine, you want to play dumb?! Then let me explain! A Thousand Star Ice Heart can kill a *cultivator* below the Fourth Realm who's dumb enough to use it. And I investigated that girl. Completely and utterly mortal, not a single cultivator within a hundred generations of her line! She should've died if she so much as *sniffed* an elixir like that, and now you're telling me she successfully cultivated it with no training whatsoever? Either she's the Empress of Heaven reborn, or you found a trick that would revolutionize cultivation forever. Either way, I want in on it, Bob."

Bob heaved a sigh.

"The trick is she didn't cultivate it at all."

A vein bulged on Xiong Huang's forehead.

"Explain. Now."

Bob held up his phone, showing an image of an Adranis Bulb illuminated by beams of sickly green light.

"Professor Mutant's work. Inspired by the Atomic Herald's elevation of his disciples, he found a way to induce rapid genetic mutation with a specific focus by imbuing plants with specialized radiation. He limited himself to Adranis bulbs as he thought their relaxing psycho-active properties were necessary to retain the subject's sanity. He was not aware there are other, more suitable bases for his project."

Xiong Huang let Bob down to the ground as she stared at the phone.

"So what, we shine this glowy light on an elixir and then anyone can take it?"

Bob shook his head.

"Not exactly. When subjected to the process the Thousand Star Ice Heart no longer passes its energy directly to the subject, but utilizes it to rebuild the subject's body from the base up."

"So? We do that with body cultivation, get to the point."

"She probably can't cultivate. At least not like you do."

Xiong Huang froze.

"Huh?"

"Her powers are more innate and biological. Her body was fundamentally transformed, including its energy pathways. She would interact with Qi differently than a regular human would, including cultivators."

Xiong Huang's brow furrowed.

"So she can't use Qi at all?"

Bob shrugged.

"If she can, it would be in an entirely different manner, such that all currently known cultivation methods would likely be useless to her. She would have to build a new one from scratch."

Xiong Huang took in a deep breath and closed her eyes as she let it out. A vein bulged on her forehead.

"So you found a second Thousand Star Ice Heart, and then burnt it to turn a mortal into a fridge and the method you discovered would destroy the user's cultivation, maybe permanently?"

Bob nodded. Xiong Huang swore.

"You're really annoying, you know that?"

Bob simply smiled at her. Xiong Huang turned to leave

with another curse.

Bob hadn't been thinking of Xiong Huang when he burned the Thousand Star Ice Heart...but he would admit he enjoyed the look on her face. Anticipated it, even. He enjoyed getting a rise out of her in general, in fact. Even after all these decades, he could still remember when she blasted him with her intent in great detail...and so he still felt satisfaction whenever he pulled one over on the now immortal demigod, all while she *still* remained unaware he was the mortal from that night.

No one ever said Bob couldn't be petty.

△△△

"Dang it! Can't I win just once?!"

"Calm down, it's just a game."

Voidspeaker opened his mouth, and then closed it. He reminded himself that he was playing with his beloved girlfriend. That he had always loved this girl. He told himself that the blue shell is the enemy. He admonished himself not to be seduced.

"Pink, please. I said I was sorry."

"Hmph!"

The door opened and Voidspeaker and Chronolock turned their heads from the game. Pink Star walked into the room, her arms crossed, her cheeks puffed, and her head turned up and to the right. Behind her came in Wonder Knight, hunching over and pleading with the girl.

Voidspeaker turned to Chronolock.

"What's up with them?"

Chronolock heaved a sigh.

"They both had a crush."

Voidspeaker raised an eyebrow.

"And?"

"The same crush."

"Oh?"

Chronolock shook her head.

"Guess who won."

Voidspeaker tilted his head before his eyes widened.

"...oh."

As Wonder Knight continued to plead with Pink Star the door opened again. All four teens rose to their feet. Director Green walked into the room.

"Relax."

Wonder Knight stood up straight but Voidspeaker chuckled at the brief flash of relief on his face.

"Director, you have a mission for us?"

"In a sense."

Director Green stepped to the side and a teenage girl stepped in after her. She had dark skin, white hair, and blue eyes behind a blue domino mask. She shyly waved her hand.

"I'd like you bunch to welcome your new teammate. Go ahead and say hello."

The girl nodded her head.

"...Hi, I'm Icy...Rose. Nice to meet you all."

AUTHOR'S COMMENTARY: To be honest I'm pretty sure at least one (probably most) of the Security Council would veto the Code if it legitimizes ILS intervention in any way but eh plots, politics, convenience, you understand. Let's just assume they all realized the way the wind was blowing and took what they could get while they had some leverage. Londyn also probably blackmailed them or something. Anyways! Will Xiong Huang forgive Bob for yeeting rare elixirs to random teens? Will Constanza find her place in the ILS? Will Pink Star forgive Wonder Knight for ruining her romantic dreams again? Tune in next time, to find out!

INTERLUDE - THE STAR AND THE ROSE

Aurora Legion walked back through the ILS Tower, just returning from another successful mission. Wonder Knight was looking at his phone and smiling, Voidspeaker and Chronolock were flirting, Pink Star was... trying to laugh and ignore all the lovey-dovey couples in the room. They were just about to reach the cafeteria when Pink Star glanced behind the group.

She paused for a moment.

Wonder Knight noticed her stop and turned to face her.

"Pink, something wrong?"

She shook her head.

"I just left something behind, you guys go on ahead."

Wonder Knight raised an eyebrow at first. Pink didn't normally forget anything.

Then, his eyes widened.

He realized what she had 'left behind'.

"Um, want me to come with you?"

Chronolock also realized what was happening at that point and nodded her head.

Voidspeaker...glanced back and forth between the team, the gears in his head still turning...

But Pink Star shook her head.

"That's ok, you have a date tonight, don't you?"

Wonder Knight opened his mouth, then thought better of it.

Because Pink Star stared blankly ahead, her eyes unfocused.

"Yes. That's right. The couples should just go on their dates. Sometimes us *single* people like to be alone, you know? Sometimes we have to be, whether we like it or not. Those of us, not in relationships, because other people can't be with us. And then those people take the other people we thought we liked and make couples with them instead. Those people should probably let us *single* people do our own thing."

Wonder Knight jumped and gulped.

"U-Um...t-take care Pink! W-We'll see you tomorrow, then?"

"Yes, see you tomorrow, Wonder."

"R-Right."

And with that, Wonder Knight, the brave and fearless leader of Aurora Legion...fled from the scene.

Voidspeaker raised an eyebrow.

"Um, hey, Pink, you ok?"

And then Chronolock elbowed his side.

"Ow! What was that for?"

"Get moving, I'll explain later."

Chronolock pushed Voidspeaker through the door. Then she turned, nodded at Pink Star, and walked through herself.

Pink Star took a deep breath, then she turned and walked back down the hallway...

△△△

Icy Rose panted slowly, her breath fogging as it left her mouth. Frost coated the edges of her hair, even creeping along the sides of her face. Her body trembled and her skin turned pale. She stood at the ILS's practice range. Icicles littered the walls, roof, and floor of the range, slowly melting. She grit her teeth, furrowing her brow.

She was weak.

Useless.

If she couldn't do this much, how could she become a hero?

And if she couldn't become Mexico's new hero, then who would?

After all, she had broken the last one.

They told her it wasn't her fault. They told her Icy Falcon made his own choices.

But she didn't believe that was true. How could they know? They weren't there when it happened.

If she hadn't gone out into that street...if she hadn't lost herself in rage...

If she hadn't been there...then maybe things might have gone differently.

She wasn't even sure why she had come here, what she thought about the ILS. But she knew she had to do *something*. Mexico had lost its hero, thanks to her. So she had to try and replace him. But she couldn't do it down there, not alone, not after what happened. Her hatred for the cartels was too great, she could not trust herself to remain in control. So here she was, hoping the *gringos* could teach her what to do.

After all, she had been incredibly stupid.

She picked a fight with the cartels, without thinking what that would mean, not really. Just like Icy Falcon said, she didn't know anything. She was so caught up in her own crusade that she hadn't even *thought* of what it would mean for Antonio and his family. She somehow thought just because they technically weren't related that they wouldn't be affected, as if the cartels would make that distinction. Not until that night, when Antonio ended up in the line of fire, did she realize what she had done.

She had ruined his life, too.

And now Antonio and his family had to leave their homes and live under ILS protection. Even though the ILS had handled any cartel dealing with Professor Mutant, everyone knew there would be someone to fill the gap all too soon. And Icy Rose had established herself as an enemy of the cartels. There was a very good chance the next one would want an angle on her.

She ground her teeth together.

Just another mistake she had to make up for.

Just another reason she had to grow strong.

Just another problem she needed to set right.

She was just about to force more ice down the range when the door opened up behind her. She glanced back and heaved a sigh.

It was Pink Star, one of her new teammates.

Probably here to check up on her, or try to convince her to stop again. She appreciated the concern, she really did, but she needed to do this. The original members of Aurora Legion were proven heroes who had saved the world, the ones who put the ILS on the radar. They were already legends. So they could afford to spend time goofing around. She could not. Not until she had caught up. Not until she had repaired the damage she had done. Not until she could take up Icy Falcon's fight in his place.

Her heart leapt to her throat as Pink Star approached, preparing to refuse the words the girl was certain to say…

But Pink Star said nothing. She nodded at Icy Rose to acknowledge her, then took up the adjacent spot in the range.

She tried to form a pink beam of light to strike the targets. The beam wavered and shuddered, barely reaching the target. She sighed and tried again.

Icy Rose watched her for a moment, eyes blinking, before shaking her head and turning back to the range. Well, if she didn't have anything to say, then that was good. There was work to be done.

The two trained in silence for a while longer. Increasingly thin and brittle icicles flew off target, while flickering pink beams occasionally hissed through the air. Eventually, Pink Star let out a sigh.

"It's hard, you know?"

Icy Rose had been panting, holding up a shaking arm, desperately trying to force more ice out when the girl spoke.

"W-What is?"

"Being the weakest member of the team, the one who holds them back and drags them down."

Icy Rose turned to face the girl, eyes wide. Pink Star wasn't looking at her but staring down the range, her brow furrowed.

"But...you're a member of Aurora Legion...you stopped the Atomic Herald...you saved the world!"

Pink Star nodded.

"We did. And they're heroes, all of them. The boy wonder who can lift a car and take a bullet to the face. The crazy cultist wielding dangerous powers we don't understand, but always using them for good. The girl who can stop time itself. And then there's me. I can, what, throw some animals around? Animals that are weaker than Wonder to begin with. And it took me months of training to even reach that stage, at first all I could do was fling some floppy beams that barely tickled while the others were already practicing joint combat tactics. It's taken every effort I can muster just to keep up with them."

Icy Rose was silent as she listened to the girl. Pink Star let out a sigh.

"But well, Director Green told me I just need to focus on what I can do, and do that. So that's what I try to do, and I guess I'm somewhat useful now. I want to do more, but for now that'll have to be enough. At least I know I can trust in the others until I get to that point."

She let out one final sigh and shook her head. She turned to Icy Rose.

"Would you like to get dinner with me? That's another thing Director Green taught me, you won't get any stronger if you don't eat adequately after a training session. And there's this place I want to try but it's all couples and families so I'm a bit embarrassed to go by myself."

Icy Rose bit her lip and looked down at the ground.

"...thanks for the offer but...wouldn't one of the others be better?"

Pink Star shook her head.

"It's date night for Void and Chrono."

"What about Wonder Knight? He...seems nice."

Pink Star's face turned dark. Icy Rose jumped a bit.

"...he rejected me."

"What?"

"I asked him out...and he rejected me. We're still good friends...but it's still too early after that for us to go to dinner alone, you know?"

Icy Rose furrowed her brow as she looked towards the ground again.

"...I'm sorry. I didn't realize..."

Pink Star shook her head with a sad smile.

"It's alright, you couldn't have known. So that's it, no one else is available, so I'd appreciate your help."

Icy Rose continued looking down, and then sighed. She was about to reject...when her stomach rumbled incredibly loudly. She felt her face flush and turned her head away.

"Um...if you're ok with me...I guess I could go with you."

Pink Star smiled and nodded.

"Great, let's hit the showers and get going then."

"O-Okay..."

△△△

The two made their way to the restaurant. Icy Rose's stomach grumbled again, even louder than before, the moment she smelled food. Her face flushed but Pink Star ignored it.

The food tasted very good.

The pair ate in silence at first, then started to compliment the food. Slowly, but surely, Icy Rose found herself talking more and more, drawn into the conversation.

And for the first time in a while, she even smiled.

But eventually, there was a lull in the conversation. Icy Rose looked down at the table and frowned. She clenched her teeth, trying to constrict her chest.

But she failed.

And the tears started to come out.

"I-I'm sorry...y-you're so nice. I-I know you're trying to look out for me but...I just don't deserve your kindness."

Pink Star silently stood up and moved over to the other side of the table.

She gently wrapped an arm around Icy Rose and began to rub her back as the girl sobbed.

"Don't say that. No one deserves to suffer alone."

"B-But...I ruined everything! I'm the girl who ruined Icy Falcon! He was Mexico's hero and I...I...if I hadn't been there...then he would still..."

"I don't think that's what happened at all."

"It is! A-And everyone's talking like he's some kind of bad guy...l-like I changed my name because I hate him! But that's not true at all! I don't deserve that name any more!"

Pink Star continued to rub the girl's back and speak as soothingly as she could as Icy Rose sobbed and told her everything she was feeling.

Eventually, as Icy Rose's sobs grew quiet, Pink Star started to speak.

"...being a hero is really hard, you know? We all mess up, sometimes really badly."

"...it doesn't seem like that..."

Pink Star shook her head.

"You only saw the stuff on TV, after we had worked things out. Our first few missions were disasters. I couldn't focus at all, couldn't even make a simple squirrel. I failed and almost died, Wonder Knight had to come save me, and the villain got away as a result. People even got hurt."

Icy Rose started to listen quietly. Pink Star continued on.

"And it wasn't just me, you know? Wonder accidentally knocked over a building his first time, you know! Luckily it was burning and coming down anyway so we can laugh about it now but it was still really scary at the time. Chrono almost got herself and Void killed because she was mad over a game and let that impact her focus! She was *really* embarrassed after that, you know? And Void..."

She looked around and then leaned in to whisper in Icy Rose's ear.

"Don't tell anyone but Void was actually a villain! Or wanted to be, fortunately the Director found him before he actually pulled anything off."

Icy Rose's eyes widened at that. Pink Star smiled softly at her.

"Look...we all make mistakes. And since we're trying to be heroes, sometimes those mistakes are very bad, and people can even get hurt from them. And people are going to talk and say whatever they want about us."

Pink Star looked Icy Rose in the eye. Icy Rose's eyes trembled but she felt she shouldn't look away.

"But we have to keep going. Otherwise...what was it even all for? If we give up...then maybe next time no one gets saved. And there's one thing I know about all this: being a hero is too hard to do it alone."

She let go of Icy Rose and slid over a bit, then extended her hand out.

"So let us help you. Don't worry about if you 'deserve' it or not. Rather, when we get in trouble, help us out too, ok?"

Icy Rose glanced between Pink Star's hand and her eyes. Her heart pounded and her chest constricted. Her vision grew blurry once more.

She looked down and to the side, but she also reached forward and slowly grabbed Pink Star's hand.

"...Please...help me. Help me fix this. Help me to become a hero."

Pink Star smiled and shook her hand.

"Let's both work hard and become the heroes we want to be."

"...thank you."

△△△

A while later, Wonder Knight was resting in the break room when the door opened.

"Oh, hi Icy Rose, how are you doing today?"

She didn't answer, instead stomping right up to him.

"Come with me. We need to talk."

Wonder Knight tilted his head but nodded and followed her to a private room.

Once the door shut she spun around and glared at him.

"Why did you do it?"

Wonder Knight jumped and held his hands up in front of him.

"Um..."

"Why did you reject her?!"

Wonder Knight's eyes widened and then he frowned.

"Oh...you see..."

"She's the nicest girl I've ever met! She's kind, she's brave, she's beautiful, and she adores you with all her heart! So...why..."

Wonder Knight hung his head.

"...I know. And honestly...I wish it could be different. But...you see...I'm gay."

Icy Rose froze.

"So...I can't be with her, even if I want to. I care about her as a friend...but I just can't see her that way. If things were different...but no...I've already tried that and it didn't work. I won't do that to her."

Icy Rose looked away.

"Oh...um...sorry. I...I didn't realize..."

Wonder Knight shook his head.

"Don't be. I know you meant well."

He smiled at her.

"In fact, I'm glad. I know she's still hurting because of this. We all want to be there for her but...I'm the cause of her pain, and Void and Chrono are dating now so..."

He took a deep breath.

"What I'm trying to say is, I'd be really happy if you could be her friend."

Icy Rose frowned but eventually, she nodded. Wonder Knight smiled sadly and nodded at her.

"Thank you. That means a lot to me. I know you didn't come here...under the best of circumstances but...whatever the reason, I'm really glad you're here now."

Icy Rose watched as he walked away, furrowing her brow. Eventually she shook her head and clenched her fists.

"And in exchange, when we get in trouble, help us out too, ok?"

"...I don't know if I can, but I'll try my best, Pink. I won't let you suffer alone."

△△△

From then on, Icy Rose truly joined Aurora Legion, sharing meals and downtime with them. She and Pink Star started to train together on a regular basis, sharing dinner afterwards. Many times she broke down and cried but Pink Star was always there for her. And eventually, some days, it was Pink Star who couldn't hold back her tears, and Icy Rose had the chance to be the one on the other side.

And like Pink Star did for her, Icy Rose was always there for her.

△△△

Bob heaved a sigh, this time of relief, as he read the report Linda had sent to him.

Icy Rose had clearly been traumatized by the situation in Mexico...but it seemed she was healing, ever so slightly. Londyn was taking good care of her, just as he hoped she would, and Aurora Legion was having a positive influence as well.

He might have to admit that he was bothered by what happened. It made sense for the world at large...but even Bob didn't want to hurt people like that. Especially not a young and innocent girl who wasn't involved until Bob put her there.

But he shook his head.

He was committed to his path now. He would not waver from it.

And he also wouldn't turn away from the tragedy and the pain that resulted.

He would *not* become like those heroes, so convinced of the righteousness of his cause that he lost sight of the people caught in the way. He would not get to the point where he saw minions not as people but as obstacles, tossing them aside as easily as furniture. He would not lose his humanity if at all possible.

He heaved a sigh.

Still, this was why he was not going to have a family of his own, not if he could help it. He needed to stay compassionate, but he also needed to remain objective. If Constanza Rubio had not been involved, had not been hurt, then Icy Falcon, and the world at large, may not have realized what he was becoming. And if that hadn't happened, he may have remained at large, growing worse and worse with each incident. How long would it have been before he was targeting the families of the cartels, even their children? How long would it have been before he wrote off the entire Mexican government, and started considering the whole thing a valid target? How long before he started destroying entire buildings for housing cartel members? Or entire blocks?

How long would it have been before another Battle of Kayserling Tower?

How long would it have been before another Destroyer of Ulsan?

No, this had been the right choice. A hero with no limits was even worse than a villain.

Not least of all because no one would stop a hero until it was too late.

People might be shocked by the violence, but ultimately no one would shed tears for cartel bosses and dirty cops. No one truly considered Icy Falcon's crusade a problem, so long as it was the bad guys getting hurt. But a young novice getting caught up in it forced the world to acknowledge the danger a rogue hero posed. That was why Bob had to sacrifice Constanza.

No matter how bad he felt for her.

And if he felt this bad for a girl he didn't know, who even managed to survive, how would he make the right choice if it involved people he was related to? People he cared about?

So long as he held this much power in his hands, he needed to ensure he used it wisely. That he held every life in equal regard. The world depended on it.

He would keep his friends. He needed to stay connected and grounded in humanity, he could not afford to isolate himself. But lovers, kids? The kind of people he might burn down the world for? That door was shut to him until his work was done.

And speaking of his work...

Bob heaved one final sigh and then took out his phone, making his next call.

He had indulged his heart long enough. It was time for the Faceless Minion's next job.

AUTHOR'S COMMENTARY: ...don't worry, Pink Star. I'm sure you'll find someone nice some day! Not Bob though. No way a faceless minion could have a family! Then they wouldn't be a faceless minion and we'd have to feel bad about slaughtering them! Anyways! Can Icy Rose find a way forward as a member of Aurora Legion? Will Pink Star ever find a boyfriend? Can Bob retain his heart as he holds to his path? Tune in next time, to find out!

CHAPTER 27 - NEW MINION ORIENTATION

"And once again the world can breathe a sigh of relief, thanks to the heroics of the Gray Slayer."

"And for our next topic, we come to the Superhero Code, as the people have started to call it. Lacey, Liam, we've had the Code with us for some time now and most nations have finished signing it into law. What are your thoughts on its impact so far?"

"I think it's been great, Brendan. It's exactly what our society needs to move forward. And it was wonderful to see such a show of unity from the international community. I believe this is proof that heroes can not only work within the law, but can be better for it."

"Liam, do you agree?"

"I agree that so far so good. I'm glad to see heroes have not been forced to stop saving the day because of this. But I still have some concerns."

"Oh? And what might those be?"

"At the end of the day, the Code is a restriction. And I just can't get behind holding our heroes back. I'm afraid of the consequences when a hero is forced to choose between following the Code and saving the day."

"I think that's the point though, Liam. Now we have a place to discuss those kinds of concerns. Laws can be amended or even repealed. But it's only right we have some process adjust in the first place."

"With respect, I disagree. The thing is, in this case, the costs of getting it wrong are too great. The heroes need to win every fight they're in. The villains only need to win once. So what if the heroes fail one day because of the Code? We might not be around to discuss the law at all."

"That's a bit extreme, don't you think?"

"Is it? What if Aurora Legion failed to stop the Atomic Herald because they were holding back? Even one missile goes off and that's a city gone, if they fail entirely then we face a nuclear apocalypse. What if the ILS loses the fight with the Necrosaurus because they have to bring him in alive? We might all be speaking dinosaur right now. Point is, I don't like heroes having to think about some piece of paper somewhere when they should be entirely focused on saving the day. It's just one more thing a villain could use to get the upper hand on them."

"Lacey, what are your thoughts on this?"

"I do admit my colleague has a valid concern, but I feel like he's underestimating heroes. Having a Code, a standard to strive for, is not such a heavy burden. It might even provide a focus for them to grow even better. Even soldiers in war have codes of conduct and standards to keep. I don't think this is any different. And the Code itself isn't just about what heroes can't do. It also says what they *can* do. The ILS is now *more* empowered to take decisive action in the situations that warrant it. And it's that give and take, that discussion and compromise, which is what society's all about."

"Thanks for your insight, you two. And now we head to the last update for our super segment: the hero formerly known as Icy Swallow returns! Now called the Icy Rose, the young dispenser of justice was seen fighting alongside Aurora Legion as they battled the nefarious Major Macho Fighter. It is her first public appearance since that fateful day down in Mexico, as well as confirmation she has officially joined the ILS. Lacey, Liam, what are your thoughts?"

"It's absolutely wonderful, Brendan."

"Agreed, she took a hard knock there, so I have the highest respect for her getting back on her feet so soon."

"And it's great to see her getting so much support from the ILS. Just wonderful to see the hero community banding together like that."

"I think we all are happy to see her recover like this. What are your thoughts on the new name?"

"I love it. It's just, she's really coming into her own. Not just as someone's sidekick or student, but as a fully-fledged hero in her own right. But also that she's keeping a bit of what came before. That she's not forgetting the Falcon entirely, even after what he did to her. I feel like that speaks to just amazing internal strength."

"Liam?"

"I agree, it definitely suits her. Not only did she survive that moment with Icy Falcon, she's overcoming it and taking up the mantle for herself. And I feel like Aurora Legion is a great place for her. She's going to do great things there."

"I think we all are going to watch her career with great interest. Lacey, Liam, as always, it's been a pleasure."

"Thank you, Brendan."

"Anytime, Brendan."

"That's it for our super segment folks. On to politics and global affairs! First off, tensions continue to rise between the United States of America and the People's Republic of China. Our analysts say a confrontation is possible if a diplomatic solution is not found soon. Join us later tonight as GNN consults the experts on how this situation might develop."

△△△

Bob rubbed his chin as he sat in front of his television, eyes on the notepad in front of him. He heaved a sigh.

Honestly, he was ready to be done.

He had achieved what he set out to do. He had accomplished things even the heroes could not.

But...it didn't put a smile on his face like he thought it would.

Because his every success came at great cost to the people in his way. And only afterwards did he realize what that truly meant.

However, he had made the world a better place for it, he still believed that.

And so...his work was not yet done.

There were still things going on that he could resolve. Problems that he *needed* to resolve. Approaching disasters that he would not be content to idly watch, not when he had the power to do something about them.

Eventually he nodded, and picked up his phone.

"You have reached Sinn Kwaigno, Director of Placements with Midnight Staffing, how may I help you?"

"Hi Sinn."

"Hi there Bob! What can I do for you today?"

"What's the status on 185099?"

"Staffing was just approved, I'm putting together a team now, will you be joining in?"

"Yes."

"Got it, I'll let Stacey know she's off the hook for that one then."

"Does the applicant have any personal staff of her own?"

"Doesn't look like it, she requested the full package. Any special arrangements we should make?"

"A standard complement will do for the most part, but I'll be bringing in the experts for management."

"Got it, should be ready by the end of the week. Anything else I can do for you, Bob?"

"No thank you, that's plenty. Thanks Sinn."

"Anytime, Bob!"

Bob heaved a sigh and rose from his chair.

Time to go meet his new boss.

△△△

Bob walked into the empty auditorium, grabbing one of

the smooth, featureless masks by the door. There was a bucket of the things with a sign indicating that they were absolutely mandatory, no exceptions. Normally he wasn't sure as to why villains found seeing faces so distasteful, but this time Miss Gabriel Le Blank's dossier made her reasoning easily apparent.

He walked into the auditorium rented for today, the sounds of dozens of conversations slamming his ears. The floor was empty of all furniture or obstructions. Other masked minions stood organized into several squares and rectangles, each with a single minion standing before them. All of them faced a stage with a large projector screen.

All the conversations died down as someone stepped onto the stage.

Bob admitted it, she was one of the most beautiful women he had ever seen. If he had to call it, she still lost to Xiong Huang, but she was definitely at the top of those who were still mortal.

She had flowing, golden hair and large, bright eyes that seemed to light up the room. Her face seemed more like a work of art than part of a real person's body. She had a gorgeous figure standing straight and tall, highlighted by her white dress that seemed to shimmer as she walked and the coat of fine white fur upon her shoulders.

She strode to the center of the room and cleared her throat.

"Rejoice, you foul peons. For today you join in the most noble and important task of your miserable little lives."

Miss Le Blank stuck out her chest and pointed to herself.

"You will take your rightful place in serving me, the most beautiful and noble person in this world."

Bob shook his head. Well, there was a reason she sought funding from EL Bank.

"You see, I have come to a realization. This world and everything else in it is ugly. Ugly beyond belief. I cannot comprehend how a world such as this is home to one such as

I."

She turned to the screen.

"This is a travesty, so we shall correct it. We shall tear down every foul and ugly thing that dares to share the world with myself, and rebuild it in my image. And it shall be..."

She pressed a button on her remote. An image popped up on the screen. It displayed a magnificent castle, towers of pristine white stone piercing to the sky. It had highlights of gold and silver that shimmered in the sun but that never felt opulent or excessive. Its gleaming walls seemed more like works of art than military structures.

"...beautiful."

The castle also floated in the air, resting upon an upside down mountain. In the center of the tallest tower was a crystal sphere, not a single blemish upon its smooth surface.

She wiped a tear from her eye and turned back to the crowd. The image of the castle transitioned to a technical schematic, detailing the inner layout and various systems hidden within.

"So get to work."

As the minions turned and mumbled to one another, Bob walked to the edge of the stage, meeting Miss Le Blank as she walked down the stairs towards the exit.

"Ma'am."

"...why have you approached me, minion?"

"Just a question, Ma'am. Do you have any specific duties or allocation of work in mind for us to get started on this project?"

"What? No, obviously not! I should expect an agency as reputable as yours to have basic competence, minion. Do not tell me that you all are so incompetent that I must micromanage every last detail. I would have words with your agency were you to demonstrate such a disappointing showing."

Bob bowed his head.

"Of course, Ma'am. I'm sorry for wasting your time."

She turned her head up.

"Do not bother me with such trifles again, minion. Now get to work."

And with that she left the room.

Bob let out a sigh as he turned around. The crowd was milling about, glancing around and conversing with one another. Bob motioned for the lead minions, who came up to him.

Chris nodded at him.

"What's the word from the boss?"

"Handle it."

"Ah, so the same as usual?"

"Looks like it."

"In that case, what's the word, Boss?"

Bob sighed once more.

"Tina will handle finances, start drawing up our budget. Sergei, get the engineers going over Miss Le Blank's schematics. Get us a list of materials ASAP. George, you're on HR duty, start setting up the shift schedule. Minh, you're on acquisitions. As soon as Sergei gets you the list, start looking up sellers. Work with Tina to figure out reasonable figures. Cikizwa, start scouting out alternative methods for anything not reasonable or not on the market. Yuhan will handle security. Chris will take construction, start drawing up a list of suitable locations for now."

He had assembled all of Cikizwa's old team for this one sans Linda and Kanna, the most experienced hands he knew. Bob wasn't in control of his target this time, so he wanted to make sure everything moved exactly on schedule.

It still amused Chris to no end that Cikizwa herself ended up on Midnight Staffing's payroll.

The group gave him a salute.

"Got it, boss!"

Bob nodded.

"All right, let's get to work."

△△△

Bob looked over several different photos. Each showed a large patch of flat, empty ground with a location and price. He nodded.

"Let's go with site C. Sergei should be far enough along that you can start with the prep work"

Chris nodded.

"I'll get to it."

Just then the door opened and Miss Le Blank strode into the room. Every minion stood at attention and gave a salute. She strode over to the table without a word, glancing at the photo.

"Minion, what is this?"

"The construction site, Ma'am."

Miss Le Blank frowned. She furrowed her brow, closing her eyes, and massaging her temples.

"Minion, why on Earth is it in the middle of nowhere?! How will we demonstrate my beauty to the world from there of all places?!"

Bob nodded.

"Well Ma'am, the final construction is going to fly around the world, right?"

"Obviously! Didn't you pay attention?!"

"We figured it didn't matter where it started, so we picked somewhere cheap and quiet. Besides, the construction won't be very beautiful until it's finished, so we thought you would not want the unworthy to gaze upon it until you deemed it so."

Miss Le Blank frowned as she looked over the photo. Eventually, she slowly nodded, and then left without another word.

Bob and Chris looked at one another, then shrugged and got back to work.

△△△

Bob stretched his arms as he left the office, minions shuffling in and out as the night shift came in.

"Minion! Attend me."

Bob watched as Miss Le Blank grabbed one of the leaving minions and then turned to march towards the garage. Bob heaved a sigh and walked over to the boy. One of the newbies, Emmanuel if he remembered correctly. The boy jumped as Bob placed a hand on his shoulder.

"Good work today, you can go home."

"B-But what about Madam Le Blank?"

"I'll take care of it."

The boy looked down to the ground.

"Don't worry about it, this isn't my first rodeo, and she can't tell us apart anyways. Rest while you can, you'll have your own crunch time soon enough."

The boy nodded.

"Thanks."

Bob waved a hand as he began to follow Miss Le Blank.

"Don't mention it."

△△△

Miss Le Blank entered a banquet hall, Bob following behind and to her side. They entered the ornate and spacious room, brightly lit by chandeliers glimmering above. The floor was filled with men in tuxedos and women in the finest dresses, chattering away and sipping at champagne. Standing behind them were numerous individuals of all shapes and sizes, wearing all manner of clothing from suits to armor. And all of their varied uniforms shared one thing in common: a mask or helmet covering their face. In the corner a string ensemble played a graceful tune.

"My oh my, what do we have here?"

A high-pitched voice rang out. Miss Le Blank and Bob turned to the side. A dark haired woman in a dark blue gown approached them, followed by a man in a tuxedo.

"I would not have thought you brave enough to show yourself here, dearest Gabriel. Don't you have another... ahem modeling session or some such thing to attend to?"

Miss Le Blank narrowed her eyes.

"My dearest Vivienne, I must say it is good to see you. I wasn't sure your father would allow you out of the house."

Vivienne hid her face with a blue fan as she chuckled softly.

"Oh, truly, Father only allows me to interact with the most distinguished of company. I must admit, it is a tad stifling at times. What am I to do with such a doting old man?"

Miss Le Blank smiled as well.

"Well, not all of us can manage to stand on our own. It is good to rely upon one's parents for as long as one can."

The pair both let out a laugh as their eyebrows twitched slightly.

"I see you have your chaperon. Alfred, it is good to see you."

Alfred gave her a polite bow.

"A pleasure as always, Miss Le Blank."

Vivienne giggled lightly.

"Only the best of the best, dearest Gabriel. Speaking of which..."

"Oh, him? I'd introduce you, but I daresay I forgot his name. 'Tis such a burden having so many loyal minions."

Vivienne raised an eyebrow at that.

"Minions?"

The edges of Miss Le Blank's mouth curled up.

"Oh, don't tell me you haven't heard, dearest Vivienne? Anyone who's anyone has minions these days, just look about you. I admit, they're a bit rough about the edges and not nearly as...personable as your butler there. But oh, the things one can accomplish with such loyal followers. I have big plans, I tell you. I wonder, you must be planning similarly great deeds yourself, are you not?"

Vivienne frowned.

"That's..."

Miss Le Blank smiled back.

"Oh my, well do not worry, I'm sure your father could lend you a hand. Perhaps you should ask him for some minions of your own, if he'll allow such things."

Just as Vivienne began to bite her lip, a voice rang out that did not fit the sophisticated atmosphere.

"Excuse me, excuse me! Miss Le Blank, could I have a moment of your time?"

All company present turned to the interloper. It was a girl who seemed barely of age. She had on a dress that may once have been beautiful, but now had faded spots and loose strings indicating age and use. The duffle bag over her shoulders likewise did not help her image. Her hair was a bit frazzled, her makeup insufficient to hide spots of acne on her face and bags under her eyes.

"M-My name is Klara Wojnicz, I'm your biggest fan! I, um, have something to show you, i-if I could just borrow a moment of your time. Y-You'll love it, I promise!"

Miss Le Blank kept her eyes to the front as the girl continued to plead with her. She motioned to Bob, who leaned over and lent her his ear. Despite the fact that she continued to speak at normal volume.

"Minion, why is such a foul...thing in my presence? Please do your job."

Klara stopped, her eyes widening. Bob sighed under his breath as he approached her.

"Miss, could you come with me for a moment?"

"What? N-No...that's...I need to show her! Please! It will only take a moment! I can definitely help you! Please!"

Klara continued to shout as Bob put a hand on her shoulder. Various participants of the ball were starting to glance over at the spectacle. Bob leaned in and whispered into her ear.

"Miss, this isn't really the best place for this. Miss Le Blank can't just speak with anyone in public. Come with me, I manage her affairs, I can help you get what you want."

The girl bit her lip and continued to glance at Miss Le Blank. But she slowly nodded her head and turned to head towards the elevator, with Bob following.

△△△

The pair stepped out onto the roof. Klara was biting her lip, eyes starting to moisten. Bob sighed and turned to face the girl.

"Now, what did you want to show us?"

The girl jumped and stared at Bob, her eyes blinking repeatedly.

"Oh, um, you...actually want to see it?"

Bob nodded.

"Oh, um, I really wanted to show this to Miss Le Blank first..."

Bob sighed once more.

"Miss Wojnicz, was it? You have guts and enthusiasm, I'll give you that. But that doesn't mean you can skip steps. There are rules to this, procedures to follow. And you just smashed through all of them, approaching Miss Le Blank like you did. I am going to give you a chance anyways, so don't waste it."

Klara jumped and then quickly nodded her head, opening up her duffle bag. She pulled out some sort of small quadcopter drone, with a large glass dome on its bottom. She then pulled out a controller and switched the drone on. It hovered in the air a few feet before her.

"Um, I was hoping Miss Le Blank would be here as I designed this with her in mind, but it's something like this."

She put down the controller and took out a flashlight, flickering it on and off a few times. The dome on the drone flashed every time the light hit it. Once she had finished, the drone took a lap around the rooftop before returning to its starting position.

"I-I heard Miss Le Blank can control light, so I programmed the drone to respond to it. I-I figured Miss Le Blank could control it intuitively on her own."

Bob crossed his arms and hummed.

"An interesting approach, but it doesn't seem more efficient than regular drones."

Klara nodded and turned on the flashlight, this time at the brightest setting. This time, the dome stayed lit even after the flashlight stopped, and then after a second a beam of light shot from the dome, illuminating a patch of the rooftop.

"It's hard to show with something this weak, but I designed it to amplify and reflect Miss Le Blank's powers."

Bob rubbed his chin and then nodded.

"You made and programmed this yourself?"

Klara nodded.

"Yes."

"Who taught you?"

Klara frowned.

"...no one. Just what I could pick up in class and then I figured out the rest myself."

"Parts?"

Klara averted her gaze.

"...just whatever I could afford or scrap."

"I see."

Bob paced back and forth once. Then he turned to face the girl once more.

"Why Miss Le Blank?"

Klara tilted her head.

"Um, sorry?"

"It's rough around the edges but it's not a bad attempt, especially for someone self-taught and self-supplied. You have potential, honestly enough potential to find employment in any number of industries. Even the ILS is recruiting for those kinds of skills. So why Miss Le Blank?"

The girl looked down for a bit, then took a deep breath.

"...she inspires me."

Bob waited for a moment, Klara took another breath.

"Her dad tried to force her into being a hero. She stood up to him, took everything from him, and made a life for herself."

Bob raised an eyebrow.

"And that's what you want to do?"

Klara took another breath, looking at her feet and clenching her hands into fists.

"My dad...my dad only cares about one thing. *Heroes.* That's all he ever wanted, and he ignores everything and everyone else."

She looked up at Bob, eyes moistening but unwavering.

"I don't care about making a name for myself. I don't want to. He might twist that too, take some weird pride out of it. I just want to ruin what he loves. He hates Miss Le Blank, very very much. So I wanted to help her rise. I want to watch him grit his teeth watching her, never knowing his own child is helping her."

Bob took a deep breath, and then let out a sigh.

"I'll be honest, there is very little chance Miss Le Blank will allow you anywhere near her."

Klara grit her teeth and looked to the ground again, her shoulders trembling. Bob reached into his pocket and pulled out a card.

"But there's something else I can do to help support your dream."

Klara looked up, her eyes growing wide.

"Call them, tell them Bob sent you. They'll get you the training and the resources you need. It won't be Miss Le Blank, but you'll help others like her. You'll be fairly compensated for your work, I guarantee that. And no one will know what you do, not unless you tell them."

Klara stood for a moment, biting her lip, clenching and releasing her hands. But, eventually, she nodded and stepped forward to take the card. Bob nodded at her and walked towards the elevator. He turned his head back after pressing the button.

"One last thing, Miss Wojnicz. You can be whatever you want to, for yourself, and yourself alone. No one else's opinion needs to matter if you don't want it to."

With that, Bob stepped into the elevator, leaving the girl alone on the roof.

This was actually very convenient for him. He had been looking for an assistant for Kanna. Tanifuji Inc. was one of the world's biggest corporations at this point and had its own R&D department, but Kanna also handled a lot of work on the side for EL Bank's...more peculiar clientele, all to support Bob's plans. The work she did there simply could not be connected to Tanifuji Inc. proper, so they had struggled to find some both trustworthy and talented enough to assist her.

But, well, it was surprising just what one could find if they bothered to listen. To see past someone's appearance and acknowledge their efforts.

Miss Klara Wojnicz might be just who Kanna needed. And so just might get her wish of pulling a fast one on the world of heroes.

Bob heaved a sigh.

He guessed this night wasn't a waste of time after all.

Though part of him wished it was, as he thought of Klara and what she said about her father.

"Heroes are so annoying."

AUTHOR'S COMMENTARY: Ah, that's better. Let's get back to the supervillains and the minion-ing! Anyways! Can Miss Le Blank get one over that vixen

AE ICALOS

Vivienne? What does life and Bob have in store for little miss Klara? Can the minions bring Miss Le Blank's plans to fruition? Tune in next time, to find out!

CHAPTER 28 - A MINION'S TOILS

It was an early morning in the ILS Intelligence Department. The room was dim, lit mostly by the glow of countless monitors, including one that took up an entire wall. Men and women typed away and answered calls at countless desks lit by small lamps, sorting tips and chasing leads. A heavyset man leisurely strolled to one of the desks, where a brown-skinned man was hard at work.

Manager Lane took a moment to savor his coffee before heading to work.

"All right, you have something for me, Kishor?"

"Possibly, sir. Miss Gabriel Le Blank is acting suspicious lately."

"Le Blank? I thought we already ruled her out. Isn't it just her normal bragging?"

"I thought so too, sir, but I can't find an alibi for her this time. She seems to be cutting down on her modeling hours, no movies in the works either. Could be a business deal but we haven't seen her with any of her normal contacts. She has also been escorted by a 'minion' type every time she's made a public appearance recently."

Manager Lane rubbed his chin.

"Hm, well start keeping an eye on her until you figure out what she's up to. I'm not sure I believe she's capable of much even if she *is* going off the deep end, but it won't hurt to be prepared."

"Yes sir."

△△△

Bob was hard at work on day when he got a call from Minh.

"Bob, we have a problem."

Bob glanced at the schedule and felt the pressure in his skull grow. Minh was on attendant duty today, so he could guess what, or rather who, the problem was.

"What is she doing now?"

"She keeps bragging about our plans. She hasn't dropped exact details yet but it's starting to get suspicious. If this keeps up I think everyone's going to catch on that it's not just a show."

Bob heaved a sigh.

"Let me think…"

Bob rubbed his chin. Eventually he let out another sigh, deeper than before.

"I think I have…an idea. Just try to follow up as best you can, I'll handle the rest."

"Copy that."

Bob rubbed his temples. He had a plan alright, a plan that would require him to do something. A very annoying something. A very annoying something he had been avoiding for *decades* now.

The things he did for people.

He heaved another sigh.

"Villainesses are so annoying."

△△△

Bob walked down the hallway of a countryside mansion, dressed in a suit with a smooth and featureless pink mask. In his hand he held a tray with tea and cookies. He stepped in front of a large pink door. He took a deep breath.

And entered into a world of pink.

Lying amidst a sea of pink cushions was a woman. Her dark hair went this way and that, her green eyes were narrowed behind round glasses. She rolled about in pink sweatpants and a pink hoodie as she typed away at a laptop on her bed.

This was the former lady Anita Laflèche de Albifort, the spoiled duke's daughter from one of Bob's very first jobs. Now a bestselling author as well, having found a way to pass her time. And technically the owner of most of his assets, so still his boss on paper, though since she had granted him power of attorney he never actually needed to interact with her.

Oh, and she was Anita Gaumount now legally, but the world at large wasn't aware of that. Even Bob was a bit surprised to hear the news, as he hadn't kept close tabs on Lady Anita ever since shoving her into a secluded estate.

And he wasn't particularly looking forward to catching up...

But he had no choice now, if he wanted to maintain Miss Le Blank's cover.

Bob heaved a quiet sigh and walked forward, carefully avoiding the cushions littering the floor, and placed the tray on a table next to the bed.

"Your afternoon tea, Mistress."

The woman started and glanced up.

"Oh, is it that time already? Thank you, my dear minion!"

Bob gave a short bow.

"Of course, Mistress. I see that Master Gaumont is out today?"

"Oh, I think so? You know Pierre, he sure loves to move about. I believe he wanted to take the boys down to the lake, for old times' sake."

Even Bob felt something warm in his chest as Anita smiled at the mention of her beloved. Something that was quickly squashed by a pounding headache.

Because if Mr. Gaumont wasn't here, then he'd have to have this talk directly. Something he had managed to avoid for decades. He took a deep breath.

"Mistress, you have a request."

Anita tilted her head.

"A request? Whatever for?"

"A screenplay."

She blinked.

"Huh? A screenplay?"

Bob nodded.

"Mister Soyer called, he was most impressed by your latest work and wants to turn it into a movie."

"Huh? Why would he do that?"

Bob held in the urge to massage his temples.

"Mistress…"

"Yes?"

"Are you not aware that you are a best-selling author?"

Anita's eyes went wide.

"Eh? What? What do you mean, minion?"

Bob suppressed a sigh and pointed to her laptop.

"Your written works are adored around the globe."

She looked over to the laptop.

"Oh, those? Oh my, I wasn't aware anyone was reading those. That's somewhat embarrassing."

She placed her hands on her cheeks as they flushed slightly.

"Mistress, did you not order them published from the very beginning?"

Anita grimaced.

"T-That was a dark time in my life, minion! I admit I was…most upset back then and wished to sully Her Majesty Adèle's reputation however I could. I, um, am trying to forget about that…Her Majesty keeps making fun of me for it…"

Suddenly Anita froze.

"Wait…you mean…we've been publishing…everything I wrote…ever since then?"

Bob nodded.

Anita turned bright red. She grabbed the nearest pillow,

brought it to her face, and began to scream.

This time Bob did not hold back his sigh. This might take a while.

△△△

Mr. Soyer sat at his desk, flipping through the last page of the screenplay Bob had acquired at *great* effort. He adjusted his reading glasses and nodded.

"Magnificent. Are you certain Miss Laflèche won't be joining us for the production? I'd love the chance to work with such an artist directly."

Bob shook his head.

"Unfortunately, Miss Laflèche prefers her privacy. I believe she is hard at work on her next project in any case."

Mr. Soyer nodded.

"Always refreshing to see one so dedicated to their craft. And so I shall commit to mine. It shall be a monumental task to live up to the source material, but I swear I shall produce a masterpiece!"

Bob nodded.

"Glad to hear it, we do have a small request, however."

"Oh? Anything."

"We like you to consider casting Miss Gabriel Le Blank in the star role."

Mr. Soyer rubbed his slightly graying beard.

"Miss Le Blank, was it? She certainly has the looks, however I'm not certain she's a great fit here."

"It's fine if it doesn't work out, just give her first crack at it."

Mr. Soyer nodded.

"That's not a problem, she's a first choice candidate most of the time anyways."

Bob stood up and held out his hand.

"That's all we ask, a pleasure doing business with you."

Mr. Soyer took Bob's hand with his right and patted it

with his left.

"No no, my friend, it is all my pleasure. Tell Miss Laflèche that this Sébastien Soyer swears he will make her proud."

△△△

Bob entered into an art gala alongside Miss Le Blank. She stood at each art piece for a second before scoffing and flipping her hair. She strolled about until she found her target.

"My oh my, fancy seeing you here, dearest Vivienne."

Vivienne turned around and frowned.

"Oh, dearest Gabriel, I wasn't aware you were coming. I didn't know you to appreciate such things."

Miss Le Blank leaned back and fanned herself.

"Well you know, we've been so hard at work, it was necessary to take a break."

Vivienne's frown grew deeper.

"I'm not sure I believe there even is a 'work', I've not heard heads or tails of anything you've done lately."

Miss Le Blank shook her head, clicking her tongue.

"Dearest Vivienne, that's just the way these things work. The only ones you'll hear about are the ones that fail. I, on the other hand, have my minions toiling away at a secret location, very remote, very private. I daresay you'll never guess what we're up to until I decide to let you see it. But soon, soon all shall be revealed. I shall cast aside all before me and rise to my rightful place. But you and I are good friends, are we not? Perhaps I can give you a sneak peak visit, I'll speak with your father to arrange a little playdate, shall I?"

Vivienne scrunched her brow as Miss Le Blank began to smirk when Bob took a step forward.

"Ma'am, sorry to interrupt, but it's almost time for your three 'o clock."

Miss Le Blank flipped her hair.

"Well, dearest Vivienne, it's been a pleasure, but duty

calls. It is so very hard having so much to do. If only I was as free as you."

With that, Miss Le Blank turned and strode away. Vivienne and Alfred raised their eyebrows as Bob remained behind.

"I'm sorry, but would you two mind keeping this conversation to yourself? The director doesn't want any leaks before the trailer, this might violate Miss Le Blank's NDA. We can invite you to visit the set if you promise to keep things quiet."

Vivienne blinked, and then her mouth curled into a smirk.

"Of course, dear minion, of course. You have my word."

Bob slouched over and let out a sigh, then bowed repeatedly.

"Many thanks, Ma'am. Now I better get back to the mistress."

Vivienne kept her eyes trained on the pair as they left.

"Alfred."

"My Lady?"

"Find out what movies are coming out, ones that haven't been announced yet. Hm, if I recall correctly, Mr. Soyer has been absent from the last few soirees, check on him first."

"Right away, My Lady."

The edges of Vivienne's mouth curled up and she giggled to herself.

"Let's see who'll be busy now, eh dearest Gabriel?"

△△△

Back in the ILS office, Manager Lane walked over to Kishor's desk once more.

"What's the word, Kishor?"

Kishor nodded.

"I found it, sir."

The man leaned over to look at Kishor's screen.

"A movie? Want to tell me why I'm reading paparazzi gossip, Kishor?"

Kishor nodded.

"Mr. Soyer finally got the rights to do a Laflèche adaptation. Miss Le Blank was auditioning for the lead role."

"Is that really it?"

Kishor nodded again.

"Mr. Soyer hates leaks with a passion, so it makes sense they've been cagey about the whole affair. The 'minion' was probably another actor who was instructed not to be seen with her in public. In fact, from what I can tell, Mr. Soyer is most upset at Miss Le Blank for giving it away. Looks like he's dropped her from consideration."

Manager Lane shook his head.

"She really can't help herself, can she?"

Kishor grinned.

"And get this, sir."

"Oh?"

"The main candidate to replace her is her old rival from university, the one she's always trying to one up."

Manager Lane let out a laugh.

"Oh, that's a good one. Twenty bucks says she's the one Miss Le Blank spilled the beans to in the first place. Well, looks like we can leave Miss Le Blank for now, good work, Kishor."

"Thank you, sir."

And so the ILS wrote off Miss Le Blank and turned their attention to higher priority leads...

△△△

And so the work continue, safely incognito. Bob stood on the empty plains, watching as minions walked around. The armored men and women were hard at work, carrying tools and supplies as they set up structures. Bob's inner circle stood by his side, tablets and clipboards in hand.

"What's our status?"

Chris gave a nod.

"Construction is on schedule, but I think Sergei hit a snag."

Sergei nodded.

"Most of the systems are underway and being installed, but there's a problem with the centerpiece. To be honest, we haven't found a suitable active gain medium."

Bob rubbed his chin and hummed.

"Minh and Cikizwa couldn't come up with anything?"

Sergei grimaced.

"There were also some snags with the magnetic core, they've been focusing on that."

Bob nodded.

"Try to do what you can to reduce the requirements. I'll get Kanna on it, see if she can come up with something."

△△△

Bob pulled out his phone and rung a number.

"Bob!"

"Hello Kanna, how's the new girl coming?"

"Absolutely incredible! She's a once in a generation genius, Bob! Let me tell you, she's going to be running this place in a bit! I wished I could introduce her to my son…"

"He's not motivated by a traumatic upbringing."

"Ugh, yes I know. Give him time, right?"

"Everyone grows at different speeds."

"I know, well, what can I do for you today, Bob?"

"I'm sending over a list of requirements for an active gain medium, I'm hoping you and Miss Wojnicz could brainstorm possibilities."

"Klara too?"

"It's for Miss Le Blank, Miss Wojnicz originally wanted to participate in her work. Consider it a celebration for her efforts."

"Can I count it as your referral bonus too?"

"...if you must."

"Well well I was kidding but if you're offering..."

"But you won't get to peek at Miss Le Blank's schematics."

"Joking! I'm joking, just a friendly joke between friends, right Bob?"

"You never joke about money."

"That's...um...I'm sorry please let me have a look."

"Call me when you have something."

△△△

A while later, Bob's phone rang. He shook his head.

Not even twenty-four hours had passed. Those two must have been up all night on this.

Bob picked up the ringing phone.

"Kanna."

"Hi Bob!"

"Got something for me?"

"Um, maybe."

Bob raised an eyebrow.

"Maybe?"

"Well, we *do* have an answer, actually. An Iesnuorium and Mablite alloy would do what you need, if processed correctly. The thing is..."

"I've never heard of either before?"

"Right. Mablite comes and goes so your people should be able to find it. Iesnuorium though...might be difficult. It's *extraordinarily* rare."

"How rare?"

"Um...you know that bullet we found in the Red Colonel's armory? The one I *specifically* told you not to use? That's what it was made of. Been hunting it ever since, but I've only ever seen it on sale twice before...and we'd *still* have trouble affording it at the prices I saw."

Bob heaved a sigh.

"Send me as much detail on the two sales as you can. Let me know if you think of anything easier."

"Will do, Bob, good luck on your quest!"

Bob sighed again as he hung up the phone.

△△△

Bob looked over the information Kanna sent over and picked up his phone.

"Miguel."

"Bob, my friend! It is good to hear from you! How can I help you today?"

"I'm looking for a package you helped bring in a few years back."

"Ah, sorry Bob, you know I can't disclose client information, even for you."

"I'm more interested in where it came from. Looking to make a purchase."

"Ah, that's a bit different then, eh? Unfortunately I'm not entirely sure, they just used us for shipping so we weren't directly involved in the sale. I can put you in touch with the guy who hired us though."

"That would be much appreciated."

"Anything for you, my friend!"

△△△

Bob walked through a marketplace in Nairobi, weaving his way through the crowd. He made his way towards a handful of men loitering outside a townhouse. The men turned to him, arms crossed and eyebrows raised at his approach. He held up a bag.

"Delivery of tacos. Extra-spicy."

The men turned away, one of them knocking on the door in a rhythmic pattern. The door opened and Bob stepped into the house. A security guard patted him down, taking the handgun he had in his back pocket, and then led him further into the house.

Bob was brought into an office, two guards flanking the door. Behind the desk sat a man dressed in a suit. He wore a ring with a large diamond on his hand.

"And who might you be? I wasn't aware our *'compadres'* out west had any business today."

"The name's Bob, I'm looking for Ashon."

The man made a wide grin, showing his teeth. The guards began to chuckle.

"Ashon is...indisposed. Turns out the ILS takes offense to smuggling weather control devices."

Bob sighed. Heroes were so annoying.

"I'm in charge now, you can call me Khalfani."

"Nice to meet you."

Bob held out his hand, then dropped it when Khalfani didn't respond.

"I'm looking for Iesnuorium."

Khalfani chuckled.

"That will cost you a pretty penny, you know? Let's talk about what you can do for me first."

Bob sighed and took out a pendant. Khalfani froze and then started to sweat.

He bowed his head.

"My apologies, sir. I-I didn't realize he sent you. I assure you, we don't want any trouble with the Scourge of Ragayanza."

"The Iesnuorium?"

"R-Right, that was a one time shipment. Ashon had this friend, one of those colonizer adventurer types, Brit I think. Settled down near the Congo rainforest. The Iesnuorium was his find, if anyone knows where to find more, it's him."

"You know where he is?"

"O-Of course, let me check Ashon's old records."

Bob took out a package and placed it on Khalfani's desk.

Khalfani opened it and stared at the sparkling contents, eyes wide.

"Your help is *most* appreciated."

△△△

Bob walked up to a dilapidated shack at the edge of the rainforest and knocked on the door. He waited in silence for a few minutes before knocking again. He waited for another five minutes before pounding on the door.

This time, he heard a crash and someone swearing.

"I'm coming, I'm coming! Hold your bloody horses!"

The door opened.

There stood a man with one eye shut, a beard that had not been trimmed in years, a stained tank top, and a pair of shorts that seemed a size too small. Bob grimaced as he was hit with the smell of sweat and alcohol.

"Sir Edmund Notfelde, I presume?"

Sir Edmund just blinked…and then swore as a mosquito bit his neck.

"Who the heck are you?"

"The name's Bob, nice to meet you. I'm looking for Iesnuorium, I was told you could help me find some."

"Well shove off! I already sold the last of it years ago!"

Bob shook his head.

"I was hoping you could help me find a new batch."

The man straightened his spine, rising to his full height, opening both of his bloodshot eyes to stare Bob in the face.

"I got that crap after months of trekking in the green hell they call a jungle, risking life and limb and who knows what else. I've gone through enough adventures for a lifetime. I dragged my partner all across this continent and we both experienced things that changed us for good, occasionally in dramatic and unexplainable fashions. Now you want me to do it again because some stranger shows up at my door and asks me to?"

Bob nodded.

"Aren't you ready for another adventure?"

Sir Edmund suddenly grinned.

"You've no idea, my boy. Give me a moment to pack my things!"

△△△

Bob swore as he swatted yet another mosquito on his neck. He, Sir Edmund, and a young guide were hacking their way through the jungle. And his boot was stuck in mud. Again.

"Come now, Bob! No time to play in the muck, adventure awaits!"

Bob swore again. Adventures seemed to involve a great deal of mud and parasitic insects.

The three finally made their way into a small clearing. Before them stood an ancient stone temple.

"And there she is. Beautiful, isn't she?"

Bob nodded, trying to ignore the itch in his neck.

"You know who built these?"

Sir Edmund grinned.

"Not a clue, dear Bob! What do you think I am, an archeologist?"

Bob raised an eyebrow.

"Don't you have a doctorate from Cambridge?"

Sir Edmund shrugged.

"I prefer to forget about pointless things. Now onward! Adventure awaits!"

Bob raised an eyebrow as the young guide started setting up camp.

"He's not coming with us?"

"Unlike you and I, he has a functional self-preservation mechanism, so he'll set up camp while we scout the premises."

Bob swore again.

THE FACELESS MINION

And into the temple they went. For once Bob was grateful for his fully enclosed helmet as Sir Edmund coughed on the thick dust in the air. Sir Edmund wrapped a filter around his mouth and nose, and then the two headed further in. The adventurer suddenly stopped and held up his hand as they approached a floor of square tiles.

"Wait, I've seen this before. These people loved to fill their temples with traps. Thought to protect the sacred places from the unworthy."

"I thought you didn't know who built these?"

"Oh I have no clue who they were. But you don't go on an adventure without picking up a thing or two. Or at least, you don't return from an adventure if you don't."

Sir Edmund spent a few moments examining the floor and the carvings on the walls before nodding. He hopped on one tile to the right, then to the left, jumped over one row, hit all of the next row in quick succession, then hit two tiles at the same time before leaping to the normal floor on the other side. He then turned and grinned at Bob, giving a quick bow.

"You got all that, right?"

Bob sighed and tapped a button on his wrist. His boots began to glow with purple light and he floated a foot in the air. A quick boost later and he floated above the tiles to the other side. Sir Edmund was frowning with his arms crossed.

"Not very sporting of you."

"My self-preservation mechanism is at least slightly functional."

Sir Edmund shook his head.

"Tourists. Where'd you get fancy boots like that anyways?"

"A gift from a friend."

"Fine, keep your secrets."

Bob shrugged as the pair headed deeper in.

A handful of life or death encounters, wildly impractical hallways, ancient puzzles, and allegations of cheating later and the pair reached a large door at the center of the temple.

They nodded at each other and opened the heavy stone slabs.

Inside was an empty room. Bob heaved a sigh as his headache grew.

"There's nothing here."

But Sir Edmund grinned.

"That, my dear Bob, is where you're wrong."

Sir Edmund strode to the far wall, shining a flashlight on it. He wiped away the dust, revealing a mural carved across the entire wall. Bob watched in silence as the man pored over the depictions.

"Aha! I've got it!"

"What?"

Sir Edmund paced as he rubbed his chin.

"You see, it turns out this temple is merely part of a wider network! They not only built a pattern into their temples, they built a pattern OUT of their temples."

Bob froze.

He trembled slightly.

"...and what does that mean?"

Sir Edmund turned to face Bob, a massive grin on his face.

"Your treasure is in another castle."

Bob groaned.

△△△

A long, annoying, and continuously life-threatening time later, and a truck finally pulled up to the construction site. Bob stepped out of the passenger seat, supervising several minions as they unloaded a large crate. He let out a sigh and walked over to Sergei.

"How's it looking?"

Sergei nodded.

"We ran the simulations, and it should work. It's just..."

Bob froze.

"What. Is. It?"

Sergie gulped and glanced away.

"...Minh and Cikizwa say they're having trouble finding that Mablite substance."

Bob turned around without a word and shuffled back to the truck. He softly closed the door, locking it with a click. He nodded to the driver, who stepped out of the vehicle. Then he checked his helmet, making sure it was fully sealed, and turned off his mic.

And then Bob screamed.

Just another day in the life of a minion.

> *AUTHOR'S COMMENTARY: Don't worry, Anita, at least everyone likes your now public secret fantasies! Can you imagine if that thing you wrote on your own was put somewhere public where everyone could read and judge it? How terrifying. Anyways! Will Anita ever leave her room again knowing the whole world is reading her musings and fantasies? Can Bob find the Mablite? Why do the ancients love booby-trapping their places of worship? Tune in next time, to find out!*

CHAPTER 29 - A BEAUTIFUL DAWN

Bob sat around a conference table with several other minions. He slouched over in his chair, barely moving a muscle. Everyone else sat up straight, avoiding his gaze.

"Please, *please* tell me we're ready."

Minh and Cikizwa looked at one another, gulped, and then nodded.

"We got most of the materials, the last one should be delivered today."

Bob looked at the pair. He closed his eyes and took a deep breath.

"Any *more* complications?"

The two rapidly shook their heads.

"Nothing we couldn't handle. We kept it quiet and shouldn't have made any waves."

Bob let out a deep sigh, the tension draining from his shoulders.

"Sergei, are the necessary systems operational?"

Sergei nodded slowly.

"For the most part. We'll need to run some integration tests once the last materials arrive, but the individual systems are running. We just need the power source and the magnetizer and we should be fully operational at about 64% efficiency."

Bob nodded again.

"That'll do. Tina, how are our finances?"

Tina frowned but nodded.

"We cut it close but we're just within budget. As long as we don't have any more surprises, we should be in the clear. Not getting the maximum bonus this time though."

Everyone around the table sighed at that.

"Villains."

"Seriously, did we really need that much gold?"

"We could've cut the cost in half if it weren't for the mountain base."

Bob cut in.

"How about the company retreat?"

Tina nodded.

"Still have enough for that, at least."

Bob turned to Chris.

"What's the ETA on construction?"

Chris looked at his notes.

"We should be done with the functional systems, the throne, and the exterior by the end of the week, minus the parts Sergei is still testing. Barracks and living systems outside of the boss's room won't be done though."

Bob nodded again.

"Good work, make sure it gets done. Senior Brother Yuhan, are the disciples ready?"

Yuhan nodded.

"I'd like to run a full on training exercise once construction is finished, to iron out the kinks."

Bob nodded.

"Should be enough time for that."

Yuhan placed his fist in his palm and bowed. Bob checked his notes one last time and nodded.

"Good work everyone, looks like we're just about ready to go. Start wrapping up and remember to finish your newbie evals."

Each of the men and women around the table nodded or saluted. The group stood up.

"I'll talk to the boss then. Everyone keep each other posted on any complications and let's get to it."

△△△

Miss Le Blank strode into her office, clenching her fists and gritting her teeth.

"That Vivienne! I can't believe she humiliated me like that! And all those imbeciles actually believe her dribble! What does Mr. Soyer and some idiotic movie have to do with anything? She's the one making up fairy tales!"

Bob nodded placatingly.

"It's most confusing, Ma'am."

She spun around and glared at him.

"Almost as confusing as your laziness, minion! What on Earth is taking so long?!"

Bob held his hands up.

"We're almost ready for you, Ma'am. Just one more week and you can visit at any time."

Miss Le Blank heaved a dramatic sigh.

"Finally! It's about time! I have to say I'm disappointed in your lack of enthusiasm."

Bob stepped over to her with a clipboard in hand.

"Just one thing, Ma'am, could we have your signature?"

"What?! What could it possibly be now?! Could you be any less competent?! Honestly, I will have words with your supervisor when this is over."

Miss Le Blank snatched the clipboard from Bob's hands and sloppily signed the sheet. Bob nodded as she thrust it back at him.

"Thank you, Ma'am. With that everything should be in order. Will you be stopping by as soon as construction is finished?"

Miss Le Blank rolled her eyes.

"Obviously! And everything better be perfect when I get there, minion!"

Bob bowed his head.

"As you will, Ma'am."

Bob left the office and headed to an unassuming janitor's room. He opened up a cabinet, flicking a switch hidden under the brooms. A low hum sounded as the privacy mode engaged. He pulled out his phone and dialed a number.

"Hello Bob."

"Hello Londyn."

"What do you have for me this time?"

"A code 26w, but it could be a 25 if left unchecked."

"Ugh, things are pretty tight here, Bob. How long do we have exactly?"

"A week."

"Hm, we should just make it. What are the details?"

△△△

Miss Le Blank sighed as the car bumped yet again. Why on Earth did the minions choose some backwater in Eastern Russia of all places? There wasn't even a functional airport in the area! All in all this had been a most disappointing affair. She expected better of the company that came so highly recommended...

And then they crested over the final hill.

Miss Le Blank's jaw dropped.

The castle of her dreams stood before her, shining in the dawn. It appeared exactly as she imagined it.

"Finally..."

Miss Le Blank remained in a daze as she toured through the castle. Then she entered the throne room. It was a golden room with a red carpet leading to a golden throne. The room was at the base of the central tower, extending all the way to the highest point of the castle. In lieu of a ceiling was a transparent dome that glimmered in the sunlight, the focal point of the castle built into the center of the main spire. She held her tongue as she strode down the hall and took her seat upon the throne. The minion who escorted her knelt before his rightful ruler.

"There is still work to be done on the barracks for your minions, but the systems are ready for you, Ma'am. Just waiting on your power and then it can activate at your command."

Miss Le Blank vaguely nodded and closed her eyes.

She began to glow, brighter and brighter until she could no longer be seen. Then she thrust her hand upwards.

Beams of light shot into the air. The throne and the walls lit up in a dazzling display of rainbow lights as the beam traveled through the air.

And then it hit the dome.

And the sun shone upon the throne.

The dome grew so bright it could no longer be viewed directly. Rainbow lights lit up around the walls and floors, traveling through the entire castle. Holographic screens appeared in the air before Miss Le Blank's face, showing the status of the facility and the views of various internal and external cameras. Miss Le Blank gave a nod.

"This is…adequate, I suppose. There may be hope for you yet, minion."

And then the whole facility shook with a roar.

"What was that?!"

The minion looked at his phone and gasped.

"We're under attack, Ma'am!"

Miss Le Blank blinked several times.

"Under attack?! By whom?!"

The minion gulped.

"The ILS, Ma'am! Looks like Tesla Titan is hitting our perimeter!"

"How did they even find us?! Those blasted heroes will ruin everything! Minion, where is the security?!"

The minion looked away.

"T-That's the thing, Ma'am…"

Miss Le Blank spun her head to glare at him.

"What?!"

"M-Most of the team is on a company retreat. We only

have the perimeter guys at the moment."

"WHY ON EARTH ARE THEY ON A BLASTED RETREAT?! JUST WHICH IDIOTIC IMBECILE APPROVED THAT?!"

The minion continued averting his gaze.

"Um...you did, Ma'am. Everyone was most grateful for your magnanimousness..."

Miss Le Blank gripped her hair.

And then she heaved a sigh.

"You know what? I don't care anymore. I'm done with you people."

"Ma'am?"

She waved her hand, not even looking at the minion anymore.

"Minion, get out there and stop the heroes."

The minion jumped.

"Me? By...myself...Ma'am?"

"Unless you see anyone else actually doing their jobs!"

"B-But...I mean...it's the ILS, Ma'am!"

Miss Le Blank rolled her eyes.

"So what? I don't expect you to win, just slow them down a bit! Trip them with your body or something!"

"U-Um..."

"JUST DO IT!"

"O-Ok..."

The minion shuffled out of the room. Miss Le Blank started pressing buttons on the holographic screens.

"If I can just get this into the air...then it won't matter. Nothing will matter! No one will be able to stop my rise! And I will make this world...beautiful."

△△△

Tesla Titan strode down the hill, his boots hitting the ground with heavy thuds. Before him, armored minions set up a barricade, guns at the ready.

"Huh, less than expected. Is good, easier is better."

He raised his right arm. A surge of lighting jumped across the barricade, sending minions convulsing on the ground as they screamed, arcs of lightning sparking around their bodies.

Tesla Titan shielded his eyes as he looked up at the castle. The glow from the centerpiece had spread, and now the entire structure was shining.

"Seems wasteful. Villain should learn to be more efficient, like me."

Tesla Titan strode towards the castle, passing by the convulsing minions. He approached the main gate.

And was struck by a purple beam.

He checked his suit for damage. There was a purple glow around the suit but no physical damage dealt. He shrugged and continued forward.

Or tried to.

But the suit wouldn't move.

"Hm...checking connections..."

The suit UI didn't respond. Tesla Titan stirred up his lightning and sent it surging through the suit. The interior of the suit was filled with crackling electricity.

But the exterior remained covered in a dull purple glow, with occasional purple lights blinking about.

And the suit still wouldn't move.

"...that's not good."

Behind the corner of a nearby barracks, the minion from the castle packed up the Anti-Ionizer Ray. He smirked and whispered.

"From the Red Colonel with love. Forgot who built your suit, did you? You should have expected the KGB to have a contingency plan just for you."

Bob shook his head and walked behind the barracks and back towards the barricade. He nodded to the minions on the ground.

"Miss Le Blank no longer requires our services."

The Outer Disciples immediately stopped convulsing and

stood back up, clearing the electricity with their qi. They placed their fists in their palms and gave a short bow, and then scattered from the area. Bob shook his head as he got into a parked car.

"A week's warning and you still barely arrived in time. Heroes are so annoying."

Just then the ground began to tremble. Cracks appeared around the castle walls, right in front of the immobile Tesla Titan suit.

The castle began to rise, the ground underneath floating along with it.

Miss Le Blank's flying castle had been activated.

Tesla Titan grimaced. The suit still refused to move. His comms were down, as they were built into the suit and so deactivated with it. He could do nothing but watch.

The castle flew into the rising sun, heading towards the sea.

Fully armed and operational.

△△△

"Breaking news, folks. We received word that America's Seventh Fleet has arrived in the East China Sea and that China's navy has set sail to intercept it. The US government is reporting that the two sides have located one another and are currently facing off. No shots have been fired yet but planes have been patrolling the skies and have had some close encounters. Experts are concerned that this tense situation has reached a boiling point and that a single accident or misunderstanding could escalate into open conflict. We'll be keeping a close eye on the situation, so stay tuned for further updates."

△△△

Gabriel Le Blank sat back in her chair, her eyes wide, hands gripping the armrests. Her light powers now spread throughout the entire castle and looped back to her, connecting her to the entire structure.

She could feel...everything.

The sun shining down upon the ramparts, the wind blowing past the spires.

She could hear the waves far below, see across the horizon.

She directed her gaze downward, following a pod of dolphins that must have been miles away. She focused in and looked into the eyes of the leader as he jumped above the waves.

She smiled.

She could feel her power coursing through every inch of the castle, the entire fortress obeying her commands as if it were her own body.

Well, almost.

She grimaced as pain spiked through her head. The navigation controls seemed to be a separate system, so attempting to control them directly had consequences. She frowned. Navigation was to be controlled by a designated officer at a more mundane terminal. A minion should have been there, changing course as per her commands.

She took a deep breath. No, she would forget those imbeciles. Nothing would be allowed to ruin this moment.

For it mattered not. The minions seemed to have programmed an autopilot with a predetermined route, at the very least. There was no need for Miss Le Blank to handle such things herself. She had wanted to head towards the world capitals directly, or maybe Vivienne's house, but there was no harm in taking the scenic route. With the flying castle at her command, all would bow before her in time.

All she needed to do was demonstrate her superiority to whoever she encountered.

She smiled once more. The beautiful dawn had arrived. And nothing could stop her now.

△△△

High above the Pacific Ocean, a squadron of Chinese jets flew in formation. The pilots sat back in their seats, speaking through their mics.

"Overlord, this is Jaeger 1."

"Jaeger 1, got some Super-Hornets approaching the perimeter near your position. Send them back."

"Copy that, Overlord. Intercept only?"

"If at all possible. If they won't deviate, give them a warning shot. If they still won't back off, you're clear to engage after they pass the perimeter."

"Copy that. Jaeger 2 and I will intercept. The rest go high and quiet, pick your targets. Don't engage until my signal."

"Copy that, Jaeger 1."

"Roger."

"Moving to position."

The pilot looked down at his radar, waiting to identify the American planes.

And then he froze.

There was something else on the radar.

Something *huge*.

And then his mic buzzed once again.

"Jaeger 1, this is Overlord."

"Overlord, this is Jaeger 1."

"We're reading a massive bogey, approaching from the north. Head over to identify."

"Copy that. More Americans?"

"Unknown. The Super-Hornets have veered off towards that direction as well. Use caution."

"Copy that, we're heading out."

The jets veered off towards the north, maintaining their formation. The huge red dot moved closer and closer on the radar.

And it was not long before the pilots could see it with their own eyes.

"...what the heck is that?!"

"Jaeger 1, are you seeing this?"

"Overlord this is Jaeger 1, come in."

"Jaeger 1, this is Overlord, we read you. What's the situation?"

"It's a...flying castle."

"Jaeger 1, repeat that. Did you say a flying castle?"

"Yes, some kind of castle, floating above the water."

"...any radio contact? Identifiers?"

"Non-responsive, no identifiers so far. Wait...we just spotted the Super-Hornets on approach. They're headed towards the castle."

"So it's American? Or are they trying to figure it out too?"

Suddenly the pilot gasped.

"...oh my god!"

"What is it, Jaeger 1?"

"It's attacking the Americans! Some kind of directed energy weapon!"

"...it's definitely not one of ours. Jaeger 1, try radio contact again."

And then the pilot saw flashes of light across the castle...

"EVASIVE ACTION!"

"Jaeger 1, what's happening?!"

"WE'RE UNDER ATTACK! WE JUST LOST JAEGERS 2 and 10! WAIT...PULL UP!"

And then the radio went silent.

"Jaeger 1, come in. What's your status?"

"Jaeger 1, please respond."

"Jaeger squadron, anyone who reads please respond."

No one in Jaeger squadron reported back...

△△△

Admiral Faulkner of the United States Navy frowned. He stood on the command deck of the USS *Ronald Reagan*, the flagship of the fleet.

"What's going on, people?"

"F-35s were on route, but we've lost contact, sir."

"We still haven't figured out what we're dealing with?"

"The Chinese reached out, they're saying it's not them, sir."

Admiral Faulkner shook his head.

"Of course they would. That means nothing until we can confirm what actually happened."

"I think it's true, sir. A Chinese squadron was shot down too. Bogey just passed over their formation, radar's reading the PLAN is in full retreat now."

Admiral Faulkner's frown grew deeper.

"Who'd be crazy enough to hit us both?"

"Sir, bogey is on intercept course now."

Admiral Faulkner rubbed his chin for a moment but shook his head. He had already lost two fighter squadrons to this bogey. Whoever it was was clearly hostile.

"Shoot it down, whatever it takes."

American jet fighters soared through the air as they headed towards the target, more of them launching off the decks of the *Ronald Reagan*, as well as its sister carriers USS *Abraham Lincoln* and USS *Carl Vinson* to the *Ronald Reagan*'s flanks. Missiles also launched from escort destroyers and cruisers.

"Sir, target is in visual range!"

"On screen, now. I want to see this."

Admiral Faulkner walked over to the closest monitor and jumped.

"What kind of Star Trek crap is that?!"

Missiles from boats and fighters detonated on a shield of light, leaving the castle beneath entirely unharmed. The castle subsequently fired back, laser beams piercing the sky from the castle's turrets. In the center of the castle was something like a miniature sun.

Jets and missiles exploded mid-air as the beams of light swept across them.

Admiral Faulkner's eyes narrowed.

"Call off the jets. We're not losing any more lives until we know what we're dealing with."

"Sir...something's happening."

He spun around to look at the officer who spoke.

"What is it?"

"Massive spike in thermal readings from the bogey!"

The monitor began to glow as the castle's core grew brighter and brighter.

Then the sky lit up, every man and woman shielding their eyes from the sudden glow.

They heard a sound like the air being ripped apart.

And then a wave of water exploded into the sky, completely blinding the right side of the *Ronald Reagan*.

"WHAT THE HECK JUST HAPPENED?! TALK TO ME PEOPLE!"

"Bogey fired some kind of weapon!"

"NO CRAP! I WANT TO KNOW..."

Another explosion rocked the ship. Admiral Faulkner turned his head to the right and gaped.

The *Carl Vinson* was torn in two, its halves drifting apart and sinking into the ocean, red hot metal visible from the cut. Steam rose across the ocean in a straight line from the castle to the sinking ship. More explosions rang out as jet fuel and bombs caught fire. Admiral Faulkner grabbed his mic to transmit to the fleet.

"*Higgins* and *Howard*, search and rescue on the *Carl Vinson*, everyone send your choppers to assist, jets run interference for the rescue op. All other ships, full retreat. We're getting out of here."

"Sir..."

"What?!"

The man was simply pointing out the window. Admiral

Faulkner turned to look in that direction.

A giant image of a beautiful woman was projected in the sky.

"Greetings, all you hags and trolls. This is your savior, Gabriel Le Blank. Rejoice, for this ugly and twisted world is at an end. I, the paragon of beauty and nobility, shall remake this world in my image, and it shall be...beautiful. As you can clearly see, there are none in this world that can match me in beauty...or in might. Please cease your unsightly thrashing, and I shall allow you to behold the beautiful tomorrow. Fail to acknowledge my rightful authority and I shall sweep you away along with the rest of the trash."

Admiral Faulkner stood in silence as his ships turned around and sailed away.

"I'm going to make a call. I want you to call up Tokyo, Seoul, Moscow, and the ILS while I do."

One of his officers raised an eyebrow.

"The ILS? From a military line? Sir, that is strictly against..."

"I don't want to hear it! We just lost a supercarrier to a freaking Death Star piloted by a madwoman! So unless you want to get in a jet and fly out with the next wave, go call the people who deal with this kind of crap! If DC calls us you just scream at them for reinforcements until they hang up, we aren't taking any orders today besides get help or go home."

The officers turned away and started making calls. Admiral Faulkner shook his head.

He was too old for this crap.

He sighed and picked up the phone.

"This is Admiral Faulkner of the United States Navy calling for Admiral Huo of the People's Liberation Army Navy. I think we have something to discuss."

△△△

"Breaking news folks! It's been confirmed that a supervillain attacked both the American and Chinese navies today! Both sides have retreated from the area, neither government has released an official statement at this time but we estimate high casualties on both sides. Miss Gabriel Le Blank, formerly actress, model, and socialite, claimed responsibility for the attack and has released an ultimatum to world leaders. Her flying fortress is currently on patrol over the East China Sea, but experts dread what may happen should she decide to make landfall. Local governments are scrambling to organize a response but with two of the world's most powerful navies already defeated a military victory seems unlikely. The public is crying out for the ILS to intervene, before it's too late."

△△△

Londyn let out a sigh as she watched the news.
"Still no word from Tesla Titan?"
Linda looked at her monitor, then her eyes widened and she exhaled her breath.
"Rescue team just arrived. It seems his suit was disabled somehow but he wasn't harmed."
Londyn exhaled her breath as well. At least there was *some* good news today. She turned to Vice-Director Carter.
"Are Washington and Beijing on board yet?"
The Vice-Director slowly nodded.
"They aren't happy but their admirals are insisting and already moving to join forces with the international fleet. Tokyo and Seoul have demanded we participate before they'll commit forces, the Russians are also saying they don't want to risk ships unnecessarily. The big two just gave us the official green light."
Londyn sighed. The cleanup for all this was not going to be fun. But she'd handle that later.

Right now she had to figure out how to bring down the sun.

AUTHOR'S COMMENTARY: They did it! The battlestation is ready! Well, minus the navigation and the security and 99% of the crew being missing, if we're nitpicking that is. Anyways! Can Gabriel Le Blank's flying castle be stopped? Will Bob be able to enjoy the company retreat? Can Londyn and the international fleet stand up to this grave new threat? Tune in next time, to find out!

CHAPTER 30 - TO BRING DOWN THE SUN

Londyn walked into a conference room aboard a neutral civilian vessel. Several commanders were seated around the room. A conversation was already trailing off into whispers and tense silence as she arrived.

"Ah, Madam Director, glad you could join us. Admiral Faulkner, USN."

"Admiral Huo, PLAN."

"Admiral Takishima, JMSDF."

"Admiral Kong, ROKN."

"Admiral Victorovich, VMF."

Londyn nodded her head.

"Director Green, ILS. A pleasure to meet you all. I wish it were under better circumstances."

Everyone around the table nodded as Londyn took a seat. She waited for a minute but no one spoke up. She bit back a sigh.

"Do you gentlemen have a plan?"

The admirals glanced around the room but no one spoke up. Admiral Faulkner gave a shrug.

"Do you have any ideas, Director?"

Londyn nodded.

"Aurora Legion can infiltrate the facility and confront Miss Le Blank directly."

Admiral Huo frowned at that.

"How do you plan to get them there? They'll never make it past her defenses. Those beams will shoot them from the sky long before they arrive, and if they make it that far then they'd have to break past that shield."

Londyn nodded.

"That's exactly why I'm proposing Aurora Legion. Voidspeaker's powers are a good match for any energy-focused powers or weapons. He can drain a portion of the shield long enough for a single craft to pass through."

Admiral Kong furrowed his brow.

"That still doesn't explain how they'll get past the beams."

Londyn nodded her head.

"It does not. That will be up to you all."

The admirals glanced around at each other once more. Admiral Huo took the lead this time.

"What are you suggesting?"

"Cause a distraction."

Silence reigned. Admiral Takishima spoke up with a whisper.

"Do you understand what you're asking?"

Londyn nodded.

"I do. But you don't need to just waltz right up to her, correct? You all have drones and standoff weapons, don't you?"

Admiral Victorovich crossed his arms.

"Will that be enough against that monstrosity? I hear American and Chinese ships already tried?"

Londyn shook her head.

"We don't need to overwhelm the castle. Just the people running it. Voidspeaker can also shield Aurora's transport from radar and visual detection. A light distraction is all they need."

Silence reigned once more, until Admiral Huo heaved a sigh.

"Well, it could work. There's just one problem."

Admiral Huo turned to look Londyn in the eyes.

"You want us to leave our fate in the hands of children? It's my country in the line of fire if we fail, Director."

Londyn met his gaze.

"I want you to leave your fate in the hands of *heroes*, Admiral. They've done this before. They will not fail."

Admiral Faulkner shrugged.

"It's the first non-suicidal plan we've heard today. I'm for it."

Admiral Huo slowly nodded his head.

"If you truly believe they're up to this task, then we will give them the chance."

Admirals Takishima, Kong, and Victorovich nodded as well. Londyn nodded back.

"Then if we're all in agreement, let's work out the details."

△△△

A small plane flew through the air, just large enough to carry a squad of people. It appeared like any other tactical military transport, save for one thing. Rather than a jet engine, the craft had a light purple glow around it, with purple light streaming from its thrusters.

This was the ILS's brand new grav-jet, a state-of-the-art transport featuring the gravity technology Londyn inherited from Dr. Kayserling. Along with some novel technologies that made it a rival for any military craft out there. It turned out not *all* the super-geniuses wanted to become villains and the ILS was a very competitive employer.

Onboard this grav-jet, four teenagers sat strapped into the side seats, while one leaned over an elaborate circular pattern drawn on the floor in pitch black ink. Wherever the lines intersected there were depictions of stars, the whole structure forming a picture of the cosmos.

Voidspeaker mumbled to himself as he poured over the formation. Wonder Knight and Pink Star exchanged glances before Wonder Knight turned to the other boy.

"Everything all right, Void?"

"Shh! Let me concentrate, I just need to check this

alignment right here..."

Wonder Knight tilted his head.

"Really? This is the twelfth time you've checked it already."

"Eldritch rituals are not something you wing, bro!"

Chronolock smirked.

"No pressure Void. We're just going to die if you fail."

Voidspeaker stared at her with narrowed eyes.

"Wow Chrono, thanks for the support."

Icy Rose gulped. Everyone else seemed very casual about something that could result in their deaths.

"U-Um, you can do it, Voidspeaker!"

Chronolock just shook her head.

"Don't coddle him, Rose. He thrives under stress."

Icy Rose glanced around as the rest of Aurora Legion chuckled.

She had to wonder...was this truly a laughing matter?

The pilot turned her head back to the team.

"Eyes up people, we're about to come in range of the target."

Wonder Knight nodded his head.

"Now or never, Void."

Voidspeaker took a deep breath.

"Ok ok, just give me a moment. Whoo...you can do this... here goes."

He held his hands out over the circle, closed his eyes, and began chanting under his breath. The area around his eyes began to glow with a dim, purple flame. His voice grew a deep and ominous echo. He began to float in the air as wind stirred up in the cabin.

His eyes shot open, glowing with bright purple light.

He spoke along with the deep echo.

"SHROUD OF THE ABYSS."

In the skies above the Pacific, the grav-jet was covered in black, and then vanished from view.

△△△

Londyn stood by Admiral Faulkner on the command deck of the *Ronald Regan*. A light flashed on her wrist.

"Aurora's in position, we're ready."

Admiral Faulkner took a deep breath.

"I hope you know what you're doing. Honestly I exaggerated a bit when I called this plan non-suicidal you know?"

Londyn shrugged.

"Every ILS op is suicidal."

Admiral Faulkner swore as he grabbed a mic.

"Great, just great. People, we're good to go here. Commence Operation Hoey."

"Commencing Operation *Hou Yi*. Admiral Faulkner, please never attempt to speak my language again."

"Screw you Admiral Huo. Try saying Susquehanna for me!"

"Susquehanna."

Admiral Faulkner dropped the mic.

"Gosh darn commie jerk."

Londyn raised an eyebrow.

"Oh don't give me that, Director. This stopped being a professional military op when we sent a bunch of teenagers to blow up the Death Star."

One of the officers turned to the Admiral.

"Planes are in the air, sir, both ours and the Chinese. The Japanese, Koreans, and Russians are reporting they've launched and are approaching from the north."

Admiral Faulkner sighed.

"Well, no one lives forever. Let's get this party started."

The officer turned back and shouted into his mic.

"All ships, open fire!"

Londyn watched as trails of smoke and fire towered into

the sky. All around them, destroyers and cruisers launched long-range cruise missiles. A monitor swapped to the view from a drone.

"Missiles on approach!"

"Send in the fighters."

"Copy that. Strike commander you are cleared to engage."

In the view from the drone, fighter jets launched their missiles and then spun around to keep out of laser range. A fleet of drones filled the sky, following the trails of the missiles.

"Target in sight!"

Beams of light lit up the sky once more. Drones exploded mid-air or fell from the sky. The castle came into view, flashes of light appearing as missiles exploded on its shields. Another wave of missiles roared past the drone.

Soon they could see the walls of the castle itself.

"Sir, we're running out of missiles!"

Admiral Faulkner turned to Londyn, who was glancing at her wrist. She shook her head.

"Keep it up! Don't stop until we're out!"

Another wave of missiles passed the drone. More missiles launched from the ships around them.

"Cruise missiles depleted!"

The drone was close enough to see the windows on the ramparts. Explosions continued to blanket the shield, but were slowly growing less frequent.

The drone's vision was filled with a flash of light, and then cut off.

"Strike commander is reporting they're out of missiles! Orders, sir?"

Admiral Faulkner turned to Londyn, who was looking at her wrist. A green light flashed and she nodded.

"Aurora has landed on target."

Admiral Faulkner grabbed the mic once more.

"Package is delivered, let's get out of here people!"

△△△

Gabriel Le Blank grit her teeth. Fools, every last one of them fools! Why couldn't they see?! Why couldn't they understand?! This ugly world could not be allowed to continue its unsightly path!

She frowned and gripped her armrests. She closed her eyes, and sent her power into the core above.

A huge wave of light surged from the castle in every direction. The assault on her shield stopped as explosions filled the air.

When she opened her eyes she saw calm seas and clear skies.

She let out a deep breath.

And then the edges of her mouth curled into a wicked smile.

It was time to show these wretches *exactly* who they had messed with.

And then she froze in her chair.

She saw them.

She *felt* them.

Bugs. There were bugs in her home. Dirtying the halls with their unclean boots.

She grit her teeth once more. But then she closed her eyes and took a deep breath.

It was fine.

It was all fine.

She had prepared for this, of course.

She focused in and fired up the security system.

Nothing happened.

She stretched her neck and fired up the security system.

Nothing happened.

This time she *really* put her back into it.

Still nothing happened.

She quickly felt around the halls of her castle, sending her power through it to explore every corner.

She found nothing.

Nothing but power lines and lights.

She pulled out her phone, scowling as it started to ring.

"Yes, Ma'am?"

"MINION! WHERE IS THE SECURITY SYSTEM?!"

"Sorry Ma'am, security system was scheduled to be installed next week. I thought Chris had shared the construction schedule with you?"

"FOR THE LOVE OF...Can any of you not be incompetent imbeciles for once?! These blasted heroes are ruining everything!"

"Oh...um, sorry Ma'am, let me see...um, if they get to the throne room you could use the core to overpower them?"

"You're saying I have to fight them myself?!"

"Sorry about that, Ma'am."

Gabriel Le Blank screamed. Then she hurled the phone into a wall.

△△△

Bob shrugged and put away his phone, turning his attention back to his rod. On the other side of the boat Chris turned from his line.

"Trouble with the boss?"

Bob shrugged again.

"ILS caught up to her it seems."

Chris sighed and shook his head.

"Heroes."

Bob nodded, and then felt a tug at his line.

Retreats are so relaxing.

△△△

Back in Miss Le Blank's castle, Aurora Legion took up formation outside the large, golden doors. Wonder Knight looked around, each member silently nodded. He held up three fingers, pumping his hand and dropping a finger with each motion.

Then he pushed open the doors.

And slammed back into the wall as he took a laser beam to the face.

"Wonder!"

"DIE!"

The rest of Aurora leapt into action. Voidspeaker and Chronolock rushed into the room, taking cover behind golden pillars. Icy Rose lifted her hands and formed a wall of ice to block the doorway. She shrieked as a beam of light pierced a hole straight through her wall, knocking her to the ground.

Miss Le Blank screeched as she thrust her arms forward repeatedly, firing beams down the throne room.

"DIE! DIE! DIE! JUST DIE!"

Voidspeaker and Chronolock glanced at each other from across the hall. Voidspeaker spun his finger around the side of his head. Chronolock just frowned and shook her head, then made some motions with her hands. Voidspeaker nodded and stepped out from behind the pillar, firing a black beam towards the throne.

Miss Le Blank turned towards the beam and thrust both her hands forward with a snarl. A beam of light overwhelmed the beam of dark as the castle's core shined above. Voidspeaker's eyes widened as the beam collided into him, sending him flying through the air.

Meanwhile Chronolock sprinted down the hall, leaping towards Miss Le Blank.

"EEK! GET AWAY!"

Miss Le Blank swung her hand and an arc of light surging forward. Chronolock was thrust back, gritting her teeth as she landed on her feet. She barely had time to dodge to the side before a beam of light blasted the floor next to her.

"JUST! DIE!"

Miss Le Blank lifted her hands into the air and the light in the ceiling grew brighter and brighter.

And then a rain of beams fell upon the room.

A pink Ankylosaurus took position over the fallen Voidspeaker, crying out as beams struck its armored back. Wonder Knight dragged Icy Rose back into the hall, he and Pink Star gritting their teeth as they hid behind the doorway. Chronolock jumped this way and that, barely stopping beams from hitting her with her powers.

"DO SOMETHING!"

She shouted into the comms. Voidspeaker shook his head and then leapt to the side, scrambling for the doorway as the dinosaur protecting him faded into pink particles.

"Ugh...that hurt. Bro, tell me you have a plan. Now would be a really good time for a plan!"

"Let me think...Pink, can you do *that*?"

"Um, I think so. Won't last long though."

"Rose, Void, you good to go?"

Icy Rose winced as she rose from the ground but she grit her teeth and stood up.

"I'll live, let's end this."

Voidspeaker grimaced and held his side.

"Ugh, no, but we have to, right?"

Wonder Knight nodded.

"You two, follow me. Pink will distract her."

Just then Chronolock gave a cry as a beam impacted the ground behind her, sending her flying forward. Wonder Knight shouted and then rushed into the room.

"GO!"

Pink Star held out her hands, gauntlets growing bright.

"I choose you..."

The pink light shone, brighter than ever before.

"Dragon!"

A mighty roar filled the hall.

A beam of pink flames cut through the rain of light, slamming into Miss Le Blank. The light in the ceiling dimmed as Miss Le Blank let out a cry.

A strand of her hair fell in front of her face, burning from the flame.

Her face twisted in a snarl.

"DEAD! YOU ARE SO DEAD!"

A pink dragon leapt into the room, roaring once more. Miss Le Blank thrust her hands forward with all her might, a gigantic beam piercing the air. The dragon let out its mighty breath, a beam of pink flame matching the golden light.

The air hissed and roared as the two beams collided, pink flames scattering around the room.

And then the golden beam began to vibrate in the air, Chronolock reaching up for it as she lay on the ground.

And the pink flames surged forth once more, enveloping Miss Le Blank's throne in a pink inferno.

Then the dragon leapt to the side and Chronolock released the beam, letting it crash into a wall.

The dragon slowly approached the flames…

And then a golden flash shot out from inferno.

Miss Le Blank was covered in golden light. Her eyes were wide as they could go, a twisted smile on her face. Her hair was frazzled and singed, with ash on her cheeks and hands. She was giggling as she pulled back a fist. Her hand pierced straight into the dragon's chest.

And then golden light exploded from inside the dragon, vaporizing it entirely.

Pink Star fell to the ground, gasping for breath. Chronolock rushed to stand before her. Miss Le Blank just looked on the ground, hair covering her face. Her shoulders trembled as she held her hands out.

She began to laugh.

"Hehehe…AHAHAHAHA! This…you…look at what you've done! Ruined…I'm ruined! Ruinedruinedruinedruinedruined! Beauty is ruined! The dawn is ruined!"

She looked up, her eyes wide and her face locked into a

massive smile.

"Hehehehe…naughty girls like you need to be punished, hehehe."

Chronolock grimaced.

"Wonder…any time now."

Wonder Knight grunted as he gripped on the side of a pillar, Icy Rose hanging from his back and Voidspeaker floating behind them.

"Ready?"

Icy Rose nodded and lifted her hand. A platform of ice grew around the pillar, Wonder Knight and Icy Rose standing on it. They nodded to Voidspeaker.

"EXPERIENCE NOTHINGNESS!"

A dark beam struck the glowing ceiling, removing just a tiny circle of the light shining around it. Wonder Knight leapt up and slammed his fist on the beam's point of impact. Cracks formed on the ceiling. Wonder Knight then pushed off the wall to land back on the ice platform. There Icy Rose was constructing a giant spike of ice. Wonder Knight grabbed hold of the spike and hoisted it onto his shoulder. He took a deep breath.

Then he thrusted it upwards with all his might.

With a crash the spike pierced into the ceiling, shards of ice falling from its sides.

Ice Rose laid a hand on the base of the spike, making it grow from inside the giant sphere overhead. She began to grunt and sweat, but she pushed her power forward with all her might. Voidspeaker grunted and widened the beam, pouring as much power into his ritual as he could. Both teens starting shouting at the top of their lungs.

""GRAAAAAAAAAAAAHHHHH!!!!!""

Miss Le Blank stopped as she heard the shout, and her smile dropped. She looked up and her eyes widened even further.

"NO!"

She held out a glowing hand.

But then Chronolock's fist slammed into her cheek.

Wonder Knight drew back his fist and crouched down. He leapt into the air as fast as he could, the ice platform shattering from the force. Voidspeaker dropped his beam, floating over to grab Icy Rose and head towards the floor.

Wonder Knight let out a cry.

And then slammed his fist into the cracking ceiling with all his might.

The cracks started to spider across the entire sphere.

Everyone heard the sound of glass breaking.

And then ceiling shattered, the core of the castle breaking apart.

For a brief moment, a second sun shone over the Pacific.

And then the castle began to drop from the sky...

> AUTHOR'S COMMENTARY: Hm, maybe I should write a villain with whose abilities are not just 'shoots beams' someday. Also should probably have Aurora Legion not solve multiple fights with 'distract villain while we break the important thing in secret'. Could probably drag the fight out that way. Eh. Maybe next time. Anyways! What shall be the conclusion of these events? What was the point of all this? Did Bob manage to catch any fish? Tune in next time, to find out!

CHAPTER 31 - PEACE IN OUR TIME

Aurora Legion were flying on a grav-jet after Miss Le Blank was apprehended. The other four were chatting with one another, but not Icy Rose. She was staring at the floor, with her hands in her lap.

She just realized how weak she really was.

She thought after being trained by Icy Falcon that she was a real hero. She had taken on supervillains and come out victorious. Even that moment with the cartels was because she let her guard slip.

This was different.

Miss Le Blank had overpowered her, easily. All of Icy Falcon's tutelage, all of her training since, and some actress had punched through her walls like they weren't there.

She grit her teeth.

She couldn't help but think...if it had been Icy Falcon, he would have taken down a villain like that with ease.

Instead she got herself hurt, and Wonder Knight had to drag her to safety. Then he had to carry her up the room, and Voidspeaker had to catch her on the way down.

As she was, she couldn't replace Icy Falcon.

She couldn't even help Aurora Legion.

She clasped her hands together, gripping them hard, and grit her teeth.

Just then someone slapped her on the shoulder.

She let out a gasp and looked up.

Wonder Knight was smiling at her.

"Nice work, today, Rose!"

"M-Me?"

Voidspeaker nodded and gave a thumbs up.

"Couldn't have done it without you!"

Chronolock nodded.

"That was smart thinking, expanding the ice inside the roof."

"B-But..."

Wonder Knight grinned at her.

"And I couldn't have smashed that thing if you hadn't given me somewhere to stand. Might have gone badly without you."

Icy Rose opened her mouth to object...but couldn't find any words to say.

Pink Star smiled at her and placed a hand on her shoulder.

"How does it feel to save the world?"

Icy Rose's eyes went wide.

"T-That's..."

That was right. They had saved the world today.

It hadn't been pretty.

It hadn't been easy.

They had been knocked down, overpowered.

And yet...

They had found a way.

They had completed the mission.

They had won.

And Icy Rose had been there, each step of the way.

Maybe she hadn't done much...

But she had done something to help.

Wonder Knight raised his hands.

"Great job, team! Another day saved!"

Aurora Legion exchanged high fives all around, and then turned to Icy Rose. They held their hands up, grinning at her.

Icy Rose slumped...but she slowly raised her hands.

And Aurora Legion celebrated with her, too.

And then...the grav-jet landed on the USS *Ronald Reagan*.

The back door opened up.

Aurora Legion stepped out into the light of the sun.

And Icy Rose blinked.

Men and women in uniform filled the deck to the brim, and clapped their hands in thunderous applause as the teens descended from the deck. Sailors from every country in the international fleet now cheered and shouted. Director Green was looking at them with a smile, and nodded her head.

Five admirals stood with her, and turned to face the crowds. They all shouted together.

"""""""ATTENTION!"""""""

And with that, every single sailor present stood up straight and gave a salute.

Waves of American, Chinese, Russian, Korean, and Japanese fighter jets flew overhead in joint formations.

The five admirals walked to Aurora Legion, each one standing in front of one of the teens.

They saluted.

"Thank you, heroes, for your service!"

Icy Rose's heart pounded.

She closed her eyes as she felt something well up inside her.

She wasn't Icy Falcon, not yet. She hadn't yet fixed the damage she had caused.

But...

She had started on the path. She had done what she could. She helped the team...and the team helped her.

And now, with their help...

She had managed to do something good.

She glanced over at her teammates. Pink Star was looking at her with a smile, and nodded.

Icy Rose stared for a moment...

And then...

She started to smile too, with tears in her eyes.

△△△

"Good afternoon all you citizens of the planet Earth! This is GNN and I'm your host, Brendan Baird. Today we're here to talk about the recent events in the Pacific, where Aurora Legion did it again! The team of heroes joined forces with an international fleet to take on Miss Gabriel Le Blank and her flying fortress! Our young heroes confronted Miss Le Blank directly, and were able to bring down her terrifying superweapon."

"In the aftermath of the conflict, the United States of America and the People's Republic of China have toned down their rhetoric. Notably, Admiral Faulker of the United States Navy and Admiral Huo of the People's Liberation Army Navy have come out in support of peace, and publicly called upon their governments to resume diplomatic relations."

"In the wake of Miss Le Blank's attack and the casualties she inflicted on both navies, the USA and the PRC have agreed to further talks. There is even word of creating a broader forum for the Asia-Pacific region to provide additional avenues of discourse."

"To explore what this could mean for the future, we go to GNN's expert on US-China relations, Stacey Shao! Stacey, how are you today?"

"I'm doing great, Brendan, thanks for asking."

"Now Stacey, a lot of people, experts included, are not particularly enthusiastic about the new peace initiatives. Do you agree?"

"Well Brendan, it's not wrong to maintain realistic expectations. At the end of the day, all nations will act in their own self-interest, and the United States and China remain the biggest potential rival for the other. Real cooperation will be difficult to achieve."

"So you agree with the critics on this?"

"To a point."

"Oh?"

"There is a new variable to this equation: supers. The

US and China are still each other's biggest potential rival in terms of countries but they are no longer the other's only or even greatest potential threat. In one fell swoop, Miss Le Blank dealt significant damage to both countries' ability to project power across the ocean. Both were forced to join hands and ask the ILS for assistance. And Miss Le Blank isn't even the worst example of what a supervillain can do."

"So you think the existence of supervillains might force countries to cooperate?"

"I think after the Atomic Herald and the Necrosaurus shocked the globe, both the United States and China wanted to assert their strength, demonstrate that they still have power and control over the world. That has backfired immensely. I think both sides will now be much more cautious about such displays of force until they possess a response of their own to the threat of supers."

"So back to the drawing board, I suppose. Will they return to the fighting once they do have a response then?"

"That's unclear, Brendan. The truth is it will take them some time to do so, and new lines of communication have been established in the meantime. Both sides have an interest in deescalating for now, which means having hard talks and developing boundaries both sides can respect. This might be easier now due to the relationship formed between high ranking members of the military on both sides. I think it is possible the relationship could stabilize by the time either side is confident in their security, and so might reduce the incentives to provoke another incident."

"So they may not become friends but they don't have to be enemies?"

"Exactly. And honestly, I think this event is going to spread beyond East Asia."

"Oh?"

"Two of the most powerful militaries in the world were shut down by a single woman. Thousands of lives and billions of dollars of military hardware were lost in an instant with no gain to either side. Before that we saw armies of monsters appear out of thin air across the globe, taking the world's cities hostage before their armies could even respond. And before that, one super nearly caused a nuclear armageddon. Every country in the world, if they are reasonable, will now hesitate to send their forces abroad. Not when their own security is at risk, not when their full strength might be needed at home at a moment's notice. I think the entire world is going to have a pause on international conflict until everyone adjusts their militaries to the new global reality."

△△△

Xiong Huang stood in one of the Eternal Night Sect's private training rooms. Across from her stood Wu Zhengkang, breathing heavily with bruises all over. Meanwhile Xiong Huang's breath was steady, and she had not a single hair out of place.

Wu Zhengkang gathered his qi, a cold fog forming around his body. He rushed forward, pulling his sword back, and then thrust it at her.

"FIVE-FOLD ARTIC THRUST!"

Blades of ice formed in the air and stabbed towards Xiong Huang along with the sword, attempting to freeze her qi and pierce her body at the same time. But Xiong Huang just yawned and casually waved a finger through the air.

The ice shattered, the blade stopped, and Wu Zhengkang was thrown to the ground with a cry.

Xiong Huang crossed her arms and frowned.

"Pathetic, Disciple Wu. You stated you were ready to become a Core Disciple now. You even received a Thousand Star Ice Heart. This level of performance is simply unacceptable."

She shook her head.

"You are focusing too much on the power of the

Thousand Star Ice Heart. You are relying on it, letting it carry you, like a caretaker carrying a helpless infant. That is not the way the Eternal Night Sect does things. We rely on nothing. We take what we want and make it our own. If you let the power of the elixir carry you, then you do not own it, you merely hold it. And one day, someone will take it from you. It might even be me, if you continue to waste my time like this. So until you display a basic understanding of our techniques, you can forget Core Disciple; in fact, consider yourself fortunate I do not put you back in the Outer Disciples."

Wu Zhengkang's brow furrowed, but he kowtowed before his Mistress.

"This unworthy peon thanks the Great Mistress for her teachings."

Xiong Huang heaved a sigh. At this point, even the groveling annoyed her. But she didn't feel like wasting any more time on Disciple Wu today, so she simply left without another word.

She went back to her chambers, plopping herself on the couch and turning on her television. She reached for her bag of chips before realizing it was empty. She glanced around, but there were no more bags in reach. The closest one was on a shelf across the room. She sighed again and lay back against her cushions, turning her attention to the television instead.

It was on the mortal news station, apparently the mortals were about to go to war when some 'super' intervened.

Then Xiong Huang froze.

She recognized that castle. She had heard about it in the reports from her Outer Disciples.

"So that's what he's been up to."

She frowned. She pointed her finger at an empty chip bag on the floor. She gathered her qi to her finger tip, condensing it until it became visible.

A beam of light fired from her finger, burning a hole in the chip bag.

"See, I can do it too. Seriously, Bob, if all you needed was someone to beat up some mortal armies, I could have done that."

She heaved another sigh, and pulled out the mobile phone Bob had bought for her.

"Like, you haven't even called since that stupid dead lizard guy. Surely you have something for me to…"

Then Xiong Huang froze.

She…*wanted* that insolent mortal to call her? To task her with some inane mortal problem?

She shook her head.

She must be *truly* bored.

She heaved a sigh and sat up. Her immortal body somehow felt heavy, but she pushed on her knees and forced herself to stand up, groaning as she did.

"Well, if I'm that bored, I guess I should get out of the house, or something. Let's see…I think the patriarch of the Luminous Ocean Sect was talking crap about us lately. Might lose some face if I let him get away with it. Guess I should go beat them, or something. Something something 'you dare' and are courting death, or whatever."

Xiong Huang sighed yet again. She pulled up her phone once more, glancing at the screen before shaking her head and walking out the door.

∆∆∆

Back at the ILS HQ, Icy Rose…no, Constanza Rubio was waiting in a room, sitting on a couch. She was wringing her hands, and glancing at the clock.

And then…the door opened.

She flew to her feet and rushed over. She opened her mouth…but all her words were lost. She couldn't remember what she was going to say…

But it didn't matter.

In front of her stood Antonio and his dad…and both of

them immediately wrapped her in a hug.

"Constanza! I'm glad to see you're safe."

"Mr. Miralles…"

Tears welled up her eyes.

"I'm so sorry! Because of me, you had to move, you had to…"

He let go of her and placed his hands on her shoulder, looking her in the eyes.

"Enough of that, young lady. The important thing is that you're safe."

He grinned.

"Besides, the ILS itself showed up at my door with a visa and a new job. You think I'm upset about that?"

Mr. Miralles turned to glance at his son, then back at Constanza. He nodded.

"I'll give you both some space. Just know, Constanza, that we love you, and I couldn't be prouder of what you've accomplished here. And I know your parents would have felt the same way."

Tears started to drip from her eyes but she nodded.

And then she turned to Antonio.

Both of them looked at each other…then looked down.

""Antonio/Constanza…""

They both flushed at having interrupted one another.

"Sorry, you go first."

"N-No, you first."

"No, you."

"No, you."

They glared at one another, and then laughed. Antonio shook his head.

"Look, Constanza, I just wanted to say I'm sorry."

Her eyes widened.

"What? What are you apologizing for, Antonio? I'm the one who ruined your life…"

Antonio shook his head.

"That's absolutely wrong, Constanza, you haven't ruined

a thing. It was my fault. I should have known that job was too good to be true from the start. If I hadn't been there, you wouldn't have gotten hurt."

Constanza shook her head with all her might.

"You didn't know, you didn't do anything wrong, Antonio! And you tried to warn me...but I rushed off to go fight the cartels without even thinking about what it would mean for you and your family."

Antonio looked away.

"Well...not just that. I'm sorry too, that I didn't believe in you. I was just afraid you'd get hurt."

Antonio shivered and grit his teeth.

"I still...can't forget that night...and when..."

He shook his head.

"What I'm trying to say is...you're a hero, Constanza. You've always been brave, and ready to stand up, and now you're saving the world. So...I won't hold you back anymore. I'm going to try and help you instead, however I can."

Antonio's eyes widened as Constanza gave him a hug.

"You already have, Antonio. I'm just...I'm glad you're safe, too."

He nodded, and returned the hug.

And then after they separated, Constanza tilted her head, rubbing her chin.

"You know...I'm supposed to get dinner with the team after this...would you like to come meet them?"

Antonio glanced at her for a second before his eyes widened.

"Meet Aurora Legion? Do you even have to ask? Do you know how much money I could sell their autographs for?"

The two shared a laugh at that.

And so Antonio met Aurora Legion. Later on, he found a new job...as an intern at the ILS. He started working to support the heroes however he could.

△△△

Londyn, Linda, and Vice-Director Carter all stood around in Londyn's office, watching the television screen as the news reported on Miss Le Blank's deeds.

Londyn turned to Vice-Director Carter.

"How are we looking?"

He nodded back.

"Not bad, actually. The US and China aren't exactly happy about being humiliated and then needing us to save their butts...but surprisingly the President is onboard. The US government won't make any coordinated attempts on us if he can help it."

Londyn raised an eyebrow at that.

"Really now? The President himself?"

Vice-Director Carter grinned.

"I think at this stage he's just happy there's someone else people might call besides the leader of the free world."

Londyn shook her head at that. Vice-Director Carter chuckled and then started walking towards the elevator.

"Well, I'm off to talk with the Chinese next. Take care, Director."

"Great work as always, Carter. Take care."

Once he had left, Londyn took a seat, practically falling back into her chair. Linda pulled up a seat and joined her.

For a moment they sat in silence.

Then they glanced at each other...and started to smile.

It was over. It was finally over. The huge wave of villains that had kept them scrambling ever since the Atomic Herald had finally started to die down. Londyn sighed.

"I guess EL Bank must be running low on funds."

Linda smiled back.

"Well, they certainly don't earn as much advertising revenue as we do."

Both women chuckled at that. Yes, Londyn pretty much

knew where all the villains came from, she had once sought EL Bank's services herself, after all. Sadly, EL Bank managed to keep everything legal on their end, but that was fine. Londyn wasn't aiming for them in the first place.

After all, she already had a man on the inside. If anything...the villains were unknowingly offering themselves up on a silver platter, thanks to EL Bank's popularity in that sphere.

She smirked at Linda.

"I wonder what those 'super geniuses' would think if they knew a pair of minions was running the League? That we've known about their little club all along?"

Linda smirked back.

"I admit, I've dreamt about telling one, just to see the look on their face."

Londyn grinned.

"As have I. I'll also admit I took great satisfaction in Captain Hot Devil's reaction once he realized he's been following Dr. Kayserling's old minion this whole time."

The two women laughed, and then fell into silence. Eventually, Londyn turned to Linda.

"Linda."

"Yes, Director?"

Londyn nodded.

"Thank you."

Linda tilted her head.

"Director?"

Londyn smiled at her.

"Thank you, for all your help. I couldn't have done all this, built all this without you. I'm truly glad I met you."

Linda's eyes widened before she smiled back. She shook her head.

"With all due respect, I'm the one who's honored to be here, Director. You are the one who made it happen. You're the one who stood up as a normal woman, a minion even, and made those supers listen to you. I'm just happy I can help you, in any way I can."

Londyn shook her head.

"All because of people like you, who gave me the opportunity."

With that, Londyn rose to her feet.

"Well, enough rest then. Carter set up a meeting with *another* Senator, unfortunately, so I'll have to get going."

Linda rose as well.

"I see, what should I grab?"

Londyn shook her head.

"This one's just a meet and greet, so you can stay, Linda. In fact, take the day off, if you'd like. Heavens knows you've earned it."

Linda smiled and then nodded.

"Got it, just let me know if you need anything, Director."

Londyn nodded and made her way to the elevator. She got into her car in the garage on her own, and then drove off towards her meeting.

And as she drove through the streets, she smiled to herself.

She loved her life now.

She, a normal woman, was now the name that came to mind when people thought of heroes. The man who once tossed her aside like furniture now reported to her. The supers she once feared now treated her with respect and admiration. The villains who once exploited her and took her for granted now could only curse her name as she put them behind bars. And she admitted it was more fun to break their evil schemes than it had been to implement them.

And best of all...she was doing *good.*

She wasn't just building something for the sake of building it. She wasn't just trying to prove to the world what she was capable of. She was now actively making the world a better place. Her efforts now saved *billions* of lives. There was no hesitation, no doubts about all the people who would be hurt by her boss's evil schemes. She even admitted she was starting to understand the heroes' mentality. It just felt *good* to be on this side of it. There was a deep temptation to believe they were always in the right, because most of the time they were.

Which is when she thought of Icy Falcon, and the girl he had hurt.

And that was the other aspect of this. The heroes could easily lose sight of who they were, and the people around them. The great power they held and the righteousness of their cause made for an insidious combination.

Which was her other purpose.

The heroes needed someone from the other side. Someone who knew what it was like to be on the receiving end. They needed to understand the people they put in harm's way. They needed to be held accountable to the people they hurt.

And that was why Londyn was here.

To remind these gods how human they really were. That at the end of the day, they weren't any different from the people they saved...or the people they fought.

They were all people, good and bad.

And so she thought of her people.

She thought of Aurora Legion, those kids she brought together and trained, who looked up to her. She thought of Captain Hot Devil, the man who now trusted her with his life. She thought of Linda, the former minion who now worked tirelessly by her side, no matter how much unplanned overtime got thrust on them.

She smiled once again.

And that's why she loved this job. Because it wasn't just a job, or a mission, not anymore.

She had all these people in her life who relied on her... and who she relied on in turn. Working together, resting together, laughing together. All striving and toiling as one, for a single purpose, a common goal.

This was her family now.

And it was all thanks to one faceless minion.

The one who had saved her life.

Who gave her the opportunity to become something more.

And who even now put himself in harm's way to support her. To get them the intel they needed and keep the world safe.

Her smile grew.

She really owed him everything.

But as Londyn drove and pondered, something went unnoticed. A small device on the bottom of her car, with a tiny light flashing red. As she came to a stop at an intersection, that light swapped to a solid green...

△△△

Bob nodded as he watched the television. He let out a sigh, leaning back into his chair and taking a sip from the mug in his hand.

It had been hard work, but he got the job done.

He flipped through his notebook, reviewing the state of the world. He rubbed his chin.

He had built a clean and sustainable future for the economy. He had made energy cheap enough to be accessed by all of humanity. He had averted a war between the world's strongest nations. He had established global peace, at least for a time. He had tamed the Eternal Night Sect. He had contained both superheroes and supervillains within monitorable systems, with laws and flows of finances that would keep them both in check. He had contained the damage and made supers accountable to the very people they had hurt.

He couldn't think of anything else that required immediate correction. Oh there was always more he could do, more that could be improved but...

He had done it.

He had changed the world, for the better he believed.

He, a mere mortal man, a faceless minion even, had accomplished things no one else had, whether hero or villain or national government with all their powers and plans and weapons.

And he had learned what the price of great change really was. Who he had to become and who he had to hurt along the way.

He heaved a sigh.

Yes, there was more he could do with this system he had built...but he decided he was done. He had achieved what he set out to do. His system was powerful...and therefore dangerous. After what he had seen in places like Korea and Mexico, he didn't think there was anything else that justified further upheaval.

He would let the world spin on by itself, from now on.

And he would let that power, with all its temptations, slip from his hands.

He just needed to set something up to forward EL Bank's data to the ILS and the system could take care of itself, barring any unexpected problems...

Just then, there was a chime on the television. Within the display, Brendan Baird's eyes went wide.

"What's that? B-Breaking news folks! There's been a bombing in the middle of New York City! We've received confirmation that Director Green of the ILS was caught in the middle of it! Details are still scarce and the Director's status is unknown, GNN will keep you posted as we investigate this shocking turn of events!"

> *AUTHOR'S COMMENTARY: Dun Dun Duuuunnnnn...welp I think that's a great place to stop. Because I'm evil. Muahahahahaha! Anyways! Will Londyn survive the bombing? Just who could be responsible for such a thing? How is Bob, the ILS, and the world going to react? Tune in next volume, to find out!*

SIDE STORY - AND NOW FOR A WORD FROM OUR SPONSORS

This is an event that occurred shortly after the ILS defeated the Necrosaurus...

Flames covered the screen as intense music played.

"He's the hottest hero in America! Captain Hot Devil!"

Captain Hot Devil punched a path through the flames, taking a stance in the center.

"Nothing gets me fired up like saving the day! But keeping the burn takes a lot of fuel."

He flexed his muscles as fire surged across his hands and arms.

"That's why I stop by Taco King after my missions! Their unique blend of spices will leave you burning for more."

Captain Hot Devil thrust his hand forward, smashing the Taco King Logo over the screen.

"And now for a limited time, challenge these Devilish Tamales with Hot Devil Sauce. It's hotter than hell, I guarantee it."

He held two tamales surrounded in flames. The screen zoomed in on his face as stared directly into the camera.

"Two for $4.99 at your nearest Taco King. If you think you have what it takes to challenge the devil."

He curled his biceps with the tamales in hand, as the flames covered the screen. Another voice spoke afterwards.

"Devilish Tamales with Hot Devil Sauce, only available

for a limited time at Taco King! It's the Captain's order! Restrictions apply, offer is not available in Alaska or Hawaii."

△△△

Captain Hot Devil pursed his lips as the video ended. He looked at Londyn, whose shoulders were trembling as she covered her face with a clipboard.

"Is this...really necessary?"

"C-Come on now, Captain, you want to make some money now, don't you? I promise you, once the corporations have some skin in your game those politicians and journalists are going to get a lot more polite."

Captain Hot Devil groaned.

"...I get that but really? Devilish Tamales, Hot Devil Sauce, 'it's hotter than hell'?"

Londyn barely contained her laughter at this point.

"Well it's hotter than a nuke, isn't it?"

Captain Hot Devil held his face with his hands.

"...the kids told you about that."

Londyn grinned at him as wide as she could.

"Yes, yes they did."

Captain Hot Devil groaned once again.

"...this isn't payback for something, is it?"

Londyn kept grinning at him, her eyes narrowing.

"Now Captain, why would you ever think that?"

Captain Hot Devil just sighed. Londyn's shoulders continued to shake.

"T-Tell you what, I'll swap you with Falcon if you can convince the deodorant guys you have better abs."

Captain Hot Devil went completely silent, slumping his shoulders. He knew a losing fight when he saw one.

Londyn continued to grin.

"Taco King it is. You'll have the hottest commercial out there, I-I guarantee it."

Captain Hot Devil groaned as Londyn burst out laughing.

△△△

Jim Roberson sighed as he opened the door. It had been a very long day, mostly spent avoiding eye contact with everyone he knew.

"Honey, I'm home."

"W-Welcome back!"

He froze.

Something wasn't right.

He hadn't heard her greet him cheerfully like that since… well a very long time.

Carefully, he crept into the house.

"We're in the kitchen! D-Dinner's all ready for you."

He had a bad feeling about this.

He had a *really* bad feeling about this.

He took a deep breath.

He spoke to himself. He was Captain Hot Devil! A superhero! He feared nothing! No matter what was in that kitchen, he would stand his ground!

He stepped into the kitchen and froze in the entryway.

"Dad! Dad! Look!"

"We got them Dad! Just for you!"

"Y-Yes, just for you."

His kids ran to him, stars in their eyes. His wife watched from behind the table, her mouth hidden behind her hand and her shoulders trembling.

On the table, they were there.

The Devilish Tamales.

"They're hotter than hell!"

"It's so cool!"

"Y-Yes. It's so…*cool* of you."

Jim Roberson groaned as his wife failed to hold in her laughter.

Now he had two mistakes he would never forget.

△△△

In a parking lot after sunset, Bob sat in a car, a box in his lap. He opened up the box. He unwrapped the contents and lifted one to his mouth.
He took a bite.
He immediately frowned.
"So much for 'hotter than hell'. Heroes are so annoying."

VARIANT STORY CHAPTER 1 - I WAS A FACELESS MINION, THEN I WAS SUMMONED TO ANOTHER WORLD!

"Good beginning of your regularly scheduled leisure period, all you denizens of the Multiverse! This is Multiverse News Network and I'm your host, He Who Proclaims! And welcome back to our hit show *Beautiful Butterflies*, where we analyze the smallest possible decision that changed your life forever!"

"And for our lucky contestant this time...it's Bob! The... Faceless Minion? You know what, that's great, Bob. Good on you. You know, there wouldn't even *be* any supervillains out there if it weren't for the hardworking men and women who went out there and did the work of villainy each and every day. You're a supervillain in my book, Bob, and don't let anyone tell you different!"

"Now let's review: what was the most fateful minor decision Bob ever made in your universe...uh oh Bob. Looks like someone took an unsanctioned break on their first job! Don't you know that was against your contract, Bob? Someone was about to get written up! If...you know...the HR department hadn't exploded shortly thereafter. But what would have happened if Bob had stuck to policy? Let's take a look, and find out!"

△△△

Bob heaved a sigh, the only sound other than the rhythmic clank of his boots on the metal floor. All around him were gray metallic floors with gray metallic walls and, of course, a gray metallic ceiling, lit by the occasional incandescent bulb. Bob swore those might be gray too, but he didn't know if that was the lights themselves or the tinted goggles of his helmet. Why he had to wear a helmet with a gas mask at all times was beyond his comprehension. What he did comprehend was that his nose itched something fierce.

Bob didn't know what he expected from this job, but this definitely wasn't it.

Bob winced as pain stabbed through his right foot. There was definitely a blister there.

He sighed and then grit his teeth. He forced himself to put one foot in front of another, wincing with each step. This was his first job and he wasn't going to let a little pain stop him!

And that would be the last mistake he ever made.

He vaguely remembered the wall exploding. Everything went black for a moment. He felt like he was floating, then there was pain. When he came to himself, every inch of his body screamed. He tried to sit up.

And then cried out as pain shot through his stomach.

He slowly reached to his stomach with trembling hands.

He felt something wet.

And a large metal rod, coming up straight through his belly.

His heart pounded. He had trouble breathing.

A red flash of light lit up the world.

A world that grew dimmer by the second.

And colder.

He felt as if he was drifting away.

He heard shouts and gunshots but everything was growing quieter. The red lights grew dimmer. The pain felt more and more distant. Was that Jenkins he saw in the air?

Everything kept growing quieter.

And quieter…

Soon all was silent.

And then all was black.

△△△

In a world of white and gold, there were white clouds as far as the eye could see, each as plump and fluffy as a pillow. Overhead there was a bright, golden sun that never faded or strayed, illuminating the entire area with warm, comfortable light.

And at the center of this world was a girl. She had pure white hair that shimmered as she moved, like polished silver. Her face and body were like works of art, with perfect proportions that seemed impossible to achieve. Her voice would move the most hardened and callous man to tears with even the most casual of greetings. Her eyes seemed to hold the entire world within them, and pierced straight to one's very soul, yet they were soft and gentle, inviting one in like an old friend.

Behold Most Holy Ione, Supreme Goddess and Creator of the World of Eirorun.

She was…laying…on a sea of pillows…in sweatpants and a hoodie…stuffing her mouth with candied nuts…and softly chuckling as she scrolled on a transparent screen hanging in the air.

There was a flash of light and an angel burst through the clouds below. She saluted and knelt before Ione.

"Most Holy Ione, I beg that you grant your humble servant some time."

Ione heaved a sigh.

"Ugh, what do you want, Miniel? Can't you see it's my

break time?"

"I'm sorry, Most Holy One, but there is a problem you must address."

"Ugh, fine, what is it?"

This time it was Miniel's turn to heave a sigh.

"The hero has perished."

Ione jumped, her eyes widening.

"What?! Again?! That's the fifth one this year!"

Miniel nodded.

"Yes, it is most concerning."

Ione stood up and started to pace around, furrowing her brow.

"What on Eirorun happened? Is the Dark Lord truly that strong?"

Miniel shook her head.

"No, Most Holy One, it was not the Dark Lord nor his forces…"

"What? Then who could've done this?!"

Miniel averted her gaze.

"Um…well…"

Ione raised an eyebrow.

"Yes?"

"The hero…got honey-trapped."

Ione froze.

"…Eh?"

Miniel heaved another sigh.

"The hero…was invited by an elven assassin to her chambers…who was a member of the famous bandit group he was hunting. Um…later that night…she murdered him in his sleep and stole the Holy Sword."

Most Holy Ione hit her face with her palm.

"His party members advised against it but he insisted it would be fine as she had clearly fallen in love with him…"

Ione started pacing again.

"Strange…this is strange…why does this keep happening?"

"Most Holy One, may I speak?"

"What is it, Miniel?"

"Um...perhaps we should stop relying on these otherworlders...if you could bless some of your followers I believe we could organize a suitable defense. I have prepared a list of candidates for your perusal..."

Ione shook her head.

"That's not possible, Miniel."

"Most Holy One?"

"Look!"

Ione thrust a transparent screen in front of the angel.

"See, it is clearly stated in the sacred texts! I am supposed to bring an unremarkable, lonely, and slightly gloomy teenage boy from the nation of Japan on the world called Earth and imbue him with great power and glorious purpose, and then he will fix everything!"

Miniel's eyes trembled as she beheld the sacred texts.

"M-Most Holy One...i-is this truly the sacred texts? It looks like..."

Ione closed her eyes and waved her finger about as she continued.

"He'll defeat the Dark Lord, seduce all the powerful and troublesome beings in the world, and then revolutionize technology, cooking, and culture! Then I can laze around all day receiving some real snacks from my followers and stop shelling out for interdimensional cable if I want to watch even one decent show! This is already happening in every other world! So why isn't it working here?!"

Miniel continued to tremble. She gulped.

"...Most Holy One...is this not...a site for web novels?"

Ione resumed pacing around, her eyes fixed on the cloudy ground.

"I don't get it...is the summoning bugged...was that guy too popular? Do I need to give them more power?"

Miniel heaved a sigh.

"...Most Holy One...if I could make a suggestion?"

Ione stopped pacing and rolled her eyes.

"What is it, Miniel? Can't you see I'm working right now?"

"What if…we use a hero…not from Japan?"

Ione froze once more.

"Huh?"

"Like, could we not find someone from somewhere else? Perhaps the committed and experienced Knight Commander of our Holy Knights…"

Ione slammed a fist into her palm.

"That's it!"

Miniel jumped.

"Yes?!"

"I'll try summoning someone from somewhere else! It must be that the other worlds took all the good candidates from Japan already! But it looks like this Earth has a lot of different nations we can choose from…ooo some took from 'South Korea' so yeah looks like it doesn't need to be Japan after all."

Miniel heaved another sigh.

"M-Most Holy One, could we not use someone from our own…"

But Ione had already started flipping through transparent screens.

"How about America? Not too many worlds picking from that one yet…oh here's a guy! Just started a job, seems kinda gloomy. Let's do it!"

"Most Holy One…"

"And summoned!"

△△△

There was a flash of light and Bob found himself standing amidst the clouds.

Was this heaven?

Light shone behind him and he turned around.

It might be heaven.

Before him stood the most beautiful woman he had ever seen, dressed in robes so bright they seemed forged from light itself. She was too beautiful in fact, a beauty that should not exist. It made him feel unworthy, as if it was a crime for one such as him to even stand in her presence. But the smile on her face and the light in her eyes filled his heart with peace, assuring him that all would be well.

He closed his eyes and shook his head.

What in blazes was going on?

"Greetings, oh noble hero."

"Um, what?"

"I am the Goddess Ione. I have summoned you here to save my world from great peril."

Bob narrowed his eyes.

"What are you talking about?"

The Goddess Ione frowned.

"That's strange, most of them were already pretty excited at this point. You've heard of Isekai haven't you?"

"Ise...what?"

"Isekai? Summoned to another world? Become a hero, get cheat skills, slay the demon king, make a harem? No?"

Bob just stared at her.

Um, was this some kind of scam?

Ione tilted her head.

"You know, you're being summoned to an RPG world?"

And then it was Bob's turn to tilt his head.

"RPG?"

"Role playing game? Haven't you played them before?"

"Role playing game? You mean like dungeons and dragons? Is that what this is?"

There was a flash of light and an angel appeared beside Ione.

"Most Holy One, may I make an observation?"

"What is it, Miniel?! Can't you see I'm in the middle of something?"

"The timeline on this one...is from a branch of Earth

during the 1980s."

"1980s? What does that mean?"

"Video games and Isekai novels were just getting started back then. I do not believe he has the requisite cultural knowledge for your normal introduction."

Ione took a step back as her eyes went wide.

"What? How can that be? Has he not read the sacred texts?"

Miniel shook her head.

"I believe he was summoned from a time before most of the 'sacred texts' were written."

Ione furrowed her brow.

"How is that possible?"

The angel sighed. Bob rubbed his temples as his head began to pound.

"Like, how can he not have read the sacred texts? Hah, I'm tired. Miniel, handle it."

"As you will, Most Holy One."

The angel bowed and turned to Bob.

"I am Miniel, Archangel and servant of the Most Holy Ione, Creator of the world of Eirorun and everything in it."

"Yes?"

"Allow me to explain the situation."

"...Please."

"You were about to die on the planet Earth."

Bob opened his mouth to refute that when he thought back to his most recent memories. After a moment he gasped, his body dripping sweat all over and his heart pounding. He moved a hand to his stomach, but the wound had vanished.

"Then...what..."

"We have summoned you here moments before your death and restored your body. Next, we will send you to our world of Eirorun. You will receive a second chance at life."

Bob's eyes narrowed.

"...what's the catch?"

"...let me see, have you read *The Lord of the Rings*?"

"Yes?"

Miniel nodded.

"Eirorun is much like Middle Earth. There are different races such as elves and dwarves, as well as monsters such as orcs and trolls. Unfortunately, there is also a Dark Lord. We are requesting that you put a stop to his reign of terror."

Bob heaved a sigh and held his forehead.

"How would I even do something like that?"

Miniel nodded again.

"You will be granted a boon, a great skill or weapon beyond what normal individuals possess in our world. Let me see, oh! You can think of it like the supers in your world."

Bob narrowed his eyes again.

"...you're going to make me a super? Ask me to become a hero?"

Miniel nodded yet again.

"The Dark Lord must be defeated, but the method by which you do so and what you do beyond that are up to you. We do have some recommendations, but before that I think we should explain more about how this world works, since you are not familiar with such systems..."

Then there was a flash of light and Bob vanished.

Miniel slowly turned to Ione.

"Most Holy One...what happened?"

"Oh, there's a timer on the summoning, you know? Can't just keep a mortal soul in my realm for too long."

Miniel held her face in her hands. Meanwhile Ione plopped herself back on her pillows.

"All right Bob! Go go! Go be a hero and save the world! Now go away, Miniel, it's time for my shows!"

∆∆∆

Bob woke up, shaking his head. He touched his stomach again, feeling solid cloth covering solid flesh. He let out a sigh and dropped his shoulders.

He was alive.

He looked up and took stock of his surroundings. He was lying in a field surrounded by a forest, with a rough dirt trail to his side. He could see mountains in the distance. His eyes narrowed.

It looked like this wasn't a dream. Or he was still in it. Or on drugs.

He sighed and stood up, and started walking along the trail. Well, there was nothing he could do now but move forward.

Just then a bright light started to shine in front of him. Bob shielded his eyes as the light grew, until the light surged in a final flash.

As the light faded Bob let down his arm and blinked.

Another angel appeared before him.

A...tiny angel?

A little angel, no larger than his hand, flew in the air in front of him.

"What in the..."

"Ah, there you are, Sir Hero! We were afraid you had wandered off!"

Bob just stared at the little angel. She cleared her throat.

"Ahem, oh noble hero, I am Adoel, a servant of the Creator Goddess Ione. I have been sent to you to aid upon your quest, and guide you as you acclimate to our world."

"...right..."

Adoel nodded.

"I'm certain you must have many questions. The Archangel said you would be most confused as to the workings of our world. Ask me your questions, and I shall enlighten you."

Bob nodded. Well, if this *wasn't* a dream or a drug trip, then a guide would be very helpful indeed.

"Which way is the closest settlement?"

Adoel blinked.

"Um, what?"

"Which way is the closest settlement?"

Adoel blinked again, then slowly pointed down the trail.

"Oh, um, that way I believe."

Bob nodded at her.

"Thanks."

"You are most welcome, noble one. What other questions may I...hey wait! Where are you going?"

Adoel flew after Bob as he started walking down the trail.

"To find shelter."

"D-Don't you want to know the mechanics of this world? What kind of races there are? The specifics of your quest?"

Bob nodded.

"Yes but I'd rather not spend the night in the forest."

Adoel frowned.

"That's..."

"Can you explain along the way?"

Adoel tilted her head.

"Um, I guess so?"

"Then do that."

"Oh, um, ok. So, um, the Archangel told me I should introduce the world from the basics?"

Bob heaved a sigh.

"That would help."

"Ok, so, have you played an RPG before?"

"No."

Adoel froze, and her face scrunched up.

"...um...well...how should I...hmmm...."

Bob just stared at her for a moment.

"L-Let's start with the status then. Can you open your status?"

Bob raised an eyebrow.

"How?"

"Oh, um, hold out your hand, imagine that you want to analyze your current state, and say Status!"

Bob raised an eyebrow but did as requested.

"Status."

A transparent, blue box appeared before him, displaying the following information:

[General Information]
[Name: Bob]
[Species: Human]
[Sex: Male]
[Age: 18]
[Level: 1]
[XP: 0/100]
[HP: 120/120]
[MP: 110/110]

[Attributes]
[STR: 30]
[MAG: 30]
[DEX: 30]
[SPD: 30]
[DEF: 30]
[RES: 30]
[LUCK: 30]

[Titles]
[Hero From Another World: +10% XP Gained, learn skills more easily, grants All-Language Comprehension Skill.]
[The Faceless Minion: Grants Presence Concealment Skill (Lvl MAX), Grants False Status Skill, Grants Trustworthy Minion Skill.]
[Blessing of the Creator Goddess: +20 to every attribute, +100 to HP and MP, Grants Favorability Skill, Grants Analyze Skill (Lvl Max).]

[Active Skills]
[Presence Concealment (Level MAX): Avoid being noticed. Higher levels increase effect and

scope of valid targets/senses. Taking action increases risk of concealment breaking.]
[**False Status:** Present a customized status when scanned by Analyze.]
[**Analyze (Level MAX):** Scan a target's status page. Accuracy and available information depends on skill level.]

[**Passive Skills**]
[**All-Language Comprehension:** Translates all languages both oral and written into wielder's primary language.]
[**Trustworthy Minion:** Your employer's trust in you grows more rapidly, effect grows if employer is of neutral or evil alignment.]
[**Favorability:** The world itself, and all in it, look upon you favorably.]

"...I have a lot of questions."

Adoel flew above Bob's shoulder to look at the status herself.

"Let me see, let me see...oh, um."

"I'm 18 again somehow?"

Adoel nodded.

"Most Holy Ione created you a new body of course. It's the easiest way to adapt you to the new world!"

Bob raised an eyebrow and pointed at one of the so-called 'titles'.

"The Faceless Minion?"

Adoel averted her gaze.

"A-All otherworlders get a powerful title and skill, so i-it must be a mighty skill and a great honor…"

Bob stared at her silently. Adoel gulped.

"S-See look, you get Presence Concealment MAX! T-That's super OP…I think…maybe…"

Bob continued staring at her. Adoel shrank under his gaze.

"I-It's not me. I didn't do it."

"Your goddess did."

Adoel stood back up, glaring at Bob.

"T-That's wrong! S-She just takes the shape of your soul and uses it as a mold for her power to grant you the skill most suited to you! So it's just a part of who you are!"

Bob stared at her once more. Adoel turned away again.

"I mean…um…sun's getting real low, we better get a move on!"

Bob let out a sigh and held his head.

And he thought to himself…

These angels are so annoying.

"Ok, so, um, your status. This shows you your current state, and the powers and abilities you possess."

"…So I get superpowers in this world?"

Adoel nodded.

"Not only that, but you can develop new ones by gaining experience."

Bob raised an eyebrow at that.

"Gaining experience?"

"There's a lot of different ways, but the most common ones are developing your skills, or hunting monsters."

"Monsters?"

"Magical beings hostile to sapient life."

Bob stopped to stare at her again.

"…Isn't it dangerous to walk in the forest then?"

Adoel shook her head.

"This area has low atmospheric mana, so it should be fine."

Bob raised an eyebrow.

"…should?"

Adoel looked away again.

"Y-You have a weapon, you know!"

"Where?"

"In your inventory, of course."

Bob heaved another sigh.

"And where exactly is that?"

"Oh! Right, so inventory is not just a physical location but..."

Bob and the angel conversed for a while longer. A much longer while. A while with much stuttering, and many headaches. But he was now able to pull some of the starter equipment gifted by the goddess from his personal inventory. Bob went ahead and equipped the basic armor, and wrapped a shortsword around his waist.

"Ok, so let me get this straight: people in this world can improve their bodies and minds as well as develop superpowers through the wanton slaughter of powerful beings that exist solely to murder us?"

Adoel frowned.

"Well...when you put it that way..."

Bob let out a sigh. This world seemed very annoying.

As the pair walked down the trail they started to hear noises. Bob could make out the clanging of metal striking metal and the shouts and grunts of men in combat.

He continued walking.

Adoel floated next to him and tapped his shoulder.

"Hey, listen!"

He continued walking.

"I think there's something going on over there!"

He continued walking.

"S-Shouldn't we check it out?"

Bob raised an eyebrow at the angel.

"Why?"

"What do you mean, 'why'? Someone could be in trouble!"

"And?"

"And? And you should help them!"

"Why?"

"You're the hero!"

Bob heaved a sigh.

"I'm a level one foreigner with nothing but a basic sword and who knows nothing about this world or its political situation. Intervening in a fight of any sort is the height of foolishness."

Adoel paused.

"T-That's...it should be fine! You have the blessing of the Goddess herself!"

Bob raised an eyebrow.

"And that's enough to defeat any foe regardless of their level, skills, weapons, numbers, or tactics?"

Adoel looked away.

"T-That's...look you have Presence Concealment, right? So no harm in at least checking, right?"

Bob let out another sigh.

△△△

Bob and Adoel hid in the bushes on the edge of the forest. Before them was a paved stone highway. The air was filled with shouts and screams and the scent of blood. A pink carriage was surrounded by knights in shining plate armor, who were in turn surrounded by a large number of men in rags. The knights were exacting a heavy toll on their assailants, but they were about to be overrun. Adoel landed on Bob's shoulder, whispering into his ear.

"See! I told you!"

Bob nodded, and then turned to leave.

"Wait! Where are you going?!"

"I'm not getting involved in a fight between people."

"Why not?!"

"I know nothing about those people, their culture, the current political climate, or ongoing conflicts. Intervening haphazardly would be foolish."

"What do you mean?! That's clearly a noble girl's carriage, under attack by bandits! What more do you need to know?"

Bob let out a sigh.

"Is this a bandit group from afar, or a local insurgency? Are they opportunists looking for an easy score? Are they local farmers driven to desperation by a malicious ruler or just plain bad luck? Members of a criminal syndicate executing a premeditated plan? An organized rebellion with a political agenda? Foreigners sent by a hostile nation? Undercover agents sent by a rival noble? Undercover agents sent by the ruling authority? Are they targeting just any carriage, any noble, or that specific person? If so then why? Maybe they just want a ransom and surrender will result in the least amount of bloodshed. Maybe the noble in question has traitorous intentions and needs to be dealt with to preserve the country. Maybe they're a malicious tyrant who drove their people to the brink for their own greed and amusement. Maybe this is a feud between two noble houses. And what is the nation's stance on vigilante justice? Are local authorities enroute? Won't they be suspicious of the foreigner with no alibi who tries to cross the border in the middle of an ambush? Am I committing to a political faction or noble house by intervening here? Will they draft me into some kind of army? Will they get rid of me as a loose end and potential threat? Will I make powerful enemies by disrupting their plans?"

Bob stopped, and pulled the angel from his shoulder to his hand so he could look her in the eye.

"So, miss angel, assuming I am capable of intervention in an armed conflict involving professional knights, which side should I intervene on and what will be the consequences in the short and long term both for myself and the nation at large?"

Adoel fidgeted and avoided eye contact.

"U-Um...t-that's...u-uh...l-let's see...u-um...i-if you help the noble, t-they might reward you? T-Then you wouldn't need to find shelter on your own?"

Just then they heard a female knight cry out.

"Why are you doing this?! The harvest is good this year, Count Demaret is offering jobs and rations to every able-bodied person of this realm! You have no reason to resort to banditry! And don't you know who this is?! We're escorting the beloved princess of the nation! The whole kingdom will hunt you down for this!"

One of the bandits crossed their arms and let out a laugh.

"Gwahahahaha! Let's kill all these suckers! We're the Green Ogre Gang! We kill and plunder, in that order, no exceptions, and we don't care who! Tremble and despair, noble knights! Today we become the gang that killed the princess! For no other reason than fun! And the whole nation will learn to fear us! Muahahahahaha!"

Bob held his head and let out a deep sigh.

"See see! You can verify their identity with Analyze! Now go, be a hero! You wouldn't just let a bunch of psychopaths murder a beloved and innocent princess and destabilize the king's mental state and thus the nation all for mere fun, would you?"

Bob just groaned.

But he did as she suggested and checked the situation with Analyze. The bandits were in fact members of the 'Green Ogre Gang' with no further affiliations. The knights were in fact knights of the kingdom. And the stats of the bandits were such that he could in fact intervene, at least on paper. He let out a sigh.

As the fight resumed he snuck up behind one of the bandits on the edge of the fight, pulling out his sword. He took a deep breath.

And then stabbed the guy in the neck.

[You have slain: Christopher Loup (Level 12 Human)]
[Gained 58 XP!]
[You have learned the skill Assassination!]
[have learned the skill Swordsmanship!]

Bob rushed back to the trees and observed the battlefield. He slowly released his breath.

No one had noticed anything.

With a relatively safe method established, Bob got to work, slaying four more of the bandits. Adoel had a complicated look on her face.

"Um...I'm glad you're helping...but this method seems a little..."

"Is there a problem?"

"It's just...this doesn't seem very...heroic..."

"And it's heroic to rush in and kill a bunch of people I don't know based solely on appearances?"

"When you put it like that...wait, where are you going?!"

Bob was walking away as the battle continued.

"Job's done."

"There's still bandits!"

"The knights can handle what's left."

"B-But, the princess! You don't want to meet her? Get rewarded for your noble deeds?"

Bob turned to face Adoel, raising an eyebrow.

"Do we need to have a talk about interacting with high-ranking political leaders with no information?"

"...no."

"Then let's get going."

Adoel frowned as she followed after Bob and the knights took down the rest of the bandits.

"...I feel like there's something wrong about all this."

Bob's Final Status (253 XP gained from slaying 5 men at roughly level 12):

[General Information]
[Name: Bob]
[Species: Human]
[Sex: Male]
[Age: 18]
[Level: 3]
[XP: 53/100]

[HP: 120/123]
[MP: 111/111]

[Attributes]
[STR: 32]
[MAG: 31]
[DEX: 32]
[SPD: 32]
[DEF: 31]
[RES: 30]
[LUCK: 30]

[Titles]
[**Hero From Another World:** +10% XP Gained, learn skills more easily, grants All-Language Comprehension Skill.]
[**The Faceless Minion:** Grants Presence Concealment Skill (Lvl MAX), Grants False Status Skill, Grants Trustworthy Minion Skill.]
[**Blessing of the Creator Goddess:** +20 to every attribute, +100 to HP and MP, Grants Favorability Skill, Grants Analyze Skill (Lvl Max).]

[Active Skills]
[**Presence Concealment (Level MAX):** Avoid being noticed. Higher levels increase effect and scope of valid targets/senses. Taking action increases risk of concealment breaking.]
[**False Status:** Present a customized status when scanned by Analyze.]
[**Analyze (Level MAX):** Scan a target's status page. Accuracy and available information depends on skill level.]

[Passive Skills]
[**All-Language Comprehension:** Translates all languages both oral and written into wielder's primary language.]
[**Trustworthy Minion:** Your employer's

trust in you grows more rapidly, effect grows if employer is of neutral or evil alignment.]
[Favorability: The world itself, and all in it, look upon you favorably.]
[Assassination (Level 2): Increases user's knowledge of stealth and vital points.]
[Swordsmanship (Level 2): Increases user's knowledge of sword technique.]

NEXT TIME ON THE FACELESS MINION...!

Bob has done it. His system is complete. Both superheroes and supervillains are now contained within organizations he can monitor and manipulate. He can minimize the damage...or use it to change the world as he sees fit. Unknown to all, the entire world now rests in the palms of one faceless minion's hands.

Or so he thought.

But success breeds envy...and challenge. New threats assail Bob and his system from the outside, forces he never imagined are on the move.

First of which is a bombing targeting the ILS!

And now Bob must scramble to identify and defeat this brand new threat while Londyn's life hangs in the balance!

For if Bob's system...and his friends...are to survive, he will need to employ all of his wit and resourcefulness. He will need to find new allies...and revise his relationship with old ones...if he is to overcome these enemies unknown!

The Faceless Minion Volume 2: Nemesis comes out whenever editing is finished! Join the newsletter at https://icalosbooks.com/newsletter/ if you want to receive updates on its progress!

Or you can check out my website at https://icalosbooks.com, my RoyalRoad profile at https://www.royalroad.com/profile/172284/fictions, or my Patreon account at https://patreon.com/icalos for more info on my other works! There's even an ongoing Faceless Minion spinoff that's based on a character who...um...doesn't show up…in this Volume…um…a-anyways! Finally, if you've enjoyed this novel, please consider leaving a review on Amazon. I'd greatly appreciate it!

Anyways!

Who has bombed the ILS? Can Bob face challenges beyond his system? Can he find and terminate threats he's never imagined? Tune in next time, to find out!

CHARACTERS AND ORGANIZATIONS

Characters are in order of their first appearance. I have attempted to avoid spoilers, but they might still be possible if you are reading about characters past your current chapter.

Bob - First Appears: Prologue - The Faceless Minion himself.

Aurora Legion - First Appears: Prologue - A team of teenage superheroes.

Herald of Ashes - First Appears: Prologue - Villain, can shoot lava

Jenkins - First Appears: Chapter 1 - Another faceless minion, the strongest man Bob knew...until he started meeting supers

Chris - First Appears: Chapter 1 - Bob's childhood friend, expert at construction management

Cikizwa Mzolisa - First Appears: Chapter 1 - Leader of a mercenary black-ops group

Linda - First Appears: Chapter 1 - Cikizwa's assistant, management extraordinaire

Sergei - First Appears: Chapter 1 - Part of Cikizwa's crew, good at engineering

Minh - First Appears: Chapter 1 - Part of Cikizwa's crew, good at sales

Tina - First Appears: Chapter 1 - Part of Cikizwa's crew, good at finances

George - First Appears: Chapter 1 - Part of Cikizwa's crew, good at HR

Kanna Tanifuji - First Appears: Chapter 1 - Part of Cikizwa's crew, a bit of a supergenius

Laurent - First Appears: Chapter 1 - Part of Cikizwa's crew, in charge of the muscle

Xiong Huang - First Appears: Chapter 1 - Young Mistress of the Eternal Night Sect, a cultivator called the Murderous Bloody Fist

The Eternal Night Sect - First Appears: Chapter 1 - A cultivation sect known for brutality

The Village Hidden Among The Trees - First Appears: Chapter 1 - A secret shinobi village, opposes the Eternal Night Sect

The Phantom Blade - First Appears: Chapter 1 - A kunoichi from the Village Hidden Among The Trees.

Coflar - First Appears: Chapter 2 - Fictional nation, an anachronistic microstate still ruled by an aristocracy

Lady Anita Laflèche de Albifort - First Appears: Chapter 2 -

The daughter of Duke Gaetan of Coflar. A bit spoiled. Likes pink.

Mister Dapper Tiger - First Appears: Chapter 2 - A hero who became a humanoid tiger after a tour in the jungle. British originally, hired by the Coflar royal family.

Prince Lionel - First Appears: Chapter 2 - The Crown Prince of Coflar

Adèle Corriveau - First Appears: Chapter 2 - Prince Lionel's sweetheart. A commoner of Coflar.

Duke Gaëtan Laflèche de Albifort - First Appears: Chapter 2 - A duke of Coflar. A bit arrogant. Likes orange.

Markus Herring - First Appears: Chapter 3 - Bob's college roommate, and only heir of a major multinational conglomerate. Likes chaos.

El Capa - First Appears: Chapter 3 - Mexican drug lord. Likes capes and swords.

Icy Falcon - First Appears: Chapter 3 - Mexican hero, creates ice and controls wind. Is also very handsome and muscular.

Miguel - First Appears: Chapter 3 - Mexican drug runner and eventual drug lord.

Xiong Zhen - First Appears: Chapter 3 - Founder and Master of the Eternal Night Sect. Cultivator of the Eight Realm and over a thousand years old. Cultivates hatred. So, you know, is dad of the year.

Zheng Bai - First Appears: Chapter 3 - One of the Core Disciples of the Eternal Night Sect. Known as the Demon of the Iron Club.

Fang Jing - First Appears: Chapter 3 - One of the Core Disciples of the Eternal Night Sect. Known as the Unholy Blade.

Old Wei - First Appears: Chapter 3 - One of the Elders of the Eternal Night Sect. Known as the Black Alchemist.

Cao Xinya - First Appears: Chapter 3 - An independent cultivator known as The Emerald Tiger.

The Red Colonel - First Appears: Chapter 4 - The most distinguished officer the KGB ever produced.

Ivan - First Appears: Chapter 4 - KGB operative. Has common sense.

Tesla Titan - First Appears: Chapter 4 - Soviet/Russian Hero who channels lightning and has big metal armor. Soviet power supreme.

Agent Tina - First Appears: Chapter 4 - American special operative who likes dual wielding pistols. The best there is.

Agent Wilson - First Appears: Chapter 4 - A CIA agent who swaps over to the super-focused BSI. A bit of a conspiracy theorist.

EL Bank - First Appears: Chapter 5 - A bank specializing in loans to a...particular clientele.

Midnight Staffing - First Appears: Chapter 5 - The staffing agency for all your minion needs.

Sinn Kwaigno - First Appears: Chapter 5 - Director of

Placements with Midnight Staffing.

Madam Toxic Kiss - First Appears: Chapter 5 - Supervillain, likes poison.

Captain Hot Devil, Jim Roberson - First Appears: Chapter 5 - American hero, creates fire.

Red Hawk - First Appears: Chapter 5 - Mexican Hero, can reinforce his body to make it super tough.

Dr. Kayserling - First Appears: Chapter 6 - Evil genius who specializes in gravity manipulation.

Londyn Green - First Appears: Chapter 6 - Dr. Kayserling's assistant. Very competent.

Brendan Baird - First Appears: Chapter 6 - Newscaster for Global News Network.

Lacey Cook - First Appears: Chapter 6 - Analyst for Global News Network specializing in supers.

Liam Reynolds - First Appears: Chapter 6 - Analyst for Global News Network specializing in supers.

Lewis McCarthy - First Appears: Chapter 6 - Mayor of New York City.

Eleanor Roberson - First Appears: Chapter 6 - Captain Hot Devil's wife.

Hungry Smasher - First Appears: Chapter 7 - Villain, big with super strength and super durability.

Chronolock - First Appears: Prologue (named in Chapter 7) -

A teenager hero, member of Aurora Legion. Can stop objects' time.

Wonder Knight - First Appears: Prologue (named in Chapter 7) - A teenager hero, member of Aurora Legion. Has super strength and durability.

Pink Star - First Appears: Prologue (named in Chapter 7) - A teenager hero, member of Aurora Legion. Can form animal constructs out of light.

Voidspeaker - First Appears: Prologue (named in Chapter 7) - A teenager hero, member of Aurora Legion. Utilizes void magic with energy draining properties.

International League of Superheroes (ILS) - First Appears: Chapter 7 - An organization founded to support heroes, especially with clean-up and legal matters.

Dazzling Vulture - First Appears: Chapter 7 - Villain, has light-based powers and a jetpack powered by them.

Electron Pirate - First Appears: Chapter 8 - Villain, can turn into lightning and has addition electricity-based powers

Atomic Herald - First Appears: Chapter 9 - Villain, channels nuclear power through his body

Samantha Roberson - First Appears: Chapter 6 (named in Side Story - What is a Hero?) - Captain Hot Devil's daughter.

Timothy Roberson - First Appears: Chapter 6 (named in Side Story - What is a Hero?) - Captain Hot Devil's son.

Sentinel of Harmony - First Appears: Chapter 12 - Villain, leader of the Order of Harmony. Communes with the Earth and can call forests and plants from within it.

Order of Harmony - First Appears: Chapter 12 - An ancient order that stives to protect the harmony and balance of the world. Not a fan of industrialization.

Bureau of Special Investigations (BSI) - First Appears: Chapter 14 - A US law enforcement agency specializing in supers.

Agent Steve - First Appears: Chapter 14 - An FBI agent who swaps over to the super-focused BSI.

Aqua Mage - First Appears: Chapter 14 - Hero, a mage specializing in water magic.

Dr. Delfino - First Appears: Chapter 14 - Evil genius who specializes in fluid mechanics.

Wu Zhengkang - First Appears: Chapter 14 - An Inner Disciple of the Eternal Night Sect.

Corrupted Claw - First Appears: Chapter 14 - Villain, has large and powerful claws grafted onto his right arm.

Gentle Gloom - First Appears: Chapter 15 (mentioned earlier) - A hero with ghost powers. Often teams up with Dragontooth.

Dragontooth - First Appears: Chapter 15 (mentioned earlier) - A hero with dragon features. Often teams up with Gentle Gloom.

Necrosaurus - First Appears: Chapter 15 - Villain, a necromancer with an interest in paleontology.

Majestic Moth - First Appears: Chapter 15 - Hero, has flight and light-based powers.

Gray Slayer - First Appears: Chapter 16 - Hero, a gunslinger with an enchanted magnum.

Master Mammoth Owl - First Appears: Chapter 16 - Hero, a giant owl-man.

Master Elegant Katana - First Appears: Chapter 16 - Hero, a master swordsman with style.

Carl - First Appears: Chapter 16 - The Necrosaurus's assistant.

Constanza Rubio - First Appears: Chapter 20 - Mexican teenager who lost her parents to drug violence. Gains ice-based superpowers.

Antonio Miralles - First Appears: Chapter 20 - Mexican teenager, his family took Constanza in after she lost her parents.

Captain Repulsive Butcher - First Appears: Chapter 21 - Villain. Super thicc.

Iron Armadillo - First Appears: Chapter 21 - Villain. A giant armadillo with a shell made of metal.

Viridian Rabbit - First Appears: Chapter 22 - Villain. A giant, green rabbit.

Bureau Chief Nathan - First Appears: Chapter 22 - Head of the DEA Bureau in Mexico.

Unnamed Crab Man - First Appears: Chapter 22 - Villain. A humanoid crab. Never thought of a villain name.

Edward Carter - First Appears: Chapter 23 - Vice-Director of the ILS. Specializes in politics.

Professor Mutant - First Appears: Chapter 24 - Evil genius who specializes in genetics.

Feverish Nephilim - First Appears: Chapter 24 - Villain. A mutant custom designed by Professor Mutant. Not bothered by the cold.

Branch Director Chavez - First Appears: Chapter 25 - Branch director of the ILS branch in Mexico.

Gabriel Le Blank - First Appears: Chapter 27 - Model. Actress. Villain. Has light-based powers. Very beautiful.

Vivienne - First Appears: Chapter 27 - Miss Le Blank's rival from college. Rich heiress.

Klara Wojnicz - First Appears: Chapter 27 - A young self-taught engineer who hates heroes and idolizes Miss Le Blank.

Kishor - First Appears: Chapter 28 - ILS Intelligence staff.

Manager Lane - First Appears: Chapter 28 - ILS Intelligence manager.

Mr. Soyer - First Appears: Chapter 28 - A famous movie director. Hates leaks.

Khalfani - First Appears: Chapter 28 - Kenyan underworld boss.

Sir Edmund Notfelde - First Appears: Chapter 28 - Retired British professor with a love of adventure.

Admiral Faulkner - First Appears: Chapter 29 - US Navy Admiral.

Admiral Huo - First Appears: Chapter 30 - Chinese Navy Admiral.

Admiral Takishima - First Appears: Chapter 30 - Japanese Navy Admiral.

Admiral Kong - First Appears: Chapter 30 - South Korean Navy Admiral.

Admiral Victorovich - First Appears: Chapter 30 - Russian Navy Admiral.

Stacey Shao - First Appears: Chapter 31 - GNN's expert on US-China relations.

Variant Story Characters

Ione - First Appears: VS Chapter 1 - Creator goddess of the world of Eirorun

Miniel - First Appears: VS Chapter 1 - Angel, Ione's main assistant.

Adoel - First Appears: VS Chapter 1 - An angel tasked with guiding the hero on his quest.

ACKNOWLEDGEMENTS

To my parents, my sister, and my brother for all their love and support. To u/Slaywraith on reddit.com/r/WritingPrompts, who wrote the original prompt that inspired this novel, and without whom none of this would have been possible. To the reddit.com/r/WritingPrompts community, who kicked started my writing and encouraged me to try something bigger. And to all my loyal readers on RoyalRoad, ScribbleHub, and Patreon, whose support, feedback, and encouragement carried me to the end.

Thank you, for everything!

Enjoy the book?

Consider leaving a review on Amazon!

Printed in Great Britain
by Amazon